JANE McBAY

cat whisker press
Boston

First Paperback Edition
ISBN: 978-1-957421-58-2

Published by Cat Whisker Press
Cover: Philip Ré, Rex Video Productions
Book Design: Cat Whisker Studio
Editor: Chloe Bearuski

To all my fur babies,
Those who are still with me and
Those waiting over the rainbow bridge

Thank you for your uncomplicated, pure love ♥

WICKED HOT BILLIONAIRES

ACKNOWLEDGMENTS

I want to give a big *thank you* to the following beta readers who gave me the gift of their most precious asset, time: Pat Robinson, G. Feldman, April Frisch, Jessica Guenther, and Miroslava Kral.

As always, thank you to my long-time editor, Chloe Bearuski, and to my line editor, Stephanie Selice.

Your combined efforts, each suggestion offered or typo found, made this a better book. I am exceedingly grateful. All mistakes, of course, are my own.

1

Brooke

As soon as I walk into the bar in Rangeley, Maine, I stop in my tracks. A tall man in a dark-gray, fine woolen overcoat may or may not be speaking with a guy in a cowboy hat, hunched on a barstool. No, this isn't the start of a joke. This is my life, and if I'm lucky, it's the start of my investigative journalist career. Cue the Emmy Award.

The man in the overcoat sticks out like a sore thumb in a town filled with people in ski parkas and shearling jackets. He's standing with his back to me. Right height as near as I can tell, he could be any build under that coat, but he has light-brown hair, just like in the scant photos I found. Somehow, the god of gaming software Jordan Asher has been all but erased from the web. This could be him, right where my cousin said she saw him.

Yet I can barely think about anything except finding the ladies' room. It's thirty degrees outside. I've needed to stretch my legs and, more importantly, to pee for the last hour of driving, and the cold I endured as I dashed from my car only made it worse.

Unfortunately, I'm in no state to sidle over there and casually order a drink. *Dammit!* I'm starting to feel nauseated from how badly I want to empty my bladder.

Seeing a sign for restrooms at the back and to the left, I take a step, then pause. Mr. Overcoat turns in my direction, maybe because of the icy draft that followed me inside the Thirsty Moose, which was easy to find due to the humongous wooden beast out front. With a close beard and wearing glasses—the man, not the moose—he's got on a gorgeous suit, underneath his open coat. It's impeccably tailored and utterly out of place in a rustic bar in this small ski resort.

Bingo! Looks like I found myself a billionaire. I was expecting a larger man, given the images and a bushier beard, but he's pretty damn close. Besides, who else would be dressed like that in the Thirsty Moose in a town with one main street?

I desperately want to go chat him up, but I desperately need to do something else even more. I have no choice. I make a beeline for the bathroom. Half hustling, half staggering, I walk cross-legged between the mostly empty wooden tables toward the sign at the back. I shouldn't have ignored the twinges in my bladder or the funny knocking sound in my engine. Nothing has ever gone wrong with Old Faithful. That's my Volvo, though at this moment, I hope it's also my bladder. But I needed to get here before dark, which in January, this far north, means way before dinner. In fact, it means right about now, at half past four.

It's been nearly five hours since I said goodbye to my cat, Mr. Busby, and hugged my cousin, who is also my roommate, Sherri. Fortified with two water bottles, a to-go mug of coffee, a bag of pretzels, a small package of chocolate chip cookies, and an apple, I started north. I should not have drunk the coffee and one water. As I wrestle with my fleece-lined pants, I still can't believe that I just saw Asher. To have spotted my quarry so quickly means I could be home tomorrow and enjoying a big fat deposit in my bank account shortly after that.

The Thirsty Moose might very well be my El Dorado. It's where Asher was sighted a year ago by a drunken ski bunny, who happens to be that same cousin and roommate *and* best friend, too. Sherri is also the same person who once swore Mick Jagger was in front of us at our neighborhood supermarket, causing me to ask a wrinkly *woman* with botoxed lips for her autograph on my T-shirt.

Sherri once thought Taylor Swift came into the bank where she works. *Was* it Ms. Swift? Highly unlikely! But Sherri declared herself a Swiftie and begged the woman to sing "just one song" before security parted them. My cousin is lucky she didn't lose her job.

This time is different. Not only did Sherri think the guy drinking shots at the bar last year looked like the mysterious self-banished billionaire, she overheard the "cute bartender with a sexy British accent" say, "Pay up, Asher."

Would a billionaire need to be asked to pay his bar tab? Probably not. Which means this could be the biggest wild goose chase of my short career as an investigative reporter. So short that this is the first time I've gone on the road and undercover for Boston Media Group, having worked there only three months.

I don't think my boss, believes this is anything other than a ski trip that I'm trying to get free lodging for.

Desperation makes strange bedfellows, including a wild goose or two. Prices have gone up for everything, while my paycheck has remained painfully low. With such scary words as *stagflation* being bandied around by talking heads who understand economics better than I do, I need a big, juicy story. The whereabout of Jordan Asher, who disappeared from his high-profile life three years ago, is the biggest, juiciest plum. Also, low-hanging fruit if I'm lucky *and* that man is really him.

Also, assuming Sherri wasn't too drunk from her après-ski cocktails last winter. She's a wicked good gamer and a *shmup* fangirl, which means something like "shoot 'em up." Asher, the software billionaire, was not only familiar to her, he's something of an idol.

"He created one of the most beautiful and exciting games ever"—again, according to Sherri. But I'm going on very little.

Even if Asher's nowhere near this pine-tree encircled bar, getting to pee was worth coming in. While I make it a quick pitstop, I take an extra ten seconds to check my teeth for bits of apple and pretzels, add a touch of lipstick, and see if my hair is still . . . Well, it's still on my head and looks the same as five hours ago. A blunt cut just above my shoulders, the hairstylist called it a "deconstructed bob." Both professional and adventurous at the same time. I think. I hope. Then, I hurry back out into the main room.

With that sorted out, I can breathe again, which brings the aroma of something fried and delicious wafting into my nostrils. But my excitement at the promise of an unhealthy, tasty meal is dashed when I notice Mr. Overcoat is gone.

Noooooo!

Luckily, the mountain man in the cowboy hat and black flannel shirt is still seated at the end of the bar, and now, he's my only hope. I walk back through the dining area. Not surprisingly, given that it's barely past four o'clock, there are only a handful of people at a few tables.

Plonking myself down on a seat two stools to the right of a guy who represents the slim-to-none chance I'll find the elusive billionaire, I drum my plum-colored nails on the bar top. The thick, glossy varnish has ancient water rings, and I try to understand why a billionaire would come all the way up here. Sure, I get the appeal of its pristine beauty, but couldn't he have moved to a picturesque foothill in New Hampshire or Vermont or any of the other closer places I passed today?

On the other hand, I'd go all the way to Nova Scotia if it meant being the first person in three years to find, interview, and photograph Mr. Asher.

For a few moments, I hope and pray he's in the other bathroom, but as the seconds stretch on, I doubt it. And where's the damned British bartender?

My stomach grumbles because I forbade myself from eating more than a handful of pretzels, along with the apple. All I could think about as I drove north were those stories when someone survives in the winter in their car by eating their leather shoes. Or maybe they have only some gum in the car and a package of those little round crackers they always give you with soup. Why are they called *oyster crackers*, anyway? I don't know, but there's a crushed package at the bottom of my purse right now.

After another moment, I glance to my right. Four seats down, a couple are very into one another, heads together, sipping what might be soft drinks and eating burgers. Unless they brought their own, there must be someone here serving something. I swing my gaze to the left. The man with the cowboy hat does not so much as glance my way, but keeps his focus trained on a newspaper. An actual paper newspaper!

I can't discern if he's twenty or seventy because his hat is pulled down so low. But by his body language, he's not my grandfather's age. He's obviously tall by the way he has to hunch in order to lean his forearms on the bar. What's more, since he's drinking coffee and minding his own business, I should do the same. But a story doesn't write itself, nor does it hand over the answers without some investigation. What if *he* is Jordan Asher?

I snicker silently at my own fanciful thoughts. As if anything could be so easy. Just in case, I try to get a better look at him while not being obvious. Of course, the hat thwarts me. In the end, I decide I have nothing to lose. I may as well be bold.

"Hey there," I say.

He grunts a greeting without looking up from his paper. Either that, or he just burped up a beer. He's got the scruffiest of beards, or maybe just a thick five o'clock shadow. And although I can tell he wants me to let him read his paper, I really do need to find the no-tell motel that my boss's assistant booked me into. Maybe this mountain man can help.

"Do you know where the Misty Slope Rooming House is?"

"Yup," he says.

"Are you one of those curmudgeonly guys who is going to give me a hard time, barely speaking, and if you answer at all, do it in monosyllabic responses designed to infuriate me into leaving you alone?"

"Yup," he says.

I snort out a laugh. Before I can say anything more, a dark-haired woman about my age comes from the kitchen and snakes her way behind the bar carrying a crate of glassware. It looks heavy, but she doesn't seem to be struggling. Regardless, the man with the cowboy hat looks up.

"You need a hand?" he asks her. I'm impressed that he spoke four words and sounded helpful. His voice is neither particularly young nor old.

"Nope, what I need are more hours in the day." She sets the crate down on the counter behind the bar top.

"Can't help you with time." He returns to reading, and the woman looks at me.

"Sorry to keep you waiting. Are you here to eat and drink or just drink?"

With her high ponytail, she's most certainly *not* the cute British guy Sherri overheard telling Asher to pay up, and I don't know the best way to ask her if or when another bartender comes on duty.

"Both, please," I answer. She hands me a menu, brief but full of everything a hungry gal could want.

"I'll have the fried chicken sandwich on sourdough, please. And a side salad."

"To drink?"

I look at what's on tap. "Epiphany?" I ask, having never heard of it.

"A Maine IPA," the bartender says. "It's fruity. Some say it's bitter, some say it's not. Do you want a sample?"

"No, I'll risk it," I say. "I'm known for trying anything once."

The woman's blue eyes flicker over to the man in the hat, then back to me. It makes me look at him again, too, but all he does is turn the page of his paper in silence.

"You got it," she says to me, and pours me a pint, setting the chilled brew in front of me. "I'll put your order in," she adds and disappears toward the kitchen door.

My beer is an orangey-yellow color, reminding me of a mango. I sniff it. It actually has a hint of mango scent, too, along with citrus. Cautiously, I take a sip. Tart and fruity. I don't think it's bitter, but it is flavorful.

With no one to speak to, I probably drink a little too quickly. Not one for drinking before dinner, I don't know why I ordered it, except it's already dark and I'm in a bar in the woods of northern Maine. To be precise, I'm on the northeast point of Rangeley Lake. *Population 1,222*, according to the sign. One long main street dotted with ski shops, restaurants, quaint ice cream shops, and bars, including this one. And lodging, which reminds me that I need to locate mine.

At this latitude, with it growing dark so early, I wanted to arrive while there was still light enough to find the place my editor's assistant booked for me. From what I was told, my accommodations are somewhere off the beaten path.

Actually, the whole town is off the path, beaten or unbeaten. There is nothing in this area apart from a lake, the Saddleback Mountain Ski Resort and, hopefully, the elusive, reclusive Jordan Asher. But because it is the closest town to the resort, it gets a steady stream of people in the evenings and all day on weekends throughout the season. Sherri said the Thirsty Moose was packed both times she was here.

Setting down my quickly emptying glass, I pull my phone out of my purse.

Yay, a signal!

Typing in the name of the lodging again as I did when I left home yields the same results. Google shows me a pin symbol in the middle of nowhere. I don't even see a road. Lizzie, my editor's assistant, said anything nice was out of the budget. Considering the budget for an intrepid reporter with nothing but a hot tip is miniscule, I'm nervous as to what type of place I'm staying in. On the other hand, I'm lucky they picked up the price of my lodging at all. Boston Media Group's generosity stopped at springing for gas or food.

"Excuse me," I say to the man on my left.

He does one of those long sighs, and I imagine he's rolling his eyes, then emits another grunt that has a questioning sound at the end.

"Hm?"

"That rooming house I mentioned before."

Silence.

"I still can't figure out what road it's on."

He turns the page on his newspaper really slowly, leaving me hanging. Right before I decide to tackle him, pushing him off his barstool just to see if it makes him speak, he says, "Take a left out of here, a right at the first fork."

A left and a right. "And?" I dare to ask.

Another sigh. "Follow the road until you can't go any farther. That's the Misty Slope."

"Is that the name of the hill it's on, or is there really a place to stay?"

For the first time, I catch a glimpse of his eyes under the brim as he raises his head to look at me. *Wowza!* Attractive gray-green color without an ounce of friendliness. If I could withdraw my question and move down a few barstools without looking like a coward, I would. In the next second, his eyes are in shadow again.

"Why are you here?" He sounds personally affronted, not curious about a fellow traveler on planet Earth.

"Just checking out the area," I say. It feels weird to lie, but I bet undercover journalists do that a lot, and I'd better get used to it.

"Not skiing?" he asks. How can *skiing* sound like a dirty word? Or maybe it's just his opinion of me doing it.

"Perhaps."

He shakes his head. "You don't know whether you're going to strap a pair of skis on or not?"

I pick up my beer. I liked him better when he wasn't talking. But I wish I had said *skiing* as my first answer. That would have ended the discussion and stopped his inquisition. Hey, I'm supposed to be the one asking questions.

"Not sure I'll have time. That's all."

"Because *checking out the area* will be so time consuming."

Opening my mouth, I close it again. He's not worth getting in a pissing contest with.

"Never mind," I say.

On the other hand, I need to be friendly, as he was standing close to the only possible billionaire in this dive.

I bide my time, hoping he doesn't leave before I can figure out my next move. More beer sipping ensues, and then my food arrives.

"Anything else?" the bartender asks.

"No, thanks." Then I think about the mountain man and what info he might have. "Not unless my *friend* here wants another cup of coffee or a drink. I'm happy to buy it for him."

I get brave enough to look his way again. "The round is on me," I add, sending him what I hope is a charming smile.

Out of the corner of my eye, I see the bartender looking at the guy, while I do the same. I'm certain now that he's not the droid I seek, and it's not because of Obi-Wan's force. This man doesn't heft the girth of Jordan Asher, no pudgy chin and belly. And he's simply too normal to have a billion dollars. Normal but rude apparently, as the silence stretches on uncomfortably for a few moments.

Damn! He's got this "grumpy local act" down pat.

"Answer the lady, TJ," the bartender says.

Another couple of seconds, and then he speaks. "Sure. If the round is on her, I'll have whisky, neat."

"Little early," the bartender says.

"Are you my mother now?" the mountain man TJ asks.

"Suit yourself." She turns and reaches for a bottle on the shelves behind her.

"Not that one," he says. "The Forty Creek Double Barrel, and don't forget to put it on her tab."

"Shit, TJ."

"The lady offered."

"She offered you coffee."

I've become invisible while they bicker. "It's fine. Pour TJ his whisky. That should repay him for giving me directions."

"And then some," the bartender says, but she grabs a bottle off the top shelf and pours the deep amber liquid into a glass.

"That's OK," I say. "Just add it to my bill." I wait until he has the drink in hand when I ask him my follow-up. "Did you notice that man in a suit earlier?"

He freezes with the glass halfway to his mouth, and as if I've said something incendiary, the bartender makes a *tsk*ing sound and wanders down to the couple's end of the bar. Then TJ downs the drink in one go and sets the glass onto the newspaper.

Getting up, he doesn't even look at me as he shrugs into a black parka that was resting on the end of the bar. While I'm sitting with half a sandwich in one hand, he walks behind me and leans close to my ear.

"Nope."

And then he's gone.

2

Jordan

The reporters are getting stupider and prettier. Or maybe I've just been up here too long, with authentic people who give a shit about one another and who don't spend an hour in the bathroom every morning. That one had gorgeous brown eyes with thick lashes that can't be real and the shiniest hair, like silky copper.

When I passed her, she smelled like sex on the beach. A coconut and sunshine fragrance—entirely out of place in northern Maine in January. It reminded me of growing up in California.

She let my Stetson and jeans blind her to her prey. And I have no doubt she was hunting *me*. Firing up my Range Rover, I head home, glad David didn't see her before he left. My lawyer loves the ladies. One look at her with her curves and he'd have been spilling his guts during a night of champagne and sex. On the other hand, she probably would've settled for more beer and giving him a blow job in the parking lot, just to learn where I live. Story-hunting reporters are no better than whores.

It's been nearly a year since the last one came snooping around. Today, I let my guard down by meeting with David at the Moose, but it won't happen again. It can't since David went straight to the Augusta State Airport and flew home to New York in my private jet. He can't tolerate more than three days away from the Big Apple, his Manhattan apartment, and his favorite deli.

Winding along the mountain road as the last rays of the sun disappear behind Bald Mountain to the west, I spare a thought for the woman I just sent to Misty Slope. Both the skies and the road are clear, and she should be fine. Although if she doesn't hurry with her late lunch or early dinner, it will be pitch black by the time she heads to Jack and Rashida's place. Like most roads out here, there are no street lamps.

I'm shocked that a reporter isn't staying at one of the motels or hotels on the main drag. Also surprised by her car, which I passed in the parking lot. Volvo, yes, but its tires were nearly bald.

Not my problem, I remind myself and turn into my long driveway, punching in the code on my phone to open the security gate. Not exactly Fort Knox, but if someone does, in fact, discover where I live, the steel gate and the high stone wall will keep out most of the snoopers. If they get inside the perimeter, they'll meet my dogs and my rifle.

The driveway lights come on as I approach and then turn off behind me for the long road to the house. And that reminds me again of the sleek-haired reporter driving off into the darkness. She had the looks I'm attracted to, making me almost wish I'd invited her over for an in-depth interview.

Down, boy. Too much time alone and too long since I last got laid, about two months ago, give or take a few days. Because even a hermit needs to run his fingers over warm skin and sink into a wet and willing woman once in a while.

This one got on the same chairlift with me. By the time we'd ridden up and skied down, we were making plans for dinner, my treat, and going back to her hotel room, which was a treat for both of us.

Vanilla sex all the way, but it satisfied the need.

My house is lit up and the two chimneys are smoking because my staff of a husband-and-wife team are home. I guess that makes me not so much of a hermit after all. But apart from cooking and cleaning, Colin and Emma stay in their section, and I stay in mine.

When the door lifts on the first bay of the four-car garage, I drive straight in and park next to Livvy's car. Three years have passed, and I should do something about it. Not sure what though. After my sister's death, I drove her car from Texas so I could feel close to her and spent two thousand miles offering up endless apologies for my part in what happened. I've been unable to part with it, a white Miata I'd given her because, suddenly, I could afford to. The car is impractical for driving in Maine nine months out of the year, but I don't give a shit. A daily symbol of how easily greedy, fucking bastards can destroy everything good.

The dogs are already barking when I enter my house, a well-crafted union of a split-log cabin and a fieldstone ski lodge. I love everything about the place, mostly the privacy. Grady, my whip-smart, female Aussie, and Beau, a whiny, loud, male husky, run toward me but stop on command, sitting two feet away, tails thumping on the hardwood floor. Duffy, a one-eyed boxer, is a rambunctious gray bundle of firm muscle and boundless energy. He doesn't stop for anything and runs full bore toward me, launching himself at my chest. On the short side, Duffy's stocky paws solidly hit my crotch, knocking me back a step.

"Dammit, Duff!" But I give him the attention he craves before pushing him off and crouching down into a doggo hug with the others. Duffy wriggles in, too. My three hard-luck rescues who've landed in the right snowbank.

"OK, guys, go run it off." Opening the back door, I let them out for as long as they want to run and give chase to whatever they find within the perimeter of thirty-five acres.

Emma hasn't started cooking, so I know dinner is hours away. Heading to my office, I use the outdated keycode pad to enter, always intending to upgrade to biometric security. From here, I run a gaming empire. Multiple screens await me, along with my workstations, all tied to a central storage network. There's a dedicated video-conferencing area, too, which connects me with old friends in Silicon Valley. They knew me *before* my life exploded as a billionaire gaming designer.

Some of them now work for me on certain areas of my games, some as beta testers, some as coders. And then there are the graphic designers—*the flakes*, as we coders fondly call the artsy members of our team.

Front and center hanging on the wall opposite the door is my countdown clock, which I take a long look at now. When I start to spend too much time skiing or playing with the seasonal ski bunnies or, in the summer, with the sexy, toned hiker-babes in their short shorts and mid-ankle boots, one glance at that friggin' clock scares me shitless. There's always a lot of work to do and rapidly depleting time in which to do it.

Bright Star, the third installment of my insanely popular gaming series, is due out in a month and a half, and a few bugs are still worming their way through the code. It should've been a Christmas release, but shit happens. So, why am I pushing aside my drawing tablet, which I doodle on while easing my way into a session of debugging, and instead pull up a map of the area on one of my monitors? I focus in on Misty Slope Lodge.

Jack and Rashida usually let rooms by the month to seasonal workers at the ski areas. It's odd that they have one available at this time of year for an overnight guest. Maybe this reporter is staying for the long haul. That could grow tedious real fast. She knows I go to the Thirsty Moose. What else does she know? Probably not that I own it and use it as my cover.

To ease whatever is digging at me, I call Tracy at the bar. The noise level indicates it's already a packed place. But she remembers the woman from earlier.

"She left about twenty minutes after you did, boss."

I let her go. Nothing worse than someone jawing at you when you had work to do. I feel better. After all, the ride is short, just a few minutes from the Moose, and that woman is probably already safely under Rashida's care. Closing the map, I don't even bother with my usual procrastination doodling. I open my workstation and start chasing my tail.

$♥$♥$♥$

After Emma's typically superb dinner, I'm back at my desk, with the three dogs lounging around the room. In the middle of running tests, breaking the game in order to find the bugs, I suddenly think of the copper-haired woman again. Punching in the Misty Slope number, I get Rashida on the phone after two rings.

"It's TJ from the Thirsty Moose," I say. She thinks I'm nothing but a fellow business owner. I guess I am.

"TJ!" Rashida greets me warmly. "Are we in trouble for not coming in there last Saturday? I hear you had an awesome Chamber of Commerce event. We had a birthday party to go to. Do you know Mike from the Zen Lodge?" She doesn't stop for a breath. "Why would you know him? He roomed with us years ago, and now he lives in town and works at the Zen. Anyway, it was his birthday over at Pepper's. Nice time, but I missed your burger and fries."

She is my polar opposite, chatty and friendly, the perfect rooming house host, but she makes it impossible to get a word in edgewise until she takes a breath.

"Glad to see you at the Moose anytime," I say, trying to match her level of friendliness. "I'm calling about a guest of yours. Did a pretty woman check in a couple hours ago?"

"Nope. She was a no-show." Rashida's words send a flood of alarm through my veins, like a surge of power through an unprotected motherboard. "How'd you know about her? And how do you know she's pretty?"

"I saw her at the Moose," I explain, "and gave her directions to your place. You have to fix that Google address glitch."

"I know, but how do I deal with a company that big?"

"I'll handle it for you," I promise. I have friends at Google. Right now, though, I'm worried about the cold temps and the woman with shitty tires.

"Thanks, TJ. Just so you don't think I'm heartless, I tried to call her to confirm she was still coming," Rashida continued, "because she never phoned in a credit card. I figured she'd booked a bunch of places and was picking the one she liked best. Happens all the time."

"No, she was definitely intending to stay with you."

"Well, shit!" Rashida swears. "I had a young man show up unexpectedly an hour ago, needing a place for two months. Since it was so late and I hadn't heard from Brooke, that's her name, I gave the room to him. Last one that I had, too. Maybe she's still having a good time at the Moose."

"No, she left." I feel like I have to do something since I may be the only person who knows she isn't where she's supposed to be. "Do you have her cell number?" I ask, getting to my feet, which makes all three dogs stir. Duffy stretches, yawning widely, before he gives me that look as though he's seriously trying to understand the situation.

"I told you I tried it," Rashida says. "The number I have from when the room was booked goes straight to a company called Boston Media Group with nothing but a voicemail."

My instincts about the woman's profession were dead-on. The only question is, where is the pretty lady?

"I know what car she's driving. I'll take a quick look on the road between the Moose and your place."

"That goes above and beyond for a bar owner and his customer," she says, "but I'll take you up on the offer since Jack's not here. I hate to leave my kids and my tenants alone."

"I'll get back to you," I say.

Rashida is still thanking me as I hang up, feeling the urgent need to get in my vehicle and find this reckless reporter.

"Stay," I tell the posse, but of course, next thing I know, I'm driving away from my house with Duffy riding shotgun, wearing his big-ass boxer smile.

Fifteen minutes later, I spy the ancient Volvo, which has skidded off a patch of black ice just after turning up the road to Misty Slope. I'm relieved to see it isn't wrapped around a tree, but my pulse speeds up at how quiet it is, resting a few yards off the road on the frozen ground. She's lucky there was a shoulder here. Up ahead, despite the gentle word *slope*, there's a steep grade and at least one turn with a sheer drop to the valley below.

Alarmed because there's no sign of life, no illumination from a cell phone, no engine sound, nothing, I pull in front of her car and leave my engine running. Grabbing a flashlight from the glove compartment, I'm springing from the Rover, slamming the door in Duffy's eager face. The last thing I need is him taking off on me.

At the driver's side, I shine the light and am met with a pair of wide-open, doe-like brown eyes. She looks scared as shit, and now I've nearly blinded her.

Quickly shining the light on my face so she can see it, I hope she recognizes me, which is a weird turnabout since I'm always hoping *not* to be recognized. At the least, she'll remember my hat. Then I start to yank on the door. It's locked.

"Open it," I order.

She rolls down the window. Rolls it down with a *manual crank handle!* I guess she's into antique cars.

"Why are you just sitting here?" I demand. "You'll freeze to death."

"I have a blanket and crackers," she says matter-of-factly. "Also, water, but I'm starting to get really cold."

In fact, we can both see our breath. "Why didn't you start walking?"

Her eyes widen again. "Because it was already dark when I got this far, and I'm not looking to get killed by person, bear, or wolf."

"It's too cold for people to be out," I remind her pointedly. "The bears are hibernating, and there are no wolf populations left in Maine." I'm just irritated enough to tell her, "Although the coyotes are hungry this time of year and wouldn't hesitate to take you down as a bloodthirsty group."

I see her nod slightly and swallow.

"You couldn't call anyone," I persist, then finish my own thought, "because your wussy carrier has no cell service."

"Right."

"And you sat here in the dark so no one would find you because why exactly?"

"My car doesn't have a phone charger, so I didn't want to waste the light in case I needed it later. And I'm pretty sure my battery wouldn't last very long in this temperature if I kept the car on. It's old."

"Why doesn't that surprise me?" I snap.

"Look," she says, starting to sound annoyed, too, maybe because her lips are turning blue now that her window is open. "I had no idea how far up this so-called slope I would have to walk. You left out that detail."

It actually would have been a long uphill hike. "Probably a smart move," I concede. "What happened?"

"I think my right front tire exploded."

I walk around her car and then back to her. "Yup, it's shredded. They all look like they needed replacing yesterday." Seems like her intelligence is about what I thought. Who would drive into the mountains on crap tires in the winter? But I don't ask.

"Get in my car, and I'll take you—" Take her where? The Misty Slope is full now. *Well, shit!* "Just get in my car."

She opens her door, gets out, and stretches. A five-foot-two doll with burnished-brown shoulder-length hair and gorgeous tits, apparent even under her jacket that cinches in at her small waist.

"I'm coming with you *only* because the bartender saw me talking to you, so I figure you're not a killer," she says. "She knew you, too."

"I *own* the Thirsty Moose," I say. "And those flimsy boots you're wearing are for pavement, not mountains." It really is a good thing she hadn't tried to walk up the hill. Her boots have a stacked heel, come up mid-calf, and are as likely vinyl as leather. She'd probably have given herself frostbite and lost all her toes by morning.

She's still looking at her footwear with a frown. "My feet are a little cold, but I'm not staying up here long enough to invest in Mount Everest–quality boots."

"Pretty sure it snows in Boston," I can't help pointing out, revealing I know where she's from. She doesn't seem to notice.

"You're right, Mr. . . . . *uh?*"

"TJ," I remind her. She already knows that, and it's all she's getting.

"You're right, TJ. But these boots have done me just fine at home, and I can't drive in big snow boots anyway." She glances at her car. "I've got some stuff to bring with me. My name is Brooke, by the way. Brooke Danbury."

I couldn't give fewer fucks about her name and consider telling her she can't bring her goddamn stuff. Then relent. Her car isn't going to be drivable till late tomorrow, and while we have barely any crime, she might lose her stuff if someone thinks her car has been abandoned.

"Put it in the back seat," I tell her. "Don't mind the dog." *He certainly won't mind you.* Realizing the last thing I want to do is help the enemy, I don't offer to carry anything. Instead, I get in my warm, plush vehicle and wait.

Since that leaves her with only her Volvo's dome light, the wait is longer than if I'd been a good guy and helped. Eventually, after two trips, she clears her car, putting all her gear on the back seat, which makes Duffy climb forward into the passenger seat. When she opens the door, he gives her a warm welcome, alternately barking his stupid head off and trying to lick her face.

"I'm sorry, but I'm . . . that is . . . I'm more of a cat person. He just makes me a little nervous."

Another reason not to like her. But since he's barring her entrance, I say, "Duffy, back."

Naturally, he does nothing but look at me, cock his head and squint with his one eye until I drag him off her seat. By the time I've shoved him into the back again, where he climbs on top of her small suitcase, the reporter has got in and buckled up.

Damn! I have a Boston reporter in my car. I must be outta my fucking mind. I make a U-turn and then a right onto the main road, and head back to my place.

"I thought you said the Misty Slope rooms were up that road."

"They are."

"So where are we going?" Her voice now holds a tinge of anxiety. I might hate the paparazzi with good cause and think most reporters are scum-sucking leeches, but I don't want to scare the woman.

"Rashida, who owns the Misty Slope with her husband Jack, gave your room to someone who actually showed up."

"What? But it was reserved."

"Not paid for, though," I tell her. "And it's Thursday in the height of ski season."

"Meaning there's no place else to stay."

"Exactly." She's caught on at last. "I can take you to the bus station where the benches are plenty long enough, or to . . . Nope, that's all I can think of where you can get warm and horizontal. Or," and I can't believe I'm saying this, "I have an extra room." Or two. Or three. Then I think better of it, consider the luxury home I live in, and begin a fabrication that's bound to get me into trouble eventually. "Well, *I* don't, but my employer does."

"I thought you owned the bar."

In trouble already, but I'm quick on my feet. "I do, but the ski season is short and most of the year, the bar does a manageable business but not a massive one. That's why I'm also an estate manager, which gives me a nice place to live year-round."

"For the man in the suit?" she asks, sounding genuinely excited.

The man in the . . . ? David. He dresses like he's got the money. Come to think of it, with what I and other clients pay him, he probably does have an estate and a manager in the Hudson River Valley.

"Sure," I say. *Why not?*

"And that's why you didn't want to talk about him. Because you're a loyal employee. That's admirable."

This is too easy. And I sound like a paragon.

"Will I be able to meet with him?" she asks. And there she goes, like the scummy reporter she is.

"Nope." Extremely satisfying to shut that door in her hopeful face. "He left town today, sweetheart. Right from the bar."

"*Oh.*"

Awwww, the snoopy lady is dejected. She doesn't get to hunt billionaire tonight. Then I think of Colin and Emma, and come up with a plan on the spot. Apart from Duffy's occasional enthusiastic bark or worse, his sneeze, we drive in silence because that's how I like it.

Turning onto the drive, instead of using my phone to open the gate, I get out and press the call button. Colin answers.

"Hello." He sounds a little surprised since no one ever comes around uninvited.

"It's me. I'm at the gate. When I come in, I'm just TJ, and I work for the homeowner as do you. Our employer is nameless. If the lady I'm with tries to ask you anything about our employer, you refer her to me. Tell Emma to do the same."

"Understood."

"And dim the lights." Colin will think I want ambience for a seduction, but I'm simply hoping to avoid being seen in bright light.

"Sure."

I appreciate Colin being a man of few words. Pressing in the code, I get back in the car, having to push Duffy off my seat. He climbs on top of Brooke, making himself comfortable on her lap, crushing her and leaning on her breasts. *Lucky dog!*

"Friendly," she says, her voice sounding a little raspy, which I suppose is from nervousness.

"That he is." I don't ask her if she likes dogs, because I don't care. But since she's tense with Duffy, I warn her, "There are two more dogs inside, but they're a little better behaved."

"Three dogs! I have a cat," she discloses.

Her and every other single woman I've met in the past decade. Only one cat though, so not a crazy hoarder with a penchant for knitting and a lack of the ability to smell that foulest of scents, the litter box.

Soon, we're entering through the garage, where I feel like apologizing to the Miata for bringing a cutthroat, unscrupulous journalist past it, and into the mudroom. Somehow, I find myself carrying her suitcase after all, realizing I grabbed it from her in the garage.

The other two mutts come to greet us, sitting on command like perfectly behaved doggos while Duffy goes berserk behind them. Then in front of them. Then behind them again. I'm thinking he needs a low-level dose of CBD.

While taking off my boots, I think if she discovers who I am, next thing I know I'll be reading about "Billionaire

Jordan Asher's Dopey Dogs." I cringe. Of course, she asks, "What are their names?"

What can I do? "Grady's on the left. The other one is Beauregard or Beau, for short." I roll my eyes for adding that little factoid like we're friends. "The crazed fiend is Duffy."

"Are they all yours or your bosses?" Brooke asks, setting down her purse and a backpack so she can take her boots off.

Her question is a good one, and I consider the ramifications of either response. Ultimately, I can't disavow my pack.

"They're mine."

She nods. "Great to have an accommodating employer." But Brooke doesn't lean down to pet them. Instead, her head is on a swivel, taking in the amber-colored, tiled floor, the bench and rubber mat, the cubbies for shoes and other gear, and the hooks for coats. I have the feeling if I wasn't standing there, she'd start taking photos and maybe even go through the closed door to the laundry room.

"Billionaire Jordan Asher has dirty laundry. Let's examine it!" Now there's a cringey headline.

Brooke can, in fact, snap photos at any moment, but she won't be able to send anything out. The house has a sophisticated jammer that blocks multiple networks at once. It'll thwart dual- and tri-mode phones so well, even Elon Musk, Bill Gates, or Steve Jobs from the grave couldn't penetrate it.

Sliding my phone out of my back pocket, I punch in the code, making everything secure under an electronic shield. I only wish there was a visual scrambler that could make me look like someone else. It's still possible she'll recognize me, if she's any kind of investigative journalist at all. I've done as good a job as anyone could, actually better than most, in wiping my photos from the web, but she's probably studied whatever she could find.

Brooke might see past the changes I've made to my appearance. Not only a fitness regimen that got rid of the programmer pounds I carried when I worked in Silicon Valley, but the lifelong desire to have my vision fixed. Getting rid of my glasses made skiing a lot easier. And like Clark Kent and Superman, apparently, the lack of them makes me look like a different person.

Still, in the light of the mudroom, I feel exposed and on display, and I'm hesitant to remove my hat. Right now, I just want to get this woman to bed. I mean, get her settled in a guest room so I can take it off.

3

Brooke

My sleuthing adventure has gone from OK to not so good to fucking amazing! I am *in* Jordan Asher's home. I just know it. There's no way there are two extraordinarily wealthy men hanging out in that same bar. Even though I missed the man himself on his way out of town, I *will* get a story from TJ, as well as a shit-ton of photos. Maybe Asher will return before I get booted out of here.

It'll help if I can win over the unwelcoming mountain man, who seems ready to shove me in a closet to wait until daybreak so he can get rid of me. I begin with a heartfelt thank you.

"I didn't say it before because I was still sort of shocked by how quickly my situation turned scary, but I'm truly grateful you came to rescue me."

His response is a glowering stare. Or maybe that's his regular stare. Hard to tell with his hat pulled low. It's partnered with the slightest nod that could mean anything. When he takes off his coat and hangs it on a hook, I quickly do the same, only a little distracted by the span of his shoulders. I love a good pair of manly shoulders!

In silence, carrying my purse and backpack, I follow the man and his dogs through an open set of French doors into a rustic foyer. The house is large, stretching back into the shadows with only accent lights on throughout the downstairs.

Wide dark-wood flooring is under my feet. I can't see any specifics, but the place is open-concept to the back wall, where a massive stone fireplace warms the house. The last embers of a dying fire are glowing in its hearth. To be honest, it looks like a big dark mouth and red devilish eyes, and I shiver. Everything apart from the cozy circles of light is in shadow.

"How about a tour?" I ask, despite how my grumpy host isn't even speaking to me. I imagine there are any number of dead animal heads and massive antlers on the walls.

Ignoring my question, TJ, also in shadow, bends to give each of the three dogs a pat on the head. Then the two who weren't in the car, flattening my lap and making it hard to breathe, come over to sniff my legs. I'm not brave enough to stroke them, but I send what I hope is friendly energy their way.

"Upstairs," he says.

No tour then? And he didn't say the word in an inviting way. More like a drill sergeant. I guess I'm a nuisance and won't get so much as a cup of cocoa, unless I ask.

"I suppose you had dinner already, while I was sitting on the side of the road."

"Yup," he says. "The chef is off duty, and the kitchen is closed."

I sigh since I would love to meet Asher's private chef.

"Besides," TJ adds, "you had a good meal at my bar. I can't imagine you're hungry again."

He can't imagine? I guess my stomach is now under his control. But mention of his bar reminds me of a sore spot.

"Your drink was fifteen dollars. In your own bar!"

He shrugs. "If you don't want to pay, next time, don't offer. I'll show you where you can sleep."

Guess I'm lucky I still have food supplies in my backpack.

Then he adds, "And no photos while you're here."

Yikes! It's like he read my mind. "Why?" I ask. "I mean, it's so lovely and unique. I just want to show my cousin where I ended up. I'm sure the Misty Slope is nothing like this."

TJ takes a step in my direction until I have to crane my neck to look at his face instead of his chest. "My employer is a private person."

I decide to catch him off guard. "You don't think Mr. Asher will mind if I stay the night?"

Without missing a beat, he says, "Who?"

Then he turns his back on me, tells the dogs to stay, and walks toward a wide wooden staircase leading up to darkness. "For the record, sweetheart," comes his dismissive voice, "I know my employer would hate the fact that you're here."

Maybe true, but here I am. With no point to taking a few sneaky pics that will be blurry shadows, I hurry after him. In an intriguingly modern touch, LED lights line either side of the staircase treads, illuminating the forest green-and-silver carpeted runner and sending up a glow toward the massive polished oak banister.

Despite being told to stay, the dog who was in the car, the one-eyed beastie, trails TJ up the stairs. Throwing caution to the wind, I slide my cell out of my back pocket. Knowing without a flash, it'll probably be useless, I take a photo of dog and man from behind, before shoving my phone back out of sight. And then I watch the tight ass of my grumpy host until we reach the landing.

Upstairs, accent sconces light up the wide hallway as we walk along, while the stair runner continues on into the darkness. I follow TJ past a couple closed doors, before he stops and opens one. After looking inside, he glances back at me and sets the suitcase down.

"You can sleep here. You have your own bathroom. I'm right across the hall," he adds, and it's definitely a warning, not a friendly "I'm close if you need me" statement. I'll have to be very quiet when I sneak out to explore.

I verbally prod him again, since I'm safely upstairs and don't feel in danger of being put out like an unwanted cat. "And where does Mr. Asher sleep?"

"Who?" he shoots back again.

"Your employer, the man in the expensive suit. The genius who made a fortune in intricately designed shooter games. When he's in residence, does he sleep on this floor, or does he have a private wing?"

"In residence?" TJ repeats. "Isn't that a term for a British royal?"

Asher's probably wealthier than most royals. I shrug since no useful information is forthcoming. He neither confirmed nor denied.

"Again, I'm really grateful. Hopefully, I can find a place to stay tomorrow night."

"No place available this weekend," he says. "I guarantee it. If you're not skiing, you should go home."

"I'll certainly take your advice into consideration," I say, trying to keep the tartness out of my tone. But, good lord, who died and made him king of this mountain?

I close the distance to the guestroom door and to TJ. He's tall, and when I'm up close, he's even bigger than I estimated. A big mountain man with the air of harsh, untamed wildness, barely covered by the thin veneer of . . . *well, hardly civility*. More like detachment, the neutral cousin to downright rudeness.

And he still has that damn hat on. I'm going to dream about a handsome man in a tan, wool cowboy hat, for sure.

But he's going to shut me in this guest room, and I won't have a chance to ask him anything. Then I get an idea.

"If I'm not ready to leave tomorrow, would you be open to letting me stay here for a few nights? Since you have the room, I mean. I'll pay you." *If he takes credit cards, that is.*

He leans on the doorjamb, in the shadows, arms crossed.

"Not gonna happen." His voice is like a low growl. TJ's feral animal vibe makes me want to gentle him, as they say, to lure this large beast of a man out of the ancient, dark forest and into the sunlit clearing. I think it'll take more than a Scooby treat since I can't even elicit a smile from his sourpuss face.

Squeezing by him because, even sideways, he's filling the doorway and not budging to make it any easier, parts of my body brush against parts of his. The lightest touch tells me he is solid muscle.

Nose to chest with this guy, I suck in a shaky breath, smelling the same clean soap scent from inside the vehicle. His employer must be a billionaire, because that wasn't merely a Range Rover. It was deluxe with a capital *D*! Not the car of a bar owner.

Thinking of cars, I stop right in the doorway, my breasts a whisker-width away from touching him. "I can't go anywhere. I have to get a new tire."

He continues looking down at me, letting the hat's shadow conceal the thoughts behind his eyes.

"I'll get it towed to a place in the morning. You'll be on your way by noon."

Too efficient for my first ploy, but wait . . . there's more. "Sadly, it's not merely the tire," I tell him. "The engine was making a weird sound by the time I pulled into the Thirsty Moose, and even worse when I turned onto the road to the Misty Slope. I'll have to get that checked out before I risk heading south."

Checked out but *not* fixed because I can't afford more than a tire. If Asher hadn't slipped away already, if I'd managed to ask him one question, it would've been my breakout story, and I'd have made bank. My next hope is to get photos of the billionaire's house, including his bedroom. That'll mean a big chunk of change. I'll be able to pay my share of the rent and my car repair.

Unfortunately, my words do nothing to soften TJ's shaded gaze. We have a standoff, right here in the doorway for a good long five seconds. And then, miraculously, as if he has a personality transplant, his hard stare melts away and he smiles.

Oh. My. God! The man was already attractive, but his wicked grin makes my knees quiver.

When I finally wrest my glance from his mouth and look up again, he's finally tipped his hat back, and I get the full force of those gray-green eyes. My insides combust. It's such a startling sensation, I gasp loudly enough for his gaze to drop to my now-open mouth.

His pupils dilate, and yes, I know what that means. We can agree on one thing, it seems—desire! Pure and simple, raw lust. I don't care that he's dressed like a woodsman when I'm searching for a billionaire.

Besides he's a legit businessman, unlikely to squirrel me away here and make me his sex slave. *Sex.* That would be nice. Take the kinks out. Take the edge off. Six months ago, I released my fiancé from his promise to wed me, and that's how long it's been. *Why?* Because not one guy I've encountered in the interim has made my heart race and my skin prickle the way TJ does.

This stranger is like a gift from a faraway land. The mountains of Maine! No one would ever know. My body is saying yes, and for once, my brain is agreeing. I turn away a moment to consider what I think is a blatant offer in his eyes. And that's all it takes to break the spell. I'm here in the middle of this craggy, pine-covered scenery so gorgeous, I almost drove off the road getting here, for one reason, and it's not to get laid.

Focus on the job. I run my hand over the wall, feeling for a switch. Finding a flat rectangle, my fingers skim over it, and the room is showered in soft light from an overhead fixture. Four-poster bed, armoire, and flat screen TV. I'm impressed, and it will be captured in photos as soon as TJ leaves. Putting my purse and backpack on the bed, I look back at him.

Maybe I read the look in his eyes all wrong. He pushes my suitcase through the doorway with his foot. I might be alone in lust, after all. Backing up, he's nearly disappeared into the dim hall when he stops.

Is he going to ask to share my bed?

"No wandering around inside or outside the house. Understand?"

His tone makes me want to mock him and say, "Yes, sir." Maybe even give a little salute. But I am still lucky to be under this roof. "Understood," I say politely.

"And stay in here until I knock on your door in the morning."

That's weird. I wonder if he's a member of a cult or something. Or maybe he changes into a demon at midnight. "Why?"

"Because I said so," he snaps and closes the door.

Obviously, he doesn't have kids or remember what it's like to be one. That line has never worked on anyone ever. And it isn't going to work on me.

After the testosterone dissipates from the vicinity, and I can think clearly, I remind myself to keep my frustrated libido in check. Plonking myself down on the high mattress, just to test it, as one does, I hear a bark, making me jump up again.

"Hey, there, doggo," I say to the hound hiding under the four-poster. "Out you go, little buddy."

Silence, then another playful bark. What was his name? *Rufus? Dufus?* I get down on my hands and knees to look for him. Despite having only one eye and a lot of slobber, I admit he's adorable on his back, with his paws in the air, touching the underside of the boxspring.

Without warning, the door swings open behind me.

"I left the damn—" TJ cuts off his own words.

Looking over my shoulder, I see he's taking in the sight of me on all fours, head low, ass high. I swear his eyes darken to charcoal, and the air becomes charged again.

"The damn dog," he finishes. "Duffy," he calls, keeping his gaze trained on mine, even when the dog comes out, and I sit back on my heels. TJ makes sure the tan and white boxer leaves before he does, then shuts the door again.

"Good night," I call after him to no response. What was I expecting? A chocolate on my pillow and a heartfelt "sleep well"?

Scrambling to my feet, I whip out my phone to look at the single photo I took on the stairs. As expected, utter garbage. But I put on the two bedside lights before taking a billion photos of the room and the bathroom, which is a luxurious mini spa. The problem will be in proving these were taken in Jordan Asher's house, not a luxury hotel. I need to find something personal of his, like a photo of him here in his house.

Selecting all the photos, including the blurry one from the stairs, I send them to my folder in the cloud. Except they don't go anywhere. The little circle turns for a while, then I get an error: "No service."

That's ridiculous. I can see I have service. I go through all the phone settings and try again. *Shit!* I can hardly ask TJ for his internet password. But I may query him on cell reception tomorrow. As long as I have the photos safely stored, I guess I won't worry about it.

Meanwhile, I have some serious time to kill before I sneak out to do a little reconnaissance. I may as well warm up with a hot shower. The sight of multiple heads at an array of levels gives me pause. I turn the water on and off a couple times. Looks like an adult's-only waterpark, causing me to undress quickly.

Sure enough, when I step into the spacious shower, my body is massaged by jets of hot, pulsating water, and my wicked thoughts turn to TJ again. First, in a lust-driven way, and then I start to wonder if I can pass him off as being the reclusive billionaire. If I frame the photos correctly, who could say he wasn't?

Wrinkling my nose and relaxing as the steam rises around me and my back muscles are pummeled, I consider the ramifications of stating in my final article that TJ is "the man who lives in Asher's house." People could make whatever assumptions they want—that he is Asher or even Asher's lover. In the next instant, I think that probably won't fly and might get me sued.

With the hot water raining over my head, I adjust one of the lower sprays until its aimed at my coochie. *Wow!* Instantly, I stop thinking about work and about being dishonest to make a dollar. At least for the three minutes it takes me to climax while leaning my forearms and forehead against the smooth stone shower wall, letting the targeted water do the work.

Then I'm back to ruminating again. Ultimately, playing with semantics and allowing people to think photos of TJ are actually Asher doesn't sit right. Besides, the photos of his house should be enough to earn some serious change without needing to pretend I met the billionaire himself.

$♥$♥$♥$

About five hours later, I wake up from a nap I didn't realize I was taking. After killing time by indulging in the bathroom that was stocked with every conceivable luxury and necessity—having shaved my legs, washed, conditioned, and dried my hair, and moisturized my entire body with rich honey-infused cream—I smell divine from head to toe. I watched a little TV and opened my laptop, which is also as much a brick as my phone with no outside contact, before dozing off on the comfiest bed I've ever had the good fortune to stretch out on.

Time to snoop around. With my jeans folded on my suitcase, I'm now wearing black yoga pants and a soft, black pullover. Like a super spy! Opening the bedroom door, I listen for a full two minutes. The hallway is dark except there are very helpful little accent lights near the bottom of the wall, like the lighting in an airplane's aisle. Cool!

I'm not going to risk looking in any rooms I pass, although maybe when I'm done on the first floor, I will. If I'm caught, I'll just say I couldn't remember which door was mine. After all, everything has been annoyingly dark since I got here. But it's the downstairs and maybe photos on the fireplace mantel or an office that most interests me.

I stop short at the top of the stairs with my heart pounding. Two of the dogs are lying here, and I've already woken them. They don't bark or growl, but just look at me with sleepy eyes. After all, I'm inside the house, not an intruder. For a few seconds, I remain frozen, staring back at them until I remember from a YouTube video how dogs might think that's threatening. Quickly, I look away, yawn, and stick out my tongue.

When I glance at them again, they each take a turn yawning. Gathering my courage, wishing TJ had cats, I step between them, while they lower their heads again. The third amigo is nowhere in sight.

Downstairs, I search for light switches using my cell phone's flashlight. All I see is some kind of high-tech, backlit glowing glass rectangle. What the hell is this? After a couple swipes, some lights turn on throughout the downstairs. *Success!*

I head into a spacious room, mountain-lodge style with big comfy furniture angled in front of the stone fireplace. No dead animals or antlers, after all. No television visible, either, but a gorgeous coffee table that looks like it was hand-hewn from a big piece of wood. Not a tree expert, I have no idea what kind, but I snap some photos and examine the mantel. No framed photos. I take pictures of the art work, mostly landscapes and one modern framed poster-size image of what I believe is the California coast.

Moving on to the kitchen, which is all stainless-steel appliances and granite countertops, I capture it from every angle. The stove is huge with a big hood vent. I love to cook, so I take extra time poking around in here. There's a closed door at one end of the kitchen, but I recall TJ mentioned staff. I don't want to risk going into their quarters and waking anyone.

Pivoting, I find a picture-worthy powder room with a glass sink and a shale wall. Then enter the dining room, which has another magnificent freestyle wooden table with a steel-and-glass chandelier hanging over it. The tall-backed chairs, each with a plump seat cushion, also appear custom-carved. Naturally, I try one out and take a photo from that perspective, and then another from one end of the room.

Wandering back into the living room, I peek between the drapes. I can't see the backyard. Nothing but uninterrupted darkness. Killing the lights by touching the rectangle switch again, I return to the window and press my face to the cool glass. I can't make out anything on the ground, but I look up and gasp. The night sky is twinkling with literally a billion stars. Pinpoints of light breakthrough the stygian black, and I am mesmerized.

Until something wet touches my ankle, making me jump and scream before I can stifle myself. Realizing it's a dog's nose, I'm fumbling with my phone to switch on the light when a voice comes out of the darkness, making me jump again.

"What the hell are you doing?" TJ demands.

Busted! Excuse ready, I don't hesitate. "I missed dinner," I remind him. "I'm looking for a snack."

"In the living room?"

"I got sidetracked. Look at that sky," I say, still with genuine awe. "Who can think of food when there's a light show? I just saw a shooting star. We don't see a sky like this over Boston."

A moment's silence, then he's closer when he speaks again.

"Go back to your room, Brooke Danbury," he says softly, making a tremor run through me. "It's two in the morning."

When I turn, I cannot see his face, nor can he see mine. "Why don't we just go to the kitchen together?" I ask.

He leans toward me, and for a second the moonlight catches his eyes, turning the gray-green to silver.

"I don't want you in the kitchen." His tone is still soft but gruff. "I don't want you wandering around this house. I want you back in the bedroom. Is that clear?"

A shiver dances down my spine. Something about him *wanting me in the bedroom* sounds like he's thinking naughty thoughts. And I'm right there with him, despite knowing he really means he wants me shut away and out of his sight.

"Fine!" Both TJ and his dog are crowding me. It's the boxer. "Your dog scared the shit out of me."

"Wouldn't have happened if you hadn't disobeyed my request. You're lucky all three trust anyone I bring into this house."

He's right on both counts. But he's still blocking me, and I notice his gaze flicker across my face, drop to my mouth, then back to my eyes again. I may be the worst reporter in the world, but I know when a man is interested in me.

I smile. This will be a lot easier if I can make him be friendly, or at least, not contentious. I lick my lips, watching his pupils dilate in the moonlight.

TJ leans close, until we are nose to nose. It's my first time seeing him without his sexy cowboy hat. That thought is quickly followed by this one: *I'd like to have sex with him wearing only his hat while I wear a pair of cowgirl boots, if I had any.*

Right now, I almost can't stop my hand from drifting up to touch his hair, which looks soft and finger worthy. I can tell he showered, too, by the same soap smell I enjoyed hours ago. I've never found soap to be an aphrodisiac before, but my brain imagines the water sluicing across his muscles before he soaps up. And I want to trace the path of the water.

I also want to kiss. Right now. And by his nearness, I'm about to get my wish.

Parting my lips, I wait, not realizing I've closed my eyes until he says my name.

"Brooke."

"Yes," I whisper. I swear I feel his lips brush across mine, sending a zap of lust between my legs as surely as if he touched me there.

"Get upstairs," he says quietly, "before I carry you up there and lock you in."

What? I open my eyes to see he's moved out of the moonlight, disappearing somewhere out of sight. *Did* he kiss me?

Maybe I've been celibate too long. All I know is I want this man, despite knowing nothing about him. And yes, it's partly because he's so cold toward me. It's a novelty. I'm pretty. Not a rock-solid ten, perhaps, although one boyfriend did call me his *dimepiece*. I have a symmetrical face except for my one dimple, good hair most days, and naturally dark, thick eyelashes around my brown eyes. Men usually drop casual compliments and sometimes downright fawn over me. They don't tell me to go to bed. Not alone, anyway. A part of me wants to crack the ice, or melt it entirely.

As I make my way upstairs, I forget about taking more photos. I have plenty of shots of everything that I've seen so far. Instead, my mind is busy wondering at the way my body is humming with sensual awareness. Sure, TJ is attractive, but it's more than that. It's magnetic, like I want to stick myself to him.

Laughing at my own desperation—the only excuse for wanting to be kissed so much that I closed my eyes and made a fool of myself—I return to my room.

Damnit! Distracted by my lust, I wasted the opportunity to poke my head into other rooms while he's downstairs. I would love to have a looksee into the master bedroom, imagining the luxury of Jordan Asher's bedroom.

I dither, then decide to risk it and go out into the hallway, exactly the moment TJ crests the stairs and appears on the landing.

"Are you deliberately provoking me?" he calls out.

Dashing back into my room, I slam the door closed. When he enters a few seconds later, he brushes past me to put something on the bureau. A package of crackers and a jar of peanut butter. He has a heart, after all!

Then TJ turns, and his expression makes me think otherwise.

"I'm this close to spanking your pretty ass and sending you out into the snow."

I feel my cheeks heat. That should not be the most erotic thing any man has ever said to me, but it is. I'm tempted to misbehave just to see if I can elicit that spanking he mentioned. On the other hand, I do not want to be tossed outdoors.

Glancing down at Duffy, the dog and I share a look like he knows what that's like. It's frigid outside, and I'm lucky not to be sleeping in my car. I should remember that fact.

"Sorry," I mumble, feeling the weird urge to add "sir." This time not mockingly, either. Obviously, I've been reading too many sexy books. But his high-handed disapproval irks me. "I guess I've broken the rules of your *oh-so-gracious* hospitality."

He shakes his head. Then he shocks me. "If you're not careful, sweetheart, you'll find yourself spread eagle on that bed, feeling my *hospitality* at the end of an oak paddle, and begging for more."

My mouth goes dry with imagining that scenario as he smirks magnificently and walks out.

4

Jordan

She's sassy, which I like. And she didn't shy away and look terrified or disapproving when I mentioned a little physical punishment. I believe Brooke got excited, in fact, gauging by the interest in her cocoa-colored eyes and the pink flush to her cheeks. It's almost a pity I have to kick her out tomorrow, because I think we could have a good time.

But I can't keep hiding under my hat or keeping my house in darkness. I tripped over Beau on my way back to bed and nearly broke my neck. Plus, as a husky, he had to let me know about my clumsiness with five minutes of complaining.

She has to go, *come hell or high water*, as my father says.

However, Dad never mentioned an unexpected blizzard, and that's what I wake up to. Despite being up at all hours, I'm out of bed early, seeing snow squalls lashing across the windows. First thing I do is call for a tow truck to fetch the reporter's car before it's buried. I should have done it last night, but I was busy keeping an eye on her.

"Sorry, TJ. Everyone has attached their plows and are clearing the roads." Neil is the most reliable mechanic in Rangeley and knows me solely as a bar owner.

I hate to flex, but in this instance, it seems imperative.

"I'll pay you double what you're getting for four hours of plowing if you get Ms. Danbury's Volvo out of the snow, fix the damn engine, and put on four new tires. Today!"

Neil hesitates, but smelling blood—and desperation—he ups the ante. "Triple pay, plus parts, but I can't promise anything until Monday. I'll start on it at seven and get it done. Unless the engine's totally shot. Then maybe Tuesday."

I start to protest, so he adds, "Today is for oil changes and small stuff, like the tires, that my guy here can handle. If I have the right size tires in stock, then he'll put 'em on if he has time today. But the engine will have to wait 'cause I don't work weekends."

"How much," I persist, "for you to work on the car today?"

"TJ, what did I just say? It's Saturday. I don't do repairs on weekends, and that's not changing, even if you were a goddamn billionaire. My wife would kill me. You wouldn't have caught me here at all if it weren't for the storm with all hands needed for plowing. But I'll get the Volvo off the road today and snug in my shop."

I'm a little surprised to have encountered someone who can't be bought.

"When's this storm going to end, do you know?" I'm grumbling like a spoiled brat, but I have work to do and a reporter to get rid of.

"Tonight, I think. Was supposed to miss us to the east. How do those weathermen always get it so wrong and keep their damn jobs?" Neil sighs. "Anyway, triple cost, and we have a deal."

Having just been fleeced—or Brooke has—I barely manage a civil goodbye before hanging up. When I head downstairs for coffee, I find my small staff of two are up. Colin and Emma look a lot happier than I feel, but they weren't up half the night, keeping tabs on an unscrupulous gossip columnist.

"Morning, boss," Emma says first when I take a seat at the island. She's a bleach-blonde dynamo, and I swear she always has energy to spare. Putting something in the oven, she has various other culinary projects started. It always looks like a tornado went through when she begins the day's prep work.

"I'm heading out to use the robot snowblower," Colin announces. Stocky, dark-haired, and so in love with his wife it's almost sickening, he sounds positively gleeful about his yard toy, the way I am after installing a faster CPU processor.

"More like heading out to play," I say, envying him. My estate manager talked me into a yard robot with multiple attachments at the end of last summer. It didn't take much persuasion, and we both stood and watched it mow the lawn before docking itself under cover when it rained.

Setting down his coffee cup, Colin adds, "I'm going to start with the walkways around the house and yard."

"*You* were?" I ask pointedly, knowing the robot does the work while my caretaker is hands-off. "What exactly will *you* be doing?"

"Monitoring the robot," he says with a laugh. "I'll leave a patch for you to do if you want," Colin adds, reminding me how I goofed around with the Yarbo's leaf-blowing attachment in the fall and set the robot to its *on-patrol* mode. The dogs had a blast, too.

"Actually, I'll be shoveling steps," Colin adds. "But I can redirect Yarbo if you need the drive cleared immediately. For your lady friend?"

As if on cue, not staying in her damn room like I asked, Brooke comes down the stairs. I know this because the dogs are barking and racing around, like the Queen of Egypt has arrived.

"In here," I call out. Otherwise, she'll probably start wandering into places, trying to find my office. If I hadn't electronically locked all the upstairs doors, I'm sure she would've snooped in the other rooms already and found my master bedroom.

"She's not a friend," I mutter to Colin and Emma. Enough said. They know who is privy to my real identity, and it's a small group. Basically, my parents, my lawyer, Cyril who manages the bar, and a couple friends from out of state. And outside this house, they know not to talk about me at all.

Brooke comes around the corner, dressed in form-fitting, black corduroy pants and a pink sweater. Like a raspberry lollipop that I want to lick. I stop gawking and snatch up the newspaper. In the bright morning light streaming through the floor-to-ceiling windows that overlook the rear snow-covered acreage, I'm practically in a spotlight. Holding the paper open in front of my face like a shield, I stay tucked behind it.

"Coffee or tea?" Emma asks by way of welcome, while Colin disappears through the door to their suite. He's a lot like me without much use for chit-chat, plus he gets the peace and tranquility of yardwork, even with sixty decibels at his side.

"Coffee, please," Brooke says. "Nice to meet you. I'm Brooke, an uninvited, unwanted guest."

"Nonsense," Emma says. "TJ never brings home strays unless he intends to keep them."

The three of us freeze at her inappropriate words. She is the opposite of Colin, which normally doesn't bother me because I can tune out her jabbering when I happen to be in listening range. And she is the best personal chef I've ever had. Also, the *only* one I've ever had. She can cook any cuisine I ask for, and probably wishes I'd ask for something more challenging than an occasional beef Wellington.

Emma has all but pleaded with me to throw a party so she can show off her hors d'oeuvres.

"Just joking," Emma says to smooth over her words. "You've met the trio."

"Yes, of course," Brooke says. "I'm not scared of them." She lifts her chin, trying to convince herself as much as my chef. "But I've never had a dog so I'm not really, you know, used to them. My cat is named Mr. Busby."

Ignoring the inanity of a cat named *mister* anything, from behind the paper, I ask Emma, "Did the dogs eat?"

"Of course." She sounds miffed, and I'm sorry I insulted her. She does her job efficiently without my butting in. "Now, to breakfast. Usual for you," Emma says, not asks, as I peer over the top of the newspaper to respond. She isn't even looking my way. I can tell she's excited about having a guest to cook for. "And what would you like, Brooke? Eggs Benedict, maybe, with a side of grilled asparagus?"

"What's *the usual?*" Brooke asks.

Even that innocent question irritates the hell out of me, knowing she'll gladly tell everyone my breakfast habits if she learns I'm Jordan Asher.

It's Emma who answers. "TJ's fond of my pancakes and a side of scrambled."

"Every day?" Brooke asks, turning her deep-brown eyes on me. "Pancakes *every* day is your usual?"

I cough. "What's wrong with that? Emma's pancakes are the best in the world. Light and fluffy. And she always adds something, blueberries, apples, even pumpkin." As soon as I catch myself defending my breakfast choice, I add, "It's none of your business anyway."

Brooke grins, and her face goes from a ten to a hundred. "I desperately need to try the best pancakes in the world, please."

For a moment, Emma looks disappointed. Then she says, "Coming right up," leaving us at the counter drinking coffee. I raise the paper again, happy to remain silent, but of course, the reporter starts flapping her gums immediately.

"So, my car," Brooke begins. "Do you want to tell me who to call?"

"All settled," I tell her.

"Can you elaborate and use more than two words, please?" she asks.

"My mechanic is picking it up, putting on four new tires, and fixing whatever's wrong with the engine."

An audible gasp makes me look over the newspaper again. The color has drained from her face. "I'll need an estimate first," she says. "Unlike you, I don't have an employer providing for my transportation."

I skate over my momentary confusion. Then I decide to ease her mind because it's going to be costly for her. "We'll split the cost. After all, you bought me a whisky."

Brooke's mouth drops open, and I would love to slide my tongue between her lips. Good thing Emma is a few feet away, playing chaperone.

"I'm surprised," Brooke begins, "and exceedingly grateful. If you're sure it won't get you into any trouble with Mr. Asher."

She thinks Asher is footing my half of the bill. I mean, he is, but . . .

"Who?" I ask because we have to keep up the charade. "Anyway, it's on me, not my employer." I send a quick glance to Emma to make sure Colin told her to be cool.

The petite redhead is acting as though she hasn't heard a word. When she brings over our breakfasts, she asks, "For dinner tonight, any preferences or dietary restrictions?" She's looking at our unexpected guest.

Brooke glances at me, then back at Emma, "I don't know if I'll be here. My car might be—"

"Not till Monday," I say, watching Brooke light up like the Christmas tree Emma took down a couple weeks ago. And my stress-level ratchets up a notch.

As quickly as she can rearrange her features, she says, "That's terrible. I'm sorry to be such a burden."

She's sorry? Sure she is, about as much as I'm a happy-go-lucky bar owner!

"Not a problem," Emma says, even though I know Brooke was talking to me. "I love to cook for new people. The more the merrier. I was thinking poached salmon or roasted lamb chops."

At the same time, Brooke says, "salmon," when I say "lamb."

Emma laughs. "*Uh-oh*, boss. Guests rule."

Then her eyes widen, and I know she thinks she's blown my cover, but I'm not worried. "You know our employer hates it when you call me that."

Emma breathes a sigh. "Right, TJ. But in the hierarchy of the household, you are, you know, my boss."

"True," I say, relieved she's playing along. "We'll have the salmon since it's the best I've ever tasted." I send Emma a nod by way of saying thanks.

"I believe you," Brooke says, "because these pancakes are fabulous. The cinnamon apple is divine, and they melt in my mouth."

I'd like to melt in your mouth, I think, and quickly shove in another bite. This is going to feel like a long weekend, and it's only Saturday morning.

I finish my breakfast and thank Emma, glad I can hear Colin clearing the driveway. Although the Rover can get through almost anything, it's imperative that the staff can get their cars out, too.

I've hardly made it to the foyer when Brooke catches up. "Hey, so what's happening now?"

I can keep my back to her or turn. I can't help sighing when I choose the latter and give up all attempt at hiding my face. She genuinely doesn't seem to know me, although any minute she might open those luscious lips in a big O and point to me.

"What's happening is that I'm going to the Thirsty Moose." Because I need to get away from this nosy woman who could ruin my life.

"Great. Can I come, too?"

"No," I snap.

She flinches slightly at my vehemence. "Why not?"

Because I want to keep her contained, away from Cy and the rest of my bar staff. And because I'm a hundred percent certain she already took photos before I found her in the living room in the middle of the night. I don't want to have a big scene about how I need to confiscate her phone.

"Because this house is a lot nicer than the bar to hang around in all day." I state the obvious while leaning down to pat Duffy, which makes Beau and Grady lean against me as well. In seconds, I'm trying to make three dogs believe each is getting all my attention.

"True enough, but I'd planned on checking out the town. Remember?" she says.

"Right." Because everyone comes to Rangeley with no intention of skiing!

She shrugs. "I'd really like a ride into town. But I can walk."

"I can't stop you," I say. I mean, I could, but I might get arrested. Turning away, I get as far as the stairs with the three dogs trailing me when she puts her hand on my arm. I don't flinch or pull away, but I do stop. "Yes?"

"I tried to go on my laptop last night and . . . and look something up, but I couldn't create a hotspot with my phone. In fact, my phone has no service here. Weirdly, it can't get or send data. Nothing you can do about that, but if you would give me the internet password—"

"No."

"No?"

"That's right. My employer doesn't want strangers on his network." With that, I shake off her hand and climb the stairs.

"But that's unreasonable," she says, following me. "What harm can I do by being on the same internet?"

"Someone skilled could do a lot," I tell her over my shoulder. At the top of the stairs, I nearly go into my real bedroom, hoping she doesn't notice my hesitation at the door before I stroll on farther.

"But I'm not skilled in . . . internet stuff," she protests. "I can barely get my browser to open."

"Tough luck."

"Really?" She sounds affronted. "Well, that's shitty." The internet seems really important to her. I guess she does have photos.

"Rules are rules."

Her pouty face isn't going to change my mind, but I guess I can bend a little.

"I'll drop you in the center of town. You can at least walk around, and there's a bus for skiers, going back and forth to the base of the mountain all day." No need to tell her that a snowmobile ride from my own back door would get her there faster without ever leaving my property.

"I guess I'll go in the shops and then find a café. I don't really want to ski alone."

I frown. "Everyone skis alone. There aren't any tandem skis."

"You're teasing me, right? Most people go together on the chair lift and then eat lunch or share an après ski drink at the lodge."

"Between the lift and the lodge, they ski alone. And you can meet new people on the lift. I ski single all the time."

"I bet you do," she mutters.

Now that makes me smile.

"OK," she concedes. "I'll catch a ride into town with you. Give me five minutes."

She hurries off, and I go back along the hall to duck into my real bedroom, grab a sweater, and am downstairs lacing up my boots when she enters the mudroom, carrying her backpack.

"Your boots are still crap," I tell her.

Her cute little frown appears. "My boots are adorable."

"Adorably crap. You're going to land on your ass, break an arm, or get frozen toes, which isn't so much fun."

She shrugs. "They're all I brought with me."

"You drove up here with bald tires and shitty boots to look around and do what exactly?"

I keep pressing her, because it would be great if she just admitted it.

"I'm a writer."

Lofty word for a low-life reporter. "Like Hemingway?" I ask, pretending not to know her profession.

"Excuse me?"

"The writer."

"I know who he is," she snaps.

"Perhaps you're more like Matt Haig? Or even Tom Clancy?"

"I write nonfiction," she says.

Now we're getting somewhere. I wait for more.

"I might write about your bar," she adds.

I have to restrain from telling her how not interested in that I am. Putting on my jacket, I notice hers is insufficient for the temperature, but that's her problem. "Then you're a travel writer?"

"I can be," she says. I'll never get a straight answer out of her, but I can try.

"What else do you write?"

"Articles," she says vaguely. "On just about anything. I write content."

"Sounds redundant? Writing *content*, like writing *writing*?"

She frowns. "It's a big world out there beyond Rangeley, and a lot of people want to read quality content every day. Someone has to write it and make an honest living while doing it."

She pulls her phone out of her pocket and swipes it, probably checking the battery.

"Make an honest living." I can't keep the condescending tone from my voice. She's almost trying to justify earning money off invading people's privacy. Speaking of which, I hold out my hand.

"Give me your phone."

"Excuse me?" Her eyes are huge like I just asked for one of her arms.

"I'm going to erase the photos you took of my house."

Her mouth opens and closes in surprise. Then she smirks. "Now, it's *your* house, is it?"

I slipped because I'm mad, but I recover. "My *employer* doesn't want photos taken inside. I told you that."

"I didn't take any," she says, and I can practically see her nose growing.

"Give me your phone or delete the photos while we stand here." If she hadn't insisted on going to town, I would have done this later, taken her phone while she was in the shower or asleep, and not even told her.

Instead, I'm trying to be honest. One of us should be. "You can't take *that* phone out of *this* house."

"I don't have any service here," she gripes. "Maybe not in town, either." We both know she had service in town.

Instead of explaining to her about jammers, I push my palm closer to her, waiting.

"Nope," she says, sliding it behind her and into her pants pocket. "Private property."

I have her backed against the mudroom door before she knows what's happening. We're glaring at one another as I reach around and remove her phone from right over her curvy, corduroy-covered ass.

"Hey! You can't do that."

"I just did. Password?" I ask, looking down into her angry brown eyes. From this angle, her mouth is a sexy bow, and her breasts are twin peaks of perfection.

"Good luck," she says.

I can easily unlock it with software in my office later, so I put it on a shelf, next to the spare gloves. Glancing at her backpack, I think about her laptop. She might've already transferred the photos over, and there's more than one internet café in town. We're going to have another battle.

"Grab your purse but leave the laptop?"

She's looking at the shelf and her phone, not really listening. "How will I call you for a ride back without my phone?"

"Not my problem," I say, opening the door to the garage. "Delete the photos or leave it behind."

"Then I'm not going." She says it like I give a damn, as though she's punishing me, putting her nose in the air. She also snatches her phone from the shelf.

Since my preference is having her stay right here where she can't ask questions in town about how long I've owned the bar or anything like that, I shrug.

"See you later, sweetheart." I slam my Stetson on my head, and I'm gone, with her furious expression the last thing I see.

5

Brooke

What an absolute asshole! How dare he want to delete the photos that he told me not to take.

After removing my boots and coat, I return to the kitchen with the three dogs circling my legs. Emma is still prepping food. Seems like she's baking bread and mixing up something else, perhaps dough for a pie crust.

Usually, I find cooking and baking to be relaxing, having enjoyed short stints in both a bakery and a small café, but I don't offer to muscle in on her territory and help. Besides, I wouldn't want to make anything for that man!

"May I pour myself another cup of coffee?" I ask her, while she's wrist deep in kneading.

"Sure, help yourself. Did you change your mind about going to town? There are some nice shops, loads of pretty sweaters and hats."

"Probably too rich for my blood," I say. "Ski resort prices aren't known for being bargains." Neither the surrounding stores, nor the lift tickets. "My dad used to take us skiing all over the Green and White Mountains. Best day of his life was when someone near the ticket office asked if he needed a spare ticket they couldn't use. It was as if he'd won the lottery."

Emma chuckles. "You're right about that. I have a season pass so it's not too bad. I'd lend it to you, but it has my photo on it."

I smile. No way I can pass for a blue-eyed blonde with a pixie haircut, not with my chestnut hair and brown eyes.

"As for the shops," Emma adds, "I tend to wait until early spring for the deep discounts on winter items."

"How long have you and your husband worked here?" I may as well get some background info before I go upstairs and start writing.

Her gaze flickers over me, then focuses again on the dough.

"You'll have to ask TJ."

So, he told them not to talk to me. *Great, just great.* How the hell did he know I was a reporter?

"Is your real boss as insufferable as TJ?"

"You'll have to ask TJ," she repeats, this time offering a small, apologetic smile. "But in an hour, there'll be pumpkin bread with caramel glaze. And this," she gives the dough a hard punch, "will be a crusty baguette to have with dinner."

I can't hold her loyalty against her, especially not with those treats coming up.

"Thanks for the pancakes and coffee." I salute her with my coffee cup and head for the stairs. Naturally, all three dogs come with me.

"*Yo!*" Emma calls out. Four of us turn at once. But she was talking to the muttley mutts. "Everyone out." They run to the back door in the kitchen. I can see a slider to the back in the living room, too, and there are probably more ways. It seems I'll have all day to figure out the house's layout and snoop in the second-floor rooms. And I'll take as many photos as I like.

Except I won't. Every damn door is locked apart from my room. Even TJ's room across the hall is a no-go. *Fine!* I sit on my comfy bed. I would have fallen asleep instantly last night, but my busy brain couldn't stop imagining myself naked across TJ's lap while he used that paddle he mentioned.

It makes me excited even now, and I open my laptop to chase those wicked fantasies away. Quickly transferring the photos via cable from my phone to my hard drive, I wonder if I'm looking at a small fortune, or at least a moderate windfall. My car might be fixed up half at TJ's expense, but the rent and my health insurance payments are due. I have got to get my financial shit together.

When the transfer is complete, I delete the photos from my phone. Let's see how he feels when he wrangles it away from me again and sees nothing but pics of Mr. Busby.

$♥$♥$♥$

By dinnertime, I've had one of the longest, most frustrating days of my life. Ironically, I'm in a billionaire's house, too, which I would have thought to be more interesting. But with no internet or cell phone connection, I've been stymied all day. When I remembered seeing other vehicles in the dark garage last night, I wondered whether Colin or Emma would lend me one.

Eventually, I went exploring, discovering a pearlescent-white Miata with . . . a pink leather interior! Pretty but odd for either a gaming billionaire or for TJ.

Is it possible that Asher is gay? Is that his big secret and why he hides up here in nowheresville? I mean, his games are testosterone driven with a lot of scantily clad, busty women, as Sherri has shown me. But that doesn't mean much. He has to design for the majority of gamers, and maybe he's worried that his true sexuality would turn off some people.

Anyway, there was no key in sight for the Miata or the other two vehicles, which turned out to be a matching pair of Subarus. Then I got spooked by Colin coming in to get a battery or something for his gardening robot. He gave me a friendly nod, then crossed his arms and stayed in the garage until I asked about the Miata. "Is this your wife's car?"

"Nope." Since no further info was forthcoming, I went back indoors.

With Emma and Colin around, it was difficult to snoop on the first floor. Every time I approached the door off the living room, Emma appeared or called out to me from the kitchen, asking if I needed something.

I wrote as much as I possibly could, describing every detail of my experience so far, including TJ and the other staff and the delicious food, I even wrote about the dogs and the Range Rover. Then I worked on a review of the Thirsty Moose—"Expensive liquor, but good chicken sandwich and a welcoming bartender"—and I ate a large moist piece of pumpkin bread for lunch. *Wow!*

I have to remind myself that I'm not a prisoner. TJ would have gladly taken me to town and probably dumped me there, if only I would've parted with my phone. As the sunset turns to dusk, I know when he comes home by the raucous barking. I've gotten over my trepidation of three energetic dogs at once, given endless belly rubs, and even taken them for a snowy walk around the property, which is huge. Despite staying on the paths that Colin's snow-blowing robot had cleared, my feet were cold, and TJ was right. I just figured I'd be in and out of Old Faithful and a bar and a lodge. I wasn't expecting that storm, fresh powder, and hiking around an estate. Naturally, I took a bunch of photos outside, too.

Glancing at my phone, I see it's just past six. I guess an owner can choose his hours and leave if he wants to precisely when the bar starts hopping. I'm in the living room, which Emma calls the *great room*. High ceiling, exposed beams, and the stonework around the fireplace extends across the whole wall and goes up forever.

"This is practically a climbing wall," I say when TJ enters with the dogs barking and circling him.

He grunts, but it almost sounds like a laugh. "You want a drink, or are you going to show me your climbing prowess? Warning, I won't catch you if you fall."

What a charmer!

"I'll take the drink," I say. A slab of polished granite serves as a bar at one end of the living room, with a fridge behind it. Photo taken and transferred to laptop. TJ goes over to it. "What's your pleasure?"

The internet, I nearly say, but that'll just poke the bear and start some unpleasantness again. "Whatever you're having. As long as it doesn't cost me fifteen of my hard-earned dollareedoos."

Another grunt-like chuckle follows my words.

In two minutes, he brings me a red drink with ice. We tap glasses before he sits in the matching leather chair on the other side of the fireplace, which I figured out how to get blazing. Just ask Colin to light it. The room was already warm enough without the flickering flames, but it's another level of cozy to have a wood-burning fire crackling in the hearth.

"Such a domestic scene," TJ quips. "Tomorrow, you can greet me at the door with my slippers."

"I'll gladly throw them at your head."

My tart response makes him smile, stealing my breath when a dimple shows momentarily. "Where's my paddle?" he asks softly.

Zing! In my mind, once again, I'm across his lap, totally naked while he's dressed and masterfully dishing out a few firm smacks. Causing myself to grow damp, I fidget.

"Try it," he says, referring to the cocktail and oblivious to my raunchy thoughts. "Tell me what you think."

I sniff first. The blend of aromas is unfamiliar. Taking a small sip, I'm not sure I like it. By the third taste, I do. "What am I drinking?"

"It's called a Negroni. Have you heard of it?"

I shake my head. "Sounds fancy."

"A traditional before-dinner drink from Italy. Gin, sweet vermouth, and Campari."

Emma comes from the kitchen and sticks a slice of orange on my glass's rim, then does the same for TJ's. "What kind of bartender are you?" the blonde chef teases.

"I'm not," he says. "I'm a bar *owner*. But thanks. That's the perfect garnish."

"I know," Emma says, before setting down a plate of puff pastries and tartlets.

"What's all this?" he asks.

"We have a guest, so I made party food."

"That's really kind of you," I say.

She smiles. "Any friend of TJ's is welcome."

He and I lock glances, and his good mood slips a little. We are hardly that, but I wonder if she's made that statement one, two, or twelve times before. He seems like the kind of guy who'd be a player, although more likely to spend the night elsewhere rather than bring women home to his boss's mountain lodge.

I try a tartlet. It's melt-in-my-mouth cheesy deliciousness.

"Wow!" I say.

"Can't be better than pancakes," TJ says. He pops one in his mouth, then chases it with a puff pastry. "I stand corrected."

I try the puff next. It has a creamy mushroom filling.

"If Mr. Asher doesn't pay you well," I say to Emma, who has hung around, waiting to be praised, "you could make a fortune as a caterer." I worked for one, lasting about two months before getting fired for various infractions, including talking to the guests.

The mood shifts again with my mention of Asher, this time to uncomfortable awkwardness. Emma looks from me to TJ.

"Who?" he asks, sounding bored.

I roll my eyes and change my words. "Thank you, Emma. This is great."

Nodding, she asks him, "Dining room or island?"

"Island," TJ says, reminding me again that only Emma thinks I'm a welcome guest. Sipping the drink, I watch him swivel the leather easy chair back and forth in a hypnotic fashion as we sit in companionable silence, not the least strained. It's almost as though he's forgotten I'm here, until he speaks.

"I'll turn off the lights so you can see those stars that so impressed you last night."

Pulling out his phone, he swipes and taps. One of the rectangular wall panels lights up across the room, receiving commands remotely from TJ's phone. The living room lights dim then darken. Another tap and the curtains swish open. I squirrel away the knowledge that the wall panel controls a lot more than the lights, and then I enjoy the view.

After a few minutes, I say something banal and cliché but accurate. "The sky looks larger, and the stars look closer," I remark. "Very cool."

He merely nods. Then TJ uses his phone again to make a super flat TV rise out of a sideboard. He doesn't say anything or give me any choice in what we watch while we eat pastries and finish our drinks. Turns out to be news from all over the world, until Emma says it's time for dinner.

A few hours later, I've devoured the best salmon of my life, and spent a mostly silent evening watching documentaries. Weirdly, and totally unremarked on as if this is normal behavior, TJ switches among three programs: one on Wyatt Earp, one on Apollo 13, and one on classic car restoration. It doesn't seem to bother him as he cuts off the various narrators, but I think he's soaking in the info from all three like a thirsty sponge.

My head is buzzing with all the space, car, and cowboy footage when I climb the stairs to bed. My bed, a scant few feet from TJ's door. The man who talked about going all slaphappy on my ass. Never experienced that before, but I admit I've read books, and I'm curious.

But because of my sad bank account, I'm more curious about Mr. Asher's bedroom, where he is, and when he'll be back.

Dozing off until one in the morning, I find myself wide awake and staring at the ceiling. Deciding to break the rules again since I have nothing to lose, I traipse along the hallway, trying doors to the rooms I cannot access. One of them must be the master bedroom. No go.

I've decided that the office must be behind the door down the short hallway to the right of the living room. Emma kept me away from it all day, except for one sneaky jiggle of the doorknob that I managed, only to find it locked. And no doubt it's locked now. But what if the control pad that works the lights also works the doors?

In a flash, I've stepped over Grady and Beau at the top of the stairs, while considering sliding down the thick, smooth banister but ultimately deciding against it. I could fall over the side and break my neck. It would solve my financial problems, but Mr. Busby would miss me. Instead, I tiptoe downstairs and go to the control panel just inside the living room.

It lights up when I touch it. Nice. A menu offers me LIGHTS, which I touch and see a bunch of choices. Both rooms and light locations are listed, even the outside and the garage. I don't turn anything on. Next on the menu is FRONT GATE and EAST GATE, followed by GARAGE DOOR. There's a red lit button next to ALARM. I assume by the way it's glowing and blinking, it controls a whole-house alarm, and I'd probably trip it if I opened a window or exterior door. Nothing says INTERNET ACCESS. That would be too easy. But there's another category: LOCKS.

Clicking it, I see a house diagram with clickable numbers for what I assume is every room in the house that has a door. That leaves out the kitchen, living room, dining room, and foyer. It's exciting. I test my theory by clicking on the door at Mud1, turning it from red to green. Running to the interior mudroom door, it's unlocked. Going back to the panel, I touch the word again, dashing back to find the mudroom is now locked. I'm giddy, as though I've cracked the German Enigma code from *The Imitation Game*.

Scanning the diagram, I identify the room at the end of the hall. It's marked 1–3. First floor, third door? Could be. I turn it green and tiptoe down the short corridor, putting my ear to the door. I can't hear anything. Slowly, I open the door to a pitch-black room with a solar system of tiny red, blue, green, and white lights glowing in the darkness.

Yikes! Using my phone, I find the small wall panel and turn on the lights.

Oh, man! The room is filled with monitors and wall screens, a mainframe and a couple laptops. A shelf has routers and modems blinking. Everything has a power indicator, creating all those colored dots of light.

I shouldn't be surprised at all. After all, Jordan Asher made his fortune in gaming software. I think this puts to bed any doubt over whose house I'm in.

Good thing I made room on my phone. I snap photos from every angle, while managing to turn off the lights and leave in under four minutes. I may try to slip in there again tomorrow when TJ is at his bar. I'd feel less nervous when I'm not risking running into him at any—

"*Aahh!*" I yell when he moves out of the shadows as I'm stepping over the two sentinels at the top of the stairs. He's barefoot, in dark-gray sweatpants and a long-sleeve, navy-blue T-shirt that fits him like a glove. All muscles on display.

"Hard to believe you needed a snack after that meal," he says.

My heart is pounding out of my chest, although I'm relieved I didn't go over backward in surprise, breaking my neck in a spectacular staircase fall.

"Nope," I say, my voice strangled with fright. I cough to clear my throat. "Just a glass of water."

He makes a point of looking at my hands, which are empty since my phone is in the waistband of my yoga pants.

"Drank it downstairs. Didn't want to break a rule about bringing water upstairs."

"Right," he says. "That makes perfect sense." His sarcasm isn't lost on me.

"Well, good night." I start to walk past him when he whips my phone off of me like a Times Square pickpocket.

"Hey," I say. "Give that back."

He strides ahead of me down the hallway, straight into my room. When I catch up, he's stretching out on that comfy mattress, crossing his legs at the ankle, and thumbing across my phone's Home screen.

"Password," he demands again, just like this morning.

"Sorry, no."

"I may have to flush it," he says.

"What? Don't be a bully. Give it back."

"How about I run the Range Rover over it a couple times?"

"I can't tell if you're serious right now."

"Serious as a heart attack, sweetheart."

For once, I'm glad I'm stuck with TJ. If he were Asher, I'd be in real trouble. That man could undoubtedly open my phone without even trying. A bar owner has to ask for my password.

But TJ can do some damage, so I need to placate this mountain man. With him lying on the bed, a few methods come to mind. With my head filled with lewd thoughts, I move closer, until I'm looking down at him.

Offering what I hope is a sexy smile, I ask as nicely as I can, "Please, will you give me my phone back?"

He sighs. "Won't do you any good." With those puzzling words, he holds the phone out to me.

I reach for it like a fool. In a classic move, TJ grips my wrist and yanks me on top of him.

I yelp, as he surprises me for the second time in three minutes. In this case, however, I'm not afraid of tumbling downstairs. I'm curious about the clanging alarm bells ringing in my body—or at least, that's what this sensation feels like.

It's a five-alarm fire, too, with heat flowing through my veins, my skin hot where I'm sprawled across him, and a spark of lust throbbing at my core.

Dropping my phone to the bedspread, he sinks his hands into my hair, cradles my head and slowly draws my face down to his. With a whisker-space between us, he says, "Password in exchange for a kiss."

What?! How arrogant!

"No," I huff. As if his kiss is worth giving up the contents of my phone.

He grins, causing butterflies to battle in my stomach. I want to relax onto him, melt my curves against his hard muscles.

"Password in exchange for showing you the pleasures of a properly conducted spanking."

I gasp as my lady bits flood with damp, fierce desire. I want that. So. Very. Much. My pussy tightens and tingles. But we're talking about my livelihood.

"No can do," I whisper because my throat has closed. I'm sure my expression is one of obvious disappointment. For a second, I helplessly curl my hips into his, letting my mound press against . . . some part of him.

"Don't look so sad," he says. "I'm happy to dish out a free sample. You game?"

Since I can plainly feel his erection, I know he truly is ready to dish. But I can't say yes. Can I? It's too tawdry and pathetic and submissive. *Ugh!* Instead, I nod because I'm inflamed with wanting him to take control and touch me.

He rolls me over onto my back and gets up, taking my phone with him. I start to say something, until he sets it safely on the nightstand.

"Be right back," he promises.

Shit! Am I really doing this? Why not? I'm an adult woman who hasn't had sex in half a year. I'm wasting my prime banging years.

A tiny part, maybe my left pinky toe, hopes TJ was joking and doesn't come back. I should've taken the time to hide my phone, but I'm too preoccupied by the much larger part of me that is throbbing, wet, and ready. *Please don't let him be joking!*

When he returns carrying a bottle of wine and glasses in one hand and some other stuff in the other, I don't move a muscle. He manages to hit the light switch with his elbow as he passes it.

The room would be plunged into darkness, except for the small bedside lamp with its warm-yellow glow.

"Are you a vampire?" I ask, trying to sound witty, but my voice is shaking.

He sets down all the things he's holding onto the oak dresser, and I try to see around him for that paddle he promised and fail. I watch him open the bottle and pour. It's a dark-red wine in a large glass.

"That's a healthy pour, as my cousin would say."

He makes a rough sound that I realize is a chuckle. Seems he's rusty at laughing.

"Neither of us is driving," he points out and hands me a glass. "Might as well enjoy the moment."

"True," I say, feeling like I'm in a dream, and we tap the rims together without making any toast.

"That's delicious," I gush, and I mean it. "I guess if you want the best, you hang with a bar owner."

He nods, looking me over in my yoga pants and pullover.

Into the silence that, to me, is thick with promise, I say, "I'm almost invisible in this light."

"Once you're naked, I'll be able to see you fine."

I was right about the promise of what's to come. While my insides do a fluttery dance from his blunt statement, TJ opens the curtains and lets in the moonlight. Just as swiftly, he steps out of the headlight-bright beam and turns off the bedside light.

I take another sip of the wine. And another. With a buzz going on, all my inhibitions just walk up the moonbeams and out into the night.

Setting my glass on the nightstand, I say, "I better slow down."

My pulse, however, disagrees with my words, speeding up until I can feel my heartbeat in my neck. Nervousness and excitement are as intoxicating as the wine, and my fierce craving for this man has me almost shaking.

After taking another sip, he sets his glass down on the bureau, and strides to the end of the bed, where he gives me a frank appraisal, practically spreading my legs with the intensity of his gaze.

"Brooke," he says. "Pretty name. Pretty woman." He places a hand on each of my ankles, curls his fingers around them, and drags me toward him until my body is in the square of moonlight.

"I was just a baby when I got it." A dumb remark that isn't sexy at all, but the wine has hit me hard. "What's TJ stand for?" I ask quickly to cover my embarrassment.

He hesitates. "Are you a reporter?"

Uh-oh! How did he know? He cannot possibly know.

"Isn't it reasonable to ask the name of the man I'm about to get naked with?"

"It's a mouthful, hence the nickname. I'll tell you later, when my mouth is empty again."

With that, he grasps the top of my yoga pants and peels them down my legs, discarding them over his shoulder. My own mouth goes dry as desert dust. If I could still reach the wine, I'd drink more. His silvery gaze across my skin is scorching, especially when it lands on my little pink thong.

"Very nice," he says, lowering himself to the bed, resting between my spread thighs.

All at once, I am nothing but sensitive nerve endings. With every fiber of my being, I anticipate this man's first touch. When it comes—the graze of his fingers across my muff as he drags my thong to the side—I'm instantly lightheaded. And wet.

He uses two fingers to part my already swollen nether lips, splaying them wide to reveal me, slick with need. With the thumb of his other hand, TJ gently pushes up my soft mound and tender hood of my aching clit, drawing it out to play.

When he blows a puff of air over the area, I groan, closing my eyes and letting him do what he wants. He doesn't speak or say anything cringey or call me *baby*. I like his silence. TJ just gets down to business. With his tongue and—*yes, yes, yes*—his teeth, he performs magic.

In moments, I'm clutching the sheets with both hands fisted, as my body tenses and draws tight as a drum. It's been way too long. When his big hands circle over my hip bones and slide under my ass to tilt me upward, giving him better access, I nearly start to cry. He feasts on me like a man starved, alternating between taking my clit between his lips and sucking on it, then releasing it to use the flat of his tongue across and around it. Finally, with his teeth, he gently tugs it, making me yell out with the painful pleasure before his hot tongue again soothes any discomfort.

I roll my head from side to side, moaning some garbled syllables that definitely could not be transcribed into words. When my body reaches its flashpoint, I fly high with a shaking, shattering, loudly vocalized orgasm.

I've had good sex before. Maybe it's because he's a stranger that's why this felt so extraordinarily wild. I came faster and harder than I can ever recall coming before. Instead of a steady, hill-climbing locomotive, my body's reaction was a lightning-fast, bullet train.

Easing off of me, TJ smiles, looking pleased with himself. Who can blame him? He gets up, stretches, and goes for his wine as I reach for mine. I can see his impressive erection bulging against the front of his sweatpants, making me eager for what comes next.

"So, are you up for something a little spicier?"

For a moment, I'm confused, but given the situation, it dawns on me what he means. I'd forgotten I was supposed to get spanked.

"I've never . . . That is, I'll try anything once."

With those fateful words, I open myself to a night of sensual surprises.

6

Jordan

When Brooke went off like a rocket, fast and intense, I thought she might be done. But when I asked her if she was ready for more, her eyes caught the moonlight and shone with naked lust. She was so ready for one orgasm, I'm sure I can tease out a couple more.

"Flip over, pillow under your hips, ass in the air. I've wanted to do this since you mouthed off in my bar."

Her face tells me everything—how horny she still is despite her first climax and how excited she is about dipping her toe into a new sexual experience.

I don't make her wait, although in some cases, that's half the fun. As soon as her rear is showcased by a moonbeam, I ease her thong down her thighs and toss them. Then I pick up the narrow, flat wooden paddle from the bureau.

She cranes her neck to see what I'm doing, and I realize I should have restrained and blindfolded her. *Next time*, if there is one.

"Close your eyes," I order, and she does. Her swift obedience is a massive turn-on.

Having thought this through while I was downstairs getting the wine, I'm about to sink to the level of the enemy.

"Don't move," I say as I balance the paddle across her trembling ass cheeks. It would've been nice to wait until they were red, but there might not be another opportunity. Withdrawing my phone from my sweatpants pocket, I snap two photos, one of only her ass, one that shows the upturned half of her face as well as her body. Insurance taken care of, I put the phone away, and reclaim the paddle.

Stroking my palm across her butt, I then caress it with the unyielding paddle. She tenses in anticipation. I begin with a tap, one ass cheek, then the other. Brooke giggles, probably letting off some nervousness. Immediately, I up the ante.

Smack. The smallest hint of pink blooms across her pale skin. The length of the paddle allows me to make contact with her entire ass with each stroke. *Smack. Smack. Smack!*

"Oh," she murmurs under her breath.

Now we have some serious blush.

"You want me to stop?" I ask.

"No," she answers really fast. "Unless you want to. I mean . . . if . . ."

She doesn't get it yet, so I tell her, "Your pleasure is my pleasure." Before I land the next swat, I drag the paddle down to the space between her legs. Lightly swinging it from side to side against her thighs, I make her part them before I run the paddle's edge over her slit. She sucks in a loud breath.

A glance at the wood shows a glistening film of her arousal, making my cock hard as a ski pole. And then, to increase her enjoyment, I put a little muscle into it.

Thwack. Thwack. Thwack!

"Ohhhhh." She emits a long, breathy moan.

I can't resist. I ease out the camera and get another shot of her, with her eyes closed, her gorgeous mouth open as she gasps, and her ass turning fiery red. Then I put it away again. Absolute insurance that she'll keep my secrets.

"If you like this," I say between smacks, "and your next boyfriend is into it, you can progress to whips and floggers."

She tenses up immediately, and I suppose I frightened her. In fact, personally, I haven't gone farther than reddening a woman's ass with my leather belt, which seems to sting more than my hand or this paddle.

"Open wider," I order.

Again, she doesn't hesitate, and I can only imagine the pulsing heat in her pussy from all the blood rushing to the area.

Dragging the paddle across her exposed lips, I give them the gentlest tap. She jumps then keeps her hips as elevated as possible, her body begging for more. Another tap becomes a firmer smack.

"Yesss," she hisses.

It's the beauty of a narrow paddle, being able to get right onto her most sensitive spot. And clearly, she loves it.

"Please," she begs, and my cock aches to come out and play.

"Please *what*, sweetheart?"

"I don't . . . I don't know. Don't stop. Harder."

But I would never strike her pussy any harder. Spanking her ass again, I watch her alternately lifting her hips for something more and grinding her mound into the soft cushion, seeking relief.

I slide my finger deep into her wet channel, rewarded when she hisses again.

"Yesssss. God, yessssss!"

I barely have a second finger inside her when I feel her second shuddering climax. She pushes back, impaling herself as hard as she can on my fingers, over and over. And then she falls silent, her entire body going from tense to limp as a pasta noodle.

"That's pretty impressive," I tell her. "*Without* any clitoral stimulation."

She laughs softly into the mattress before turning over, blinking up at me with a gratified smile. Maybe she's entirely too satisfied. I hope Brooke is ready for more. Although, if she wants to stop, I'll return to my room, take myself in hand, recall her sexy sounds and the look of her bright red ass, and go off in record time.

But I don't have to go it alone. Reaching up, Brooke runs her hand over the front of my sweatpants.

"That's pretty impressive, too," she says. "I'm happy to reciprocate."

"Happy to let you," I say. I keep thinking I should be repulsed by the fact that I'm having sex with someone who came here to expose my life to the world and make money while doing it. But I'm attracted to her despite her profession. Honestly, I can't remember any woman stirring me up inside this much in years.

So, I guess we need to decide what we're doing. "Do you want to blow me or have intercourse?"

She wrinkles her nose, which is sexy and adorable at the same time. "I've never been asked that question before, not like that, so straightforward and frank."

Seems only polite. I shrug, using the movement to pull my shirt off over my head. Whatever we're doing, I intend to be comfortable.

"I guess I'll go for door number one," she says. If this is our only time, then I'll never know what it's like to sink balls deep inside her. But I'm definitely not disappointed. For me, either way, it was a win.

Sitting on the edge of the bed, Brooke unties my draw string with her delicate hands and those sexy, dark-grape-colored nails just made for raking over my skin in the heat of passion. Then she tugs my pants down my hips.

"Nearly poked my eye out," she jokes, when my cock springs up.

I roll my eyes. Joking isn't exactly an aphrodisiac, but my pent-up lust combined with the way she's looking at me causes pre-cum to pearl up on the tip. Kicking off my pants,

I stretch out on the bed. It's been an unexpectedly long day, and the second night in a row that I'm up at two in the morning. Yet instead of exhaustion, I feel exhilarated, especially when she settles between my legs.

Before she gets down to it, I ask, "Will you take your top off?"

Brooke actually looks shy, which is hilarious considering what we've done tonight. Slowly, she pulls her black sweater over her head, and I get a look at her beautiful breasts for the first time. Fuck, she's gorgeous! The moonlight makes her skin luminescent, practically glowing. I can't help reaching out and palming her, while rubbing my thumbs over her nipples until they harden into perfect pink buds.

Closing her eyes, she leans into my touch, but with accurate aim, she wraps one hand around my cock and squeezes while I play. Her glossy nails are an extra visual aphrodisiac. Eventually, I have to give in to the intoxicating sensation of her fingers' firm grasp. My heart is pounding as I release her tits and let my arms fall to the bed in surrender.

Without my touch, able to focus, she drops low, her forearms resting on my thighs as she takes the length of me between her lips. With one of her hands tugging on my balls and the other squeezing my shaft, she sucks me in, licks me over, drags her teeth down the length of me, and then nibbles on the head before starting again.

I almost tell her how amazingly good this feels, but I think Brooke has enough power over me without my feeding her ego. Instead, I close my eyes and give in. She glides smoothly up and down my erection with her hand *and* her mouth, while tugging and squeezing my sack. I'm surprised how quickly I'm ready to come.

With her lips stretched around my cock, I feel her begin to hum, sending a tantalizing vibration down my shaft. It's the last fucking straw, and my control snaps. As my balls draw up, ready to shoot their load, I start to pull out. After all, I didn't ask to come in her sexy mouth, and I'm not going to assume she'll appreciate it.

But Brooke makes a warning sound to stop me. In fact, she takes me deeper and sucks harder while I surge uncontrollably into her mouth, feeling the tip of my cock against the back of her throat as my cum starts spurting.

She lets me finish pumping into the hot, wet heaven between her lips. The only saving grace, as I lie there, feeling wrung out and exhausted, is knowing I didn't do anything to break her trust. I didn't grab hold of her head so she couldn't retreat. She took all of me by her own choice.

Flopping down beside me, she doesn't try to snuggle. She simply rests her arm over her eyes and yawns widely.

"I can take a hint," I say, getting up. "Do you want to finish your wine?"

"Sorry, too tired. I feel like I ran a marathon. Out of practice, I guess." Maybe realizing she has said too much, Brooke laughs. "OK, out. This girl needs to sleep."

It's my house, so I don't bother dressing. I snatch up my clothes in one hand, making sure my cell phone is still in my pocket, before I take my glass of wine with me. I leave the paddle. After all, her car won't be fixed until late Monday at the earliest.

Reaching the door, though, this feels a little unfinished. I'm not the "sleep well" kind of guy. I don't have fairy dust to make her sleep any which way, and if she wants to toss and turn, that's her business.

Since Brooke gave me a great night, I say simply, "Thanks."

"Right back at you," she says, clutching the down comforter to her body, shielding herself from view, as we return to being strangers.

It's not a good time to remind her I don't want her roaming my house, and I know I blew it by working late and forgetting to lock down my office. I'm pretty sure she was inside, and I'll check the security camera in the morning. I doubt she would touch anything, but I'm certain she took photos.

I'll have to get her phone soon and erase everything, but it can wait until tomorrow. At least I don't have to go back to my room and jack off.

7

Brooke

I sleep better than I have in months, maybe years. Maybe it's the downy soft flannel sheets that almost make the frigid winter worthwhile. I don't try any of the doors on my way down to breakfast, but later, after TJ leaves for the bar, I intend to go into Asher's office again. Maybe I'll even turn on a laptop. By accident, of course. Just a little bump against the button and presto. *Oh* dear! My bad.

TJ is already there, reading the paper.

"Good morning," I say, because I wasn't raised by rude wolves.

He barely looks up and only grunts in reply. No one would ever know I had his cock in my mouth last night by this frosty reception.

"What time are you leaving?" I ask, pouring myself some coffee.

He puts the paper down. "Why?"

I shrug, not bothering to reply. Two can play at this game. Emma comes out of the generous pantry I peeked into the first day, and she's carrying a bag of potatoes.

"Good morning, Brooke. It's a beautiful sunny day. Let's get you on the slopes."

I wasn't expecting this. "No, that's OK. I don't have the right clothing, and I'm not a big skier."

Emma tilts her head. "You said you loved it when your dad took you."

TJ is listening, his gray-green eyes fixed on me. I don't particularly enjoy the way his gaze all but peels me like an onion, trying to get beneath my confident exterior. Anyway, he needn't try too hard because I'm going to confess the truth.

"I'm mediocre at best. It's been a while."

"Good thing I'm an expert," he says unexpectedly. "I can teach you a few things."

I bet you could. He taught me a few things about myself last night. All we do is stare long and unwavering until Emma breaks the stalemate.

"You should totally go," she says. "The powder is fresh, and the views are outstanding. I'll be going for a couple hours tomorrow."

I scrunch up my face. "I haven't skied in years, to be honest."

"Isn't that why you came up here?" Emma asks.

My expression freezes as I dart another look at TJ, who returns it with a raised eyebrow as if he knows exactly why I came up here. They're both waiting for my answer.

"I wasn't sure I'd be brave enough to ski."

"But why else would you come to Rangeley?" she asks, all wide-eyed. "Not for the expensive shops we talked about."

I pointedly don't look at TJ this time. I can't bear to see his smug face. But he chimes in anyway. "Brooke's a travel writer, among writing other *content.*"

I should've said that to Emma in the first place. But I add, "My cousin, Sherri, skied here last year. She had such a good time, especially in the watering holes *after* skiing, that when I had a few days off, I decided to check Rangeley out for myself."

"So, more for the nightlife?" Emma persists, but she shakes her head. "I can tell you it's a lot more fun in the bars if you're one of the skiers. The après-ski crowd tends to shun the non-skiers. Let TJ get you acclimated to Saddleback Mountain. I promise you you'll have a blast."

Probably have more fun going back upstairs with TJ than to Saddleback. So how come forty minutes later, wearing borrowed ski pants and a warm parka from Emma, am I on the back of a snowmobile? *Without* my phone! I guess because I couldn't come up with a reasonable excuse for driving all this way north not to at least go to the ski area. And I wasn't going to argue with him about my phone in front of Emma. Besides, with all the photos I have on the laptop, I'm less concerned about sending them to the cloud.

On the ride over, I'm having a pretty good time, with my arms around TJ, my front pressed against his back. We leave from the property without ever going to the road. About two acres from the house, we go through what TJ calls *the East Gate*, which I remember from the alarm setting on the house control panel. Even though we're now outside the fence, the land we're on is still Asher's, a clear shot to the base of Saddleback Mountain. The crisp air, the pristine forest around us, it's magical, and I feel as though I'm on another planet, holding onto an alien—a sexy, strong, male alien.

All too soon, I'm strapping on rental skis and making my way to the chair lift. TJ had equipment in a locker at the lodge and a season pass. He paid for my ticket and my equipment. I try to be grateful, but the mountain looks steep, and despite what Emma said, the sun has already disappeared behind heavy, gray January clouds.

We take our places at the end of the lift line, which moves quickly. In no time, the choice has been made and I'm dangling in the air.

"Wow! Look at that view."

He nods, not much of a talker in any situation, which doesn't bother me. I watch people of all skill levels on the blue-tinged winding trail beneath us and crane my neck around to look behind me as the lodge becomes smaller. The scenery is just as beautiful in that direction, over the valley, and to neighboring mountains. Peering past TJ, I can see the way we came on the snowmobile and think I can even see Asher's house.

Which reminds me, I've had sex with someone whose name I don't know.

"What's your last name?"

For a moment, I think he's not going to answer. He's looking in the same direction as me, to the right, which mean I'm staring at the back of his black helmet. Finally, he turns to me with those gray-green eyes. "Linter."

"Linter?"

"It's Scottish."

"Mine's English, from Essex," I say, but he barely nods, plainly uninterested. I glance ahead and feel a twinge in my stomach. It's a familiar sensation, because I live up to what I say. I do try anything once, from sky diving to para sailing to getting my nether regions waxed. But that doesn't mean I enjoy the feeling of being uneasy.

Except I really, really did enjoy last night, both the anticipation *and* the actual spanking. Mind-blowing, in fact. But I need to stop reliving being paddled by this sexy man next to me and focus on skiing. Or I'll be landing on my slightly sore ass.

Adjusting my goggles, I scoot to the edge of the bench, preparing for getting off the lift. I hate this part.

"Relax," he says.

"Easy for you to say, Mr. Expert." His goggles are up on his helmet, and he's leaning back, looking like he wouldn't care if he had to jump from here and start skiing. I confess to him why lifts make me anxious. "I've been knocked over by the chair while trying to get on."

He looks like he's trying not to smile.

"It was humiliating. In front of everyone waiting behind me. They had to stop the entire lift by pressing that big button."

He snorts out a laugh. Glad I can amuse him.

"And a couple times, when I've disembarked, or whatever you call getting off this contraption," I continue, "I fell. Right on that little smooth plateau before it angles down. Again, they had to stop the lift so other skiers weren't forced to ski over me. I could feel everyone's irritation, not to mention being on display and entertaining a mountain of people."

"Fuck 'em."

Did I hear him correctly? "Excuse me?"

"Don't worry about what anyone else is doing. You got on the chair just fine. Not to mention being the sexiest skier in line."

I wasn't expecting that weird pep-talk or boost to my confidence. I feel my cheeks heat up. That was kind of him, and I'm not used to him being even the smallest bit kind, except in the bedroom.

"Enjoy the ride, we're almost there," he says, bringing me back to the side of a cold mountain where the blue shadows make everyone look muted. "When it says 'tips up,' I want to see your gorgeous tits perk up under that jacket and your ski tips go up, too. Then keep your poles out of the way in one hand, and push off the chair seat with the other. Easy."

I ignore the remark about my breasts, although my nipples decide to harden because last night is still so fresh in my mind. "You make it sound simple."

"It is. And the little kids do it *without* poles."

"They don't have so far to fall."

He shakes his head. "Nearly there." He draws his goggles down off his helmet. "Ready?"

"As I'll ever be."

"Let me check," he says, and runs his gloved hand over my chest.

The shock of his bold move—in public—wipes the fear from my mind. Next thing I know, I'm gliding down the small incline from the lift and following TJ to the left, out of the way of those disembarking behind us.

There's a big three-foot by five-foot map of the mountain and all the trails, and I start toward it.

"You don't need to look at that. Come on, this way. I'll show you one of my favorite runs. Hope it's not too advanced."

The last thing I hear is "advanced," as I ski past a sign with the iconic black diamond. I was hoping to see the friendly blue square of an intermediate slope. Right away, I'm in trouble. He's skiing like we're in an Olympic competition, and I recall what he said about no one skiing together. I guess I should have got on a different lift, one that only went up halfway.

As he disappears while I start to curse Emma for butting in, I begin my slow descent, trying not to get in the way of the experts. I'm not a dreadful skier, just a timid, out-of-practice one. The steepness of the slope makes me turn every few yards so I don't pick up speed. With each turn, I go horizontally across the ski run, reach the tree line on the other side of the trail before doing another graceless turn in the other direction. Crossing over in front of those going down in a more vertical fashion, I continue the same routine until I reach the other tree line.

After ten minutes of this, I've only gone down about a football stadium's length, and I have a long way to go. A few people have yelled "right" or "left" as they came from behind and warned me of their approach.

Another ten minutes, and I wish I was at the lodge, drinking cocoa and having a rest. My calves are tight and aching already. If I can just get off this bowl-shaped section, I'm sure the rest will be smooth—

I fall spectacularly, with a ski coming off and sliding a few feet down despite the auto brakes that pop down to claw at the snow. I ponder my choices. Eventually, taking off the other ski, I look up the mountain and when it's clear, I dash to the edge of the run, getting out of the way. I'll need to retrieve my other ski, but skiers are whizzing by.

Despite not being injured in the least, it seems a good idea to remain where I am, if only to catch a breather. I've strenuously made the least possible progress and am going to have to start going downhill instead of across, or I'll still be on this run when they close the lifts.

Plopping my sorry self down by the trees, I look around, enjoying the fresh air, contemplating putting my skis over my shoulder and walking down. Or I could ditch the damn things all together. After all, I don't own them. I didn't even pay for the rental.

A skier comes to a stop just below me. "Need help?" he asks.

"Thanks, no, I'm good."

"'K." And he skis away.

This happens another time, and I am starting to think these are the friendliest people when a couple of kids go by, laughing and shouting "fucktard" and "bunny sloper."

After a few minutes, I hear my name and look up. There's TJ, on the lift over the trail.

"Are you hurt?"

I raise a hand and wave. But I'm still sitting there when he skis down to me about five minutes later, laying down a spray of powder as he stops just below me. My mouth drops open. TJ must have got off the lift and skied straight down. I mean really straight and very fast.

"Are you injured?"

"No, I waved. That meant I was fine."

"It doesn't mean anything. Why aren't you standing? Why aren't you skiing?"

"I only have one ski," I point out.

He doesn't even have to remove his to reclaim my ski and sidestep back up the few yards to give it to me.

"I didn't realize you were a beginner," he gripes.

"I'm not. You may not have heard me earlier, but it's been a number of years."

"And when you last skied, back in the dark ages, what level were you? A double-diamond expert or a beginner?"

I sigh. No point in lying. "Upper-level beginner to mid-level intermediate. Also, different resorts classify their runs differently," I point out. "I've skied Bretton Woods blue-square slopes. But it was many—"

"Many years ago, I know. Well, you can't live here. Get your skis on."

He's right. Although, it might take me less time to hike up and see if the lift operator will let me ride back down.

"No," he says, guessing my thoughts by the way I'm gazing up the mountain. "You can't go down that way." He jabs the pointy end of his pole at me.

"Hey," I protest.

"Grab hold, sweetheart."

I do, and he pulls me to standing. My muscles are already tired. I guess I'm a marshmallow.

"Lay your skis parallel and get them on," he orders. "Are your hands cold?"

"A little." I put my boot toe in the top of the binding and press down with a satisfying snap and do the same with the other one. *Oh, yippee!* I'm back on my skis.

"You let your gloves get wet. Here." TJ has stripped off his large man gloves and he's offering them to me.

"What about you?" I ask.

"Let's get a move on."

I strip my gloves off and jam them into my jacket pocket before donning his. They are big and incredibly warm. My fingers are so happy, like each just went from a freezer to a down sleeping bag. Meanwhile, he has put on some plain slim leather driving gloves, but I guess they're better than nothing.

Away we go in the most embarrassing fashion. TJ is skiing backward, doing a reverse snow plow, and he lets me snow plow facing forward. Between. His. Legs!

I think I saw some toddlers given this same treatment on the gradual slope near the chairlift entrance. And I'm positive I hear laughter from other skiers. Ignoring them, I'm finally getting somewhere, even if only because my fisted hands, holding my poles, are resting against his fisted hands. I marvel at his thigh strength as he manages to keep himself from speeding up while keeping me at a slow pace down the steep grade.

"You win," he mutters. "We're skiing *together.*"

I'd laugh if I wasn't so mortified. But also, grateful.

We don't do this for too long, only until we've traversed the steepest part of the run. And then, ever so gracefully, TJ arcs away from me and to the side while I turn the other way and stop.

"Don't stop," he encourages. "Let's see what you've got."

I just want this to end, so I point my skis down and . . . fall.

"You can do this," he says. Is it my imagination or is he sounding a little desperate? Like me, he's probably starting to think he'll never get off this damned mountain, not unless he ditches me.

"I can do this," I say to myself. And then I do. I'm slow but steady, and I spend more time with my ski tips pointed downward rather than across the mountain, and less time going side to side like a deranged duck in a shooting gallery.

TJ stays with me. Sometimes he's in front, sometimes behind, occasionally making sharp turns in the space beside me, then waiting below until I catch up. Finally, we come around a curve, and the tree line disappears. There's the main lodge and three other runs feeding into the same space, with chairlifts on both sides of our trail.

Without telling him my intention, I ski directly to the lodge, where there are racks to rest your skis. Silently, not caring if he agrees, I take them off, lean them against the rack, and loosen my boot buckles to make it easier to walk.

"You've had one run," he points out. "Granted, it took an hour and a half, but still."

"I'm done," I say. "Thanks for breaking your rule and skiing with me. Now go have fun, and I'll wait here for the ride home."

Strangely, he's removing his skis, too. "I'll come with you. I have something to show you."

"Perv," I joke.

Amazingly, *that* elicits a laugh from him. Soon, we're inside, drinking hot cocoa, eating chocolate chip cookies, and watching the other skiers come down through the big windows. We're not chatting like best buds, but he's not being hostile, either.

Finally, having regained my equilibrium and achieved a happy place due to all the chocolate, I ask, "What did you want to show me?"

He grabs a glossy brochure from the stack on the table. "Take a look." TJ opens it to the trail map and points to a trail that goes three quarters of the way to the top. Then he drags his finger down it to the lodge. "You skied that."

I read the map. "Peachy's Peril?"

"If you can do that, you can do nearly all the runs on the mountain. Don't you want to ski one more run?"

I recall my father always wanting to get another run in, but that was because he wanted to squeeze every moment out of the cost of that ticket. I doubted TJ cared about the cost.

"You go, and I'll stay here."

He gets up and takes our empty cups to the trash. A part of me is disappointed in myself. Maybe I'll never ski again if I don't get back out there. As if that matters! I may never afford a ski ticket again, either.

But TJ doesn't walk away. He comes back and holds his big hand out to me. I stare at it for a few seconds.

"I thought people didn't really ski together," I say, although I'm already placing my hand in his. The feeling of being female, petite even, in comparison to his maleness is exciting. More so when he gives my fingers a gentle squeeze.

"I guess I was wrong. Twice. Come on. It won't be any fun on the high-speed quad without you."

I shrug. "The ride up *is* the best part of skiing. I guess I don't want to miss the view."

With that, I walk out of the lodge with him, ready to put on those wretched skis again, face my fears, and beg him to let me ski down a blue-square trail.

8

Jordan

We ride the snowmobile back to town after three more
runs that take Brooke forever, but I stay with her.
What I did on the first run, abandoning her at the top, was
mean, but I was feeling mean at the time. Being lied to 24/7
is grating. Being forced to make up a last name makes me
feel hunted. Then I got over myself.

When I gave her pointers, she listened and corrected her
form. She's a better skier than I—or *she*—first thought.
Simply rusty, and her teenage skiing years have given way to
adult fears lessening her confidence, which grew the longer
she kept trying.

No surprise, she wants to go back to my bar for après-
ski. After all, that's where she last sighted her billionaire
prey. Despite living in my home, naturally she wants to talk
to anyone who'll blab about Asher. Good luck! Emma is
more of a loose cannon than any of my employees at the
Thirsty Moose.

Nice to see the place is packed. Lately, I've spent more time in my office at home, getting the game out of the beta stage, than I have here. Tracy is carrying a tray full of drinks. I raise a hand, and she nods in my direction, then looks twice when she sees Brooke trailing in after me. Cyril is behind the bar. He's a couple years older than me, British, and named for a popular TV character in his native country.

The first time we met, he said, "My name should be chucked in the rubbish bin of ugly old monikers. Call me Cy, or I'll clean your clock."

"OK, Cy, you're hired." The only one here who knows who I really am, he's mostly careful. However, Brooke is the second person to track me down to the Thirsty Moose, and I intend to find out precisely how next time I have her in a helpless situation. Hopefully tonight.

"Bar or table?" I ask.

"Bar," she says. "And no top-shelf whisky."

I can't help smiling because she's serious. "No worries. Tonight is on me."

I don't even know why I say that. Maybe she has an expense account through the Boston Media Group, and I'm being taken for a ride. After all, she's saving on lodging. Perhaps I'm funding my own demise.

On the other hand, at this moment, she's just Brooke, with her fun personality, full tits, pretty smile, tight pussy, and sexy laugh. I can treat her like any other female for another few days and then send her on her way.

"You want to try a house specialty cocktail?"

She perks up. "I'll—"

"Try anything once. I know." An admirable, open way to live, but it would give any guy pause as to how far that extends, wondering what she's done and, more importantly, what she'll do. I guide her to one empty seat by the taps and stand between her and the customer seated beside her.

"Cy, this is Brooke. Let's make her a Snow Bunny."

"Excuse me?" Brooke says.

"Cheers, Brooke. So, you're wanting a Snow Bunny, are you?" Cy is in jovial form tonight. I can see he's bored and ready to give me a hard time to entertain himself. "You're in for a treat, love," he tells her. "TJ only orders it for the rare, peng birds he's trying to impress."

Rolling my eyes, I tell her, "He's messing with you."

Brooke shrugs. "No idea what he said, but I don't care if you order it for every woman you bring in here," she says. "As long as it tastes good and I'm not paying for it."

"I'll make sure of the former, and TJ can take care of the latter," Cy says. "Did you enjoy the slopes today?"

"Surprisingly, I did, after a rocky start."

"She did well," I tell him. "And she started the day on Peachy."

Not a great skier himself, Cy looks impressed. "I bet you taught him a thing or two, love."

Brooke laughs. "No, honestly, TJ was really helpful." She looks at me. "Thanks again."

I can tell Cy is determined to stir up something. "Did you know he's got an Achilles heel?"

My insides turn cold. What now? I'm trying to make solid eye contact to shut him up, but he can't take his gaze off Brooke, all the while making her drink. He's a whiz at the bar, having grown up in his father's pub.

Leaning over the counter, he says, "Sushi."

I actually feel embarrassed. Damn him.

"Sushi?" she repeats, then glances at me. My smile is forced because even the word has my stomach churning.

"The man's afraid of a helpless piece of raw fish." Cy laughs, and pushes the finished cocktail, all creamy pink and frothy white, toward Brooke. "Take a sip," he orders. "Tell me how I did."

She does and then moans softly, making my groin tighten.

"That's delicious. Better than a Negroni."

Cy is smirking. "Our fearless leader made his one and only cocktail for you, did he?" He's laughing again.

"Bartender," comes a call from the other end.

"I'm chuffed you like the drink," Cy says. Then he slides a menu over to Brooke. "Take a look-see. Let me know what makes your mouth water besides me, love. You won't see any sushi. If you wait around till my shift ends," he adds, "I'll take you to a place that has it."

"You're closing tonight," I remind him with glee. "Also, you didn't get me a drink."

"Sorry, boss, got a real live customer to tend to." And he strides away to torment someone else.

"Do you want to share mine?" she offers.

"I can get my own." When I'm on the other side, however, I get stopped by a few customers. I nearly pretend I'm a lowly bar-back who's not allowed to pour a drink, but I hand out a few beers, which will be on the house since I don't do the register or have an order pad. Come to think of it, I don't even know the prices.

When I'm in front of Brooke, I can see she's getting happy from her drink. Cy must've made it a strong one.

Cheeks pink, eyes bright, mouth giving a little crooked smile that shows her dimples. No doubt the prettiest woman in here. Maybe who has ever been in here.

I pour myself a whisky neat and lean on the bar. "Did you lie about enjoying the Negroni?" I ask, not meaning for it to come out like a serious question, but it does. It's hard not to wonder if she lies about everything.

Her smile dies, replaced by earnestness. "I liked it. I promise. But it was an acquired taste. This is simply easier to enjoy. Like dessert. Here, take a sip."

Since she's pushed it across to me, what can I do? I drink the fruity, sweet drink. It's freakin' delicious. But I don't let on, even though Brooke is smiling again.

"I'll stick to this," I say, holding up my glass. We touch rims, and I feel . . . content. Until she asks the next question.

"So, what's up with you and sushi?"

I nearly heave up the couple sips of whisky, which would be a real shame. I'm going to clobber Cy. "Not much to tell. Bad experience, food poisoning."

Her expression clouds over. "That's terrible. I've never had food poisoning." She knocks on the bar top superstitiously.

"Then you are one lucky woman. I always thought eating anything raw was a stupid idea, and then I have to be the example that proves it."

"Other fish, you're fine with, though? Like Emma's salmon. I also noticed fish and chips on the menu here."

"Cooked fish is fine by me. And Cy said we needed to offer a decent fish and chips to call ourselves a bar. Are you hungry?"

She nods enthusiastically. "What's the best thing on the menu?"

"The pork ribs, hands down."

"Sounds good. If you have a salad and mashed potatoes, I'll be in heaven."

A woman who knows how to eat. "I'll go put the order in." I trust she can't get into any trouble here for a few minutes, nor will Cy say anything about who I am.

When I get back, however, she's got a fucking phone in her hand. My heart nearly stops. I rush over like I'm in contention for a downhill gold and Brooke is the finish line.

Snatching it out of her hand, I glance at a text that just got sent.

Staying in Asher's home! Eating at his fav bar. No internet or service at the house. Photos coming soon.

Even worse, there's a picture attached to the message. In it, Cy is leaning on the bar, grinning like a fool. Luckily, no identifying slogans are in view. Nothing that says "The Thirsty Moose." Cy's wearing the bar's requisite black T-shirt, but luckily, the moose logo is on the back.

"Hey!" Cy and Brooke say at the same time. I grit my teeth, trying to tamp down the blossoming fury.

"Problem, boss?" Cy asks as I hand his phone back to him.

"See if you can delete that message."

"It'll only delete on my phone, not the recipient's," Cy says. "Ask me how I know." Then he grimaces.

I don't ask. I just regret the crude gadget my chief bartender owns. On my phone, I've installed software that lets me recall a message from someone else's phone within a reasonable timeframe, which this would be.

"Text me the phone number she sent that to."

"You are being unreasonable," Brooke chimes in, drawing my focus back to her. *The sexy ski bunny is a scummy reporter,* I remind myself.

"I told you no photos."

Shaking her head, she gets off the stool and faces me. "No, you said Mr. Asher doesn't like photos being taken of his *house*."

She's good. I almost let something slip. "No, I said *my employer* doesn't like his house being photographed. I never mentioned this Asher guy you're obsessed with."

We're toe-to-toe, except her face is at least a half foot beneath mine.

"What's more, I *never* gave you permission to take photos in my bar. *My* bar, sweetheart! If a bunch of people turn up looking for someone who isn't here, then maybe I'll just sue your ass."

"That's crazy!" she says, then she looks at Cy, who is watching this as if it's a tennis match. "He's nuts, isn't he?"

Cy is smart enough to keep his mouth shut, unlike this reporter. Pocketing his phone, he moves away quickly, knowing he has fucked up.

"You know what they say about publicity," she says, poking my chest with a curved purple-painted nail. "All publicity is good publicity. This place would be hopping with people trying to catch a glimpse of Jordan Asher."

I'm sure my head is going to explode. I ignore my name casually spoken by her luscious lips and explain to her the obvious. "In case you hadn't noticed, this place is already packed. Even on a Sunday. With *paying* customers. And reporters are notoriously cheap or broke. They'll nurse one beer all day and night, camped out at my prime tables, taking up space. All because you brought them here, waiting for some guy who plainly is not here. How will that help me?"

I've rendered her momentarily speechless. Finally, she looks around, sees the full place and the customers waiting for a seat, and sits that same pretty ass back down on the barstool. Either she understands my point, or she wants that free drink and meal and a ride back to my house. Asher's house.

Maybe because I'm plainly seething, she says, "Sorry. I really didn't think you'd mind me taking a photo of Cy behind the bar. I was just . . ."

"Doing your job."

Sighing, Brooke finally comes clean. "Yes, I'm a journalist."

Hallelujah! "From Boston Media Group."

Her eyes widen. "How'd you know?"

"Someone from there booked you in at the Misty Slope Lodge."

She shakes her head. "You knew all along."

"Yup."

Crossing her arms in front of her chest, she looks pissed off. I can't imagine what gives her the right. Then she asks, "Are you kicking me out of Asher's house?"

"Who?" I ask, then add, "I won't kick you out of my employer's house if you follow the rules. It's only for tonight, anyway." To be honest, I'll miss seeing her striking face, but I won't miss worrying she's about to tell the world where I live. "Food will be out in ten."

Dragging my glass toward me, I take a healthy swallow. I do need her gone. Soon. No matter how much fun she is with her clothes off. She's been an unwelcome distraction. I should be debugging, not skiing. Luckily, the guy sitting on her right gets up and I take his spot. With the mood as sour as a lemon, we eat in silence, although it's hard to be too miserable while eating spareribs.

By the end of it, she's chatting again about Mr. Busby, who she found in a cardboard box beside a garbage can in Georgia. And I tell her about the shelters where my three dogs came from, all down south, too. By the time she finishes her mashed potatoes and I've wolfed down my fries, we're nearly back on an even keel.

I'm not sure whether to bring up the photos she referred to in the text or wait for her to bring them up. They're an elephant between us, to be sure.

Bundled up, we're back on the snowmobile for the short ride home.

"Shower time," she says. "Long and hot."

Mercy! I'm hoping we do other long, hot things afterward. Or during. Maybe she'd like company in the shower. But she dashes off to her room without offering an invitation. I guess my righteous outburst cooled her off.

Getting my head back in the game, I go on offense. When I decide enough time has passed and she's in the shower, I tap lightly on her door. No answer. Slipping into her room, I take her phone that's lying on the bed. Five minutes in my office, I've cracked her password—four numbers that are probably her birth year—and searched her photos.

Well, shit! Nothing but photos of her cat. Some pics of another woman, who is probably her cousin, *with* the cat. And some close ups of . . . the cat! Brooke must have put the photos on her laptop. I send myself a text so I have her number, then delete the message. Not wasting a moment, I race back upstairs and return her phone to her bed while I can hear the shower still running.

Do I have enough time to break into her laptop?

It's on the bedside table. As I approach it, the shower stops. Considering my options, I take a seat on the bed and wait. By the time the bathroom door opens two minutes later, I'm lying down flat, mulling over an integer overflow that's causing a kill screen in the latest iteration of the new game. She comes out wrapped in a towel. Hair up in another towel, which she has turned into a turban the way women do.

"TJ!" Brooke exclaims when she sees me.

"I was hard on you at the bar," I say.

She sets a hand on her hip. "And now you want to go hard on me in the bed?"

Wait, what? I sit up. Does she want sex again or is Broke just teasing me? "I'm here to apologize," I tell her. "You didn't know the bar was off limits for photos."

"You're right, I didn't."

Getting to my feet, I take a step toward her. "But you do know this house is off limits for pictures, right? You're not snooping around here, taking photos, are you?"

Grabbing her phone, she punches in the four-digit code and opens her photo app. "Look for yourself." Offering me the phone, she maintains an expression of innocence on her face about as convincing as Duffy when he tries to pretend he didn't chew through yet another one of my hiking boots. I don't take the bait. Two can play at this game.

"I don't need to see." I sound like a saint. "Your word is good enough."

She looks confused, obviously convinced I would grab her phone and thumb through it. For extra persuasion, I add, "Unless you have a photo of your cat you want to share. Mr. Budgie, isn't it?"

"Busby, as in the fuzzy black hats that certain royal soldiers wear in Britain."

Next thing I know, she's showing me the stupid cat, and as punishment for lying, I have to pretend not to have seen the photos already. I mean, as far as cats go, it looks . . . catlike. Black and furry. But I'm a dog person. Finally, when my stiff face and unenthusiastic noises convey my utter disinterest, she closes her phone.

"Now what?" she asks.

Good question. I reach out and edge my finger between her breasts, right where the towel is fastened over them. She inhales a quick breath, which tightens the towel. Pity. I give it a gentle tug, testing it, but it doesn't fall. I could easily make it come loose, but that's up to her.

"You want to enjoy another round of playtime?" Was that too crude? By the interested look on her face, I'd say no.

9

Brooke

A hot shower helped me think. I was psyched to see Cy at the bar tonight, knowing by his accent he was the one Sherri must have overheard. As soon as TJ went to order the food, I was all over the Englishman like white on rice.

"You can tell me the truth," I began, "Jordan Asher is a frequent patron, isn't he?"

Cy narrowed his eyes. "Are you trying to get an interview?"

"Of course. I'm as dead broke as he is filthy rich. An interview with him will jettison my career into the stratosphere and fatten my bank account."

"Seems like a fuck-all way to make a living," Cy had said.

"Enough about my prospects, you didn't answer."

"No, I didn't."

I may have had a mini-tantrum and slapped the bar top. "Why is everyone protecting him?"

Cy laughed. "Because he's—"

He caught himself, his face drained of color, and I leaned across the bar. "He's what?"

"He's obviously not here," he finished. But we both knew that wasn't what he was going to say. We both knew he'd slipped and all but admitted Asher hangs around here sometimes.

"Never mind," I said. "Let me take *your* photo instead. *Oh*, but I don't have my phone."

Next thing I knew, I had Cy's phone, took his photo, told him I was sending it to myself as a memento, and sent the text off to Sherri. Right before TJ caught me. I wish I could have sent it to work, but I'm lucky I can remember my own cousin's number, let alone one from a place I've only worked at a few months.

I'm still shocked TJ didn't toss me out into a snowbank. Even more astonished he let me stay here again tonight. Strangely, however, I'm not nearly as surprised to find him in my room.

When I come out of the bathroom to discover the man lounging on my bed, I surmise he's no longer pissed off at me. Or rather, that he *is*, but his libido is stronger than his annoyance.

He apologizes for being mean at the bar. In a hot minute, we're standing toe-to-toe, and I'm showing him there was nothing on my phone but photos of my fur baby. I hope I've made him feel bad about doubting me, even though his accusations were true.

When TJ touches me, right between my breasts, my body experiences an instantaneous lava melt down. Then he tugs at my towel and asks me a question that makes all my lady parts twinge and throb.

"You want to enjoy another round of playtime?"

But I know deep down, all the way down to where I ache for another exquisite encounter with him, that I need to take a hard pass. The unexpected sex last night was over-the-moon awesome. I would describe my orgasms as nothing short of spontaneous combustion.

So, how can I say no? Because despite being horny after a six-month sabbatical from sex, I'm not loose. I've rarely been a one-night stand kind of person. I like to meet a guy and see potential for a future relationship before I give my body to him. Even once.

TJ is a different scenario. I know for sure there is not going to be an *us*, so I allowed myself to have some adult fun. Out of character, yet with no regrets. But to do it again when I'm leaving tomorrow . . . seems kind of slutty. Also, vaguely pathetic, knowing he doesn't like me very much.

Decision made. I take a step back and another until the dressing table is pressing into my hips. Because what would happen next is predictable. He'd crook his finger, first to bring me nearer again, then up inside me to reach my G-spot.

I catch my breath, as we lock gazes. Thinking about it makes me want to feel those skilled fingers of his. And his tongue. And his—

Stop!

"Not gonna happen," I say, managing to grow a backbone, despite how my body thrums with disappointment.

Giving me a rueful, crooked smile, TJ swaggers impressively to the door, before calling over his shoulder, "See you in the morning."

Whew! Denying myself and him was harder than I let on. By the time I've slid my nightshirt over my head, dried my hair, and climb into this glorious bed, I've cooled down. That's when I notice my laptop has been moved.

Oh, hell no! Sure enough, I open it to find the folder labeled ASHER is now empty. Before I can think, I'm on my feet, throwing open the door, and marching across the hallway to TJ's room.

Pounding on the door yields a quick result.

"You're going to wake Emma and Colin."

I reach out to slap him for his intrusion into my privacy. I don't know where the unusually violent notion comes from, but this man infuriates me beyond measure. It must be his smug face, his easy life in someone else's house, his profitable bar, his superior good looks, and his generally charmed existence.

Some of us have worked every possible job trying to find out where we fit in. And failing. Literally, during college and ever since, I've tried everything from factories to farming, assistant to a chef, assistant to a baker, even office assistant. From a doctor's front desk to a hotel's front desk to selling desks at a furniture store. A psych degree can only take a girl so far. But this journalism gig seems like a good fit if only I can get my first big story. So, yes, I'm pissed.

He snags my arm midair because I telegraphed my action and even hesitated. And then he yanks me off my feet to fall against him. I practically roll my eyes at my own stupidity, as his hands slide down my back to rest on my rear.

"Playtime?" he asks, but his expression is more guarded than passionate.

Momentarily, I feel too defeated to deal with TJ. A good night's sleep is what I need. That is, unless he pushes the issue. Maybe tosses me onto his bed and touches me like he did last night. His mouth on my skin, his teeth on my nipples, his tongue flicking over my clit. SO much for cooling off. I'm making myself wet with the thought of writhing beneath him.

I mean, I could say yes. But somehow, I don't.

"No playtime," I finally manage, my voice raspy.

Immediately, he releases his grip on my ass. Crossing his arms over his chest, maybe to keep from touching me, he cocks his head. "Then what can I do you for?"

God, he's conceited! I can't say the words I want to. "You erased the photos off my laptop." Because I'm not supposed to have taken any. In a lose-lose situation, I shouldn't have come flying over here, ready to fight. I should have counted myself lucky that I've already copied them onto an SD card. And that's tucked safely in my makeup bag in the bathroom.

"Nothing. Absolutely nothing," I spit out. "Asher's flunky is of no use to me." Seeing his eyes narrow, I turn on my heel, and go back across the hall. At least I got the last word in.

As I go to sleep, I wonder if I can find a job as an estate manager somewhere awesome, like Hawaii. Maybe I could get free housing and a car, too. When I have internet again, I'll do a search because Boston Media Group pays me peanuts to do stories around Boston and the greater New England area. And that's being generous to peanuts!

$♥$♥$♥$

My first thought when I awaken is of my Volvo. It's Monday. I survived the weekend without phone service or internet or a car. Now I just need to get the three together again, and maybe I can rescue this mission and revive my fledgling journalism career. Maybe.

I'm downstairs early, but Emma is already in the kitchen, and Colin is eating at the island.

"Good morning," she says. "Coffee?"

"Yes, thanks." Colin smiles, but he's uneasy around me. Probably because, like Cy at the bar, he knows he'll face the wrath of TJ if he lets anything important slip.

"My car is ready today, and I'll be out of your hair," I say.

"Not a problem." And he runs a hand over his head as if checking to make certain he still has plenty of it on top.

"I need the name and number of the mechanic, please."

"You'll have to ask TJ," he says, then darts a glance at his wife, who is frowning.

"Hold up," I say. "I'm not asking about Jordan Asher or prying secrets about this place. I want to know where my car is. That's all. *My* car."

98

"Sorry," Emma says. "You're right." She glares at Colin before telling me, "We all use the same place. It's called Neil's Garage." She looks it up in her list of contacts.

"Thanks," I say, giving Colin the stink-eye. "But my phone doesn't work in this house."

"Right," she says. "Fortunately, we have a landline."

"You're joking!"

She grins. "Nope."

"But everything else is high tech."

It's Colin who says, "It was already here when . . . our employer bought the place. So, he decided to activate it. Just in case."

"Just in case?"

"If the internet goes out and the cell towers, too."

That's some high-level prepping. "OK. Where's the phone?" I ask, half expecting some huge, old-fashioned, dial phone tethered to a wall jack.

Emma laughs. "No problem with you using it, but Neil's only been open for like a half hour. He gets cranky if you pester him." She widens her eyes. "I did that once."

Colin smiles and gets up with his plate. "I think he added a hundred bucks to her bill because she called him twice. Honestly, Brooke, and not because I'm trying to put you off, but give the man until at least lunchtime."

He's right, and now that I have the name and a phone available to me, I don't feel so out of control.

"You hungry?" Emma asks.

"I've never eaten so many great meals in a row. But yes. How about those eggs Benedict you mentioned?"

"Pancakes aren't good enough for you?" comes TJ's voice as he enters with all three dogs. The mere sound of it, kind of growly, has my pulse picking up. After all, I tried to slap the man and then insulted him. And I have to check to see if he's serious with his question. By his expression, which appears totally neutral, he's not.

TJ pours a cup of coffee and takes a seat at the island. "The usual," he says to Emma, before picking up the folded newspaper.

I guess we're back to where we started, except now he knows I took photos inside the house, and I know he's an overprotective asshat! Who also happens to be paying for half my car repair and who gets my *other* motor purring like nobody's business. When I'm driving home later, I'll probably regret not letting him take me for another spin last night.

"Is the bar closed on Mondays?" I ask, half expecting to be told that's classified info.

"Yup."

"Is Neil's Garage in walking distance?"

"Nope."

"You're not one of those guys who only answers in single syllables, are you?" I ask him like I did in the bar.

Emma chuckles, but keeps her back to us as she makes our breakfasts. TJ doesn't say anything more, scanning the pages, getting caught by something that interests him. Normally, if Sherri's home, we're on our phones at breakfast while talking, or we put the TV on. I watch his profile for a few moments, thinking he has a really flat ear.

Finally, I ask, "You want to share?"

Slowly, he glances over, and when his gaze catches mine, it sends a zinging sensation straight between my legs. *Jeez!* What is wrong with me? Worse, it's like he can see my discomfort, knows that my heartbeat has sped up, and that I want him so badly I'd forego eggs Benedict if he brushed the dishes off the island and took me right here.

Not with Emma in the room, of course. Shaking my head at my crazy, lustful thoughts, I'm grateful when TJ slides another newspaper toward me. Not to be a twenty-first century snob, but newsprint makes me feel like I'm in the world of the Great Depression. Still, I read until my breakfast is ready. Captured by a long article on migratory birds, I keep reading while I eat, pausing only to thank Emma and tell her how wonderful her hollandaise sauce is.

I almost do a hand-to-mouth *chef's kiss* gesture, but wonder if that's insulting to do to a real chef. When I've finished, after Emma's left the kitchen, I put my plate in the dishwasher and turn to see TJ looking at me. Thinking it's a good time to make peace—after all, I broke the house rules—I snag his plate and rinse it, too.

"Thanks," he says.

"Still too early for the mechanic?"

"I believe so." He folds his arms like he did last night, seemingly content to watch me. Naturally, that makes my face heat up. Thankfully, he doesn't remark on it. Instead, he asks, "Eager to get home?"

Then it hits me, I don't have to go home. He can't make me leave Rangeley. Once I get my car back, then I'll be free to drive around and ask questions. There have to be other people who've seen him, perhaps shopkeepers or restaurateurs who aren't under TJ's big thumb. God, do I love it when he brushes his thumb over . . . any part of me.

With my cheeks feeling even hotter, I say, "I do miss my cousin and my cat."

He nods. "Might as well enjoy your last day here. Borrow some boots from the mudroom and take the dogs for a hike. Or go for a swim. There are also cross-country skis, which you can use all over the property, or snowshoes or—"

"Hold on," I tell him and walk over to the large living room windows. "Swim? Do you mean here?"

"There's a covered pool and hot tub to the right."

"And snow over the cover," I surmise, craning my neck to see.

"Yes, but the cover slides on a track, so it's not a problem."

He has come up behind me, and I shiver from his nearness. "Heated, of course."

Leaning close, his arm comes around me but only to point. "See that bump there, and then that pole?"

I can hardly focus on shapes when he's standing so close, but I say, "Yes."

"The bump is the edge of the cover. And that pole is actually a heater with a cover over it. There are eight of them out there, and that's so your head won't freeze, especially if you swim at night."

"That's a lot of words for you. You must have used them all up for the day."

Something like a chuckle rumbles through him, and I can feel it in my back. Then he backs off. "I have to get some work done."

"What do you mean?" I ask, turning to face him, already missing his warmth. "Are you going to the bar?"

"No." And he gives me no further explanation, but turns on his heel and goes toward Asher's office. "Let Emma or Colin know if you want the snowshoes or whatever."

Then he's gone. I go to the back door and poke my nose out. It's not unbearable. While I have no intention of going to the trouble of uncovering the pool, I do think playing outside with the dogs sounds like fun.

To that end, I get as bundled up as I can, borrowing from the mudroom whatever I don't have, and call the muttley mutts. "Duffy, Grady, Beau."

They're with me in seconds, and we head out into the endless white of the landscape. I couldn't imagine that an hour later I'd be on my back under TJ's magnificent body, wishing my car wasn't going to be ready today.

10

Jordan

I can hear Brooke's laughter outside my office window, and it's driving me nuts. It's out of place when I'm deep in the violent world of my game, where players are almost always fighting for their lives and for those of their loved ones. Laughter in my life is actually so rare, it's insanely distracting.

I also keep thinking she is too joyful for someone who lost all her precious photos off her laptop last night. She must have a backup, either an SD card or a thumb drive in her room. Luckily, the delay in her car repair means I'll still have time to find it.

Running the debugging linter on a specific segment of code, finally, despite Brooke's *loud* happiness, I've got clean results. Ready to give myself a break, even though I've only worked for an hour and a half, I should simply get some pumpkin bread from Emma and more coffee.

Instead, I put on my boots and coat and head out back to see what can possibly be so funny. Only then do I realize that the dogs have been barking more than Brooke has been laughing, but I'm immune to hearing my noisy pack.

Turns out, she's been creative with snow. Duffy is barking incessantly while sitting in front of a crude snowcat, twice as big as he is, with its long, thick tail curled around its front feet. And the other two numbnuts are circling a snowman, with twigs for arms and pinecone hair. Her last work is a small doghouse, shaped like the one Snoopy used to sleep on. The pointed roof has caved in.

"Did you try to put one of my dogs on the roof?" I ask her, already stooping down to scoop up some snow.

"Yes," she says, sounding gleeful, "but Duffy didn't cooperate one bit."

I pack this perfectly sticky snow into a tight snowball and whistle to the dogs. They pay attention long enough to watch me send the ball flying, and all three chase it down. They're mystified by its disappearance and start digging.

Brooke is laughing again. "They are so silly. And great companions, too."

"Unlike a cat," I can't help pointing out. "Don't cats just stay inside on a cushion?" I make another snowball and send it flying, and the dogs go after it again.

"Hey, don't disparage Mr. Busby," she says. Next thing I know, she's packing her own snowball. Instead of throwing it for the dogs, though, she lobs it at my head. Not a bad aim, it explodes on my shoulder. I shudder and flick some snow out of my ear.

"You don't want to start that battle, lady."

I can see the mischief on her face, along with her cheeks pink from the cold, despite wearing a knitted, navy-blue hat pulled down over her silky, thick hair.

Another snowball comes my way, right at my chest, and I dodge to the side. What can I do? I retaliate, but not at her face. My snowball lands in the middle of her jacket despite how she tried to sidestep it. When she dives behind the Snoopy doghouse, I know the game is on.

Ironically, the closest cover is the snowcat, and I crouch behind it, with most of me still visible. Rather than making one snowball and sending out my only ammunition, I start to make them as fast as I can, stockpiling while she lobs one after the other in my direction. Most hit the cat, but some find their way to my head and chest.

When I have about a dozen, I switch into assault mode and let her have it. Brooke doesn't have time to make any snowballs in between dodging my blitz. Not only is my aim great, but I gather my ammo in a pouch I make from holding up the bottom of my jacket. Now, I'm mobile, too. Like a snowball firing machine, I approach her while throwing, and she has no choice but to try to make a run for it.

Rookie mistake. In the open, I cream her until her entire torso and legs have been hit. She's laughing hard, trying to fend me off with her gloved hands and moving zigzag, although it's hard to run in the deep snow of the past couple of days. Ultimately, hearing me close behind, she turns and collapses into the snow.

Naturally, unable to stop my momentum, I go down as well, right on top of her, although I brace myself from squashing Brooke by shoving my arms into the deep snow on either side of her head.

"TJ!" she squeals.

Her rich, chocolate-brown eyes gaze up at me, and she parts her lips. I want to do the unthinkable and kiss her. Instead, I take another moment to enjoy looking down at her, and then . . . three dogs pile on top of us.

"Hey," I yell, but they don't know what I want or whether I'm simply messing around. Duffy starts digging beside us, showering us both with snow.

"No!" Brooke screams, while still laughing.

Meanwhile, Beau is lying across my ass, and Grady is going around sniffing. Her cold wet nose leaves trails on both our faces, and Brooke is turning her head side-to-side to escape the onslaught.

"Off," I say, not waiting but rolling to dislodge Beau and get to my feet. Just as Duffy showers Brooke with snow again.

"*Ohhhhh!*" she yells. She's not laughing anymore. Probably freezing, more like.

Holding out my hand to her, Brooke grips it, and I pull her up quickly to get away from the idiots. Her hat is gone, her hair is wet and dark, and it seems that snow, melting from her warm skin, has slid down her neck and into her jacket. That has to be uncomfortable.

Right about now, she's probably wishing I'd never come outside. Like a gentleman, I recover her snow-crusted hat and brush it off before handing it over. But she doesn't snatch it and storm away. Amazingly, she's smiling.

"I am freezing," she declares. "Not to mention hungry from all this fresh air and exercise. But first, a hot shower. My last one before I leave."

With that, Brooke dashes off toward the house.

Damn. She's only been here a few days, but I'm actually going to miss her. I look at the dogs. Now the fun human has gone indoors, they're subdued again. I feel the same way.

$♥$♥$♥$

With my mind finally focused again on work and a half-drunk mug of hot cider making the room smell good, I've been zipping along for hours. I'm tackling what I hope are the last of the finicky issues with the game when there's a loud knock. Forgetting myself and the workstation in front of me, filled with strings of code, I almost invite the person in.

But the interruption must be my house guest, and I think of the original Star Trek with Dr. McCoy's famous line reworking in my head, "Dammit, Brooke, I'm a bar owner, not a billionaire game designer."

How do I explain working in here all day? Locked in Asher's office where I'm definitely not supposed to be debugging code. Sick of jumping at my own shadow, I decide I don't have to explain anything.

When the knock becomes the thump of a fist, I close the multiple screens, get up, and open the door, just enough to identify her and slide through the opening, pulling the door closed behind me.

"You should have asked me first!" she fumes.

"I beg your pardon." I'm already lost, but glad she's not questioning me about having my own office to work in. Spinning on her heel, she strides to the living room and plops down on the couch. Then she covers her face with her hands. I follow because she seems genuinely upset.

"Brooke?"

She waves me away with one hand, keeping her head low and her face turned from me.

"What's up?" Then I realize the awful truth. She's crying. My gut twists. I am a sucker for a woman so upset she's shedding tears.

"My car," she mumbles, then wipes her face with her sweater sleeve. Finally, she levels me with a red-eyed stare. "What did you give the mechanic permission to do? A full Volvo makeover? Without asking me? The estimate is huge, and I won't be able to afford even half the bill. Plus, my car won't be ready for another few days because of some stupid transmission part. Even if I could afford the repairs, which I can't, I'm stuck here," she slaps the couch. "An unwelcome intruder. Unless I call my cousin to pick me up or hitchhike home."

I'm a little shocked by her vehemence over staying in my home, until I recall her one sole purpose, which certainly wasn't to have fun with me and my dogs.

"You have really screwed me," she adds, unironically. Considering what we've done in the bedroom, I'd have thought she'd be referring to that with some bitterness. But there's no sexual connotation to her sad words at all. Leaning forward, she doubles over, face covered by her hands again, blocking out the world.

Dropping beside her on the couch, I lift my hand to rub her back and manage to stop myself. Instead, I decide to alleviate her problems, although for the life of me I don't know why I give a damn. If she hadn't been out to destroy my privacy, she'd be back in Boston with her crappy tires, her bad transmission, and her cat.

"I'll pay for the whole repair."

Slowly, she raises her head. Instead of being instantly grateful, she sniffs, narrows her eyes, and asks, "Why?"

I shrug. "Happy to get rid of you." Not really the truth because I've enjoyed her company. On the other hand, once she's gone, she's gone. I'll forget her and go back to my old routine in a heartbeat.

Her deep-brown eyes grow wide. Then she nods. Despite my rudeness, she says, "Thank you."

I'm still staring at her, wondering why I want this woman so badly. Why *her* of all people? As soon as Brooke leaves, I can hook up with a shapely ski bunny any night of the week and fuck her lights out.

But then the other part of what she said suddenly filters through the reptilian, sex-crazed part of my brain and up to the higher-functioning, cognitive part. "Neil said a few more days?"

"Yes. Maybe two, maybe three."

Silence as we look at one another. I'm back to the sex-crazed lizard again, probably looking like I want to devour her. Jumping to my feet, I tell her I have to get back to work. Knowing she's going to be around for longer is too tempting, and I need to get my head in the game. Figuratively and literally speaking.

Back in my office, I know I'm not good for any more debugging or run-time errors today. I'm starting not to know the code's *while loops* from its *conditional statements*. With another pressing project still to finish before the game's release, I print out notes from the beta players, listening to the hum of the printer and the sliding of the pages as they shoot out into the tray. My one quirk that made fellow Silicon Valley tech-bros laugh at me, I like paper. *Newspapers, books, and notes.*

My beta gamers identified some hollowness to the non-player characters. Their words were: *thin, 2D, unrealistic, shallow.* Obviously, they actually are 2D characters, but I know what the gamers mean. Even though you have to suspend disbelief, you still want a solid experience. No distortion, no glitches, and you want to connect with the game's characters, whether they're archetypal, custom created, or controlled by the software.

I switch on one monitor again and pull up the database of nonplayer characters. With a pen—a real pen, *not* a stylus—in one hand, hovering over the printout, I get to work. For all of a minute and thirty seconds, at which point Brooke strolls into my office. I'm being sloppy. Door was ajar, PC's on, and I'm obviously working on something that isn't Thirsty Moose payroll or estate management.

"Whatcha doing?"

I need to get her out of here without raising her suspicions.

"Just . . . *um* . . ." What *am* I doing? How close to the truth can I get? "My employer has regular people test his games." I still can't get myself to use my name. "When I was in here earlier, I noticed some pages of feedback come through the printer and contacted him." So far so good. Sounds plausible.

"You spoke to Asher today?"

"Who?" I ask, just to maintain the charade.

She rolls her eyes, then sits her perfect ass on the edge of the desk and holds out her hand. "Lemme see."

My brain is spiraling, but I can't think of any harm it could cause. With a little dread, I hand over the top sheet.

"Is this your doodle?"

The blood drains from my head. What did I draw mindlessly in under two minutes while thinking of a characters' shortcomings? When she starts to laugh, a perfectly wonderful sound, I relax.

"That's quite a bodacious little creature," she points out, tapping it with a painted nail, and I peer over the paper to see what it is. I recognize it's *her* body that I was stupidly doodling without any obvious flaws at all, character or otherwise, but I keep my mouth shut while she reads.

"How many pages of these do you have?"

"Three and a half."

"And Asher will let us help?"

Us? Would I let us help? I think I would. But first, I say, "Who?" And then add, "Yes. After all, I'm his flunky," I shoot back.

She winces. "You obviously are a capable and valuable employee. Plus, you have your own business. I'm sorry for what I said."

"Apology accepted." And I shouldn't dismiss her offer without finding out if she could be helpful. "Are you game?"

"I love this sort of thing. We did exercises like this in my psych classes."

I perk up. "Sounds promising."

"Hey, it's not like I'm a practicing psychologist or anything. I might be utter crap at this."

I doubt it. I've always winged it, creating entire worlds and populations without any type of sociological training. So far, it's worked out fine because all other aspects of my games, storyline and graphics, are stellar. I'm not boasting. Sales and reviews don't lie. But Brooke could take my latest characters to the next level if she has a knack for understanding people's personalities. And tweaking them.

"You actually want to help?"

"Sure. After all, I've been enjoying free lodging and food."

"You've paid me back in sex." Instantly wishing I could take back that lizard-brain thought, I expect her to be annoyed.

She offers a sideways smile. "Hardly payment, since we give and take pretty evenly."

I really like this woman.

"If you can assist me, I'm sure my employer will appreciate it."

"Why does he let you meddle? Even if it's not anything technical. I mean, you're surrounded by what I can only assume is top-quality, super expensive workstations, and you're sitting in here with some paper and a pen like a neanderthal."

Neanderthal! But I'm thinking. Why would I let myself meddle? "Because of my years in a bar. I've seen every type of person. They say bartenders are like psychiatrists." I hope that extends to bar owners, too. "He knows I can give him advice on characters."

Brooke nods. "Makes sense."

Thank God!

$♥$♥$♥$

With only a dinner break, we work until eleven. Brooke pens in a bunch of emotional and behavioral traits for the inhabitants of Bright Star, fleshing out their motivations better than I could. Understanding individual personalities allows us to create authentic interactions amongst them. We spend a lot of time on the dialogue. Gamers will better recognize which non-player characters to avoid and who to team up with for honest info and clues and for genuine help.

The day and evening flies by, and what I haven't typed into the descriptions or fed into the AI-assist that makes these characters come to life, I can easily do tomorrow.

"I can't believe how much we've achieved," I tell her, switching everything off and closing the door behind us. "That was like a high-level think tank of two."

Brooke laughs. "It was fun. Glad I could help. You'd be surprised how much psychology I've used in various jobs, especially retail and being an office assistant. Lately, as a journalist, it's been useful for getting inside my subject's head to frame an article."

"And when you came up to find this Asher dude, how were you going to frame your article?"

We reach the top of the landing before she answers. "I pictured a techie guy, an introvert. Kind of awkward maybe, socially super-quiet, and from the photos I've seen, maybe a few too many cheeseburgers at his desk."

I almost smile at how well that describes the old me. Instead, I nod neutrally.

"He's also probably a bit of a control freak. After all, he creates gaming worlds and all the people in them, which allows him ultimate godlike control."

I lean against the wall beside the guest room door to listen to her explain me.

"But I think something traumatic happened that made him go into hiding," she continues. "Something beyond becoming a billionaire."

"You think becoming a billionaire is traumatic in itself?" I'd never thought of that. It happened so fast, and then Livvy's death occurred the moment I became super wealthy and instantly famous. I never considered that, even without the accident, I'd have found having unfathomable wealth difficult to handle.

"Could be, don't you think? Obviously, you know the man and I don't, but becoming a billionaire must be life-changing in almost every aspect. If you're not prepared for it, it might be overwhelming."

Her forehead furrows, and I want to smooth the line between her eyebrows with my thumb, but I urge her to continue. "You said you think there's some other trauma?" I'm basically inviting her to pick at my scab like a sadist.

"I think it's something more than being an overnight billionaire, for sure. Asher can afford to be an introvert *out* in the world. He could travel where he wants and buy out a movie theater or a museum to enjoy it for as long as he wants. Take a jet to a private beach. Sure, people would hear about it, but he could buy his privacy just about any place. The fact that we don't hear of it, I think, means that he doesn't go anywhere."

She's right. I've hardly left Maine since I moved here after Livvy's death. Then Brooke cocks her head, and levels me with that warm, brown gaze. "So, the question is, TJ, where is he now? How did it happen that as soon as I came to town, he walked out of the Thirsty Moose and vacated his house?"

Good question. "He does have another home," I tell her. I don't know why I'm disclosing my private info, but I add, "Somewhere else to live and work privately."

"More remote than this?"

I have a uniquely beautiful island home. After the first twelve straight months here in Rangeley, I contacted a real estate guy who can find anyone what they want, or build it if it doesn't exist. Marcus Parisi came through when he understood what I needed, and I bought the half-island estate, sight unseen. I've hung out exactly two times there. Both stays were with my parents, and the second time included some other close family.

Suddenly, I'm itching to get out of this frozen town and take Brooke with me to a sunny paradise. No bathing suit needed there.

"Is Asher there now?" she asks.

For a second, because it's late and I'm tired, I almost believe Asher is someone else, maybe on the island. I even forget to retort with "who?"

"Yup. And he's not coming back until you leave." I wonder if and when she does, she'll try to find a record of my real estate purchase and pursue me internationally.

"Wow. I guess I'm pretty powerful," Brooke jokes before covering a massive yawn with her hand. Funny how she no longer seems to care if she meets him. I mean meets *me*.

"Bed," I order, and again, I feel like kissing her sweet lips. Weird, unwanted, affable, almost-tender thoughts. But we're both tired, so I gesture to her room. Still, we stare one another down for a few seconds before she sends me a sleepy smile and goes in.

When I'm lying in my guest bed, I consider the peaceful feeling of having her as a friend, no matter that it's based on one big lie. I enjoyed playing with her and the dogs outside and working with her on the game. I can imagine us in the same bed, our bodies touching, and being able to fall asleep together. *Without* sex.

Like people who care for and about one another.

Then I laugh. What the fuck am I thinking? I must be more tired than I even know.

11

Brooke

When I awaken, I glance at my phone to see it's only four in the morning. But I feel refreshed and wide awake. Not to mention super aware that TJ is across the hall and would do wonderful, wicked things to my body, if asked.

I'll try anything once, including bearding the lion in his den. Uninvited. Also, it might be my last chance to see his bedroom. I was so angry last night, I didn't even take a look around while trying to slap him. I bet I could learn a lot about TJ Linter by seeing where he sleeps. Same about Asher if I could get into the master bedroom, which I've decided is behind the double doors at the top of the stairs.

I pace my room a little. Should I or shouldn't I? And go to TJ's room or make another attempt to get into Asher's?

When TJ answers my knock, after five agonizingly slow minutes of debating with myself, he's wearing nothing but muscle-hugging boxer briefs and a knowing smile. My brain empties. As his hands snake out to take hold of my upper arms and draw me slowly against his body, my hips curl against him. There's that magnetic effect again.

The soap fragrance has become a wildly stimulating aphrodisiac. I'll never again catch scent of it, earthy sandalwood and something indelibly woodsy, maybe pine, without growing wet between my legs.

He leans down as though he might kiss me. Although my mouth has been on his cock, and his has blazed hot trails across my curves and devoured my pussy, we have not kissed on the lips. It seems too intimate, too personal, too much like we care about one another.

I realize, with a flash of yearning, that I would love it if he kissed me, open mouthed, plunging his tongue between my lips. I wait, eyes open, but it's my neck that he targets. With his lips, tongue, and teeth, he teases the skin exposed by the deep *V* of my nightshirt. Without any sexy lingerie, I'm wearing what I brought for motel sleeping. TJ doesn't seem to mind.

His hot tongue on my skin causes me to arch, giving him better access, while my knees start to tremble. A volcano of heat erupts low in the pit of my stomach, flooding my body, north and south. An instant and utter conflagration. I'm more than ready to lie down, or fall down.

When TJ is done nibbling my neck, he draws me farther into his room, which, at a quick glance, is oddly impersonal. In fact, it's the same as mine, right down to the low lighting of the lamp beside the bed and the same thick comforter. The curtains are a different shade of blue, but there aren't any knick-knacks or photographs. Before I can give this much thought, he asks me a riveting question, one that snags all my attention and holds it . . . captive.

"How do you feel about a little restraint?"

A small prickle of uneasiness is swiftly washed away by my large and intense curiosity.

"I'll try it," I say, as if I've been offered a new dipping sauce or shade of nail polish. "Anything once," I add, which makes his grin briefly appear and then vanish.

He narrows his eyes. "I'll stop whatever I'm doing if and when you say so."

"OK."

He looks appreciative, as if I've met his expectations and exceeded them. And then his demeanor grows serious, causing a shiver to dance through me.

"Strip," he orders.

Suddenly, I feel stupidly tentative, but I nod. Whipping my nightshirt over my head, I immediately rest my arms across my breasts, hiding my nipples from his gray-green gaze.

His smirk tells me this will do me no good. "Get on the bed, on your back."

Another shiver races down my spine at the tone of his voice, firm, in command. When I do as he asks, TJ produces a couple of silk ties from his dresser. He loops one around each of the bedposts on either side of the headboard and fashions a practiced, silken knot at both of my wrists. He leaves my restraints slack so I can move my arms around, maybe even flip over onto my belly.

Admiring my body, his glance lingers long enough on my breasts for my nipples to pearl. Now, I wonder about my ankles, thinking that might be a bridge too far as I consider my vulnerable state. I needn't have worried since he doesn't tie my legs.

"Blindfold is non-negotiable," he says. "Ups your sensation factor into the stratosphere, not to mention your focus."

If it's non-negotiable, I guess I needn't say anything. I simply wait while he rests a silk scarf over my eyes and tucks the ends under my head.

"What's next?" I ask, a little waver in my voice.

"I don't want you to be afraid, only excited," he says. "Nothing but pleasure," he promises.

To prove it, he runs his fingers up and down my rib cage and brushes the sides of my breasts, as I drag in an already-ragged breath, hollowing out my stomach.

"Beautiful," he says. Then I feel his fingers under the small elastic waistband of my thong.

"*Oh, um,*" I begin, as he slides my thong down my legs and off. I mean, what did I expect? But somehow, that tiny triangle of satin was like a suit of armor. Without it, I'm entirely naked for him to look at. What's more, I can't even see him looking.

It's both disconcerting and . . . thrilling. I shiver as though a breeze has kissed my skin.

"*Um*, TJ," I begin again, but he draws my left nipple between his lips and sucks.

"*Mmm,*" I murmur, instantly happy, apart from the deep and persistent ache between my legs. I'm shocked by how needy I am.

He massages my other breast, before pinching its nipple, all the while continuing to suck on the first one. When that turns to a gentle bite, just a nip, I gasp, enjoying the exquisitely sharp sensation that's over before I register the pain.

"Settle," he says, and I realize I'm yanking at the ties. Calming immediately, I focus on his mouth switching over to my other nipple while his hand slides down the length of my body, blazing a trail of prickling heat, before he cups my mound. I cannot help the way my hips lift against his hand, seeking greater pressure. And more. Spreading wide for him, I invite a more intimate touch, no longer concerned that I'm stripped and laid out.

TJ slips a finger between my slick folds, then circles the taut bundle of nerve endings, which are ready for the next sensation.

"Greedy little clit," he whispers against my breast, then flicks my hardened nub. I buck like a horse, but when he doesn't touch my clit again, I whimper.

"Don't worry, sweetheart. We're just getting started." His finger slides deep inside me.

"God, yes," I say, despite wanting so much more.

"You are sopping wet," TJ comments. He has raised his head, no longer feasting on my nipples. The titillating knowledge that he's looking at my bare body while I cannot see him nearly makes me come. "It's like I've turned on a river of desire," he adds, "a slippery, lubricating river for my tongue to glide on. And maybe my cock, too."

"*Mmm-hmm,*" I encourage him, entirely ready for that cock he mentioned.

"Pity for you," he says, "I want to drag this out for as long as we both can stand it."

That sounds like torture. But instead of making me wait for more stimulation, he inserts another finger and massages me from the inside, making sure to stroke my G-spot.

He finds the mark perfectly, and I go still, breathing hard but unable to catch my breath because I'm teetering on the edge of an orgasm.

"I love watching your breasts rise and fall."

I guess he saves all his talking for the bedroom, while I'm helpless to stop my body from doing a sensual, undulating dance for his eyes only. As he continues to finger fuck me, he licks my nipples again, one then the other, with quick flicks.

"Don't come yet," he orders. "Hold on."

What? No! Why? How?

"I can't," I confess, feeling the gathering release like a tidal wave in my hips. Suddenly, no part of my body is being touched. His mouth has left my breasts. His fingers are no longer pumping inside me.

I fall back from the precipice of my climax and cry out something mindless. I'm annoyed, frustrated, and pleading, all at once. Then, without speaking, while I am unable to guess what's coming next, I feel a puff of air across my coochie. I spread my legs even farther, hoping to tempt his touch back to where I want it most.

"I love how wide you've opened for me, sweetheart." Then his fingers are on my left ankle, and he ties it with more silk. Before I know it, both my legs are secured to the posts at the bottom of the bed, and I have lost all my freedom.

I swallow with my mouth suddenly parched, but I trust him. He works with friendly people. He drives a great car. He lives in a nice house. All stupid reasons, but he helped me when we skied and earned my trust.

I wait, but nothing happens. I hear movement but can't tell what he's doing.

"TJ?" I ask.

I'm answered by what must be the flat of his tongue rasping over my clit.

Dear God! I wait for more. Nothing happens.

"Again," I say, sounding like a plea because it definitely is. "I'll come if you lick me again."

He chuckles and strokes the sensitive skin of my lower stomach with light swirls of his fingers. "I don't want you to come."

"Gah!" I exclaim.

"Not yet," he clarifies. "Patience."

That single word is infuriating. I can't squeeze my legs together to help myself, can't get my fingers close to touch my clit. And now that my legs are spread, I can't turn over and grind my mound on the comforter. I was right. It is torture. Silk restraints might as well be chains.

"TJ," I say, ready to bargain. "Why wait? I'll come again afterward with you deep inside. Just touch me. Please!"

He doesn't do anything. No touch. No words. Nothing. This stretches on like a battle between us, which I don't know how to win or if I want to. I just want him to release the built-up tension coiled in my body. I swear my clit is straining for . . . him.

"Say something," I beg. "What's happening next?"

But he doesn't answer. I picture him standing at the foot of the bed, directly in front of me, watching my frustration build. Is that turning him on? Is he masturbating while looking at me?

"TJ," I whisper into the silence. I think minutes go by, but I'm not sure. Finally, I wonder if he's even in the room. Could anyone be so quiet or so cruel? A tear leaks from my closed eye.

A second later, his fingers trail across my stomach. "Why the tear, sweetheart?" His voice slices through the blackness.

"I thought you'd gone," I accuse him.

"I'm here. And you can come now."

Picking up where he left off, TJ slides two fingers inside me while drawing my clit between his lips. It's a button of desire and pleasure he can turn on at will. Despite how I was prepared to remain outraged, to deny myself this orgasm in order to punish him for abandoning me, I can't quell the climax. Clearly, that's fucked up.

In seconds, my channel clamps around his fingers, and I fly off the side of the mountain as if I tried to master a double diamond on newly waxed skis. Forgetting I was mad at him, I shudder.

"Yes, yes, yes." I pray he doesn't let up on the perfectly timed strokes. I even forget I'm being watched while I tremble and moan, before beginning to float back into myself.

Strangely, as soon as I start to relax, still sightless, I feel claustrophobic.

"Blindfold off," I say. It's whisked away in a heartbeat, before I have the chance to add the word *now*.

Blinking up at him, I'm shocked by how seeing his face again affects me. Something tender unfurls deep inside. Before I can examine such a dangerous and silly emotion, he smiles. A welcome sight.

"You're beautiful when you climax," TJ says. "Are you game for more?"

I am. I want him deep inside me for the first time. He was right about the sensual impact of waiting, combined with the blindfold and the restraints, but now . . . "Will you untie me? I'd like to touch you."

Tugging on the extra tail, the loose end of each silk tie, he sets me free.

"Magic knots?" I ask.

"Classic slip knot," he says. "You OK?"

"Good so far." I am very good. *Very, very* good. But I'm also curious to see how we fit as lovers in the traditional sense. "Condom?" I ask. "And do you want a history?" I really should have asked those in a different order.

I'm treated to a chuckle again. "Sweetheart, if I was worried about that aspect, I would never have let you suck me."

My cheeks heat, recalling him pumping into my mouth. It made me feel powerful and pretty at the same time.

"And you're clean, too, I assume," I say, as I push myself up to sitting.

"I promise you that I am," he says.

"Let's do this, then," I reply, eagerly.

No second request needed, TJ grabs a condom from the JIC stash all guys have. In this case, top drawer of his bureau. Then he stands in front of me at the end of the bed.

Having been passive long enough, I reach eagerly for his snug boxer briefs. Hooking my fingers in the waistband, I tug them down and release the Kraken. I don't think I'll ever get used to this tall, muscular, mountain man's massive size when he's aroused.

I also have a split-second remorse that I'll probably never encounter anyone as well-endowed again. Then I cheer up. He's all mine right now. Enthusiastically, I lean forward and bury my face in his crotch. One of his hands drops to the back of my head, his big palm cradling me.

Without thinking twice, I lift his cock out of the way and give his balls a gentle lick while he groans above me. But very quickly, he releases me and jerks away.

"It'll be over before we start," he mutters, making me laugh.

TJ flops down and kicks off his briefs, then tears open the foil package. I hope he got the XXL. "Do you want to do the honors?" he asks.

I swallow. I haven't had a lot of experience with them, since I was on the pill the whole time with my fiancé. Before that, in college, my boyfriend took care of it.

"That's OK. I'll watch you do it."

He gives me a look like he wonders if I've ever put one on a guy. Answer: *I haven't.* I think it was a good thing I left it to an expert, as TJ has the condom unrolled down his shaft while I would still be getting the little package open.

I lick my lips, not because I'm trying to be a seductress, but I'm a tad nervous about that tree trunk of an erection he has. Also, I don't think I've ever had sex with someone without having kissed them first. I'm tempted to throw my arms around his neck and go for it, but I don't. This isn't about romantic emotions.

Besides, he's already pressing me back onto his bed, and I part my thighs so he can nestle between them. I'm ready for whatever he gives me. He fits the head of his ramrod cock to my quivering pussy, which is about to get pounded.

Then TJ hesitates, leaning on his forearms, looking down at me, while I can feel my racing pulse and his at the juncture of my legs. His unusual eyes, like shadows on the mountain, are studying my face. Again, I wonder what it's like to kiss this man. I think I'm about to find out, but instead, he sinks into me with one smooth, penetrating thrust.

Gasping, I keep my gaze locked on his. Good thing I was already wet and turned on, or that might have felt like being impaled. And not in a good way. Rearranging my body under his, I tilt my hips, while adjusting to his girth. I can't help my next words, stating the obvious.

"You're big."

A small smile lifts one corner of his mouth. Then TJ breaks eye contact, tucking his face into the sensitive area between my neck and shoulder. With steady rocking movements, he draws back, like an archer with his bow, then surges in, stretching me, filling me, and back again. Each time he pulls out, his erection drags at my clit because of his size and the angle.

It is simply exceptional, and my entire body quivers with each demanding stroke he makes. Letting my fingers range over the smooth skin of his back, I curl my legs around his waist, sending his shaft even deeper.

Wow!

It doesn't take long before I feel his body tense under my fingertips. I'm right there with him, reveling in the way the length of him keeps grinding across my hardened nub. Closing my eyes, arching back, I start milking his cock with my channel.

As I climax, with every muscle in my body growing taut before releasing, I can't help hanging onto his ass with all my fingers *and* my nails. I've never felt more like a true member of the animal kingdom. Intense and utterly natural. While a river of endorphins rushes through me, he groans and thrusts faster.

His orgasm chases mine until he loses control, banging me harder before he freezes, buried deep inside me, and I can feel the spasms of his powerful ejaculation.

Double wow! And simultaneous, too.

And then it's over. Once again, we're two strangers with our heartbeats still racing, and a thin piece of latex between us. TJ pulls out and rolls off me.

12

Jordan

I want to gather her in my arms and tell her that was incredible. Perfectly ordinary, missionary-style sex, sent me into an orgasm that felt like flying off a ski jump.

Tonight was special. Hell, we were in sync so well, we came at the same time. And that's why, while lying on my back, eyes closed, still breathing hard, I reach for her hand and hold it in the silence.

However, I know what she is and why she's here. No holding her close or kissing—none of that bullshit—is going to change the fact that Brooke is still determined to expose my home to the world. I now have the proof in the form of an SD card.

After a few minutes of enjoying the aftermath, I feel her turn toward me. Opening my eyes, I glance over and am taken aback by her big brown gaze. Those same eyes that earlier were glazed with desire are now looking at me with satisfaction. And perhaps something else.

Releasing her hand, I vault from the bed like it's a hot frying pan. No way, no how do I want to see affection in her glance. Soon, her car will be fixed, and she'll be on her way. Although she hasn't recognized me due to my own damn good bleaching of the internet, and how well I altered my appearance, I shouldn't be so cocksure it will last. I'd be worrying a hell of a lot more if Brooke was a gamer chick, into all the pre-release hype of my upcoming game. As it is, the couple blurry images of me that are still out there don't seem worth worrying about.

But pretending to be my own assistant, my own flunky, is getting old. I need her gone and my privacy restored. I should have found her a motel as soon as I found out her car was going to take longer than anticipated, instead of inviting her to stay.

Yanking on a pair of sweatpants, I give her time to cover up. In seconds, Brooke is on her feet and covering her shapely figure with her nightshirt. She smiles at me, and I swallow the unwanted twinge of guilt. Even though she's the one who came up to Rangeley trying to make money off of me, I betrayed her trust with what I did tonight while she was tied up.

Opening the door, I all but kick her out, by leaning on the door frame and saying, "Goodnight."

Her smile dims. Maybe she was hoping for an alcoholic nightcap or that we'd sleep together.

"'Night, TJ. Thanks."

Inside, I cringe. She will *not* be thanking me, not when she notices what I took. It's sure as shit going to ruin her postcoital blush and the halo of good feeling. Hopefully, it won't happen tonight. If it does, it means Brooke is checking to make sure the photos are still there. Yup, things could get ugly.

Once she's in her room, I grab my phone and select the whole-house lockdown setting. I don't want her taking more photos now that I've deleted all hers from her phone and laptop and taken her SD card. On the other hand, what if there were an emergency and she needed to leave her room?

Changing my mind, I swipe my thumb across the screen again, locking all the downstairs rooms, and all the other rooms in the main section of the house, leaving only hers and mine unlocked.

I lie on my bed, waiting for the inevitable fallout. Five . . . four . . . three . . . two . . . one. I take a breath. Guess she didn't immediately go into her bathroom and look in her makeup bag that was sitting open on the counter.

"No. You. Didn't!" comes her shrieking voice. A moment later, she throws my door open without knocking.

"Did you go through my things?"

"Why would you ask that?" I rest my hands behind my head, cross my legs at the ankles, knowing my relaxed look is annoying as shit.

She clenches her fists. "Because something is missing."

"How strange." I level my hard stare at her. It usually makes people fall silent, but not Brooke.

"You tied me up and then went through my things. I knew you left the room. I just knew it!"

"More files missing from your laptop?" I ask, so innocent-sounding that butter wouldn't melt in my mouth, as my mom says. For a few minutes, while Brooke lay blindfolded and restrained, I'd searched her room, easily locating an SD card in the bathroom. Sliding it into her laptop, which, despite my having erased her photos before, still had zero security apart from the same password as on her phone. The folder labeled ASHER remained on her desktop. Empty. But on the card was a ton of pics of just about every corner of my house. Even my dogs! And a blurry one of me from the first night, going upstairs.

That wench!

When I'd picked a few file names at random and searched her laptop, there were no other copies hidden. One click and the SD card was erased, but then I thought better of it and took the whole damn card. After all, she still has her phone, and I don't want to start this entire ridiculous spy game over again. It's like fucking whack-a-mole!

"You *know* what's missing," she hisses.

Pretty ballsy considering it was a card full of forbidden pictures. She's also impressively worked up, like a wildcat. Makes me want to try kissing her more than ever, if I wanted my back clawed, that is. Come to think of it, I think she stabbed my ass with her nails, all ten of them, when she came. It was insanely erotic.

"How could I possibly know?" I ask just to infuriate her. *She* knows that *I* know what she's talking about, but this is too enjoyable. Not in the same league as when she was waiting on my bed, panting and begging. But a good time nonetheless.

"You invaded my privacy," she fumes.

"That's rich," I snap back. "Are you really going there?"

"Look, this isn't even about you," she says. Not for the first time, I'm tempted to tell her that it is. That I'm Jordan Asher, and how little I appreciate her trying to make a buck off me, and how much I despise reporters.

Then she lifts her chin. *Uh-oh.* What did I miss?

"Neither your prior act of sabotage to my laptop, nor this thievery will stop me doing my job. Not even close. I'm a cautious person at heart." She finishes with a satisfied smile.

Cautious meaning multiple backups? Perhaps she has another copy. I am instantly weary because this means I have to extend the war. Not that I'm averse to tying her up again and enjoying our special brand of fun, but I have work to do tomorrow. And she has been nothing but one massive distraction. Full of sensuality, passionate beyond my expectations, yet unswervingly intent on ruining the peace I've found here in northern Maine.

"I'm going to get some sleep," I tell her.

Looking as though she was expecting more of a fight, she shrugs. "As long as you know that's the last time I'm letting you tie me up."

I clutch my chest as though she's wounded me. "*Oh, sweetheart. We'll see who holds out next time you beg me.*"

"You're a prick!" With that, she turns and walks out, right back across the hall into her room before slamming the door. Grady and Beau come running to my room from the top of the stairs, but Duffy, who has been under the bed the whole time, starts barking like he just got woken up.

"Calm down," I tell all three. "Just a woman having a tantrum."

A woman who might have another SD card or a thumb drive, or both. I can't let her leave until I find out.

$♥$♥$♥$

Brooke doesn't come down to breakfast. At first, it doesn't concern me. But now it's half past nine, and there's no sign of her. Maybe she slept in. A watery sun is hidden behind gray cloud cover, and I may hit the slopes for a couple runs before I get back into the game. After all, the bar runs itself, and Emma and Colin run my house. I consider inviting Brooke, although I think she'd rather shove a ski pole through my heart than ski with me again after our latest blowup.

Regardless, I'd like to keep an eye on her while she's still in the vicinity. Maybe look through her phone again. Heading upstairs, I knock on her door. No answer. Feeling a little awkward, I put my ear to the door and listen for the shower, but I hear nothing.

I have a bad feeling about this. Another knock with no response, and I swing the door open. Empty, not just of Brooke but of all her things, too. *Shit!* Before I can think, my feet are carrying me down the stairs, through the kitchen to Emma and Colin's side of the house. It's empty. What do they usually do at this time of day?

After five minutes wasted poking around, with all three dogs at my heels, my brain tamps down the panic and thinks clearly. It's Tuesday—supplies morning. They often go together. It's a long trek to a big box store for groceries and everything else. But would Brooke have gone with them? I punch in Colin's number.

"Hey, boss."

"Where is our houseguest?"

"Gone," he says.

Alarm bells go off in my head. "Gone?"

"She was waiting in the living room bright and early, all packed. I turned off the alarm, gave her directions, and let her go."

"You let her go?" It comes out harshly.

Colin frowns. "You never said she couldn't leave. I draw the line at helping you keep someone prisoner."

He's right. One hundred percent. "It's fine. I just didn't say goodbye. How long ago did she leave?"

"About forty minutes. She refused a ride, by the way."

As I head for my vehicle, I think about this situation. She's on foot, but within walking distance to town. About two miles—plenty of time for her to have made it out of jamming range. She could have used her cell to call an Uber. Brooke could be anywhere.

My rising heartbeat fuzzies my thinking. Then I realize I haven't paid for her car yet, so she's stuck in town at least. No way Neil's releasing the Volvo until he has my credit card. But it's Tuesday, so she might be able to get a place to stay tonight.

I start driving and think about what damage she can do if she goes to an internet café with her laptop and has any photos that I missed or that she took since I wiped her phone.

"Fuck!" The last thing I want is her blathering to the world that she's found where I live. Not only will reporters swarm my perfectly low-key world, but every goddamn CEO will send investment offers. Startup business owners will be hitting me up to finance their passion projects. I'll be tripping over suits who look like my New York lawyer every time I turn around.

And then there are the gaming groupies. Nice people when kept at a convention, but they can get a bit freaky when they meet the creator of Bright Force and Bright Quest out in the real world. And I'm under no illusion that they won't make the pilgrimage to camp out at my bar and on my doorstep.

Brooke has forced my hand, and I fully intend to use my pair of aces. Pulling over, I find her number that I sent myself from her phone, and text her the two photos from the first night, with her ass showing rosy red and the paddle in view.

It's a scummy thing to do, right up there with her coming up here and sneaking around my house, documenting my existence. As if the outside world has a right to know anything about me. As if me and my family don't deserve a little peace after what happened to Livvy.

I start driving again, and my phone begins to chime about ten seconds later. I continue toward town. When it rings, I hit the button on my steering wheel and answer.

"You bastard!" she shrieks.

"I thought I was a prick," I say glibly despite not feeling at all light-hearted about this.

"If I wasn't in a public place, I would scream."

Meaning she's probably in a café. With internet. "Have you sent any of your photos to the Boston Media Group yet?"

"No," she says, and I believe her because I need to.

"If you're lying and I find out, I want you to know that I have more than the two I sent you." Now I'm lying. "And I'll upload them worldwide with your name attached. So, make sure you're telling me the truth, sweetheart. Because although you look good in black silk ties, you might not appreciate everyone seeing how beautiful you are when spread wide."

"I am telling you the truth." Her voice sounds small and defeated. Good!

"And if you gave the address where you were staying to anyone or the name of the town or even my bar—"

"I understand."

"Do you? Because I've been telling you since Friday, and yet you still betrayed my trust. If you leak any information, your embarrassed face along with the rest of you will be all over the internet for eternity."

She barks out a sad laugh. "Eternity, eh? Is that what Asher would want, or are you overstepping? A bit power mad when you're left in charge of protecting your boss, aren't you?"

I don't bother denying the name of Asher again, despite the temptation to ask, "Who?" simply to infuriate her. "If you release the photos or any info, then the house will simply be sold. But what will you do? Get a new face? Seems a pity when you have such a pretty one already."

"You're right," she says. "You are a prick *and* a bastard. Not to mention a bully. This story is . . . *was* important to me."

Livvy was important to me. "Tough shit."

"Where the hell is my car?"

"Where are you?" I counter.

"At the Double Diamond Café."

"Then you're not too far from Neil's Garage, but he hasn't called me yet to say it's ready."

She hangs up without another word, and I'm betting she's calling Neil directly. Since I'm now around the corner from the Double Diamond, and since we've come to an understanding, I head over there. When I enter, I spot her directly. She's hunched over a table in the corner, head down on her backpack next to a cup and a plate.

"Hey, TJ." It's Jeremy, who works behind the counter, is a crack skier, and drinks too much most Saturday nights at my bar. I'm lucky never to have gone that route after the tragedy in California.

"What'll it be?" he asks.

But I just wave and continue on toward Brooke.

"TJ," Jeremy calls after me, and I glance back. He exaggerates wide eyes then circles a finger around his ear, in the universal sign for a crazy person. Warned, I continue to her table.

"Brooke," I say to let her know I'm there.

"My car," she mumbles. "Still not ready." Then she looks up and dabs her face with a napkin she's holding, scrunched in her hand. "Maybe tomorrow." She puts her head back down on the table, appearing utterly dejected.

Dropping onto the chair opposite, I tell her what has to happen. "You have to give me your SD card or thumb drive or whatever you still have."

"You took everything," she says, quietly.

"I don't believe you. You're a *cautious* person, remember? This crazy fixation you have on this one particular subject has to stop."

"I told you," she says. "You already took the SD card."

But Brooke sounds too calm, too confident. "I think you have another backup, and I'll go through your bag or strip you naked right here to search for it."

She raises her head again, and her deep-brown eyes flicker to mine. "You wouldn't dare."

"Watch me," I say.

I hold out my hand, palm up. I'm fully prepared to hand Jeremy my credit card and buy everything that is currently for sale and everything he would sell for the entire day simply to close the place down for half an hour while I search Brooke and her belongings. I'm that fucking desperate.

Luckily, I don't have to. Brooke knows me well enough by now that she can read the determination on my face. After a few moments, she unzips her backpack and draws the laptop out halfway. Then she presses the slot on its side and out pops an SD card.

"Is *everything* on there?"

"Yes." Her tone is bitter and believable.

"And you've sent none of it to anyone, not even the person you texted from my bar?"

"Not yet. I was going to, but I called Neil first. And then I screamed loudly since there's no one else in here."

I think I can now tell when she's lying, and she's not. And no wonder Jeremy thought her nuts.

"Why don't you look at the bright side," I say. "You're getting your car fixed for free, and you had great sex. Seems like a winner of a weekend. Plus, I'll even let you stay at the house until the Volvo is fixed."

"Aren't you just Miss Mary Sunshine?" she gripes. "If I don't go back with a story, I might as well not go back at all. I need to make money. I get paid by the word for the stupid little articles I write. But for photos of Asher or his house, I could name my price."

I ignore the hungry look on her face. Not my problem. So why am I trying to help her again?

"What did you plan to do after this article? Surely, it couldn't mean enough money that you wouldn't have to work again."

"Of course I'd have to keep working!" she says, tucking a lock of hair behind her ear. I never realized what sexy ears she had until she does this. "But I'd have journalistic credibility. BMG would probably start paying me a small monthly retainer. If not, if this was a one-off, then I'd find my next job. Believe me, I have experience in every field."

"Why?" I ask, interested despite myself.

Brooke sighs. "I've tried and quit at a lot of places, about a hundred starter jobs, trying to find the right fit. Nothing meaningful. Some lasted weeks, some months, rarely years." She ends on another sigh that makes me feel sorry for her.

"What did you do before you became a scummy reporter?"

She glares at first, but she answers. "Just another job, but I was also engaged for two years before working at BMG."

This is news, which I *should* have zero interest in. "What happened?"

Her eyes lock with mine. "Are you a reporter?" she quips, echoing my question when she asked me, quite reasonably, for my name.

I should tell her to forget about it. I don't know why I asked. I don't give a damn. I don't. But I wait. Finally, she shrugs.

"We seemed like a good couple. Our friends thought so." Her frown is back. "After two years, I wanted more."

Now I understand. "More money?" I feel sorry for the guy. Captured the interest of someone as gorgeous as Brooke but was unable to keep her.

Without another word, she pushes to her feet, gathers her things in silence, and walks out, backpack over one shoulder and suitcase in hand. No one has ever done that to me before, and I admire the hell out of her for it. Guessing she found my question insulting, I slide the SD card into my back pocket and follow her.

Brooke is standing on the sidewalk as if she's waiting. *What for?* When I approach, she reaches out and slaps my face.

Another first.

13

Brooke

"Shit!" TJ says, backing up a step because he didn't see it coming this time. I felt the satisfying impact, and my palm is stinging. I don't care that I'm on a public street. That's how furious I feel at his assumption, not to mention how he has finally managed to take the last copies of the house photos that I had.

"You destroyed my chances of making some decent money from photos of Asher's house. His goddamn living room. Photos of his *furniture*, not even of him! Whatever you think of reporters, I work to support myself. How dare you pass judgment or think you know anything about me or why my engagement ended!"

I don't expect his next words. "Sorry, I was out of line."

"Too right." I heft my backpack higher on my shoulder since it slipped when I struck him. As I cool off, I'm growing appalled for slapping TJ's face. I've never done anything like that before, and yet, he's incited me twice to the same act of violence. Later, I know I'll feel revolted with myself. But right now, I still think he deserved it. "Why do you care so much? It's not even your house."

Then I think of a solution. "Why don't you let Mr. Asher decide?" I hold up my hand. "If you say 'who' one more time, I swear, I'll . . . I'll tell everyone in town how you like to paddle women."

His expression is stony and unflinching. "You'll have them lining up, sweetheart, and I don't have the time right now."

"*Ha-ha.* Look, just call Asher. Tell him I'm a nice person, which I am."

"When you're not slapping people," he gripes.

"When I'm not driven to bizarre, uncharacteristic behavior," I add. "Were you serious that he won't return until I leave?"

"Yup. I suppose you want to sleep with him, too. That would be a unique take on *exposing* a billionaire."

I can't believe he went so fucking low. I guess I've given TJ the wrong impression, and he thinks it's perfectly normal for me to jump into bed with a stranger. If I told him he was my first sexual partner since the break-up, he'd be so full of himself. Insufferable. He has no idea how attracted I am to him or how downright irresistible I find him, which is kinda sweet. Well, except for him thinking me a tramp.

The fight goes out of me all at once. Although his smug face provoked me to doing something I'm not proud of, he holds all the cards, and he knows it.

"Why are you so petty and mean?" I grumble. "You're like a Taylor Swift song."

I'm amazed when his expression softens, then he smiles. With his gray-green eyes amused and his sensual mouth relaxed, my treacherous stomach flips. I am going to miss having sex with this man.

Not for the first time, it seems we're on the same wavelength. "Why don't you come back and stay with me . . . with *us*, the dogs, Emma, and Colin, until your car is ready? Free gourmet meals and nice lodging. Now that we're absolutely clear on what you aren't allowed to do, you can use the internet to job hunt or write some articles about the area. Maybe some food reviews. Will your employer be able to use them?"

Frankly, I'm flabbergasted that he's trying to help me. But the small, crooked upturn of his mouth, showing his one dimple, explains it all. "And in return for your hospitality?"

"We have sex every night."

At least he's brutally honest. The sex is hotter than I've ever known. I'm interested to see if he can up the ante. My imagination wonders what we could do tonight, and my lady bits clench. But I should say no. Or I should lay down a rule of my own.

"No more photos of me, either."

"No reason to," he said. "They had one purpose, and they achieved it."

I feel irate again, but it's not as though he didn't warn me not to take photos of Asher's house. Hearing my texting app ping and then seeing myself in living color was shocking. The guy behind the counter heard my scream of disbelief. But I got the message, no pun intended, loud and clear. I suppose I have no right to be angry.

"Come on," TJ coaxes. "Aren't you a little curious what Emma's serving up for dinner?"

I sigh. If I had all the money in the world, what would I do? Honestly, I'd still like to eat Emma's food and have sex with TJ Linter. Plus, I'm starting to like dogs, his in particular, more than I thought. Obviously, they're not as great as cats, but Duffy, Grady, and Beau are pretty sweet.

When I hand him my suitcase, TJ knows I've given in.

Grilled turkey tips with roasted brussels sprouts covered in caramelized maple syrup and onions is the answer to what's for dinner. Turkey and talk, in fact, after not speaking to one another once we got home. TJ spent the day in Asher's macked-out office, but didn't invite me back in.

"Payroll and bills," he said. "I just try not to knock into any of the important tech stuff." Then he closed the door.

I curled up on the sofa with my laptop and endless cups of cocoa, writing about anything Rangeley, Maine, that I've experienced, including the café where I had my meltdown and the skiing. Of course!

When we meet for dinner, it's in the dining room for a change. With the fireplace lit, TJ starts asking me legit questions about myself and my living situation with Sherri and Mr. Busby.

I clue him in on what a fan my cousin is of the Bright games, and even let him know that's how I found my way to the Thirsty Moose. Belatedly, I regret mentioning Cy and that Sherri overheard him say Asher's name. But TJ didn't lose his shit over it, so I guess it was OK. Once I've exhausted the topic of my boring existence, in about five minutes, he circles back to asking about my fiancé.

"So, you were engaged?"

I roll my eyes, but tell him how Juan and I met in a meet-cute way. When TJ frowns at the term, I say, "Juan and I called for the same Uber. We came out of different buildings a block from each other. That was in Savannah, where I moved after college. Just to try it. After a twenty-minute ride, he asked for my number. He was nice, so I gave it to him."

"That's a meet-cute?"

"Yes. Every girl's dream. The opposite of how you and I met, with you being rude in your bar, letting me buy you a drink, and walking out."

He nods thoughtfully. "Gotcha. I'll have to remember that next time I see a woman in a potentially meet-cute situation."

I have no doubt TJ will succeed in conning some unsuspecting female, and it pangs me. I answer his next question about my ex. "Juan stayed in Georgia. He's in Atlanta now. Super smart, I'm sure he'll end up owning some big company."

"Keep your hands where I can see them when I ask my next question," TJ says. "You told me you left him because you wanted more. More what?"

I'm a little vague on that, myself, but I try to explain it without sounding shallow, selfish, greedy, or clueless. "More out of life. More *oomph*. More adventure. And between me and him, more spark. I felt like I was settling."

"Did you get what you wanted, after breaking the man's heart?"

I glance up to see whether he's serious. Juan was definitely hurt, but not devastated. He knew deep down he could do better than me, with a woman who wanted to devote herself to him and *his* career.

I sip the burgundy and confess. "No, I didn't get *more*. I got the spare bedroom at Sherri's condo. Definitely less room than the two-bedroom house Juan and I shared in Savannah. But I am so grateful for a place to sleep and getting to live with my best friend. I had just moved into a small apartment after the engagement ended when, two weeks later, I got fired from my job. That's why I ended up moving to Boston."

"*Ouch!* What were you doing?"

"Working in a private testing lab." Then I hold up my hand. "Don't get that look like, *wow, she's a scientist*. I literally punched data into spreadsheets all day while wearing a stiff, polyester lab coat." I groan because . . . my life!

"Why were you let go?"

"Not my fault. Funding dried up for the project. I was the last hired, first fired." Thinking about that lab, I add, "It was just like every other job. Not a career or a passion."

He's nodding along, and I see that look in his eye. The look a guy gets when he wants to fix something. Sure enough, TJ's next question tells me he's determined to distill me down into a manageable problem and figure out my future.

"You said you took psych classes. So, college grad?"

"Yes." Here comes the obvious question.

"Did you just take classes in psych, or was that your major?"

"My major. I have a B.S. in BS. Not totally useless, but I like to think it pretty much ensures that any potential mate I have will make more in a year than I ever will in my whole freakin' career. Juan did, and he was only thirty."

TJ shakes his head. "You're dissing yourself before you start."

"Au contraire. I'm dissing myself *after* reality has set in. I've wasted my time." I almost say *my life*, but I'm not that dramatic. I still have time to do something fulfilling.

"I could've chosen sociology," I say, making a face. "Or become an English major."

"Or gone for a communications degree," he adds.

Wait. Is he talking about himself? "What's your degree in?"

TJ pours the remainder of the dark-red wine into our two glasses. "Bartend-ology and babes."

"No, really?" I press.

"I didn't graduate," he says, surprising me. He's clearly not the least bit embarrassed. "Seemed a waste of time after I got a good job my first summer."

"You started working in a bar, under age, and then decided that was the path for you."

"Not exactly. But when I considered the next year's tuition with all the loans and shit, I told the college, 'Thanks but no thanks. I'm good.'"

I snicker. It's not because I'm on my second glass of wine, either. It's the image of a young guy not buying into the system that says we all have to put off life for four years and go to college. Also, the idea of him tearing up his tuition bill. Who didn't want to do that?

"Your bar looks to be successful."

"It is," he agrees. "Even in the off season, we have campers, hikers, fishermen, and hunters. Someone always wants a drink and a burger."

"Then I guess you made the right choice."

"I know I did," he says, with an unwavering stare that warms me all over, mainly due to how we're talking like friends.

Then Emma comes in, "Dessert in the living room or in here?"

TJ doesn't take his gaze off me. He's asking me a different question. My answer to him is yes. Now, please. I'm ready.

My answer to Emma is, "Maybe later. I'm super full. It was really delicious."

Rising to my feet, I pick up my plate because she doesn't work for me, after all. A second later, TJ is standing, too, but I take his plate before he can. "I got these," I tell him. "I've never had anyone wait on me, and this seems a weird time to start. After all, neither of us is a billionaire."

Emma chuckles and steps aside, so I can go by her to the kitchen. I load them in the dishwasher, and turn to reclaim my wine from TJ.

"I'll leave dessert in the fridge," Emma says. "Chocolate mousse cake with raspberry sauce."

I groan. "Sounds amazing."

As soon as she leaves, I add, "I'll definitely be down for that in an hour or so."

"Or so," TJ agrees, and I shiver. We weave our way through the lounging dogs to the stairs.

"My room or yours?" I ask as butterflies take flight. I hope I sound sufficiently sophisticated and blasé, as if sexual shenanigans are nothing too rare for me.

"Mine. I've got the toys."

I trip. So much for sophisticated and blasé. "Toys?"

"Good, all-purpose word for anything used to enhance sex."

I nod. "How are we *enhancing* sex tonight?" I can barely say the word without slobbering, let alone conceive of what we might be doing.

"How do you feel about temperature play?"

Color me confused. I shrug as we reach his bedroom.

"Ice cubes, for instance, can be a novel sensation," he says.

"I'm generally a cold person," I confess. "Maybe in the heat of the summer?"

After closing the door behind us, TJ leans against it. "The opposite is heat."

I'm imagining matches and firebrands and boiling water. Nothing in the least enticing or sexy.

"Melted wax," he adds softly.

Oh! I've heard of that. My pussy responds with a flutter.

TJ's watching me, I guess to see if I'm game. Then he says, "Should I bother to ask, or will you give your standard 'try anything once' answer?"

"You can assume that's still the case."

In the few moments it takes for him to close the curtains and dim the lights—while changing their color to rose—I yank the comforter off his bed, revealing sheets identical to those on my bed. Then I down my wine while watching him open his bedside drawer and bring out what looks like a small candle in a glass pot. When he lights it, a sensual aroma immediately laces the air.

"Powerful little thing," I say, trying to identify what I'm smelling. Somehow, it's the essence of warmth. When he moves away, I pick it up to see the wax melting quickly, and

I read the label aloud, "Amber, cedar leaf, tonka bean, medjool date. Seriously?"

He laughs behind me, and the sound is warm and rich, too. After I set the candle down, his arms come around me from behind, and he begins to nuzzle my neck.

"You have the silkiest hair I've ever touched," he says. "It's like a shiny, brandy waterfall."

"That might be another sex enhancer," I joke.

"Damn right it would be," he agrees. "Brandy-dipped nipples." Cupping my breasts with both hands, he presses his arousal against my rear, and I lean my head back onto his chest, breathing in the erotic fragrance and enjoying the moment. The best is yet to come.

When he's rolled my nipples until I am a prickly bundle of neediness, wet between my legs with my entire body humming, I turn in his arms and . . . forget for a second that we don't kiss. We are not on that path, nor ever will be.

I look down when I want to look up into his granite-green gaze. But if I do, we'll be too close. He'll think I'm asking for him to kiss me. *Awkward.* Instead, like a spaz, I reach between us and grab for his erection under his fly.

TJ makes a sound of surprise, and I release him as quickly as I grabbed him. Better to let him lead.

"That's OK," he says. "You can touch me, sweetheart, whenever you want." Then, he strips off my clothing—a sweater and jeans—before backing me onto his bed. He removes his own clothing down to his boxer briefs that stretch over his muscular thighs like a second skin.

"Skiing," I say. "That's why your legs are so toned."

"At this time of year, yes. But my body is like crude clay compared to yours. You are a work of art."

I stop myself from mentioning my flaws, the mole on my right shoulder, my general lack of firm muscles where I'd like them to be, and my long toes. I'm blessed with a classic woman's shape, small waist, generous breasts, curvy hips, and so far, haven't needed to work too hard to look good. If TJ thinks I'm art, who am I to stop him?

"And art shouldn't be covered," he says, segueing into sliding my bra straps down before unhooking it and letting it fall. It's deliciously arousing to be undressed so boldly, as if he has a right to do it. When he hooks his fingers into my thong and whisks it off, this time, I don't want to cover myself.

"Lie back," he orders, and I quickly comply, eager to experience temperature play.

"This isn't really wax," he says. "If you ever do use wax, make sure it's soy, not beeswax. That burns too hot."

I ignore the fact that he knows about this stuff on a granular level of what type of candle to use. I also don't let my thoughts drift to doing this with someone else. Neither him, nor me. Knowing he's totally fine with that when we're about to get intimate is unsettling. What's more, I can honestly say I don't want to think about him doing this with the next woman in his life.

Taking a deep breath, I focus on the now. "So, what *is* in that jar?"

"Solidified massage oil." He picks up the jar and blows out the wick. Although he doesn't restrain me, he says, "Close your eyes and lie still." When he straddles me, I peek up at him.

"Eyes closed," he reminds me, and I do so. "Now, you'll have to be spanked for disobedience later." The promise of that makes my heart rate speed up. At the same time, I feel the fragrant, slippery heat drip onto my right breast as he circles my nipple with melted oil.

"Good?"

"Very good," I say.

TJ proceeds to give my other breast equal treatment, like a liquid caress. I hear him set the candle down beside us on the nightstand before he begins a frontal massage like I've never had before. He kneads my breasts, plucking at my pearled nipples, then rubbing away any tension as his hands smooth the oil up and outward over my shoulders.

"*Mmm.* You could be a masseur instead of a bartender."

"I'll take that into consideration." I love the timbre of his voice, and hearing when he's amused by his tone.

After another few moments of this stress-relieving touch, he climbs off me and the bed. Without opening my eyes, I wait for the next dribble of oil. It slides onto the flat of my stomach directly below my navel. Then TJ takes it south.

"Spread your legs."

I don't hesitate to do as he demands, certain he's not playing games any longer with cameras and photos. I cannot believe how much I trust this man. Maybe it's because I can open my eyes or move if I want. Perhaps he didn't restrain me tonight for that reason.

Holding my breath as he creates a heat-infused trail, I gasp in some needed air when he drips oil over my mound. The slippery heat trickles between my folds, warming my clit. It is magical.

"Wow," I say softly.

"You look gorgeous," he says.

His capable fingers begin to spread the oil over my stomach in circles around my navel, and over my hips. I raise them in hopes of encouraging his touch where I desperately want it. But all I get is more oil, just a few heavy, hot drops.

"*Ooohh*," I protest. "Is it hotter?"

"A little. I relit the wick. You seemed too comfortable."

"Thanks for the warning." But honestly, it's been amazing so far.

"Supposed to keep you a little on edge, sweetheart," he says, his voice coming from the end of the bed. When his fingers part me, I jump. But when he drips the fragrant oil directly onto my clit, I can't help a low groan.

"Good?" he asks.

"Great."

"Your pussy is glistening in the moonlight. It's fucking fantastic." He's still holding me open, exposing my hardened clit, when he sends a puff of air directly on it. I buck. He trickles oil again, and I moan, ready to beg him to—

TJ touches me before I can ask. Lightly at first, his fingers glide on either side of my sensitive nub. Then they dip inside me, before circling my clit again. It's a mini, mind-blowing two-fingered massage.

"I need to kiss you there," he says a second before I feel his mouth close over the center of my entire world. For the first time, I lift my hands from where I was grasping the sheets and sink my fingers into his hair. I'm holding him, terrified he'll stop when I'm so close to coming, when I need to grind myself against his mouth.

With the slight turn of his head, I'm treated to the abrasion of his short beard.

"*Oh*, God!" I'm totally out of control, rubbing my coochie on him mindlessly, until his hands slide under my ass.

Holding me still, he sucks my clit between his lips and flicks it with his tongue at the same time. This finishes me off, sending my consciousness flying out of my body.

Shuddering against him, I feel safe, sexy, and utterly taken care of. I recall his words, "Your pleasure is my pleasure." If that's true, then he must be having a great time.

14

♥$

Jordan

Nothing like edible massage oil. This one is from the UK, and worth sending a friend and his wife in a private jet to buy it, seeing how they were going anyway. They enjoyed the luxury, and I received some necessities, including Cadbury chocolate bars that taste better than those made in the U.S. and a new panoramic roof from Range Rover's Liverpool factory. Definitely a necessity after a short-term female acquaintance put her skis out the roof and then tried to close it while we were driving along.

If I hadn't had my mind on her changing out of her ski clothes and into a sexy dress for dinner, it never would have happened.

With Brooke's easygoing nature, she'd be great to travel with, not to mention how I'd enjoy spoiling her rotten. I've never traveled with someone who had a try-anything-once attitude, either. And lately, since Livvy's death, I have barely traveled except to my island home. Pre-planned, extended fun, like a vacation to Italy, seems disrespectful.

As Brooke comes back from her short orgasmic trip, I settle between those slender legs and look down into her beautiful brown eyes. They make me think of enjoyable things like my childhood Labrador, a perfectly toasted marshmallow, and decadent chocolate mousse waiting for us in the kitchen. But none of those things seem like the right compliment.

"Your eyes are like burnished mahogany."

Amazingly, her cheeks turn pink, right over her high cheekbones. She's naturally seductive, and I wonder how I'd feel if she was making a concerted effort to turn me on.

"When you look at me like that, I want to . . ." I trail off. It's just my sex-crazed brain coming up with garbage. I nearly told her I wanted to kiss her. Who does that with essentially a one-night stand that has turned into a weeklong stand. Still *not* a relationship that warrants a kiss.

But her gaze and her lips are beckoning me. I ignore them and drop a kiss on her collarbone. I've discovered she loves that. As I nibble my way to her breast, I feel her intake of breath. Again, I want to cover her mouth with mine. To stop myself, I need to put a little distance between us.

"Turn over." I've also noticed she likes commands. It makes her nipples harden.

Just to cool myself down and negate any stupid thoughts of getting attached to Brooke, I trickle a line of oil down the middle of her back.

"More massage?" she says, when I straddle her thighs. Keeping my weight off her, I begin to rub her muscles, splaying my fingers away from her spine. "Thank you," she adds. "I am one lucky lady. And happy to reciprocate."

A massage isn't exactly how I want her to return the favor. We'll see. I knead and use the heel of my hand. Knowing what I like when I have a professional massage, I copy that. Eventually, when she's a limp rag and I wonder if I've done too good a job, I move lower and begin to knead her tight ass. Her butt cheeks are truly perfect, and my wicked thoughts want to play.

While I'm considering all options, she asks, "Any more condoms?"

Even as my erection stiffens, I can't help laughing. She keeps doing that—out of the blue, surprising a laugh out of me.

"I think I can scrounge one up."

In under a minute, I've put a pillow under her hips and am taking her from behind. Brooke keeps adjusting her angle and making sexy noises each time my cock contacts her G-spot.

"*Mmm—uhhh.* Yesssss! *Ohhh!*"

I lean down, nose aside her silky, chestnut hair, and nip her shoulder as well as the soft nape of her neck, feeling strangely territorial. Not something I'm familiar with. Leaning on one hand, I slide the other under her and slip between her soft folds to caress and circle her clit. She goes off first, which is good because I'm beyond ready. When Brooke stiffens under me, lifting her ass and grinding into my groin, I piston inside her and climax as fiercely as if we hadn't had sex yesterday. And the night before, too.

She's like a new piece of code I want to run over and over. Except at this moment, I need a break because my heart is still hammering. Rolling off in one direction, Brooke rolls the other way, off the pillow, which I grab and put behind my head. Curling onto her side, she faces me, a contented smile on her serene face.

After a few moments of silence in which we take turns opening our eyes and looking at one another, then closing them again, she says, "I like temperature play. A lot."

I nod. Then she adds, "You know what I want right now?"

Inwardly, I groan. In what way did I fall short? I gave her my all. Still, I'm only teasing when I ask, "Dammit, woman, what can you possibly want that I haven't already given you?"

Her smile grows. "Chocolate mousse and a Negroni."

I chuckle. "You're right. That's exactly what I want, too."

$♥$♥$♥$

Today is like yesterday. I work in an office that I pretend is someone else's and try to focus. To my credit, I do pretty well. The last fifty runs of the game, I can't break anything. No demand yields an error, nor can I stumble into any of my own backdoors in the code. After I upload files to the sandbox, where two of my trusted buddies from my Silicon Valley days will try their best to crash the game as they've been doing for months, I decide to reward myself with a dose of Brooke.

While I'm proud of my superhuman ability to work despite the presence of a gorgeous female, I can't deny thoughts of Brooke snagged my attention about once an hour. When I leave my office around four o'clock, she's not around. Then I realize the dogs aren't, either. They must be growing on this cat lady.

Shrugging into a shearling coat and putting on some hiking boots, I head out into the long blue shadows. The sun is going down fast, and I hope she borrowed one of my heavy-duty jackets, no matter how ridiculous she looks.

After tromping around for a few minutes, passing my buried tennis court, I hear the dogs in the distance toward the tree line and speed up. Brooke suddenly seems like a greenhorn, a dyed-in-the-wool city dweller, just as I was a few years back. A California transplant, I didn't know black ice from a frost heave. She has no business alone in the snow any distance from the house. I enter the trees, following the sounds of the dogs, and there she is. I stop because she steals my breath away.

She's built a pile of snowballs and is sitting beside it, probably getting a cold wet ass. I watch while she picks one up and heaves it. Duffy jumps for it and misses, and the other dogs bark like crazy while Brooke laughs. She tosses one toward Beau, who dodges while the other two bark. Being fair, she tosses the third to Grady, who jumps high and catches it, crushing the snowball in her jaws.

"Good girl," Brooke says, as Duffy smells my approach and starts barking again, racing in my direction. The other two follow, but I ignore them and make a beeline for the pretty woman wearing one of my coats with the sleeves rolled up.

"You shouldn't sit on the cold ground. If you get wet, your skin can freeze." And I hold out my hand to her, which she takes. After hauling her to her feet, light as a feather despite all the bulky clothes she's wearing, I see now she's not in any danger of getting wet. She has on waterproof nylon pants, probably Emma's.

"I'm fine," she says. "It's so beautiful and quiet. Apart from these three nuts, that is."

I haven't let go. Still holding hands, I draw her close, and she's looking up at me. Her cheeks are ruddy, her eyes are bright, and she's wearing a silly knitted hat with a pom-pom, which I've never seen before.

When Brooke falls silent, we stare at one another, ignoring the dogs who are running and barking around us like mad things. She licks her lips and must know what I'm thinking—that it would be good to finally try a kiss.

Of course I don't give in. I don't want to give her the wrong idea that we have something. Since I don't even want her to know my real name, we clearly don't have anything but great sex. A kiss could plaster a layer of emotion across the satisfying games we're playing. And that would be a disaster.

Oddly, she looks away first, shuttering her eyes with those long dark lashes that I've watched sweep her cheeks as she climaxes. Her gaze has dropped to Duffy, nudging his way between us. I release her and step away.

"I'm getting a little cold now," she says. "Ready to go back indoors and stop swishing."

"Swishing?" I ask.

"Listen to me." Brooke walks ahead a few feet and comes back. Sure enough, her pants and coat sleeves make swishing sounds.

I grin. "The natural sound of winter clothes."

"Nothing natural about nylon, but I appreciate that I'm warm and dry under all this."

"I thought you were making a stockpile for a revenge snowball fight."

"Nope," she says. "That's only a quarter of what I made and threw for these clowns. They legit never get tired of the same game."

We start to walk back with the dogs ahead of us, when I get an idea. "You up for some night skiing?"

"I thought they closed at four."

Yes, you idiot. She's right, except for Fridays and Saturdays. I shrug as nonchalantly as possible. How do I explain this? "I know the manager there. He'll keep the lifts running. It'll be fun."

While she's considering, I add, "Plus, I need to move after sitting down all day."

As if my welfare matters, she nods. "Ok, let's get you some exercise. I've never tried night skiing before."

"And you'll try anything once."

"Absolutely," she agrees.

That may be why our sex is the best I've ever had. Because she just goes with it, relaxes into each moment. Brooke lets it happen and reacts with a pure response that leaves no room for thinking, judging, or worrying about what happens next.

I make a phone call while she changes, and then we take the Range Rover over to the base lodge.

"It's magical," she says, as we approach. The lights illuminating the trails look like Christmas luminaries along a walkway. On a giant scale.

After parking in the all but empty lot, I take her hand in mine. Heading over to the lockers, I retrieve my stuff. Since the rentals were closed, I had the manager put equipment for Brooke into the adjoining locker.

"Wow!" she says when I surprise her with boots and skis. "Apparently, you have a really good friend here."

"Upper management," I say. "You ready?"

It's a first for me, too. Not night skiing, but pulling strings and spending a shit-ton of money to do something that's super elitist just to impress a woman. We stick to the trails with lights, mostly blue-square runs. Two lifts are open with the four lift operators, top and bottom, looking pretty stoked to be making a healthy bonus for a couple hours extra work.

"You've improved," I say, as we swish down our third run.

"It's easier when I'm not scared of getting in someone's way or hitting an unsuspecting skier below me." Then she laughs. "I guess all I needed was my own private mountain."

I could buy the resort tomorrow and give it to her, and the thought flits through my brain as we ski over to the lift again. I would do that for the woman I love, in a heartbeat. But for a no-scruples reporter? An expensive treat of night skiing seems like the perfect gift.

"Tell me when you're done," I remind her on the lift. "Or if you get hungry."

Brooke waves away my mention of food. Her eyes are bright, and I can tell she's really enjoying herself. "This is a blast. Thank you. If the other chair was open, I might even try that black diamond run again."

"That's the spirit," I say. "Not stupidly fearless but thoughtfully brave."

She nods. "So, no flask of brandy?"

"Do I look like a Saint Bernard?"

When Brooke smiles, I feel a tug in my chest that I don't quite like, and I counter it with a disapproving tone.

"Drinking during skiing isn't my thing." But my censure is reserved for myself. I've never let a pretty face get to me before, not even when it's attached to a killer body. Still, her expression falters.

"No worries. Just thought a nip would be nice." When we get off the lift this time, she calls out, "I'll race you to the bottom."

I almost decide to let her win, but I've never been a fan of false victory. I do, however, ski beside her, effortlessly keeping pace, until the end when I zoom past. Unfortunately, she'd been skiing her hardest. When I look back, I see her lose control. Surprised by my sudden spurt of speed, she stands too straight, the edge goes out on her right ski, and suddenly, she's falling hard. Luckily, there are no people and no trees nearby. Just Brooke falling sideways, skis coming off, and getting the breath knocked out of her.

Removing my skis, it takes me a moment to climb up ten feet to where she's lying flat, looking up.

"Join me," she says unexpectedly.

"You're not hurt?" I ask, although that seems obvious.

"Nope. Lie down and look up."

Well, OK then. Another first, I'm lying at a slight incline, helmet on, as is hers, staring up at the early evening sky, dressed in our ski clothes.

"Even with these nightlights, the cliché of black velvet and diamonds is totally true," she says.

"Which is why it's a cliché," I remark, like a smart aleck. What the hell is an "aleck" anyway? Luckily, she fell in between two of the poles housing lights, so we can actually look up without being blinded, and see some stars. "It's the same view from my . . . from Asher's house."

"I know, but we're on the side of a mountain."

"The bottom, if we're being accurate."

Finally, she swivels her head to look at me. "Can I just enjoy this moment please?"

"Sure."

She looks at the sky again in silence. "Look. A shooting star."

"Technically, that's a—"

"Don't. Please. I know it's a meteor." She sighs. "And it's spectacular." Then she adds, "I didn't notice before that you're kind of a pragmatic geek and not in the least bit romantic."

A laugh escapes me. "You're right, I'm not."

"That's OK. I've been with romantic guys before. Flowers and cards and all that. But they didn't know their way around hot massage oil the way you do."

Preoccupied by her half-assed compliment, I almost miss her next words. "I am falling in love."

Before I make a fool of myself, she finishes, "With this view. With Maine. With living in the mountains. A starry night is common, but so freaking many stars and so close I believe I could touch one, that's special. It's not really black velvet yet, though, is it? More like navy blue. Give it another hour."

"If we give it another hour, ski patrol will find our frozen bodies in the morning." I get to my feet and offer her my hand. "Come on, Galileo. Let's get some dinner."

On the short drive home, my cell rings. Seeing it's the bar, I answer over my car's mic.

"Hey, it's TJ and you're on speaker phone."

"It's Cy, boss, and we have a situation. Who's with you?"

"Brooke." I'm glad he asked before saying anything more. I haven't forgotten she mentioned that it was Cy's slip of the tongue that her cousin overheard. I'll definitely be talking to him about that in private. "What sort of problem?"

"There's a horde of people here to see a mutual friend of ours."

A horde! My blood runs cold. "What kind of people?" I imagine paparazzi with those massive, old-fashioned cameras and their flashes going off in rapid-fire fashion, like at a red-carpet event.

"Gamers, boss."

"Gamers?" I quickly erase the notion of flashing reporters and think instead of rabid Bright fans.

"About a baker's dozen, at least. They all came in together. They've taken the center tables."

"How do you know they're *gamers*?" I say the word like they're a different species altogether. My species. My people.

Brooke giggles at my tone. But to me, it's no laughing matter. Unlike her, this segment of the population might recognize me. She's going to wonder why I don't drive straight there to sort out whatever's bothering Cy about the bar's guests.

"Because they're odd ducks," he says with his distinctly British understatement. "Most of them have set up their laptops and are playing, right here in the bar! Every once in a while, they yell out, 'Where's Asher?' 'We want Asher.' And then they chant 'Bright Star, Bright Star, Bright Star,' like creepy cult members."

Damn! "Apart from the chanting, are they causing any problems?"

"They're not spending much," Cy complains, "but no, they're not doing anything, except demanding to see you . . . *your* boss."

I grit my teeth at his slip. Then Brooke chimes in, "If you need TJ, we're all done skiing."

How nice of her to offer me up to the horde, but I can't go anywhere near the place.

"Make friends," I order my bar manager. "See if you discover how they found out—" I cut myself off and glance at Brooke who's watching me intently. I guess there's no point in pretending any longer that Asher isn't a part of this community. "Find out how they knew to come to the Thirsty Moose. OK?"

"I already know how, boss."

My stress level ratchets up a notch as I wait to hear.

"It was some female gamer, known as Busby's Aunt, who posted it on the Bright gaming chat boards."

Brooke gasps. And I don't need to look at her to see her large, guilt-laden eyes.

15

Brooke

My text to Sherri has come back to bite me in the butt, and I'm trembling in my crappy, fashionable, impractical excuse for winter boots. Also, a photo I snapped of TJ talking to the Saddleback manager is burning a hole in my pocket. But I didn't break any rules. It wasn't taken at the bar, nor at Asher's house. Just a memento for me personally.

"Sounds like you have everything under control," TJ says. I can tell by his voice that he's really pissed off. *At me!* "Call if you need me. Otherwise, don't let them drink over the limit because we don't want police involved or any publicity about this. And after another hour, if they're not spending on food, tell them they have to give up the tables. Use your British charm. You got this."

"And if they keep asking about Asher?" Cy asks.

"Who?" TJ says as we pull into the garage before he glares at me. But Cy laughs.

"Got it, boss."

After he hangs up, the silence in the car is what I would call *thick*. Is he waiting for me to apologize?

"I guess Sherri got excited," I begin.

This causes him to bang his head back against the headrest a few times, eyes closed, muttering under his breath.

"She's a big fan," I continue.

"No shit!" he says. "And now a bunch of other *big fans* are in my bar!" Then he asks, "Why not your cousin?"

"*Busby's* Aunt," I remind him of her gamer handle. "Someone has to stay home with him."

More silence.

"I don't see how this is so terrible," I say. "Asher is on Gilligan's Island somewhere, and some mostly well-behaved gamers are drinking at the Moose. Not the end of the world."

"Unless this is just the opening of the tap. Unless they come in bigger numbers and it becomes a story. Asher," he annunciates the word like it's distasteful, "will be royally pissed!"

I almost point out that's the first time he has said his boss's name. It gives me a little thrill to know I was right all along. Instead, I say the other thought that's bouncing around in my head.

"Have you ever considered that Gilligan is kind of an unusual name? If you say it a few times, I mean. And was it his first or his last name?"

TJ gets out of the car and slams the door. He doesn't even wait for me as he heads inside.

"I'm sorry," I finally say, as I trail after him. "I didn't think texting Sherri would be a problem. It didn't break any photography rules that I knew at the time. Just Cy's picture, remember?"

"She knew which bar you meant," he says as he removes his boots in the mudroom. "And she couldn't wait to form a posse to track Asher down."

I don't mean to, but I smile at the word *posse.*

"Not funny, Brooke," he growls and goes into the foyer.

When I catch up, the aroma of something delicious for dinner makes my mouth water. I know TJ was caught off guard and isn't thrilled by gamers at his bar, but no real harm was done. I don't see how he can stay mad at me for too long.

Ten minutes later, I realize he's a natural at the silent treatment. He's radiating his displeasure, even when we sit down to eat the most fabulous chili and cornbread I've ever tasted. We're at the kitchen island, and he's got his tablet, scrolling through emails while he eats. Not that I can see them without craning my neck.

Eventually, interrupting the quiet meal, I say, "I really enjoyed the night skiing. Thanks for taking me."

He grunts but doesn't look up from his tablet.

After another few minutes, I apologize again. "

I didn't know Sherri would post anything, but I should have thought to tell her not to. Anyway, I really am sorry it's made you unhappy." Strangely, I truly am. We were having such fun and getting along so well until Cy's call. I already miss the easy camaraderie.

TJ nods, so I know he's listening. Then he turns off the tablet and pushes it away. After eating another spoonful of thick chili, he sips his beer and asks, "What type of punishment should you get?"

Zing!

"The paddle," I answer quickly, since he asked my preference. I'm a bit shocked at myself for being able to request what I want. But I very much *want.*

His slow grin sends a shiver up my spine and causes an immediate tingling between my legs. I'm ready to shed my clothing here at the kitchen island.

"I think restraints are in order, too," he says, and my body's reaction goes into overdrive, instantly drenched down below and throbbing with desire. We finish our meal in a hurry, like a pair of star-nosed moles, the fastest mammal eaters. I know this after doing an article for kids about various animals when I first got to BMG. Those moles have nothing on TJ and me, as we eat, drink, and head off to be merry.

"Strip," he orders as soon as I'm in his room. I do, fast and in a probably not-very-sexy manner. He stays dressed, which makes this naughtier and hotter. Meanwhile, he has grabbed his bed's two pillows, arranging them one atop the other in a high pile.

Glancing at him, I can see TJ's erection already pressing against his jeans. We lock gazes, and his pupils are dilated. I imagine mine are, too.

"Climb on, ass high," he says, no hint of humor, which I like. It's as if he steps into character, as do I, blocking any embarrassment *regular Brooke* might experience. I get on the bed, situate my hips on the pillows, and wait.

"Great view," he says, trailing his fingers over my exposed pussy, making me gasp. I wish he'd dip them deep inside me. Instead, as promised, he ties my wrists with silk ties, and I have the strange notion that he's taken these from Asher's room, because why would a bar owner have so damn many?

He ties my ankles to the bottom bedposts, and I am so turned on by this, I start to hump the pillows.

"Stop," he commands, and I freeze. "No coming without permission."

I smile into the comforter, but am taken by surprise by the first, sudden whack of the paddle, which I hadn't even seen him pick up. There wasn't any torturous wait time, either.

"Oof," is the only sound wrested from me, as the smack is followed by warmth permeating the area.

Before I can turn my head to peek at him, TJ brings the narrow wooden paddle down again. A mild sting brings even greater heat seeping through my cells, gushing into my lady parts. It's magical.

"Were you good today?" he asks.

Is this a trick question? Today, I think I was. "Yes?"

He smacks me again. "Are you sure? Did you think of having sex with me?"

"Yes."

The pain from the paddle is increasing, but so is the tingling of my clit.

"How many times?"

"A lot." It's true, too. Every time I looked at him or thought of him, I dreamed of this moment when I was in his capable control.

"You *were* a good girl," he says, dragging the narrow paddle across my engorged folds. Then he gives them a few light taps that nearly sends me over the edge. But I'm learning, so I ask first.

"May I come now?"

He pauses. "Are you ready so soon? I was just getting started." With that, he leans over and puts his open mouth on my muff. When he spreads my lips open and touches his tongue to my clit, I can't hold on any longer. The climax is a long, shattering unwinding that leaves me exhausted for such a brief experience. Brief but intense.

Then TJ surprises me again. "Go for a swim?" he asks as he starts to untie me.

$♥$♥$♥$

Being in a hot tub in winter, nestled in a valley with mountains all around is simply spectacular. We're treated to a light show of stars winking in and out of sight behind what looks like a rippling curtain of multi-colored Northern Lights. It's like no other hot tub experience, especially being with TJ and mulled red wine.

But we didn't start here. We started in Asher's heated pool. It's about half the size of an Olympic pool, which is still massive for anyone's private enjoyment. It's not a silly shallow splashing pool, either. It has a deep end, a diving board, and quite unexpectedly, a slide.

"Hard to believe you can heat a pool that size. It should be an ice rink this time of year," I tell TJ when he first suggested we go for a night swim.

"It's a perfect eighty-eight degrees this time of year."

I cannot imagine how much that costs each day. While we were still indoors, he tapped a switch to open its massive cover, then lit the path to the pool. There are four heaters on poles, but he would have to go remove their snow-capped covers and wait for them to heat up, so we decide not to bother.

The pool area is close to the house. Under the snow, there must be an impressive deck for summer outdoor living. Pity I won't see that, but I'm definitely down for a winter swim.

In a flash, I'm wearing a stunning bikini. No, I'm not! I'm wearing my only pair of non-thong underwear that I have with me and a bra, a thick robe, snow boots, and a woolly hat. Very sexy. Also, *not!* After a few laps and showing off our swimming moves, with neither of us wanting to find out if we'd stick to the frigid slide, we hopped the tiled dividing wall. Now, in the hot tub, which is more like a hot pool, the jets melt away any tension. That's when TJ uncorks the red.

"Après swim?"

I grin at him. "Yes, please."

Reclining seats line one side, with a place for one's head cradled above water. Leaning back, I look up at the bright sky. Not simply a billion stars tonight, the Northern Lights steal the show.

"Directly over Saddleback Mountain," I say, reverently. They're vivid green with shimmers of purple. Truly the definition of magnificent and awe-inspiring.

"Honestly, that has to be one of the best displays I've ever seen," he says.

Sipping the wine, relaxing, I can see how this could be a danger if alone and tired. Too much alcohol and one might slip under the hot water. However, with TJ's wicked smile, I am anything but sleepy. Although, my head is decidedly cold. No longer caring about my appearance, I put the woolly hat on my wet hair, so I can enjoy this experience without freezing my brain.

"*Oh*, baby!" he says. "How that hat turns me on."

I laugh. "You're lucky. Your hair dried with a couple swipes of the towel. Mine would be frozen stiff in a few minutes."

"Something else is getting stiff," TJ says.

This statement gives me pause. "Wait, really? But not because of the hat, right?"

He smiles enigmatically and drinks his wine. Still, I'm curious. "For some reason, I didn't think you could get an erection in really hot water. Not that I've spent much time considering it," I add.

TJ shrugs, pulls his swim trunks off, then lifts his hips out of the water so I can see an impressive pole spearing the night air.

"Wow!" I say, as he sinks back into the bubbles.

"Must be the way your breasts are spilling over the top of that bra. Your turn," he adds.

I glance around, but we're obviously alone, and no one can see us, unless they have a telescope trained on the tub. Not taking any chances, I ask, "No peepers?"

"Colin and Emma have their own life. I'm sure spying on us isn't part of it. And there are no neighbors or you'd see their lights."

Fair enough. I divest myself of my nude-colored bra and set it aside.

"Come on," he urges me. "Go completely native."

I giggle from the wine and the heat and the freedom. "If I were going native, I'd have on layers of fur and be sitting around a campfire, not exposing myself to frostbite." But I wiggle out of my panties. Reaching out his big hand, TJ seeks the juncture between my legs and rests his fingers on it, which naturally wakes up my desire from mildly aroused to pulsing neediness.

"Put your head back, Brooke, look at the sky and relax."

I do as he suggests while he sips wine with one hand and slides his fingers between my folds with the other. I can trust that he knows how to handle me, beginning with the ideal pace and speed, the correct finger position, and the perfect touch as he circles and strokes my clit. When I can't keep my eyes open any longer no matter how gorgeous the night sky, I arch against his hand, close my eyes, and moan loudly into the frosty air. With that, he captures my clit between two knuckles and tugs me into a fierce climax.

What's more, he's so good at this, as if he knows my body as well as I do, he doesn't stop until he's milked out every last ripple of my orgasm, letting me ride it as long as I can.

"Yes." I breathe out the word and finally open my eyes. TJ's no longer casually drinking wine but looking at me with an intensity of passion that makes me immediately grab hold of his cock. He has already set aside his empty glass.

"Watching your face was magical," he says, "and the way your tits bobbed up and then disappeared again as you breathed and squirmed, like a teasing mermaid."

I love how beautiful he makes me feel.

"I want to come between your breasts," he says without a hint of embarrassment.

I wasn't expecting that, but the idea is novel. I sit up as he straddles me, leaning his arms on the edge of the hot tub on either side of my head.

"Won't you freeze up there?" I ask.

Ignoring my question, he situates his cock between my breasts. "Squeeze it between your tits," he orders, beginning to move up and down, stroking himself with my flesh.

I get the hang of it, pressing my breasts together so they encircle his erection. When I realize I can reach the tip of him with my tongue, I say, "Come higher." With each thrust he does, and I take the head into my mouth for a few sensual seconds before he retreats again.

Each time, I can lick or suck, but only for a moment. He's moving faster, and I can feel his body tensing.

"God, yes," he says. "That's it." The first spurt touches my lips, then the rest goes everywhere as he continues to pump until he's spent. Then he sinks back into the water.

"Good?" I ask.

He goes under completely before bobbing back to the surface. "You were right, my back was frozen."

I laugh. "But you manfully struggled through your suffering to achieve an orgasm."

"Damn right," he says. "Now my head is freezing, too."

"Grab a towel," I suggest, "and wrap it around your head before you have no working brains left."

Soon, he's wearing a turban. Utterly nonplussed by our odd appearance, me with my hat and him with the towel, we enjoy our second glass of wine.

"Getting out will be a bitch," he says. "I think we'll need to move fast and take hot showers."

"You didn't think this through, did you?" I like that. Maybe he's not so practiced at all this, and perhaps he hasn't done what we just did before with anyone else. But I don't ask. Instead, I say, "I bet that pool would feel frigid after this."

"Probably. But some people practice hot and cold therapy. In Bozeman, Montana, they have a natural hot spring that's been used by visitors since the late eighteen hundreds, including by yours truly. The outside pools are most popular with lights and live music, but the inside has two of the hottest pools sandwiched on either side of a cold pool. Bathers dunk from cold to hot and back again."

"Yikes," I say. "Not my cup of tea."

"I'd love to take you skiing at Big Sky and go to the Bozeman hot springs." His words come out while his head is back, and he's looking at the shower of transparent colors, undulating over our heads.

I can feel how much he wishes he hadn't said that. The regret radiates off him for sounding too friendly. It makes me a little wistful because being with TJ in Montana would probably be great.

An awkward silence follows, and we don't look at each other until he speaks again.

"Not that we'll ever be in a position to do that," he adds, causing a pang of yearning to dampen my mood. "But I think you'd like the view from the chairlifts. If you ski there or make it to the hot springs, you can think of me and this night."

Way to smooth over an unintended invitation. I guess he did as well as he could.

"If I find myself in a hot spring, I'll think of you," I say softly. Also, the next time I'm in a hot tub or a pool or a bed or having sex or letting my mind wander to the best experience I've ever had. But I'm obviously not going to disclose all of that. Instead, I turn to look at his profile.

"Tell me something," I say. It's a game I used to play with my parents on car rides.

"About what?" TJ asks.

"Doesn't matter as long as it's something you haven't told me before." Which covers a lot of ground since I know next-to nothing about him.

"Like a story?" he asks, turning his head and training his gray-green gaze on me.

I shrug. "A fact, a memory. Just something."

He frowns. "I can't think of anything interesting."

Rolling my eyes, I say, "OK, what's the T in TJ stand for."

For a moment, he looks shocked, and in the next, I wonder if he doesn't want to tell me. Then he takes a deep breath. "Don't laugh."

Which of course puts me in the grips of a big guffaw that I wait to let out.

"Tiberius."

I slap the water, making a big, loud splash. "What? No! That's an amazing name. You're the first Tiberius I've ever met."

"Me, too. Maybe there are a lot of them in Rome."

If I were him, I'd have looked that up before this moment. "Is there a reason behind such a magnificently unusual name? Were your parents James T. Kirk or *Star Trek* fans?"

He laughs. "No, they weren't. I mean, I'm sure they liked the show but they weren't Trekkies or anything. Why are you called Brooke?" he asks me.

"Easy. Because my father's mother was known to everyone as Nana Brooke, even though it was her maiden name and not her first name. Apparently, I looked like her as a baby. It suits me. I can babble with the best of them."

He nods and takes a drink of wine.

"Hold up," I say. "You distracted me. If not from Captain Kirk, what's behind your mouthful of a name?"

This time, he shoots me a smile. "I tried and failed to distract." He runs his finger down my arm, then over my breast, making me shiver.

"Stop right there, Tiberius," I say, clamping my hand over his to halt its progress.

TJ sighs. "My mom worked at the Getty Villa Museum in Pacific Palisades, California. Her specialty is ancient Rome. She thought this guy's story was interesting, a Roman general who became emperor." He pauses before adding, "And he was adopted."

I turn my entire body toward him, still gripping his hand against my chest. "You're adopted?"

"Yup."

I think about this a moment, letting it sink in. It would be nosy to ask more about how he came to be given up for adoption if he doesn't volunteer the information. But I'd like to know about the rest of his name. "And the *J* in TJ?"

His jaw does that clenching, jumping thing. Finally, he says, "Guess? Think ancient Rome and the most famous general."

I know my eyes widen when I guess, "Tiberius *Julius*?"

He nods. "That was Tiberius's actual name."

"Very cool."

"Thanks," he says quietly. Then he tilts his head and sends me a questioning smile. "You ready to get out and run?"

16

Jordan

I'm a little surprised by how easily the lie came to me, although I did say to Brooke that Tiberius Julius was *Tiberius's* name, which it was. But it's not mine. Jordan is my adoptive father's name, passed on to me since I had no name of my own.

The rest is true, as my mother is obsessed with Rome, and thought this man's life particularly interesting. Not exactly happy, however, nor was the old Roman someone to emulate, but that's another story. In every way that mattered, my parents gave me the best childhood from the moment they brought me home as a four-month-old baby. They'd adopted Livvy the year before. With both of us from different hard-luck orphanage situations, we were lucky to end up with the Ashers.

Then Livvy's luck ran out because of my fame and greedy reporters who wanted a piece of me.

While I'm showering, I wonder how long I can keep up this entire lie. When I told Brooke my first name, I half-expected her to have dug up my records and know I'm Tiberius Jordan Asher. I've never used the name, apart from still answering when my father calls me Tibs. And since only a few thousand gamers found the Easter egg in the first Bright Quest, disclosing my real first name, I was willing to gamble and tell Brooke tonight.

Seems she has no idea. In fact, she's more convinced than ever that I'm TJ Linter. Turning off the water, I shake my head. That was a stupid lie. If she talks about me with anyone who knows coding, they'll tell her a linter is a tool that analyzes code for problems, bugs, and syntax errors.

But why would I think she'll talk about me to anyone? I've managed to button her up as tightly as an aim-assist locked onto a target. She won't mention me or this house or Asher for fear her cute naked ass will be all over the internet.

Not that I ever would, even if she were a scheming bitch, which I don't believe. I no longer think Brooke is anything but a good person trying to make a living in a crappy way. Plus, she doesn't seem to have any skill at being a ruthless reporter, though she was damn good with analyzing my psyche. Spot on about my control-freak personality. And I feel most out of control when I think people are going to start invading my space, with nothing I can do about it.

Brooke's skilled in other areas, too. She makes me happy, which isn't easy. Ever since I was young, I've been told I'm on the serious side. Maybe that's why my games are uplifting and whimsical, despite being filled with conquest and elite fighting forces. I'm working out all my mental issues. Or at least shooting the hell out of them. I've laughed with her, or at least smiled, more in the past few days than I have in the last three years since Livvy died and I moved to Maine.

Her other set of skills, I cannot get enough of. I don't know whether she's up for sex tonight. I didn't ask her as we were both running for the showers. Just in case, I put on sweatpants and a shirt and find myself in the hallway outside her room.

Silence inside. Maybe she went to bed. I groan at the thought of her between the sheets. I can't remember ever being so infatuated with a woman's body, but I'm starting to understand it's because I like the woman herself. Not that I haven't cared for someone before, though not deeply since college. Usually, a week in and a half dozen fucks later, I'm thinking of the *speedrun*, a gaming term for getting to the end of play as quickly as possible. In the real world, that means reaching the part where I tell someone it's over.

And this game between me and Brooke definitely has an end. Instead of knocking, I go back into my room and call Cy again. He's closing up, and I want to make sure the gamers haven't overwhelmed him. Maybe they barricaded all my bar staff in the kitchen and are laying siege to the exit until they get their demands. Classic Bright tactics.

"Nah," Cy says. "Apart from chanting your name every once in a while, they weren't rowdy. Some only drank soft drinks because they wanted to stay sharp." He laughs. "You know, for getting to the next level or some such rubbish."

"This is all because of you, you know?" I tell him.

"Pardon?"

I can't help smiling at his Brit talk. "You mentioned my name out loud like a year ago, and that gamer, Busby's Aunt, overheard. She's Brooke's cousin."

"*Ah*, I see. *Hm*. Not well done of me, I suppose."

"No, not at all. I guess no harm was done. How'd the night turn out? Were they satisfied I'm not there?"

"Honestly, I think most had to get back to school or a job. They all came up from Boston, part of a university gaming club."

I feel instant relief. Maybe Brooke's cousin's reach is really small and local. In other circumstances, I'd like to meet Sherri and these other diehard fans. Although I'm not certain what those other circumstances might be.

$♥$♥$♥$

In the morning, I invite Brooke to go into town with me. Cy reminded me last night of a few things I've neglected at the bar, although not in those exact words. And while Bright Star is being played by my team of game-crushing testers, I have a window of free time to keep up the pretense of being a bar owner.

Brooke is happy to walk around Rangeley, having decided to write short articles about the town. When she says she'll come with me first to the Thirsty Moose, I let her. I'm not concerned about gamers since we're not open yet.

Tracy is already here, along with a bar back, and a prep cook. She smiles when she sees me, but her eyes widen and her smile falters when she sees Brooke. I'm not sure if she recognizes her from last Friday.

"Hi, Trace. Everything OK?" That's the extent of my usual greeting.

"All good, boss," she says as always. But her curious gaze is fixated on Brooke.

"This is Brooke Danbury. Brooke, meet Tracy Pelletier."

The two women exchange greetings, but I don't really want them chatting. When I hook up with a woman, typically a tourist, I don't bring them here. The last thing I want or need is the scrutiny of my staff. I should've thought of that before I brought Brooke in, especially during closed hours. During a loud, crowded happy hour a few nights ago was a different matter.

At least Brooke isn't clinging to my arm. Maybe I should tell Tracy she's a reporter doing a story about Rangeley. Then I remember I don't have to fucking explain myself to anyone. Having a female around me for so many days, especially a nosy one, has twisted my thinking.

"You want the tour?" I ask, sounding gruffer than I mean to. Brooke doesn't seem to notice.

"Sure." We escape Tracy's questioning stare. I show Brooke the spotless kitchen, the walk-in freezer, and the alcohol stores.

"That's a lot of booze," she remarks.

"You'd be surprised how quick the turnover is and the need to replenish it."

Next, I take her downstairs to see where the draft beer kegs are stored in our cellar. There's a network of beer lines and air lines, regulators, and CO_2 tanks. It reminds me of the complexity of cables attached to the back of a mainframe server.

"Wow!" Brooke sounds impressed. "Like veins in the body."

I guess we all have our own frames of reference.

"How many pints of beer in a keg?" she asks.

Shit. I have no idea. If I really owned and ran this bar and didn't rely on Cy, I would know that. "Enough," I say, hoping I sound like I'm telling her not to worry her pretty little head.

Then I hustle her out of the cellar in case she has other questions. Taking her to my office, which is more often Cy's domain, I forget how cramped it is until we're both standing in it. It's old and ugly, with paneled walls, a drop ceiling of aged and stained foam tiles, a four-year-old wildlife calendar hanging beside the small desk, and a dented, gray metal file cabinet that has God-knows-what inside it. All on a beat up narrow-plank floor. On the desk is a high-end PC tower and a large monitor. Of course!

She shakes her head. "It's like high-tech tried to take a stand in a 1970s accountant's office and lost."

I agree. I ought to spend a little money and redo the room. It's authentically terrible.

"You are hands-down the best-looking thing in this room," I say.

"Hey, wait a minute," Brooke says, grinning back at me as she takes another look around. "That's not saying much. Plus, I'm not a *thing.* Also, that PC might actually be better looking than I am." She runs a sexy purple nail across the top of it.

Just like that, I'm horny as a freshmen college student. The office is small enough that I can reach out and run my hand down her back. She stands taller, stretches her shoulders up and back, making her tits rise and fall.

When she looks over her shoulder at me, I see we're simpatico. Shutting the door, I am grateful there's a lock, which I never noticed before.

"You are not a *thing*," I agree. "You're a freakin' goddess."

Her eyes widen, her lips part, and in about half a second, I have backed her against the one bit of empty wall space, between the front of the desk and a floor lamp. Another second later, I'm pressing her hands over her head onto the ugly paneling while I grind against her.

"TJ," she whispers. "Can we?"

Can we? Is there a condom in this office? "God, I hope so."

In a flash, I'm rifling through the office drawers until I find a box. Inside, there is exactly one rubber. I hold it up in triumph, and she smiles. While I undo, take off, and slide on, as needed, Brooke takes off her jeans, leaving her sexy thong barely covering her.

I can feel my blood pounding and hear my own heartbeat in my head. Sinking down to the floor, I drag the wisp of silky fabric aside and nibble her clit. Already softly moaning, Brooke splays her fingers in my hair and lets me bring her to the edge of a climax.

When she's wet and her thighs are visibly trembling, I rise to my feet, hook one of her legs over my arm to open her and glide inside.

"Tiptoe," I order, which she does immediately with the foot that's still on the ground while I keep my knees bent so we line up. After a couple thrusts, I think, *Forget this shit*, and hoist her high. Now I can stand straight, letting the wall support her upper back. Instinctively, she wraps her free leg around my waist, and we become a writhing, two-backed beast, getting a little sweaty, both grunting as I spear her over and over.

"Never done this," she mutters, draping her arms over my shoulders and hanging on.

Not as easy as it looks, still, it's worth the effort. But I can't speak and give her the fucking she deserves so I say nothing. Her pussy feels so tight, I'm seeing stars and ready to come.

But ladies first. Her pleasure really is mine, too. If I went off and she was left hanging, I'd regret the whole thing and feel like a failure. I hold back and grind my pelvis against her tiny, sensitive clit, knowing at this angle, I am hitting her G-spot, too.

A tap at the door causes us both to freeze, although Brooke can't stifle another moan. I hear the handle rattle, but the ancient lock holds.

"What?" I call out, hoping I sound casual while straining to maintain our position.

"It's Tracy." Long pause. "Do you have a minute?"

Brooke and I lock desperate eyes. "Please," she mouths. We're both caught on the edge of our respective orgasms.

"One sec," I call out, trying for a normal tone. Starting to move again, slowly, deliberately, I pull back before sheathing myself in Brooke's slippery heat. She bites her lower lip, but keeps her cocoa-brown gaze on mine as I continue this motion. When she nods, I know she's ready for me to speed up, which I do, pumping into her until we're back on the climax cliff.

"TJ," she whispers again. "That's . . . it!" I feel her quivering release as her body squeezes my cock, and I can no longer refrain from coming. A little out of control, I thrust like a piston engine and bury my face in her sweater at her collarbone, trying not to be loud, with my final driving onslaught.

And there it is, the best stand-up sex I've ever had, adding to all the other bests we've enjoyed.

Brooke is hanging limp, still anchored to the wall by my body, until we uncouple and separate. Condom in trash can, clothing on, we're still breathing hard and her cheeks are pink. My face is probably ruddy, too, from the exertion.

"Very much worth it," I finally say.

She laughs softly. I unlock the door and open it, but Tracy has disappeared.

Brooke is going to go exploring. "Now that I can barely walk," she pretends to complain. I doubt there's a man alive who doesn't feel proud of himself when his woman says that.

Not that she's *my* anything.

"I'll be OK in a few minutes," she adds. "I'll probably end up finding a place to have a cup of tea and recover."

"The Double Diamond?"

She wrinkles her nose, which I find adorable. "I don't think that guy wants me back in there anytime soon. I made kind of a spectacle of myself. Not in a good way."

That makes me smile, then I add, "I guess we made a spectacle right here. Definitely in a good way."

Brooke rolls her eyes. "See ya, TJ."

I can't help myself. I follow her into the bar's dining area.

"Give me a couple hours. Then call me when you're ready to go home," I tell her. It sounded weird. Like we're in a relationship.

Watching her ass as she leaves, I make sure to remind myself that we're all about coupling, *not* being a romantic couple. Back behind the bar, Tracy coughs after the door closes behind Brooke.

"Isn't that the same woman from last week?" she asks me.

"Yup." And that's all I say as I head for the office. My private life is not anyone's business. Then I recall that we are, in fact, in my place of business, and I say, "Sorry, I was on the phone earlier. What did you need to speak with me about?"

Her blue eyes flicker over me. "Nothing important."

17

Brooke

My phone pings as I exit a combination bookstore and tea bar. I spend forty minutes in there, thoroughly enjoying some dragon pearl tea, but unable to focus on any of the titles I was browsing. I can't stop thinking how much I'll miss this crisp air, the beauty surrounding me, and . . . TJ.

Drawing my phone from my purse, I see it's Sherri. And there are about fifteen previous texts from yesterday that I didn't receive because of the lack of service in Asher's house.

Scrolling through, they're warning me that her gaming group is coming. Too late! Her final one last night read:

Sorry. Hope I didn't ruin your scoop for BMG.

In the rest of the texts, she's been bombarding me with questions. My silence is driving her crazy.

If you don't tell me what's going on, I'll pack Mr. Busby in a suitcase and drive up there.

She'd do it, too. Sherri, born a scant one month before me, is not only my cousin, she's truly my closest friend and, occasionally, my protector.

Are you being held captive?

I grin as my brain considers how awesome sex is when TJ restrains me. Then I spill my guts in a long text.

I've been having fun with a guy named TJ. Skiing and OTHER stuff. 😌 😌 He owns the bar you saw Asher in and also manages Asher's estate. No sign of the billionaire himself.

She sends me a wow emoji: 😲

This makes me laugh because she has been pushing me to go out with someone, *anyone*, for months.

Photo of the guy who has managed to break your celibate streak of six long months. NOW!

I nearly tell her I can't send one, but on second thought, I decide I'm not breaking any rules. After all, I'm not trying to make money from it. A barely discernible photo of TJ won't earn me a cent. Plus, the photo isn't in the house or even on Asher's property, nor is it at the bar.

I send the only one I have, which I took when we were night skiing. TJ was talking to the resort manager, thanking him for letting us ski. He didn't notice, and I just wanted one picture so I'd know this wasn't a dream, once I returned to my real life.

She texts back immediately.

Hottie! Name?

I can't help smiling to myself. It's not like I'm going to say Steve or Rick.

Tiberius J Linter

A few exclamation marks mixed in with question marks hit my messaging app. I know it's an unusual name, but she seems to be fizzing. I quickly text her:

What? Can't a guy have an old Roman name?

She shoots back:

Pretty BIG coinkidink

She has lost me.

What is?

The three dots are jumping, then her next message appears.

Asher's first name is TIBERIUS!

After reading this nonsensical text about five times, I hit the phone symbol and wait for the call to connect.

"Sherri, what are you saying?" I demand as soon as she answers. "Asher's first name is *Jordan*."

"I'm a gamer, remember? Asher created my fav game of all time. Twice, actually."

"So?" But I know Sherri isn't stupid, and my heart is beating out of my chest already as the truth circles my brain.

"So, I know his name. Asher goes by *Jordan*, because who would go by *Tiberius* if they didn't have to?"

Good point. Now my mind has completely stopped working after rearranging everything I thought I knew and putting the puzzle back together. I already know she's right.

"What did TJ say the *J* is for?" Sherri asks.

Obviously, I have been neglecting my reporter instincts in favor of my sexual ones.

"Julius, as in Caesar." And I believed him because I'm an idiot. But . . . "What about Linter?"

"Dunno," she says. "Sounds legit. Just too weird, isn't it? Asher left an unlockable in Bright Quest."

"A what?"

"You know, an Easter egg. A hidden extra in the game. It was a little thank-you note to us gamers for believing in him enough to shell out fifty dollars for his first game. And he signed it *Tiberius Jordan Asher*."

Standing on the snow-crusted sidewalk, I feel dizzy, still wanting her to be wrong. "But TJ doesn't look like any photo I saw of Asher." Granted, I only saw two blurry ones that were basically him crossing some campus in California. But I have intimate knowledge that TJ is all lean muscle, sculpted thighs, and brawny arms, not to mention a long, hard cock when needed, stamina, and staying power.

"Asher is . . . *um* . . . chunkier and heavily bearded," I point out. "With Clark Kent glasses, right?"

Sherri says, "Hold on."

I wait and wait. Then she comes back. "I'm doing a little photo manipulation. A man can lose fifty pounds, shave his beard, and get Lasik surgery so he doesn't need glasses."

I don't know what to say except of course he can.

"A billionaire could do all that without even blinking," she adds.

She's right. While anyone can alter their appearance, it's easier if you have unlimited funds. Next, she sends my TJ photo back, altered to add those pounds and the bushy beard and the glasses. *Fuck!*

"Your hottie is Asher," she says. "No doubt. Also, my bad, but when I thought I saw him last year, he had lost the chunk, like your TJ, and I forgot to tell you. Although, at the time, he had glasses on and his beard was bushier, so I recognized him on the spot. Did I ever tell you I once shook his hand at a PAX East?"

Did I tell you I once sucked him off? I shoot back silently.

"You told me," I respond woodenly, feeling ill. "Thanks for your help. I have to go." Sticking my phone in my purse, I don't respond to the next few pings before Sherri stops trying.

I've been staring at the situation from a thousand miles up, and suddenly, I've zoomed in, as close as our naked, wet bodies in the hot tub last night. Taking off the filters of diversion and desire, I walk back along the street, directly to the Thirsty Moose, not seeing the various stores I wandered into before I went for tea. It's all a blur anyway. Everything except Jordan Asher doing me up against the wall in his office. That's still crystal clear.

Whose place is it, though? Does Asher own the Thirsty Moose? Is he really a billionaire with a wood-paneled, squidgy little office that looks like it was last redecorated in the seventies?

Tracy is behind the bar, her dark ponytail high and tight. They've just opened for lunch but no one is here yet. I greet her as I cross the plank floor. I'm heading for the back when she says, "He's out. Gone on an errand."

Diverting my footsteps, I take a stool directly in front of her.

"How's the Misty Slope?" she asks.

Funny that she never got the word the way it all turned out. Or rather, didn't turn out. She doesn't know where I've been staying. That's good. I avoid an answer with a shrug, but to keep our conversation going, I say, "The chicken sandwich I had the first time I came in was delish."

"First time?" she asks.

"I came in one night and met Cyril."

She nods. "I think I saw you." Then adds, "Don't let Cy hear you say his full name."

Right. Names can be tricky things.

"You here for another chicken and fries?" she asks.

I am not here to eat, but I don't tell her that yet. "When I came in the second time, I was with TJ." I wait for her reaction. Is she going to gab and gossip with me or stay cool?

Tracy nods. "I noticed. How'd that happen?"

"He gave me a ski lesson." Among many other lessons.

"He's a great skier. Nearly as good as me," she adds. "Which is a pisser, since he barely ever skied before he moved here."

Apart from learning he was adopted, it's the first nugget of personal info about the man I've been getting naked with. He's not from here. That would have been useful to know.

"I skied as a teen," I say, turning the attention away from my burning need to learn more. "Mostly in New Hampshire at Pats Peak or Gunstock. Before that, I lived all over the place on military bases, none with ski resorts nearby. What about you?"

"Skied all my life," Tracy says. "I grew up about half an hour from here."

"An authentic local." I try to sound impressed, but I'm confused, not sure what I want to find out from her. "With

TJ being such a great skier, I would've mistaken him for a local, too. Also, because he owns this bar."

"He moved to Maine a little over three years ago. Decided to buy the Moose, even though he knows nothing about bartending."

Nothing? What did he say about his degree? *Bartend-ology and babes.* Cy said TJ knew how to make *one* cocktail. I should have known he wasn't a bartender.

A couple of guys come in and sit at the other end of the bar. I'm not surprised when they look us over. Tracy rolls her eyes at me before she wanders down their way to chat a moment and give them menus. I wonder if she knows that TJ is Jordan Asher? More than that, I can't help being curious as to whether they've had sex. Has she enjoyed one of his masterfully sensual playtimes? My stomach churns at the thought.

"How long have you worked here?" I ask when she returns.

"Ever since TJ took over and started hiring. He's a good employer. Pays well. If I want to keep my job, I better start doing it. What can I get you?"

She pulls a tablet from under the counter.

"You didn't have that gadget the first time I came in," I point out. "You had to go to the kitchen with my order."

She nods. "Good memory. We haven't used these devices very long, and last week, whatever day you came in, I'd managed to wipe the program from mine. Honestly, no idea how I did that. Luckily, TJ is great around anything to do with computers. Obviously, given his past and how he made his money, he would be." She swipes at the tablet. "He said I'd 'corrupted the code.'"

I nod. She knows about TJ's time in Silicon Valley before he released the game he'd been working on. But does she know he's the filthy-rich gaming designer?

"With his love of newspapers," I say, "I thought he was technologically helpless with anything more than a remote control."

She doesn't laugh. "You've seen TJ with a TV remote?"

Oops, too much info. "At the ski lodge. He was trying to eat his lunch in peace and read a newspaper," I add, thinking quickly. "He grabbed the remote to turn down the sound on the TV."

She nods, and her face relaxes. "Sounds like him. Anyway, we're lucky he chose Rangeley. Before he bought the Thirsty Moose, it used to be a rundown dive with fistfights spilling out into the street. That sort of clientele. Can you believe it?" She glances around at the nicely laid out surroundings with large, leaded windows in front letting in the natural light.

I shake my head. There are a lot of things I can't believe in this very instant. Like what a gullible twit I've been.

"Quite honestly," she adds, "I'm surprised he took you skiing. He can be a bit standoffish, even prickly."

His prick has not been the least bit standoffish.

"I can see that," I agree. "The first time I came in, he wasn't exactly welcoming and fleeced me out of an expensive drink."

"Yeah, that wasn't nice. I'll comp your lunch today."

Flustered by her generosity, I protest, "Thanks, but I didn't come in for free food."

"What then?" she asks, frankly. "Another go at TJ?" Her tone is definitely a little frosty when she adds, "I have to tell you, he doesn't *do* relationships." It makes me think she's tried and failed.

"I wasn't looking for one," I insist. "I'm heading home shortly. Besides, if I were, it'd be with that dapper guy who was in here when I first came in, last Friday."

Since we're talking like gal-pals, I add. "I came in here to pee and noticed TJ in his cowboy hat. He was next to a guy who was his polar opposite. Definitely *not* a skier. Gorgeous suit, dressed to kill, which is why I remember him. He stood out."

I could have added, "And was my usual type," because the gray suit guy was exactly the type I've always dated.

Dressed well, nothing scruffy, looking like he was going places. It still seems impossible that *he* wasn't the billionaire Jordan Asher.

Tracy's forehead creases, then smooths. "That was probably David. He's a lawyer. Handles things for the bar. Not exactly sure what his deal is, but he's always dressed like he's about to get married."

Laughing at her description, I want to kick myself. I assumed incorrectly and never changed my assumption, nor even examined it properly. I convinced myself David was Jordan Asher because I thought a billionaire would dress to show the world that he has money. Of course, TJ spoon-fed me all the confirmation I needed, and I lapped it up.

Now that the simple truth is in front of me, I can see everything clearly. I've been in Asher's home *and* in his bed all this time. Technically, though, I'd say not really in *his* bed. I bet his real master bedroom is vastly superior to the guest room he's been staying in to fool me.

Tracy goes and gets the men's orders, then strolls back down to me. I think she must be bored and happy to have someone to talk to, especially now that she knows I'm leaving and have no designs on TJ.

"Personally," she says, "David does nothing for me. I *loves* me a mountain man vibe, even if he came to it late, like TJ." She sighs. "Sadly, the boss is off-limits. Still, a girl can dream, and I do! Because he's undeniably H.O.T., hot! I know he hooks up occasionally with a visitor." She looks me squarely in the eyes. "You know, a meaningless fuck with a weekend skier. But it obviously never means anything."

Damn! She's warning me off big time. Too late, Tracy. *Waaaaayyyy too late.*

Then she blinks her blue eyes. "But I haven't seen him legit dating anyone in town." She sounds wistful again.

Ugh! I hate hearing her gush over him, wanting him after what he and I have done over the past five days. It's not like I can say, "You're not missing much."

"So, the lawyer guy, does he work in town?" I ask.

For some reason, of all the words we've exchanged, this makes her narrow her eyes. "Why?"

"I have an issue back home, and I'd love to get some legal help before I leave."

She relaxes. "Gotcha. Unfortunately, David—Mr. Wilson—lives in New York. TJ consults with him whenever the guy is up here skiing, although I've never seen him in ski clothes."

Probably because the lawyer simply flies up when summoned by his billionaire client. I'm fairly certain that skiing doesn't come into it. But all I say is, "Pity."

She glances over at her paying customers. "I have to go check on their food."

"OK. It was nice talking with you." Sliding off the barstool, I'm glad that TJ didn't reappear in the last ten minutes. I really want to get away from here.

"You, too." But she hesitates. "You said you're leaving soon, right? Not hanging around?"

The way she says "hanging around" like I've been a nuisance makes me explain to her at least half the story.

"I was waiting for my car to be fixed. Should be any day now."

This makes her nod, looking satisfied. "If I don't see you again, safe travels." Hurrying off toward the kitchen, Tracy is clearly not broken up about the quick end to our friendship.

Wandering outside, unsure exactly what to do next, I set out toward the mechanic's garage. Maybe my car will be ready by later afternoon, and I can wait for it.

$❤$❤$❤$

A half hour later, I'm driving back to Asher's house for my stuff in my repaired car. Paid in full and sitting ready for a couple hours. According to Neil, he called TJ to give him the final balance and get his credit card number. Funny that TJ didn't call or text me. Did he know *before* he pounded me against his office wall?

And why didn't he text me immediately? After last night, I'd say the answer is obvious. He likes having a willing sex slave who'll try anything he throws at me. I'm not saying that facetiously, either. I have enjoyed every minute of what we've done.

But fun and games are over.

TJ, who I have to start thinking of as Jordan Asher, paid for my Volvo and kept an entire ski resort open for me. He has fed and housed me, and he has strung me along like a clueless cow. Despite now having a story to top all journalists' stories, I can't deny that a small part of me wants him to be TJ Linter. Because with him, despite what Tracy said, there was a chance for a future. And that's what my heart started wishing for on those falling meteors.

But with the billionaire, I'm definitely out of my league. I could never be anything more than a temporary plaything. The office that TJ uses should have awakened my suspicions. No way a master game creator is going to let a bar owner hang out in there, even if he was also the estate manager. I get to the gate and press the button I saw TJ use the first night. Colin answers.

"Hey, I picked up my car. Can you let me in?"

Amazingly, he does, although I'm fairly certain he'll be phoning TJ in a minute. He's out somewhere, expecting me to call him for a lift home.

Home. What a sap I am! I missed being Juan's fiancée so much, I was playing house with the first guy who floated my boat. I'm never going to forgive myself for my lunacy. But I also wouldn't be able to rest if I didn't finally peek into his bedroom.

I park in the driveway and enter through the front door, going straight for the staircase. I don't want to run into Emma, recalling how she called TJ *boss*. She and Colin know who they really work for. It's humiliating.

What else do they know? That he spanks me, and I love it? Do they facilitate all his hook-ups with gourmet food and clean sheets?

Racing upstairs, I use the opening sequence I learned on the keypad and break every rule I promised I would follow. Pushing the door open, I gasp. I know I'm being dramatic, but *Jeez Louise!* Finally, a room with personality, and it's huge—both the room and the character it evokes.

A vaulted ceiling with massive floor-to-ceiling windows on two sides, and a spiral black iron staircase to a loft. I can't see what's up there from the door. Instead, my gaze is caught by the huge stone fireplace and the even larger king-size bed.

With four hand-carved, free-form bedposts reaching skyward, the mattress is high off the floor, covered in a black flannel comforter with a couple of black silk-covered pillows on top. The bed anchors a thick, cream-colored carpet that makes me wish I was barefoot. Walking slowly toward the magnificent bed, I imagine the escapades which have taken place in this room.

Red-hot jealousy streaks through me. No way he hasn't had women in here. No possible way he takes them along to the guest room, either. Only me.

Above the headboard is a large, framed four-color poster of a Bright Quest scene. I remember when Sherri had a similar one as her screen saver. Finally, visual confirmation. *Hello, Mr. Asher.*

My glance is drawn upward because of the way the light is coming in. *Whoa!* The steep cathedral roof has massive skylights. I know the roof has heating coils because I asked Colin how come he didn't have to clean off any of the rooflines. Heat must keep the skylights snow free, too. Anyone in the bed will have a view of the stars. A couple tears prick my eyes, and I blink them away. I would have liked to have seen that view. Again, *wowza!*

Invading his privacy further, I yank open a bedside drawer and find a couple more of those solidified oil candles and slam it shut. I'm sure there's other "fun" stuff to be found, but I don't need or want to see it. Instead, I pull my phone from my back pocket and snap photos of basically everything I can see. *Fuck him!*

Wandering toward the mantel, I look closely at a framed photo of TJ with his arm draped around a pretty female. Not the current TJ, but the one whom Sherri described, glasses, beard, a little heavier, so I know it's a few years old. But now I can definitely see it's the same man.

Another more recent photo shows TJ with an older couple whom I assume to be his parents. It was taken right beneath my feet, in the living room downstairs. Normal, regular people who raised a software genius who, in turn, became a billionaire practically overnight.

I decide to climb the open staircase, circling to the loft, although I can see bookshelves. Nothing outrageous like a BDSM chamber up there. But as I reach the bottom step, I catch sight of the man himself entering the room out of the corner of my eye.

Facing him, I ask, "Hard day at the bar?"

His expression tells me little about what he's thinking. If I had to hazard a guess, I'd say he's perplexed by my behavior. Maybe gearing up to be furious that I invaded Asher's privacy. But all he says is, "You were supposed to call me for a ride."

"Turned out I didn't need one." I shrug. "My car was done. But you knew that."

"So, you just drove home without telling me?"

That word again, a word that means so much to me because we moved around for my dad's military service through my entire childhood. When Mom put her dishes in a new kitchen, she would declare the place *home*.

"Home?" I repeat. "Not *yours*, though. Asher's home. Don't you want your own, where you don't have to sleep in a guest room of some cowardly billionaire who's afraid to face the world?"

"I don't think of him as cowardly," he protests, looking like he's unsure which way this is going. *Do I know, or don't I?* That's what he's asking himself. "More like fed up with the world's bullshit," TJ adds.

Oh, poor baby! Is the world mean to the billionaire?

"Not a coward, huh?" I press the matter. "Yet he's hiding at one of his other properties until I leave. That's what you said. While you're here, waiting like a 1950s wifey, taking care of the place, even doing his work. A bar owner and an estate manager whom Asher lets help him with perfecting his upcoming release. Tell me how that works again."

TJ's gaze narrows and his jaw tightens. He knows that I know.

"Are you going to come up with something creative?" I ask. "You know, so this all makes sense without you really being Jordan Asher?" I gesture at the photos on the mantel. Then I take a step toward him. "Say it. You're him, aren't you?"

TJ sighs. "It was only a matter of time. I was playing with fire by keeping you around."

Keeping me around. A stray rescue with benefits! "Were you waiting for me to figure it out? Like this is one of your games? Because that's all you know, right?"

"Brooke," he reaches for me, but I sidestep. And then I push past him. I'm done with him. Humiliated, regretful, angry, schooled in the art of deception. Going to my room, knowing he'll follow, I not only close the door, I tuck a chair under the handle, like I've seen in movies.

When he asks me to let him come in, I ignore him.

"Sorry, Asher. I'm busy."

While I pack, I have to fight off tears. Un-fucking-believable. I am so not crying over this asshat. I'm too annoyed at failing in my latest endeavor. *Crack reporter?* Not even close. I didn't really want to be an investigative journalist anyway, and I'm certainly not the type to get the scoop of a lifetime.

On the other hand, I'm leaving with a lot more than I came with, namely four new tires and a tuned engine.

Also, a shit-ton of new sexual experiences and a desire for more. Sadly, that's going to be tough—finding a guy who can rev me up like Tiberius Jordan Asher.

And then there's *our* story. Am I brave enough to publish an exposé as an embedded sex partner? He has mortifying photos of me. I have a long drive in which to consider that extremely difficult dilemma. I would certainly become rich *and* infamous.

Packed up, playtime over, I can't wait to get home and see Sherri and Mr. Busby. I wheel my case to the door. It's been awfully quiet out there, so when I open it, I'm a little surprised to find him leaning against the wall opposite, arms folded, head back, eyes closed. Like he's meditating.

At my appearance, his eyes snap open, piercing me with their gray-green intensity. And they look . . . uncertain.

"Remember when we started talking about Tiberius?" I ask. "You said Julius was Tiberius's middle name. You never said it was yours. I guess I really am a sucky reporter."

"But a really super human being," he says quietly, his voice gruff.

That makes me hesitate, but only for a second. "Because you can fool me so easily?"

He shrugs. "I don't tell anyone who I am."

I nod at his choice of words, thinking of him melting oil onto my nipples. "I guess I'm just *anyone*."

I almost ask how many women he's had in that big bed over the past three years. He had a pretty good supply of that fragrant oil. But I don't. That would be pathetic.

When he says nothing more, I turn and rather ungracefully for a grand exit, drag my suitcase along behind me to the stairs, letting it bump down the entire flight before I head for my car. I hope I haven't forgotten anything.

I sure left it all on the sheets last night. My pride, for one thing, and I'm starting to think my heart, too.

18

Jordan

I let Brooke leave. She knows who I am, which strips me of any semblance of armor. Simple as that. I'm defenseless against her bringing the world to my door, which makes me mad as hell. On the other hand, I find I'm really not thrilled that she's vacating my house and my life. I hate to identify this feeling, so I won't.

In fact, squishy feelings arising in me lately are getting tamped down and paved over. All unfamiliar territory. *Emotionally attached lover* is not a role I've played in any of my games or in real life. While I can't deny any longer that I care for her, I know I was first nothing but a lucrative story and then a new toy.

When Colin called to tell me she was home, I knew in my gut something had happened, and it wasn't going to be good. Finding her looking at my stuff was disconcerting. But having a reporter in my bedroom was not as disturbing as I imagined it would be. Because it was Brooke. Enigmatic, fearless, curious, she's taken to the sex games like she's been waiting for them all her life. And I can easily imagine playing them with her for the rest of mine.

Looking into her eyes when she climaxes has been like seeing into her soul. Sappy as that sounds, it's the truth. Suddenly, I'm taking the stairs two at a time and getting in the Rover.

By the time I catch up and flash my lights, Brooke is about ten minutes out of town, driving too fast on her new tires. When she pulls over, I jump out of my vehicle and jog up to her driver's side, still not sure why or what I intend.

"I considered not stopping," she says when I come alongside the open window. She remains staring straight ahead while she talks.

Unfortunately, I have nothing to say that will keep her here, away from her real life. From her family who loves her and her cousin and her cat. Then she echoes my thoughts.

"I have nothing more to say to you." At last, Brooke's glance leaves the road as she turns to look up at me. For a few moments, we're silently staring into one another's eyes. Weird, uncomfortable, exposing. I want to lean in and kiss her. It might actually solve everything.

"Why did you come after me?" she asks.

"I don't know." A lame answer, but the best I can do. I'm not about to delve into anything more profound on the side of the road with someone who's driving out of my life. Then I ask a question that, for some reason, isn't as crucial as it was a week ago.

"Do you intend to write about me?" I keep my tone neutral, like I haven't tasted every part of her except her lips, finding the most intense pleasure while pleasuring her.

"You don't trust me," she says flatly. "Why should you? It's not like we really know each other."

I haven't made up my mind whether I trust her, but that would be a stupid thing to say so I say nothing. Obviously, I'm never going to release the images I took of her the first time we had sex. She must know what an empty threat that was. So, what leverage do I have?

"I don't know what I'm going to do," she says, sounding glibly unconcerned, as if she's not in a position to blow a hole through the middle of my serene life. Then she points out, "Your jaw is doing that clenching thing."

It's the last thing Brooke says before she looks ahead again. In the next instant, she nearly runs over my foot when she steps on the gas and speeds away.

$♥$♥$♥$

I spend the next forty-eight hours waiting for my face, my house, and my whereabouts to be on the news. Nothing happens. I think about sending her a *thank you*, but I don't. I consider and dismiss a dozen reasons to contact her. All because I don't know what to do with this unfamiliar wanting. In the short time we've been hanging out, I've fallen for Brooke's face, her smile, her laugh, her body, her thoughts, and those gorgeous eyes. I've never known anyone like her, and haven't wanted anything long-term before.

Having gone my whole life without truly missing anyone except my sister, it's difficult not to act. With Livvy, there was no remedy. She was here one minute and taken the next. Brooke, on the other hand, is a mere couple states away and only a few hours' drive. Much less if I take a jet to Boston. Yet I do absolutely nothing except finish Bright Star and release it.

Over the next few weeks, the accolades and the money pour in. I'm certain her tweaks to the characters' depth and emotional range helped tremendously. I want to share Bright Star's success with her. Hell, I want to share the revenues with her, too.

Finally, I have a solid pragmatic, *business* reason to contact her. Still, I can't let my mind settle on or accept the ultimate goal. If I initiate interaction, then I better know what I'm really intending and follow through. Or leave her the hell alone.

In the end, I get her address, which is easy as she has no internet security whatsoever, and I send her a check. A big one, which feels wrong in some ways but right in others. I cannot imagine how she will take it.

A week later, an envelope arrives at the Thirsty Moose addressed to me. When I open it at the bar, shredded pieces of check drift down onto the polyurethane surface, and I understand exactly how she took it. Maybe I shouldn't have had the bank fill in the memo line with "For services rendered."

Boneheaded move! I thought it would be funny, maybe even an amusing reminder of us. Nope.

"Someone's mailing you confetti?" Tracy asks.

"Brooke," I respond, without thinking. I can only guess she never got my exact address at home so sent it here. After all, there's no number on the house or the gate.

"Looks like you two made a connection," Tracy observes, lifting up a small trash can. "Shall I?"

When I nod, she brushes the pieces away.

"You need a whisky, boss, or an ear? You know what they say about us bartenders."

I can't manage a smile, but then I'm not the happy, grinning kind, so I doubt she or anyone else has noticed I've felt a little blue lately.

"Thanks, but I'm good." Actually, I have too much time on my hands, and too many goofballs are up for spring skiing. They're all over the slopes in rowdy packs, many drinking too much and not waiting for après ski to do it. It must be their presence that has put me in such a foul mood.

Another week later, my deep-search internet scout program sends an alert that something new about me is on the web. *Damn!* With dread, I click open the report and see my own profile in a photo taken at the bar. Is this payback for deigning to send her a check?

My security program caught it because of the ALT text, an image's label, which can be read aloud for those with visual impairment. In this case, it's my name as the photo's subject. Even if it had been a full frontal of me on my own doorstep with my address showing in neon, I wouldn't have retaliated. But I am curious. Did she release this innocuous image to bait me? Is she hoping that I go see her? Maybe begging to be punished with a paddle?

Before I can decide whether she's provoking me into making contact—perhaps because she misses me as much as I miss her—the worst happens. When I go downstairs a week later, powering on my phone, Colin meets me in the kitchen where Emma is making breakfast.

"You are not having a good day," he says.

He's right that I haven't had a good day or a great night since Brooke left. But I'm not sure how he can be so prescient on this particular morning.

"No point in hiding it," Emma says. "Read the paper, boss."

A chill settles over me even before I pick up the *Portland Press Herald*. Photos of my face, along with the front of the Thirsty Moose and—*son of a bitch*—the driveway to my house have succeeded in pushing the latest political fiasco and military conflict below the front page's top fold.

The headline screams: "Billionaire Software Gaming Designer Has Come Out to Play!"

Not particularly clever, I'm transfixed anyway and keep reading as I sink onto a stool at the kitchen island.

"Eccentric recluse Jordan Asher has been living in Rangeley, Maine, for three years, where he owns a bar, the Thirsty Moose, boosting the local economy while living a mostly isolated life."

It goes on for a few paragraphs, then the article continues a few pages later, with a full-body photo of me in ski clothes nested around a single long column of writing. I don't remember Brooke taking that photo. Also, I cannot imagine how there could be that much to write about me.

At least there are no images of the inside of my house, but the front shot makes it recognizable to anyone who knows the area. Although, I suppose, only to people who have been let in past the security gates and driven up the long drive.

Feeling like I've been kicked, I flip the pages to the front of the newspaper again and look at the byline. Expecting to see *Brooke Danbury*, I'm surprised by a man's name I don't know, along with the words, "Original source: Boston Media Group."

Emma pushes coffee toward me and a plate of scrambled eggs.

"Comfort food," she says, adding a slice of hot, thickly buttered sourdough toast.

"Thanks." I doubt anything is going to comfort me, but I won't turn it down.

"Aren't you going to read the whole thing?" Colin asks.

"Why should I? It's my life." Then I think about everyone who might be impacted. "Are you and Emma in it?"

"Yup."

"Shit! I'm sorry." I let my libido endanger the people I care about. Also, everyone who works at the Thirsty Moose. What's more, except for Cy, who already knew, I must have some shocked employees and some explaining to do.

"Brooke was a better reporter than I thought," I mutter.

Emma tops up my coffee and says, "It doesn't say anything about her. In fact, the writer mentions an anonymous source."

I make a face. "I don't believe in coincidences, Em."

She nods, looking sad.

"What happens next?" Colin asks.

"I'll sell the Thirsty Moose to Cy." It'll be more like a giveaway, but I know he wants it and will make sure it succeeds.

He and Emma exchange a glance, and I put their minds at ease. "I'm going to go away for a while. I'd appreciate it if you'd continue to take care of this house."

"Then you're not selling it?"

"Not at the moment, no. If I do, I'll give you six months' notice. Fair?"

Their relief at not having to go find jobs in the current economy is palpable. "And I want you to enjoy everything as usual. Tennis court, gym, and"—I can barely spit out the last words—"the pool and hot tub, of course. And if you would look after the dogs until I send for them."

"Goes without saying," Colin says, as Duffy chooses that moment to run over and knock into my leg. I'm going to miss my three companions. A lot. That alone, having to be without my little pack, sends a burst of anger through me.

But I'm not going to slither away and hide. Not much point now. I'll find somewhere else discreet to live, but first, I'll be dropping in on the person who has betrayed me so spectacularly. She once called Asher a coward. Time to teach her that she mistook my detachment for weakness.

First, I contact my lawyer and have David draw up the papers to transfer the bar to Cy. Then I text my parents that I'm coming home for a week's visit, making sure the timing suits them. My father calls immediately from their home in Virginia.

"Your mother said you'd be coming. She already has the guest room ready. I swear that woman is psychic."

Despite everything, I smile. "I just want to make sure you're OK."

"We've been through it before," my father reminds me. "See you soon."

Lastly, I make arrangements for a stay in Boston at my favorite hotel. The same real estate developer who found me my island home, Marcus Parisi, owns a hotel in Boston. By the time I get there in a couple weeks, I hope Brooke is well and truly rattled, looking over her proverbial shoulder. I want her wondering whether the photos I took of her red-hot, paddled ass are about to show up in public.

They won't, but I don't want her to know that. Not yet. I hope she squirms. To that end, I open a fake number in Messenger, attach a cropped photo of just that, her ass in the air, and hit send.

19

Brooke

"**S**top sniveling," I order myself and shove another dripping peach slice into my piehole, wishing it was actually peach pie. I cried when I drove away from TJ. Not heaving sobs, nothing loud and gross with my nose running. Simply tears streaming down my face because my heart hurt. I didn't want to leave the sanctuary of his house and his bed. I didn't want to leave *him*. If he'd said, "Hey, you know what, I'm really into you. Let's keep doing what we're doing," I totally would have given in.

But all TJ was concerned with, as usual, was keeping his whereabouts a secret from the world. He really thinks he's all that and a bag of donuts. That anyone who found out about him would immediately be knocking on his door for an autograph or something.

Of course, that's pretty much exactly what happened with those gamers flocking to the bar when Sherri let the cat out of the bag. She has apologized so many times, and even offered to talk to TJ, but I told her to forget it.

While eating breakfast and watching TV, with Mr. Busby on my lap, I see that someone finally won the state lottery after it's been growing for months. Staring at an older guy with his daughter and her son hanging on each of his arms, accepting a massive three-foot by six-foot fake check, Sherri says, "I wish he was *my* uncle." Then she dashes out the door to work.

It hits me that *anyone* who ever knew TJ before he became a billionaire probably crawled out of the bushes three years ago to declare themselves his best friend. "Hey, good buddy, how about a few hundred thousand?" Becoming famous as a gaming tycoon earned him the right to a big portion of paranoia, part of the trauma I mentioned to him from my psych studies.

And then there's the potential for blackmail or kidnapping. Being rich is an entirely new world of danger. No wonder he hides from everyone.

Weirdly, watching a little old man get rich causes tears. I wipe them away with my napkin that smells like peaches, which I'm eating straight from a can. I am jobless again. It was pretty obvious I'm not reporter material. I could not get myself to write about our sexual escapades or post photos of his bedroom.

After Sherri leaves for her gainful employment at the bank, I start hunting job websites. Maybe I should play the lottery, too, but I kind of won it when TJ sent me that stupid check. It felt wrong. I'm proud to be firmly in the camp of those who would never take advantage of someone, even though Sherri made her opinion known quite strongly.

"Keep it!" she screamed while I was still staring at those three rude words: *For services rendered.* I know exactly what services he was referring to and felt mortified down to my toes. Then she held up Mr. Busby and pretended to be him: "Please, Mommy, deposit the check for my cat food and future vet bills."

Too late. Rip, tear, and dramatically place in envelope! That was when I realized I didn't know his address and had to look up the Thirsty Moose.

Some mornings, I look at my reflection in the mirror while brushing my teeth and think, *You idiot!* That money was nothing to him. And I earned it by helping him make his moronic characters into believable three-dimensional people with heart. Something I'm not sure he himself has.

I sniffle one last time and then sigh, crumpling up the napkin, and scrolling through jobs on my laptop. TJ doesn't need a heart. He has *mine.* Either I'm in love with him or utterly obsessed. I know while I was in his presence, I was obsessed with pleasing him and letting him please me. Obsession does not make for a healthy relationship, nor does a billionaire pretending to be a bar owner.

Regardless, I know what I feel is love because I don't want to track the man down to spy on him or send him locks of my hair or, worse, sneak into his house and cut off some of his. I want him to be happy. Just like I wanted for Juan, who recently texted me that he's fabulously in love with someone else and grateful that I set him free. He even said he would mail me a wedding invitation.

I would go if I had a plus-one besides Sherri.

My phone pings, and I stop looking at warehouse and assistant clothing store manager positions and click on the unfamiliar number. It's a single photo. My heart nearly stops.

"You bastard," I say out loud, making Mr. Busby lift his head and look at me. Ever since I came back from Maine, he's been stuck to me like glue. But only after he stomped around the place for days, yowling at me, launching himself onto my lap or chest at all hours.

Quickly, I delete the text. Even if my cat saw this image of my red butt cheeks with the paddle lying on top, I would be embarrassed. What is the meaning of this? Is TJ threatening me? And why now, after all these weeks? Is he just making contact so I'll do the same? I hit delete on the image, and then try to put it out of my mind by filling in a couple applications for jobs I will hate.

Forty minutes later, Sherri calls me. "Are you sitting down?"

I feel guilty that I'm still in the same position as when she left, seated at our small dining room table from which I can view the entire second-floor condo, including the TV. Meanwhile, she has probably bought a coffee, taken the T, and made it to work at the bank.

"Mebbe," I say. "Why?"

"Turn on the TV."

"It's still on in the background," I confess. "But I promise you, I'm job hunting."

"Well, switch it to that morning show with the women."

"That's like all of them," I grouse, but I pick up the remote next to my can of peaches and start surfing channels. "Why?"

"All over the news, girlie. Asher is out in the open."

"What?" Mr. Busby jumps again at my tone.

"They're going to be talking about him any second," she adds, and I start clicking faster and faster, like the pig on *Toy Story*. Sherri is still talking. "I saw his face on a newspaper on the train, front page. Some people actually thought he had died, so this is big news. And then when I got to work, given the fact that everyone around here is obsessed with money, people were talking about Asher's resurrection into the real world. Some think it's a publicity stunt, so close to the release of Bright Star, to fuel sales."

Wow! I know that's not true. I also have a feeling it might be why he sent me that revealing photo, which has gone from mystifying to definitely a threat. He's probably waiting for an apology for something I didn't do. If he doesn't get one, that photo may become *un*cropped and show my face.

"I see him," I say, as an image appears of TJ in ski clothes. "Talk to you later." Ending the call, I get to my feet, dunking Mr. Busby to the floor, before taking four steps into the living room and turning up the volume.

"That's right, ladies. One of America's most eligible billionaires has been found."

My mouth drops open. The TV women are grinning at the blatantly opportunistic slant to the story, starting to speculate on whether he'll date a recently divorced starlet. It's creepy. Regardless, my eyes are glued to the screen as if I hadn't lived with the man for a short while, eaten at his table, and had a ton of great sex.

"Jordan Asher has revved up his style from techno dweeb to fit-and-fantastic bad boy. Look at that sculpted physique. Not the body of a man who stays indoors writing code, is it?"

I long for his sculpted physique. *Dammit!* And I don't like all the other women in the world—and obviously some men—ogling him. Another photo is a close up of TJ at the bar, unsmiling as usual, but I can tell from the way his eyes look that this is a light moment.

"He's lost the baby fat," another of the TV personalities says with a wink. Because at thirty-two, TJ is too old to classify for "baby" anything, even three years ago when I guess he was last seen with extra poundage.

The same woman continues, "Also gone are his Bigfoot-inspired beard and the metal-rimmed glasses, revealing a face that ships have sunk for. Even without those glasses, we sure hope Mr. Asher can see what's right in front of him. Because with this unexpected resurfacing and the wild success of Bright Star, his bar will be packed and probably his driveway, too. I see a bevy of single ladies lining up for summer hiking in Rangeley, Maine."

I cringe at the mention of the little town. On the other hand, the influx will be great for business, not only the Thirsty Moose but everywhere else, too. It won't be great for TJ though, not if the tenor of this broadcast is any indication. They did everything except show his own front door.

Oh, shit! Just before ending the segment, they show an image of the front of his driveway. No number or street address showing, but still. *Jeez!* Why not do a drone flyover while they're at it, streaming coordinates? Poor TJ. I can picture how furious he is, and rightly so. Except not at me.

Leaving the TV on, I return to my seat, fill in a couple more job applications, and contemplate calling *him* about every other second. My brain cannot really focus on anything or anyone else, so I give up trying and search the web. Every single story, from the AP to the BBC, shows the same few photos and has no new text with anything substantial, except one that offers the bar's menu and links to the Yelp reviews. Talk about scraping bottom.

After making myself another cup of coffee, and chewing my lip unproductively, I call the number that texted me the photo. No one picks up, and there is no voicemail attached. Then I mentally pull up my big-girl pants and call the number I know is TJ's. It's disconnected, which shocks me to the core. For weeks, I've known I can contact him if I ever decide to, for whatever reason, such as groveling for another night of sex.

Now that I know I'm not any different from every other person in the entire world with no idea how to reach him, I'm sad all over again. Suddenly, it's like whatever we shared never happened.

Then I put on my reporter's hat and call the Thirsty Moose. If I speak to Cy or Tracy, surely, they'll at least give him a message. And what will that be exactly? Something like, "Tell TJ I didn't do it."

In any case, I dial and get a recorded message. I recognize Cy's charming accent, but he doesn't sound amused.

"You've called us before business hours, but even if you call when we're open, we can't pick up to every crazy billionaire hunter. He's NOT here. If you want to come in for a drink and a pub lunch or for amazing cocktails and comfort food at dinnertime, then we welcome you Tuesday through Sunday, eleven-thirty to closing, which varies. You can't leave a message so don't try. Good day."

I hang up. Now what? I guess there's nothing I can do apart from driving up there and knocking on his door or simply waiting for the other shoe to drop, if there is one. I choose the latter.

$♥$♥$♥$

When our doorbell rings a week later, I don't move. Sherri is closer by a few feet since she likes the other end of the couch, and I'd have to be willing to wake Mr. Busby, who is currently curled on my lap. Expecting a large, hot cheesy pizza, we have our wine glasses filled already. But when I hear my cousin's shriek followed by a familiar voice, I know who has arrived. The other shoe!

Still, I don't get up. This is who I am, lap full of feline, no makeup, hair pushed back with a novelty headband that looks like blue butterflies are springing from my head. It keeps the hair out of my eyes and amuses Mr. Busby at the same time.

When TJ comes around the corner from our short entrance hall, I can see nothing is amusing him right now. Sherri is on his heels but rushes around his tall form to state the obvious.

"Jordan Asher is in our living room." She makes a sweeping gesture, which I attribute to nerves.

"I can see that," I say, looking directly at him. He looks great in his familiar cowboy hat, worn jeans, and a leather jacket. My body responds by tingling before I can warn it to be chill. "*Why* is he in our living room?"

Sherri turns to him, then back to me. TJ and I are doing one of our staring contests, which I don't think has ever been witnessed by a third party.

"Mr. Asher wants to speak to you," she says.

"We have this great invention called the phone," I say, being snarky.

The little muscle in his jaw jumps, but he doesn't look fazed by my attitude. In fact, he looks perfect on this cool New England spring evening. Perfectly dressed. Perfectly sexy. Perfectly larger than life. Perfectly annoying as hell.

"Except your phone has been disconnected, and some nasty, petty ghost is texting me as if he's you," I continue.

"I don't know about any ghost," he says, his gaze level, unflinching and unapologetic. I had to change my cell because too many untrustworthy people had the number."

Meaning me, obviously.

"Anyway, I was in the neighborhood," he says, which makes me cock an eyebrow at his blatant lie, before realizing he's saying it as a joke. Meanwhile, Sherri plays hostess.

"Please, have a seat. Would you like anything? Soda, water, but not soda-water. *Haha.* We don't have that. We have some Pepperidge Farm cookies, unless Brooke ate them all. She's been scoffing our snacks lately, probably due to being home all day."

I make a cutting gesture across my neck for her to shut up, but she continues. "Or I can whip up some peanut butter on crackers. Remember how Jamlin and Arte lived on the peanut butter they brought with them from Earth in the first Bright game? I bet you love the stuff, the crunchier the better, or why would you put it in the game?"

I stare at this alien creature who used to be my placid cousin.

"Thanks," TJ says, having torn his gaze from mine and now given his attention to Sherri. "I don't need anything. Did you get the latest Bright release?"

My cousin's cheeks turn pink. "I can't believe I'm talking to you. I want to mash your head between my fingers, just thinking of all those creative ideas floating inside there." She lifts her hands and makes scrunchy finger movements.

TJ's nostrils flare, and I think he may be ready to bolt. Instead, he takes a step backward away from Miss Crazy Fingers. I might have to banish Sherri to her room and lock her in. Then she recalls the question.

"Yes! *Oh*, my God, yes! I've been playing Bright Star pretty much nonstop. When I'm not at work, I mean. Haven't I, Brooke? I'd preordered it six months before release so was one of the first to get a copy."

"I hope it didn't disappoint," TJ says. I think he looks smug. But then he says, "Brooke told you how she helped, didn't she?"

Sherri's eyes are as big as frisbees. "She did, which is why I thought she should have kept that check."

"Sherri," I warn because this is not her business. In fact, I think it's time I separated these two.

"This is Mr. Busby," I say, as I scoop the black furball off my lap and put him back on the warm couch in the place I just vacated.

"I guessed," TJ says, not a glimmer of warmth in his gray-green eyes.

"No dogs with you?" I ask.

"They don't travel well."

"*Oh!*" Sherri suddenly says enthusiastically. "*Duh!* Seeing you made me lose my mind a little. We have pizza coming any minute, and we have wine. Would you like a glass?"

"No, I don't want to interrupt your evening," he says. "I simply want to speak to Brooke for a moment."

He glances around our condo, takes in its size, and realizes for privacy, we'd have to turn on the shower water and talk in the bathroom or maybe in my closet. But I don't want it to be weird for Sherri or make her feel in the way.

Knowing it'll rattle his cage, I suggest, "Why don't we go for a walk? There's a park nearby if we need a destination."

"That's fine."

What? No protest? He's going to walk around here without a disguise? I guess he did at home, too, but now that his image has been everywhere, I thought he'd be more cautious.

I glance at my plain black leggings. No holes, so they'll do. And I'm wearing a long-sleeve T over the top. Grabbing a fleece, I precede him to the door.

"Brooke," Sherri says. I turn making a big-eyed what-is-it-now face. She points to the top of her head.

I frown, until TJ says, "She's trying to tell you that you have blue butterflies exploding out of your head."

"*Oh.*" Snatching off the headband that I never wear outside, I toss it toward Sherri who, with her quick gaming hands, catches it and slides it onto her own head.

"Me and Mr. Busby will be right here," she says. "Nice to meet you, Mr. Asher. An honor, actually."

"Really, I'm the one who's honored that you enjoy my games," he returns, like Mr. Charming. "It's been a pleasure to meet you."

Once downstairs, I head toward the grungy little park nearby, and he falls into step beside me. But a couple yards down, I realize I can hear a slow car and glance over my shoulder. Shocked, I see a man driving beside us in a midnight-blue Cadillac sedan. Leaning closer, I say, "I think you're being followed. That might be a reporter." Although it seems too nice a car for any reporter I know.

He doesn't turn. "That's a driver and a limo."

I double-take.

"I knew parking is difficult here," he explains. "So I got a ride."

"It is," I agree. But it's weird. I haven't really thought about the money side of TJ since finding out he's Asher, but this perk makes it clear.

"Your cousin seems nice," he says.

"She is." But chit-chat seems silly, given the circumstances, so I ask, "Why are you here?"

"A few reasons. First, to apologize to you."

Not what I expected. "For what?"

"For not telling you who I am *before* we had sex."

"That was a shithead thing to do."

"Agreed." He shoves his hands in his jacket pockets.

We walk up the block, past a Dunkin' Donuts and a dry cleaner. "I'm waiting for the 'but,'" I say.

"None coming."

"*But* you didn't invite me to Rangeley. And you had to protect yourself because I was a prying reporter." One who loved every minute of what we did. And by the way, *I think I love you.*

"I didn't invite you at first," he clarifies, "until I did. I asked you to come back to the house to wait for your car to be fixed. I shouldn't have traded staying with me for sex, and I should have let you know your car was ready that morning."

"Why didn't you?"

"I was having fun," he says in a grim voice.

I nod. "Me, too." We reach the small two-block length of greenery with a swing set and a slide, two picnic tables, and an overflowing trashcan. Compared to his front yard, it's a joke, but the neighborhood parents and kids appreciate the small park on weekends. Right now, it's empty. There's aren't any lights, because no one wants people hanging around there at night. We sit on an attached bench, side-by-side, looking at the street, at his limo, and resting our elbows behind us on the table.

"You could have apologized for being a shithead by phone or text."

"Not my style," he says. "Also, I really want you to take payment for the work you did. I know that your insights improved every aspect of the gaming experience."

I sigh. "I don't want to be patronized. Anyone could have fleshed that out the way I did."

"Don't be absurd. I worked on that for the better part of a year, and at the last moment, literally, you swoop in and see how to fix the problems."

I don't want to get a big head, but I did think it was super easy. And because I really need the money, I say, "If you're not lying to me about my having helped, then I'll take a check, but for half what you sent before."

"OK." We're still not looking at one another, but staring out at the road. He lifts his hat with one hand and runs a hand through his hair with the other, which I watch out of the corner of my eye.

He is the sexiest man alive, and I could go down on him right here and be perfectly willing. I mean, if we went behind a tree and that creepy driver wasn't circling the block.

Then he says, "Are there any more photos of me?"

"I could ask the same thing," I say and finally stare at his profile. He turns to meet my gaze, and I suppress a gasp.

His pupils are dilated due to the dim light, but I see that glimmer of desire I became familiar with. The tick in his jaw is followed by his glance going unexpectedly to my lips. That sends a shiver up and down my spine. More than anything, I would like him to kiss me.

"Anyway," I say, "the photos that came out a week ago weren't from me."

20

Jordan

I shake my head. "You don't have to lie. To answer your question, I'm not going to do anything more with the photos I have of you. I sent you the cropped one because I was angry, and I wanted to scare you."

"You succeeded," Brooke says, "But I'm not lying. I don't know where those photos came from. Nor did I have anything to do with the news story."

My face must indicate my disbelief, because she raises her voice. "I'm telling you the truth."

"Brooke, the original byline I saw in the newspaper *before* the story was picked up and sold to every media outlet in the world was your editor at Boston Media Group."

"That's not possible."

"If you say so."

She gets up from the bench and clenches her fists. "I do say so."

"Then call your boss and ask how it happened. He must be in line for a massive raise, proving there's no honor among thieves. You took from me in the form of photos and he took from you by stealing your story. Should have been *your* raise."

"I don't work there any longer."

This is news. "Is that why your cousin said you were at home a lot?"

She doesn't go into details about her lack of employment. "I promise you it wasn't me."

It's so great to see her, from the first moment I walked into the small, second-story apartment in a Boston brownstone. Despite being loaded for bear, as soon as I saw her on the couch with that ridiculous butterfly head thing, I didn't care about what she'd done. Now, I *want* to believe her, but the timing is crazy coincidental.

"What about the first photo? In the bar."

"No idea what you're talking about," she insists.

"A few weeks ago, this popped up on the internet with my name attached to it." I hold out my phone with the photo, and she comes nearer. Standing right in front of me so close I want to touch her.

Glancing from my face to my phone and back again, she shrugs. "No idea."

I have to believe her, mostly because I want to. The limo comes by again, and I decide to get to the point.

"Like I said, I wanted to see you first to apologize for acting like a shithead. And second, to ask you not to release any more photos or delve any deeper into my life."

That doesn't come out right. It sounds like I want to keep her at arm's length when more and more, I want to hold her close. It's not her delving into my personal details that bothers me, as I've realized I'd like to have her in my life on a more permanent basis. It's the sharing with the world that I need for her to stop.

Brooke raises her chin and an eyebrow and crosses her arms. "I've told you that I didn't release any."

"Except the one to Sherri."

She uncrosses her arms and looks uncertain. "It's true. I'd almost forgotten about that. That's when she told me who I was sleeping with."

"Have you forgotten any others?" Immediately, I wish I hadn't asked that. I sound patronizing at best.

"No. I haven't," she snaps, sounding annoyed. Spinning on her heel, she starts to walk, out of the park and toward her home.

I'm right behind her. "Do you want a lift back in the Caddy?"

"No, thanks," she says coolly. "Are you going back to Maine tonight?"

"No." I don't tell her I'm not going back to Maine for a while. She is still someone I don't entirely trust. It's not wise for me to tell her anything more.

Except I'm still talking. "If I stay around for a few days, may I see you again?"

When she glances at me, her eyes are wide. "Why?"

"Now that we have all this out of the way, maybe you could show me around a little." I came to apologize and to get an apology out of her. She's sticking to her claim of innocence. I'm going to choose to believe Brooke, to get over being angry, and try to start something fresh with her.

"People will recognize you," she points out.

It's true that my perfect disguise of lost poundage and vision surgery has been obliterated, but I haven't yet noticed a massive uptick in people staring and pointing.

"We'll see," I say. "I'll wear my hat. There's a good science museum in Boston, isn't there?"

Her expression softens. "The best." For some reason, despite my accusing her of things she says she didn't do, Brooke agrees. "OK. Let's do it."

"Only if you get in the limo right now," I tell her, slipping into the voice I use when I order her to strip or get on the bed.

Her gaze darts to mine, but I don't waver. "It's full-on dark now. I'm not letting you walk back even a block, never mind four." I think she'll put up a fuss, but she barely hesitates before climbing into the back seat.

That's how I find myself sitting next to Brooke, our thighs touching, for a tantalizing, tormentingly brief journey. There's no time to even make a move, but I've secured her company for tomorrow. That's a win.

I walk her to her door. "I'll pick you up at eight."

"*Whoa!* I haven't even fed the cat at that hour. I told you, I'm out of work."

"I was kidding." If she'd said yes, we would've shared breakfast like old times, but I can wait a few hours longer. "You pick the time."

"Ten is good," she says. "In case there's a problem, where are you staying?"

I'm so used to protecting my privacy, I hesitate.

"Really?" she asks. "Are you giving me that look right now?" She tucks her gorgeous, silky, copper hair behind her right ear, and I want to nibble on that exposed lobe. "Do you think I'll be on your balcony taking photos through the window?"

"How do you know I have a balcony?" I shoot back. "Spying on me already?"

"Look, TJ—" Then she realizes I'm teasing her.

"I'm at the Parisi," I tell her.

"Never heard of it," Brooke says, "but I'm no expert on Boston lodging."

"Small hotel, owned by an associate of mine."

"Of course it is. The rich stay with the rich."

Barely listening, my gaze lands on her lips again. This would be the time a boyfriend would kiss his girl. But that's not us.

"My pizza's probably getting cold," she says, her own cocoa-colored glance flitting across my face.

"Right. Yes, sorry. I'll see you tomorrow."

Without a backward look, she disappears indoors.

$♥$♥$♥$

For some reason, I was expecting her to be waiting on the front steps, as if she didn't trust me to come upstairs to her condo, but the sidewalk is empty. I go up and knock on her door.

It takes a minute, but finally she answers. Despite it being just after ten, she's clearly not ready to go, still wearing a bathrobe and blue slippers. I've never seen anything sexier, and if nothing had gone wrong between us, I'd be sliding her robe open to satisfy my curiosity about whether she's naked underneath.

"Everything OK?" I ask, when she gestures me in and turns away, obviously expecting me to follow.

"I'm sorry," she says. "I'm fine now, I promise, but I had a bit of a rough morning. I think the pizza didn't agree with me."

"Are you sure? If you want to stay here and recuperate, I'll leave you in peace." Disappointed as hell, but whatever she needs.

"No, unless you're grossed out. I really do feel better. I just had a shower and need to dress."

She *is* bare under that robe. I clasp my hands behind my back, recalling how she didn't find humor in the off-handed note on the last check. In the real world outside Rangeley, I need to be more respectful than assuming I can grab her at will. Which is also why I don't bring out the new check yet.

"There's coffee. Help yourself."

I would love to help myself to Brooke, but she disappears into a room and closes the door. Message received. Taking off my jacket, I wander into the tiny kitchen, find a mug, and pour some coffee. It's actually very good. Turning to go back into the living room, I'm ambushed by a furry missile landing on my shoulder, making me spill the entire contents of the cup onto the hardwood floor. Luckily, I wasn't close enough to hit the sofa or the area rug it's on.

"Fuck!" I set the empty cup down, while Mr. Busby sinks his claws into me. "Get off, fiend."

After freeing myself by grabbing the cat by the back of his neck and pulling, leaving holes in both my skin and my shirt, I look around for a roll of paper towels. I'm still cleaning up when Brooke reappears, looking sexy in dark jeans and a top the color of pine needles, which sets off her hair.

"What happened?" she asks. "Clumsy when you have to get your own coffee? Where's Emma when you need her?"

Are the rich man jokes going to follow me the rest of my life, as though I didn't live a normal existence before creating the most popular game series in history?

"Your demonic cat is what happened," I explain, standing with a clump of sodden paper towels dripping into my cupped hand.

"Really? That's odd. I always took him for more of a tea drinker."

She's in a good mood, and now that we're going out, I feel happier, too. "He dove on me from somewhere. I never even saw him until he was trying to tear my throat out."

She laughs, a sound that makes my groin tighten with wanting her. "Where is he?"

"I don't know. I ripped him off me and threw him out the window."

Her expression freezes. "I'm kidding. Follow the coffee tracks. He ran through the mess he made."

"I'll go see if he's all right."

"What about me?" I ask.

"Big, strong mountain man like you," she says as she disappears again, hunting for him.

"Mr. Busby," I hear her calling. She returns a minute later. "He's OK, just curled up on my bed."

"Jackass," I mutter.

"What?"

"Fantastic," I say, wishing I was the one curled up on her bed. "Let's go."

We're in the back seat of the Cadillac and heading for the Museum of Science in downtown Boston when she finally says, "He was probably on top of the cupboard. Sometimes, he jumps onto me or Sherri on his way down. He must have thought you were one of us."

"Super," I say, and she laughs again. Her lilting laughter sets the tone for our time at the museum. There's a lot to see, and I'm fascinated by all of it. After a few hours, we eat at the museum's café, which has a panoramic view of the surrounding neighborhoods of Cambridge and Boston's Back Bay.

"I'm impressed," I confess, thinking of the slightly goofy but still entertaining and informative electricity presentation and the nanotechnology exhibit we saw.

"I don't know," she says, "this lettuce is a bit wilted."

"You're easily amused by your own wit. I didn't realize that until today."

She grins and eats from her pile of potato chips. "I guess I'm more relaxed here than I was at your place. Being a snoop wasn't really my bag."

That's the best thing I've heard all day. "What do you plan to do next?"

"Remains to be seen."

"I'd be happy to collaborate again," I say without thinking it through. My next game release is at least two years away, so what the hell am I talking about? But she doesn't brush it off as a stupid idea.

"You've got my number," she says lightly.

We have a choice of a movie in the five-story Omni Theater or a planetarium show, which we decide is a bad idea. After all, we've already star-gazed together on a mountaintop with one of the best light shows in the world. The planetarium could only be a letdown.

The movie is spectacular, although not due to the subject, Cities of the Future, which I thought was a little tame, but because I casually drop my arm around Brooke and she lets me leave it there. It's been nearly four years since I played the part of a boyfriend, but she brings it out in me effortlessly.

We leave the theater, hand-in-hand, funneled out into a discovery center, and the shit hits the fan.

"Jordan Asher!" shrieks a female voice. I should've known better than to choose a film that might attract my people—futuristic nerds. Actually, in that moment, when I hear another person say, "Really? Where?" I realize the entire Museum of Science was a bad idea. We should have gone to a straight-up art exhibit.

Knowing how bad this can go, I grab Brooke's hand and run.

21

Brooke

It's like one of those Beatles movies except with a mere sliver of a crowd chasing us. And they're not all crying, screaming women, either. These are not billionaire bachelor chasers. They're gaming fans who don't want to tear off TJ's clothing. They want to offer tribute and get info.

"Asher," some call out. "You rock!"

"Bright Star rocks," others yell.

"When's the next one?" That becomes a chant.

"Any cheat codes online?" becomes the most popular question coming our way.

We don't stop until we're out the exit and searching for the Caddy. No one follows us out of the museum so we slow down.

"Sorry about that," he says, as if he had any control over what just happened.

More amused than upset, knowing he has nothing to be sorry for, I don't see the big deal until we get in the back of the limo. When I look at his face, he's clearly shaken. I realize it's precisely because he had zero control over the mob, no matter how small and harmless they were.

TJ is not a guy who enjoys life happening *to* him, without him having an ounce of say in the matter.

"Are you OK?" I ask.

"I never should have taken a risk with your safety. Take us back to Ms. Danbury's residence," he tells the driver in the voice that makes me want to obey. I shrug it off.

"I didn't feel unsafe," I tell him. Apart from TJ running a little too fast and nearly pulling me down a flight of stairs in the parking garage.

"Bad things can happen when someone's chasing you," he states.

Ohhh-kaay. "But we're fine. I had fun."

He's silent, looking straight ahead, unsmiling, reminding me of the TJ I first met in his bar. Untouching, we don't talk again until we get back to my place. And then I don't want to let him go.

"Come in for the coffee you missed this morning," I offer, hoping I don't sound desperate, although my body is. All day my thoughts have gone to sensual places until I think I'll break down and beg if he doesn't touch me. I know Sherri's not home, out on a date with a new guy. And I'm going to try my best to get TJ indoors.

He walks up the steps with me, but instead of being relaxed, he's glancing around behind us. Gone is the man who walked to the park without looking over his shoulder.

"Probably not a good idea," he begins, and I cut him off.

"*Definitely* a good idea. Let's get inside and off this busy street." It's obviously a quiet residential street with literally no one in sight. "You can tell me about the next game and how I can help." I'm babbling but at least his focus is directed on me again. I see the instant he realizes how much I want him.

The smallest of smiles quirks one side of his mouth. One word signals the ecstasy to come. "OK."

As we enter the condo, I drop my purse, shed my jacket, and kick off my shoes.

"Get comfy," I start to say, but he's already doing so. When his shoes are off, he puts his big hands on my waist and brands my neck with an open-mouth kiss.

In return, I palm the front of his jeans. *Yippee.* There's my favorite toy.

"Bedroom," he orders.

I lead the way to the tiny second bedroom where Sherri was storing stuff before I broke off my engagement and moved in. Her exercise bike is still here under my untidy clothes. Although my bed is only a double, at this instant, it looks palatial because it's a horizontal mattress and TJ is with me.

After closing the door, he reaches for my long-sleeve top and removes it, then tugs my bra cups down, exposing my breasts.

"I've missed your tits," he says.

"They've missed you," I say. Then I'm rendered speechless when he closes his mouth over one nipple, while pinching the other. Against my skin, he says, "They're even more glorious than I remember."

Glorious? Ha! What a word. How sweet. Eyes closed, I grab hold of TJ somewhere on his torso and tug him with me until I feel the mattress behind my legs and let myself fall, bringing him down on top of me.

Mr. Busby, who I didn't notice through the haze of lust, yowls at the intrusion before settling down again beside my head.

"Not sure I can continue with your cat taking up half the damn bed, and threatening to flay me alive again."

Damn! Mr. Busby has broken the mood. Jumping up and pulling my bra cups back into place at the same time, I scoop him into my arms and race to the couch, where I deposit him with a little less care than usual. I think I'm really quick, but when I return, TJ has already removed his jeans and is taking off his crewneck shirt.

Whoa! While all of his sculpted body is a turn-on, every rippling muscle and taut plane, I've loved watching every time he has divested himself of a shirt. It's so masculine, with that overarm movement when he grabs the back, showing biceps and triceps in action, and then inch-by-inch revealing his six-pack. I sigh with appreciation.

His stony-green gaze locks on mine. "Strip for me."

I don't know why, but my hands shake a little as I comply. Probably the long weeks between the last time we satisfied one another. Also, knowing how good the climax will be has me wanting to skip to the end. In a moment, I'm in my panties and bra. I wait, hands on hips.

TJ cocks his head. "I think you disobeyed me just a little." Leaning forward, he unhooks my bra and lets it drop. "Take them off," he orders, and I shimmy out of my panties.

Sitting on the end of my bed, he reaches for my arm and drags me over his lap, face down. *Oh!* When he rubs his big palm over my ass cheeks, I whimper with need. It's embarrassing how much I want him. So is my body's obvious quivering, which he must be able to feel, along with the gush of desire that's leaving droplets on his thighs.

"Why did you disobey?" he asks softly, still caressing my skin.

"I want . . ." My words trail off.

"I know what you want." He lifts his hand. "I know what you need."

Smack. It's very different from the paddle, that's for sure. Different but not better or worse. *Smack.* A warmer, broader sensation of his entire palm and fingers, heavy and firm, on my soft flesh. I relax into the spanking, knowing he's going to take care of me and all my desires.

Smack! That really stung, causing heat to flood between my hips. His taut erection presses against my lady bits, too, like I'm sandwiched between everything TJ.

Smack. That one takes my breath away, but as soon as his fingers caress my wet pussy, I moan and spread my legs for more. He begins a rhythmic repetition, alternately spanking me and fingering me until I cannot stay still despite him demanding that I do. I'm writhing uncontrollably, trying to simultaneously grind my mound against his lap, open myself to give him better access since he keeps purposefully eluding my clit, and lifting my butt for his palm's next slap.

I don't exist anymore except for those three points of contact. I don't want anything except release.

"Please," comes out on my ragged breath.

"Please what?" TJ stops everything he's doing.

"No!" I cry out. "Please!"

Suddenly, it's clear to me that I don't want to climax this way. "Please *fuck* me," I whisper, hoping he hears.

In seconds, he stands, catches me from falling, and I find myself on my back looking up at him. Where the hell has that condom come from? Not that I care when he deftly rolls it onto his erection. Spreading my legs to welcome him, he settles between them, edging the head of his large cock at my entrance.

"Thanks," I say, as if he's doing me a favor, but it's all part of the game.

When he sheaths himself inside me in one burst, I nearly go off. I have to hold my breath and fight not to come immediately as he glides in and out, leaning on his forearms to brace his upper body. The force of each deliciously filling thrust rocks my body as each time he penetrates a little deeper. It's exactly what I want.

Reaching up to him, I feather my fingers across his chest and his nipples, which are tight, raised nubs. His eyes open at my touch, and I am captured. Yes, I love this man. For how he makes me feel when we're together. Seen and understood. Then I notice the marks.

"You're all scratched up," I say, running my fingers over the pricks and lines on his left shoulder.

"Busby," he mutters.

Of course. I should feel guilty, but it's kind of sexy. Everything is sexy while my body is revved and trying to charge across the finish line. Also, intoxicating, as if I've had a few too many glasses of wine. I'm contemplating blurting out my tender feelings. I can pretend they're mindless words in the heat of the moment.

Before I decide whether it's manipulative to tell him, knowing he only came to Boston to apologize and to ensure I'm not about to write an exposé, TJ slides one hand between us.

For the first time since we entered the bedroom, he makes direct contact with my throbbing clit. It's like he presses a magic button. I utter some strange sound I've never heard before and fly off the edge of the mountain in my mind. Right into the heart of the billion stars we saw together.

"*Ahhh*, yes!" I say loudly, shuddering against his hand even as he continues to drive into me, stretching and filling until he, too, finishes on a sexy, low groan. After his final thrust, he rolls off me and nearly ends up on the floor.

"Mercy," he says, making me smile.

"Sorry for the small bed," I say, not really sorry about anything. I decide never to have sex again if it doesn't measure up to TJ Asher. And how could it?

$♥$♥$♥$

He finally gets a cup of coffee, and I do, in fact, dig out some packaged cookies. No thanks to Sherri for making me sound like a human vacuum cleaner yesterday. *A snack-uum cleaner!*

"You feeling better?" he asks.

"Sure, why?" Does he think he was too rough? "It was perfect."

He smiles, and I think I see a little red tone over his cheekbones. I must compliment this man more often to see if it happens again. Which reminds me he's not *my man*, nor does he live anywhere near me.

Maybe we can be long-distance friends with benefits.

"I meant the pizza poisoning," he clarifies, munching on a chocolate sandwich cookie.

"I'd forgotten, what with the museum and then the . . . *that?*" I point behind me toward my room. "Yes, totally better."

"Good. I have a few things to do in the city. But since you don't have to get up for work early, you want to have dinner with me later?"

"Yes," I snap, way too quickly. But he doesn't embarrass me by appearing to notice my eagerness.

"I was hoping you'd say that. Select somewhere you like or somewhere you've always wanted to go. Might as well get some use out of all the gaming money."

"I'll think about it." I rub my hands, pretending to plot. "The more expensive, the better."

He laughs. "Not necessarily, but I just want you to know there are no limits."

"No one has ever said that to me before," I tell him somberly.

"Then it's about time."

Just then his phone pings. He drags it from his pocket, then smiles, presses the talk-to-text button and says: "Can't talk. Ran into Brooke, and we're making dinner plans. Talk another time." He hits send.

"Who was that?" I ask.

"Back to your inquisitive self again," he teases. "Just Tracy. The minute I'm not in driving distance, she and Cy become like needy children. Anyway, eight o'clock, I'll be back."

Taking him at his word, I think about somewhere I've wanted to try. But how will I get a reservation on such short notice? *Duh!* I will namedrop the hell out of *Jordan Asher.*

I choose Mooo on Beacon Hill, not the most expensive but well out of my price range and boasting great reviews.

Plus, it's in the heart of the historic area. As it turns out, I do need to drop his name for a table for two. *Voilà.* I have a feeling it would annoy him, but he doesn't have to know.

I'm ready and on the sidewalk at eight, because if TJ comes in to fetch me, I'll drag him into my bedroom, and we'll miss what promises to be a fantastic dining experience. I'm dressed in a black dress that *almost* reaches my knees, a simple silver necklace, and a black wool coat. I hope I'm not too severe, but I think my pale-pink patent leather pumps give me a little pop of levity. Luckily, he had the good sense to wear a suit, and he looks like a slightly scruffy James Bond.

His driver takes us through the famous streets of Beacon Hill with their cobblestones, brick sidewalks, and gas lamps. He drops us by the Beacon Street front door of the cast-iron paneled, black-painted steakhouse.

Mooo is written in gold letters over the corner entrance. The second story and the limestone band above it support the Roman brick floors of an exclusive hotel, XV Beacon Hill, which shares the building. We read this on TJ's phone on the car ride over.

"That's another coincidence," I say. "Roman numerals and brick, seeing how you're Tiberius."

He rolls his eyes and holds open the door.

"Mr. Asher," someone greets us immediately, and I feel him startle beside me. Placing my hand on his arm in case he's about to do a runner, we follow the host to our table. Everything is as I expected and as I saw in the online photos. Understated elegance of wooden tables and comfy padded chairs, a long white-marble bar filled with patrons, and scuffed brick floors paired with newer plank flooring around one edge of the sophisticated dining room. Our table for two has wingback chairs, giving us a modicum of privacy.

And then we feast. I don't have to worry about showing my unfamiliarity with this level of fine dining because, as it turns out, my billionaire date has rarely gone out since he made his fortune.

Regardless, we know we like good steak, ordering both Japanese Wagyu and American grass fed. "We can share both," I say, like a child, ignoring the server's raised eyebrow. I guess he would have preferred we ordered two of each. TJ chooses a bottle of wine that seems to be missing a decimal point in the price and orders a Caesar salad.

"Don't," he says, when I'm about to mention Tiberius Julius. I bite my tongue and order the iceberg salad.

"Are we going to make it to dessert, or do you want an appetizer?" TJ asks.

"Definitely dessert," I say, and we send our server on his way with one last request for truffle parmesan fries. I'm hoping there are bread rolls, but I fear that's too crass for this place.

To my delight, another server brings out a cast-iron loaf pan with four freshly baked rolls and a pot of butter. My insides dance excitedly as we each tear off a warm, perfectly browned bun.

"Wow," I say as the roll melts in my mouth.

TJ snickers. "I doubt many people say that about the bread in here. Maybe we should hold our enthusiasm for the steak."

Wine comes next, and we toast to seeing each other outside of Maine.

"I'm really glad to be with you again," he says, which for some reason brings tears to my eyes. I have to set my glass down and flutter my hands toward my eyes because my mascara is not waterproof.

"I had a great day, too," I manage when I've recovered. Taking a sip, again, I say my fav all-purpose word, "Wow."

"What?" he asks.

"I can't tell the difference between this and a Trader Joe's five-dollar bottle."

We grin at one another, and the rest of the meal flies by while we exchange stories about our families. I have a lot because of the different military bases I've lived on, both in the states and internationally. He tells me that he bought his parents a nice house outside of Charlottesville, Virginia, as soon as the money started pouring in. Then TJ grew quieter when he tells me he had a sister, also adopted, who has passed away.

Reaching out my hand to touch his, my heart hurts for him. He lets me squeeze his fingers on the tabletop before drawing away. I can see he wants to drop the subject, so I do. I tell him about my few previous trips to Maine, once to Bar Harbor and Cadillac Mountain, and the requisite drive up Mount Washington.

"Because everyone makes that trek at some point if they live in New England."

"Never been," he says, which floors me.

"What about to southern Maine where the outlet malls are?"

He makes a face. "Never going to happen."

"Other than that, I probably wouldn't go back myself," I confess. "I can eat lobster and go to the beach without leaving Massachusetts."

He nods, still seeming a little morose, so I tell him the story about Sherri and Mick Jagger and his lopsided, dimpled smile appears.

"Do you still have the t-shirt the woman signed?"

"Of course," I say, and his smile grows.

During the course of dinner, we see a movie star and a TV star, not at the same table. At least one woman stares too long at TJ. He's about to ask her if she's a reporter, maybe punch her husband in the face, until I tell him she's looking at him like she wants to jump his bones because he's such a damn studmuffin.

"That man's going to come punch *you* in a minute if you don't rein in your oomph."

"My *oomph*?" TJ looks surprised.

"Just telling you like it is." Despite having changed since those photos from a few years ago, I wonder if the man doesn't realize he's a ten plus. That's kind of refreshing.

All too soon, it's time to order dessert. "Strawberry tart," I say, surprising myself. "I was sure I was going to order the chocolate cake, but look at that description."

"I'll have the chocolate cake," TJ tells the server. "The lady and I will share."

And as soon as we're alone again, he asks, "Will you spend the night with me in my hotel room?"

"Damn straight I will," I say, quick as a whip. "I even brought my toothbrush."

TJ's laughter sounds loud in the restaurant of subdued diners and servers, and neither of us cares.

22

Jordan

My try-anything-once girl in a sexy black dress that has been driving me nuts all night is riding the elevator of the Parisi. I wasn't planning on inviting her back to the hotel, but I wasn't ready to drop her at her home and say goodbye, or even goodnight. She's one step ahead of me apparently, with a toothbrush in her tiny purse.

At the restaurant, I asked her the question without too much thought. And I should ask the next one that's been in my brain all day. *May I kiss you?* But I don't ask. I give in to the overwhelming urge instead, hoping she's willing.

Pressing her against the elevator wall, my hands at her waist, I insert my thigh between her legs and lean down.

"What are you doing?" she asks, eyes open, looking shocked.

Her words stop me cold, because it seems obvious what I'm doing. So, why are her hands on my chest, holding me back?

"Kissing you," I say, sounding idiotic.

"*Oh.*" Her eyes are huge.

"Is that OK?" Because now I'm losing the will to live and wishing I'd never made my move.

"Yeah, sure. Are we doing that now?"

"Doing *that?*" I ask.

"Being a couple who kiss? Because that's a whole different ballgame, don't you think?"

"*Uh . . .*" I'm so slick and cool I can hardly stand myself. "I guess so."

But the moment's over, and I step back when the elevator doors open.

"Hey," she says, putting her hand on my arm. "I didn't mean to put you off. I was simply surprised."

"I understand. We'll pick it up again in my room." I hope. Or we can have a sexless sleepover because I may have gone and ruined everything. Not really sure at this point. Where before, we were in sync and I had no doubt she wanted me each time we were together, now because I want to kiss her, I have a case of nerves like we're on a first date. Maybe we are. And perhaps I should have been a gentleman and taken her home.

"Do you want to go home?" I ask, pausing at the door of my suite.

"No. Why? Because I stopped you kissing me?"

"Not that, but I don't want you to think I asked you out because I expected sex in return."

"I don't. I wasn't thinking *TJ bought me the most expensive dinner of my life and now I owe him a good time.*"

"OK." I swipe the card and let her in. Brooke takes a few steps inside and does a long, slow sweep of the hotel suite.

"Nice," she says. "I mean, *really.* Your friend, Mr. Parisi, knows how to build a hotel."

"Not exactly my friend, but I'll tell Marcus you approve. He's the same real estate developer who helped me find my house in Maine and the half an island I own."

"One of those realtors for the rich, then?" she quips.

"I guess so." We're standing in the sitting area, and I want to make things easy and casual like they were before. "I don't have to leave tomorrow. Do you want to show me around Boston a little more? Maybe do something outdoors?"

"I have a job interview midmorning," she says, making a face. "Kind of interrupts the day, but we can play it by ear." Then she shrugs. "I could cancel it."

"No," I blurt. I don't want to be responsible for her losing out on a job. Not when I'm still unsure where we're going with this. "You should go to the interview. Are you prepared?"

Brooke's face breaks out in a smile. "No worries. It's nothing I can't fake my way into."

Since she's not telling me what the job is, I don't ask. "Do you want a drink?" I gesture vaguely to the thoughtful stash that came with the room, a couple bottles of red next to a mini-fridge that holds white wine and champagne.

"No, thanks. The wine at dinner was plenty for me, but go ahead if you want to."

"I'm good. I thought it might relax you."

She smiles. "I promise you I'm relaxed." To prove it, Brooke kicks off her pink shoes and comes closer. "Let's get you out of this suit, then you'll be more relaxed, too."

I let her act the part of a valet, taking my coat and laying it across the sofa. Next, she eases my tie loose before removing it. After all, she was engaged and is obviously used to helping her man get undressed. That gives me a surge of irrational jealousy, but also relief the guy let her get away.

My desire for her is evident. When she takes my hand and leads me to the only door, which is the bedroom, I snap out of it. Kissing is unnecessary, as we've previously discovered, and I think we can go straight to the main event. I don't take long getting out of my shirt—maybe losing a few buttons in the hurried process—before everything else comes off under her watchful eyes.

I turn Brooke gently away from me so I can unzip her dress.

"I like this," I say, fingering the straps of her lacy black bra, which are only half cups with her breasts nearly spilling over. In fact, from my vantage point looking over her shoulder, I can see the upper curves of her dusky-pink nipples. Along with her matching black thong, her sexy underthings are the perfect accessories for her beautiful body. If I'd known all this was happening under her dress during dinner, I wouldn't have been able to calmly eat and talk. We probably wouldn't have made it to dessert.

"Ready for skirmish mode?" I ask.

She laughs softly. "A gaming term? Now? I've heard Sherri say it. But never in this context."

Brooke turns in the circle of my arms and looks up at me. Here's the moment again to kiss her. I ignore it, refusing to stop our momentum by making it weird again. Instead, I grab a condom from the side pocket of my leather bag. Task accomplished, sitting on the end of the bed, I draw her to stand between my legs where I can set my mouth on the smooth skin of her stomach instead of her mouth. She sinks her fingers into my hair as I work my way up to her breasts with a trail of kisses. With barely a tug at the bra cups, I expose her tits to my lips and teeth.

Her body trembles against my thighs. I might be a gaming geek, but I have figured out how to please a woman, this one in particular. As I latch onto her nipple, I pull down her thong, dropping it at our feet. My hands on her shapely ass, I guide her to straddle me, a knee on either side of my thighs. Then I slowly pull her down onto my erection, which she guides into her wet channel.

Brooke grabs onto my shoulders, including Mr. Busby's scratches. She starts to ride my cock, rising up and slamming down, with little assistance from my hands at her waist.

"Lean back," she says, after a few moments. "Then I can see you watching me."

Resting on my elbows, the view is fucking amazing. Her sleek hair floats around her collar bone as she moves. Her tits look fuller in the bra, pushed upward by the cups I tugged under them. I appreciate how they bounce with each movement she makes.

With Brooke gliding effortlessly up and down my length, my balls are tightening already, and I'm nearly ready to blow.

"You are so perfect," I say, and her cheeks grow pink. "Will you grab your breasts for me?"

The briefest pause before she takes them each in hand. "I've never done this before. Touched myself in front of someone."

Good! That's what any man wants to hear. "Now, pinch and tug your nipples."

She does, well enough that she makes herself moan, closes her eyes, and tilts her head back. She's a siren, a sex goddess, a vision of sensuality riding me fast.

After another few moments, she murmurs in a raspy voice, "Will you touch me, please?"

In a flash, I'm stroking her clit, keeping up with her movements until I feel her body tense and her pussy tighten around me.

"Yes!" she says. "Don't stop."

"I won't," I promise. "I've got you." I caress her through the duration of her orgasm as she quivers on my lap. The gyrations send shockwaves through my cock to the base. As soon as she slows down, practically limp, dropping her hands from her breasts, I grab her by the hips.

"Hang on." She grabs my shoulders again. Fast and fierce, I drive into her, lifting her as needed and bringing her back down hard until my own climax takes hold of me. Anchoring Brooke against my thighs, I grind inside her as deep as I can until the sensual madness lets go and my satisfaction is complete.

Together, we fall back onto the bed. She looks down at me with an unfathomable expression before climbing off. I think it was admiration. We crawl to the top of the mattress and flop down on the pillows, exhausted, satiated, content. And I'm struck at how natural and normal this feels. How right my life is when I'm with Brooke.

$♥$♥$♥$

When I awaken, she's in the bathroom showering. A glance at the clock tells me I slept longer than I usually do. It's almost nine. Then I remember her job interview. *Shit!* I hope she's not nervous. By the time I've dressed and made two cups of coffee in the room's Keurig, she's strolling out of the bedroom dressed in the black dress, which I want to now categorize as "famous." Or maybe "infamous." I know I'll never forget it or how she looked at dinner or how she let me strip it off her.

Down, boy.

"Coffee, thanks," she says, but she sounds a little off.

Regrets? I wonder.

"You OK?"

"Yes, definitely. Just a lot of rich food last night." She sips the coffee, makes a face, and puts the cup down.

"Sorry, I think I've got a case of nerves. My head is already thinking about what to wear to the interview and that's putting my stomach on edge."

"Let's get you home ASAP," I offer. I feel like apologizing for not having offered her clothing to wear home. At least sweatpants and a T-shirt, but there's nothing I can do about that now.

Brooke is putting on her shoes and I'm admiring her ass, when I recall the check I have for her. Is she going to blow up if I offer it to her after last night? Only one way to find out. After shrugging into my jacket, I open my wallet.

"Will you take a check for your help on Bright Star?"

To my relief, she smiles. "Yes, thank you. Kind of takes the edge off worrying about the interview. I'm sure I have the necessary skills, but you never know. Not being in desperate need will allow me a measure of confidence."

"I'm glad." As we head downstairs to grab a taxi *together*, I take her hand. She tenses, but I don't let go. I'm not letting her ride alone dressed like that. Someone will mistake her for a paid escort.

By the time the doorman has summoned a taxi, since we don't have time for my limo driver to arrive, she's relaxed and leaning against me. But she also insists on going home by herself.

"I've been living in this city for like seven months now. I can get home in a taxi without help. Plus, I can go over my canned responses to lame interview questions."

"OK." I hand the driver two hundred dollars. "Get her home safely," I tell the guy, whose eyes are bugging out.

Brooke's cheeks are scarlet when I stick my head in the window to say goodbye, and I wonder if I've made her seem more like a prostitute by overpaying.

"I'll call you this afternoon," I tell her.

She mumbles, "Goodbye. Talk later." And they drive off.

Damn me if, once again, I don't want to kiss her.

23

Brooke

When TJ calls, I'm unsure whether to tell him that I didn't make my interview. My stomach was roiling again, and I had to lie down. I'm pretty sure the interviewer didn't believe my excuse, because he said he couldn't reschedule. He informed me that he had plenty of applicants who could make their appointments. But the generous check from TJ means I don't have to worry about it. Not for a while.

It's a really great feeling, too. Money can't buy you happiness, but it can sure alleviate stress. I wish I could have called TJ as soon as I felt better so we could have gone out earlier, but I still don't have his new number.

When the phone rings at two, I'm stretched out on the couch channel-surfing with Mr. Busby on my chest.

"Hi, pretty lady, how'd it go?" The mere sound of his voice makes me happy.

"Hey there." I dodge the question despite knowing I'll have to answer later. "There's still plenty of sunlight and time to walk around Faneuil Hall and Boston Harbor. You game?"

"I'm game."

Hard to believe I'd been sick to my stomach a couple hours earlier as I do a last fluff and spritz while waiting for TJ to pick me up. But the time drags on, and I'm back on the couch waiting, waiting, waiting. I've reapplied perfume to my cleavage for the second time. Still, no knock at the door. *WTF!*

Without realizing it, I close my eyes and drift off to sleep. I know this because when Sherri comes home, she startles me. For a second, I think it's TJ at last. Mr. Busby sits up in the middle of my chest and stretches before beginning to groom. It's growing dark, and I'm confused why I'm still here, unable to reach him. When I tried the number he used for calling me, it didn't even ring.

She clicks on a lamp, and I see concern on her face.

"What's up?" Has Armageddon occurred outside the condo while I was drooling in a cat-induced stupor?

She glances at the TV, and I see TJ's face. At first, I think the worst—he was in an accident. He's dead. My throat seems to close. What a selfish bitch I am, getting worked up over him not coming over as planned when he was possibly injured while trying to get to me. Then I realize the gist of the story: a flood of photos, or so it seems because there are about four new ones, along with facts about his parents' whereabouts, his old boss at Silicon Valley, and his current trip to Boston.

Boston! He must be furious.

"I don't understand," I say.

Sherri shrugs. "I don't know, either. What's going on? Were you with him last night?"

"Yes, for dinner and then," I hesitate, but Sherri's not going to think less of me. "I went back to his hotel room afterward."

"Did you tell anyone?"

I must appear shocked, because Sherri ducks her head. "Sorry. I didn't mean intentionally, but . . . well, the scripted radio news that repeats every half hour names you as 'an intimate friend.'"

She sits on her end of the couch, leans her head back, and closes her eyes. "And it said you were happy to talk to the media because you think Mr. Asher shouldn't have to be in hiding. Like you were trying to help him by bringing his life into the open."

"What!" I jump to my feet, sending Mr. Busby crashing to the floor. "I have to go."

"Where?"

"To the Parisi Hotel."

"You want me to come," she offers, "for moral support?"

"No. I'll be fine. This is a misunderstanding. I didn't do anything."

$♥$♥$♥$

I t's not fine. That's obvious when I see reporters clustered around the entrance to the hotel. Even worse when one of them asks me who I am. Thinking they may actually figure it out, I make a dash for the glass doors. Passing the front desk, I try to go to the elevator, but I'm stopped by a hotel employee.

"Are you a guest here?"

I've never seen this woman before, nor do I recognize the man behind the front desk. But the doorman from this morning would know me.

"I'm a friend of Mr. Asher's," I say carefully. "I was here last night and . . . and . . . this morning." I straighten my shoulders as I feel the heat rise up my neck. "If the doorman is around, he'll remember me."

"I think he's on break," she says. "In any case, Mr. Asher has checked out."

Shit! I nearly ask her if she knows where he's gone. Luckily, I manage to refrain from embarrassing myself. I think about our evening. He'll know it wasn't me. He can't possibly believe I had anything to do with this latest story. Any minute, TJ will contact me.

I'm disconcerted as I make my way through the reporters. Without my consent, they take photos of me, just as they do a hotel guest who's leaving at the same time. But all I can do is hurry away to catch the commuter rail home. Cursing myself for not getting TJ's number last night or this morning, it hits me that he could have—*would have*—given it to me if he'd wanted me to have it. It's not my fault I don't have it. It's his!

At home, Sherri has started dinner. "Any luck?"

"He's gone."

"What about calling him?"

I feel like an idiot telling her I no longer have his number. But my expression says it all, and I hate the look of pity.

"Let's have a good dinner, and everything will seem better tomorrow. How was the interview?"

"I didn't feel well enough to go. Maybe there's a bug going around. Not COVID, but something."

"Never mind. It wasn't your dream job."

Then I remember something that will cheer us both up. Opening my purse, I recover the check and lay it on the kitchen counter.

"I'll be able to pay my share of everything this month, and for the next four, in fact."

"I'm glad you came to your senses and let him pay you. You earned it."

I wish I hadn't spent any time on my back, I think to myself. *Or over his lap. Or all fours,* as happened about three this morning.

But I *did* earn this. What's really bothering me is TJ being out in the world thinking I had anything to do with this latest media blitz. My need to set him straight has me fidgeting all evening, unable to settle, checking my phone, and even trying that stupid number again.

Now what? I love him. And all I can think of is how I ruined what would have been our first kiss. So surprised in the hotel elevator, I'd pressed my hands to his chest simply to get my bearings, not really to stop him. Then it got weird, and the moment passed.

With a sharp pang, I wonder now if I'll ever get another chance. He's a billionaire, meaning he could go literally anywhere and disappear. After all, it's not as though he ever said he cared for me, either. I don't know if that was because TJ was hesitant or because it was just sex for him.

What wouldn't I give if I could tell him now how I feel.

"Do you have another interview tomorrow?" Sherri asks.

I shake my head, wishing I'd cancelled today's and spent the day with him. If we'd been together when the story broke, he would've known it wasn't me.

"I have an interview on Monday, and haven't heard back from anyone else."

"No worries," Sherri says. "You'll figure it out. You always do."

But I don't care about my next job. I just want to talk to TJ. When I awaken the next morning at six, with my stomach roiling again, my feet hit the floor before I'm really awake. In the bathroom, I heave up bile and not much else. At the sink, I wash my face with cold water to feel better.

As I catch sight of my reflection, I stare into my own eyes and tell myself the truth.

"You're pregnant."

And there's no doubt who the father is.

Blasted, fucking, unreliable condoms!

24

Jordan

To say I was surprised by the betrayal would put it mildly. I was floored like I'd been hit by a snowboarder. It was worse this time because I wasn't at home with my dogs. Far worse to be in a strange city in a hotel room when you hear that the woman you love has just spilled her guts about stuff you told her at dinner. I think I've sprouted gray hairs.

From the back of my limo, I arrange for my jet to take me back to my parents in Virginia. I want them safely away from the house I bought them. They've endured enough pain because of me and what happened to Livvy.

Maybe if I'd told Brooke how I lost my sister, she wouldn't have done this. But I shouldn't need to convince anyone to keep their mouth shut. I know now why she didn't want me to accompany her home. She was in a super hurry to get to her "interview."

A few hours later, and I'm charging through my parents' front door.

"Tibs," Dad says, just to tease me, knowing it's not my favorite moniker. "I think you're overreacting."

He's talking about my phone call from before I jumped on the jet. But I'm too busy hugging my mom to argue with him. When I'm done almost suffocating her, I tell them what I fear.

"Any moment, a throng of reporters will show up."

"So, they'll stomp your father's lawn or a few of my flowers," my mom says, but she's not fooling me. I can see the worry in her eyes. We all know that even one jackass can cause a car accident and change everything.

"I don't want you two staying here, even if all the reporters do is touch a single blade of grass."

My father rubs the back of his neck. "Your mother and I like it here. We have friends and a life."

Anger at Brooke bubbles up. I hate like hell that I'm the cause of disrupting my parents' happiness. But it is what it is, at least for now.

"Come with me for a couple of weeks."

"Charlie," my mom begins to protest, referring to her spaniel.

"Charlie is coming, too. Of course."

Even though I was here for a week after the last media storm, no one knew about their whereabouts. We played board games and talked a lot, and with a hat and sunglasses, I could walk Charlie with my mom and play golf with my dad at his favorite course. This time, I'm rattled. Brooke's disclosure of my parents' town was unforgivable.

"Have you packed anything yet?" I ask, feeling as though reporters are converging on the place.

Dad rolls his eyes, but my mother, now that Charlie is included, springs into action.

"Tell me the weather where we're going, and I'll have a couple bags packed while you two button up the house and figure out how to set the alarm."

"Figure out?" I turn to my father again. "Dad, don't you set it every night?"

He shrugs, looking sheepish. "We've never felt the need to live inside Fort Knox."

His stubbornness makes me want to tear out my new gray hairs, along with a lot more. "But you do know how to set the alarm, right? And you understand it's important to go away with me now, don't you?"

"If you say so."

"I do. Mom, pack for the island. Basically, balmy and warm. Charlie's going to love it."

This makes my father smile. "I'll bring my clubs and some golf balls. I can work on my drive."

"Great idea." And I'll work on calming the vengeful, furious thoughts that are plaguing me. And to think I was imagining bringing Brooke to the island. Thank God I never told her where it is.

My phone pings, and I see it's *her*, again calling the number that is invisible to the world, unattached to my name. I can't believe she's still trying it. *Persistent bitch!*

I hate being right, particularly in this instance. However, as we lock up the house, activate the alarm, and drive away, I see a van with a local news station's logo on its side pulling up to the curb. I'm seething again. Despite my internationally bestselling games featuring every kind of conceivable weapon, I'm not a violent man. Yet I could cheerfully shoot out its tires. We can't get to my island home fast enough.

$♥$♥$♥$

"Bring it here, and I'll fix it," I tell my cousin's little boy. Four-year-old Josh is having kite troubles, enough to turn his sweet smile into a frown. With a little untangling, he's laughing again. I can't help but join in.

I've been on the island for months and have just about regained my good humor. I flew Beau, Grady, and the Duff-monster down even before my parents left. Mom and Dad went home after three weeks, when the short attention span of the media hounds had long forgotten why they were camped outside an empty house in Virginia. Charlie was ready to go home, too, having been chased around by a different kind of hound, three of them, often getting rolled.

Since they left, I've had a sporadic trickle of guests, including some from California. Currently, I'm playing host to my mother's sister's family, including a cousin my age and his wife and their boy.

I've done nothing toward developing a new Bright game. Can't summon the interest. Don't need the money and not sure I have anything new to bring to the game's devoted players. I know I can't stay here forever. On the other hand, I can.

Since this time of year is easy on the Rangeley property, I've only had a few calls from Colin. No frozen pipes to worry about or frost heaves chewing up the driveway. All three calls were regarding trespassers looking for me. Nothing crazy, though. Each time, they rang the bell at the gate and then went away when told I wasn't there.

Cy has been weaned off of asking me every damn question that pops into his British head. After all, he always knew more than me about the bar. It just took him a couple months to believe it. The crazy billionaire hunters, both reporters and females, have tapered off, too.

"I almost miss the notoriety," Cy said last time we spoke.

Tracy contacts me more often than I like. While she was one of my first acquaintances in Rangeley, Maine, we're not exactly buddies. Still, as I watch Josh run up the beach toward his mom, when I answer my phone, it's nice to hear her familiar voice.

"Hey there, TJ. Missing you up here." She always says that, making me smile.

"Missing you down here," I reply, which is as much of my whereabouts as I will give away, even to her.

"Thanks," she says like she means it. After about five minutes of shooting the shit about local business news, including closings and openings, her tone turns a little husky. I know what's coming. She dances around a certain topic of wanting me to come "home" or of letting her join me in my "mysterious locale" each time we speak. This time, she comes out and says what she wants.

"You know, since we're not boss and employee any longer, we could pursue this thing between us."

Fortunately, I don't respond with "What *thing*?" I may be a clueless man, but I'm not that stupid. She'd hand me my head on a bar tray right over the cellular network. How do I tell her that's never in the cards for us without hurting her?

She's good looking and has a sense of humor, but I feel zero interest in starting anything with her. I don't even want to paddle her ass. Thinking of that only brings Brooke to mind. And thinking of Brooke makes me irritated, which is why my response is gruff when I say, "I'm thousands of miles away, Trace. I don't see that happening."

"Then come back. Come home." Her voice is a little pleading now, and I feel sorry for her. I hope to hell she isn't as deeply into me as she sounds.

"Home is here right now," I say firmly, as I have in the past.

"Then let me come there and keep you company."

Not getting the hint, no matter how many times I gently tell her no. "You have to look after the bar and help Cy. Maybe sometime, I'll get both you and Cy here, but not now." Her *and* Cy. Why doesn't she zero in on him as a possible partner? Is it the boss-employee barrier again? "If you and Cy are getting closer, I won't be upset. In fact, it would make me really happy for you two."

"That's not happening," she says flatly.

Well, OK then. An awkward moment of silence ensues while I stare out at the turquoise water. Suddenly, Josh is back.

"Daddy says your turn." My cousin wants me to clean the fish while he gets the charcoal going.

"I gotta go, Trace. Talk to you later."

"Sure. Bye." And she ends the connection before I can.

Women! Then again, what if I'm missing out on the right one while hung up on the wrong one? I acknowledge how infatuated I still am with Brooke, who makes cameo appearances or plays starring roles in most of my dreams. Sometimes, she's in trouble and I can't help her, making me awaken in a cold sweat. Sometimes, she's coming into my room here on the island, wearing nothing but a smile.

My body reacts, waking me up to a boner and a big disappointment. Occasionally, as the weeks pass, I have to remind myself what she did. Yet I find myself curious as to how she's doing and what job she found.

Standing, I hold Josh's kite for him as he takes off running on those skinny legs. At the right moment, I toss it as high overhead as I can and watch the kite catch the gentle breeze in the bright blue sky. Then I follow in his direction to the path that leads through the beach grass to my house.

On the back deck, there's family, cold beer, and some fish that need prepping. Everything but Brooke, her dazzling smile, and her squeeze-my-heart brown eyes.

Come to think of it, she probably didn't need to work this year after getting paid to send me into exile. She once said she could name her price for photos of me or my house. One big story, and she made bank. I need to stop worrying about her. Stop thinking about her at all.

If only that were possible.

25

Brooke

"Got it, boss," I say. "I'll be back with the coffee in a jiff."

"No, hurry," Mrs. Moxley tells me, as I amble away from her desk toward her office door. "Remember, no running or skipping. Definitely no jiffing. Don't forget your tea this time. And a bag of cookies."

I adore her. She's the oldest boss I've ever had, and so knowledgeable I could just listen to her talk for hours. My new position is still merely a job, but it's the best one I've ever had. The very married CEO, Adam Bonvier, is eye candy of the finest kind. Not that I see him much, but his painting is in the company's lobby, meaning I get my fix of dark-haired, dark-eyed handsome male each morning and afternoon. These days, all I want to do is look anyway.

The workplace, an international marketing firm, situated in Boston's financial district near the wharves, is beautiful, an easy T ride from home, and the work is interesting and varied. I could use my degree to get inside the heads of potential buyers and assist with the ad campaigns if I stay around long enough and get promoted. But basically, I'm a junior assistant to the VP of Accounts.

I'm totally fine with getting coffee from the corner barista, or proofreading the final ad copy, or hand-delivering product samples to the conference room. I'm never bored.

I'm also seven-and-a-half months along in my pregnancy. Not a massive weight gain, although as TJ once noticed, my breasts that he thought were fuller during the second month are now quite impressive. *Ha!* Knowing what a breast man he is, it serves him right, missing out on my lusciousness.

Serves him right, except I'm the one paying the price and missing him every moment. I wish he could come again between my breasts like that perfect night in the hot tub.

When I let myself into the condo, I walk in on Sherri's panicked face.

"What's wrong?" I check to see Mr. Busby's in his spot on the couch.

"I can't make the baby checkup with you. Emergency meeting tomorrow afternoon."

"How can it be an emergency if you already know about it?" I joke, but I'm not bothered. "I'll be fine. It's routine. Baby will be perfect as usual."

She nods, sniffs, and goes into the kitchen without asking her usual question: "Do you want your special tea?"

My morning sickness is over, and I feel great. I no longer drink gallons of herbal tea, a ginger, red raspberry leaf, and spearmint blend, but I know her sudden quietness means I've hurt her feelings. Trying not to make her feel bad about tomorrow, I've underplayed how much I love having her support when she comes to my wellness checkups.

"On the other hand, I probably should reschedule," I say, following her into the kitchen. "What if the doctor gives me important info? With my pregnancy brain, I might forget everything I'm told."

She frowns with concern. "You should go, but you're so big I don't like you going alone. And what if you get on the wrong T line. What did you forget today?"

I have to hide my smile. "I got the order wrong for Mrs. Moxley's coffee this afternoon. I swear I said it right, but I was daydreaming about putting the crib together."

"*After* the birth," Sherri insists.

I've been letting her superstitions guide us along this path, although I definitely have the nesting urge lately. Her exercise bike is no longer in my room, stored away somewhere she'll never use it. That corner is now dedicated to the few baby things I've gathered, awaiting the deluge from the baby shower next month. Knowing my family's and friends' generosity, it's going to be tight in my room.

Sherri puts the water on for the tea that I don't need but love, and adds, "I promise you Dan will put the crib together as soon as I text him that Baby Boy or Baby Girl has arrived. Even if it has a billion pieces, he'll put it together before you come home from the hospital."

Dan is her steady guy now of five months. I think I love him nearly as much as she does.

"He has already read the instructions," she adds.

Now I can't help but laugh. "He must be the only man in the universe who has."

Sherri laughs too, but she also blushes with how much she loves him. "Yeah, probably," she adds with a dreamy tone to her voice.

We're going to push the long side of my bed against the wall so I can only get in from one side, making space for the crib against the other wall. I can hardly wait to share my room with this peanut. But Sherri used the word *billion*, and my heart did the weird squeezing thing it does when I think of TJ.

I don't want to be a weak-willy, but I very much miss that man. I'm pretty sure he would want to know he's about to become a father, but that's out of my hands. I texted the number no one ever responds to, and I even called the Thirsty Moose, more than once.

Sitting at the kitchen table, I do it again, always keeping my fingers crossed that I'll get Cyril or even better, TJ, himself. No such luck. It's Tracy's voice that greets me.

"Hi, Tracy, it's Brooke."

"You have some nerve."

"I didn't sell photos or info to the media." I've told her this before.

"What do you want?" Her voice is clipped. She's always ready to hang up on me.

"I need to get a message to TJ."

"Not on my watch."

I guess I should be thrilled he has such protective friends, but I can't help sighing.

"Shouldn't that be up to him?"

Silence.

"Do you have his number, Tracy?"

"Of course I do."

"Will you please deliver a message to him? It's important." Tracy has made her annoyance crystal clear and conveyed that TJ no longer lives in his house, so I gave up trying to get the exact address.

"Gotta go. This place is always hopping since *you* put the Moose on the map."

"I didn't—"

She hangs up. Of course I will try again, but I never get Cyril. Sherri gives me a pat on the shoulder and sets my tea in front of me. I could send a letter to the bar, but Tracy would probably intercept it and not pass it along. I shudder at the thought of her reading about our baby before TJ finds out about it himself. On the other hand, perhaps she'd soften and tell him if she knew he was going to be a father.

"Try later," Sherri says. She, too, thinks it's important for TJ to know about the pregnancy, but she has her own reasons. Number one being that he should be paying for every expense.

After dinner, I'll call again when she goes to meet Dan for a . . . well, *hm*, I think she said a drink, but she wasn't really dressed for going out. I'm assuming she went over to his place for something else. Good for her. It's none of my business, but I'm thrilled she's found a great guy.

When Cy answers, I nearly cry with relief. But then, I also cry at insurance commercials and real estate ads, so the bar isn't very high ever since the pregnancy hormones took over my emotions.

"Cy, please don't hang up. It's Brooke."

"Why would I hang up?"

Thank God, he's not a fanatic *warrior for TJ* like Tracy.

"First of all, I did not sell any story or photos to the media, not once, not twice."

"OK."

"OK? Just like that."

"Why would you lie?"

"I wouldn't, but how do you know that?"

"Because I can't see any angle that would make sense. You guys were building up to something. At least that was my impression the couple times I saw you in here and by how upset TJ was. So, why would you ruin it? Not for money. If you two hadn't broken up, you'd be a billionaire's wife with all the money you need."

"Cy, you are some kinda clear thinker. Thank you. Tell that to Tracy."

"She's bonkers," he says cheerfully.

Maybe she lied about TJ's whereabouts. "Does he still live there?"

"He's away, long term."

Well, crap! He could be anywhere. "I don't suppose you want to tell me where I can find him."

"I can't do that, Brooke. TJ has asked me not to tell anyone. Not just you."

Probably *especially* me, but Cy doesn't say that. "Does TJ ever come back to handle anything bar related? As you can tell, I'm trying to reach him. I've called before, but this is the first time I've managed to get you and not Ms. Bonkers, who is uber-protective of him."

"She has a thing for him. Big time. And she was tamping when she found out he's a billionaire under her nose for three years."

"Tamping?" Sometimes I can't believe we speak the same language.

"Absolutely, and gutted. She's kicking herself for not acting on her feelings. Anyway, you don't usually reach me, love, because I'm the owner now."

This is news. "Since when?"

"TJ sold it to me for a dollar after the first story came out. He didn't even keep a share."

"Meaning he may never come back there." My heart sinks. How will I find him?

But Cy laughs. "I think TJ will be back for the skiing and he loves his house."

"He didn't sell it? I'm glad." I wish I had Colin or Emma's last name or their numbers. "Not just for skiing, he said he likes the hiking and . . . whatever else you do there all year." I'm rambling because I don't want to hang up without getting more info. "Look, Cy, you don't owe me anything, but I . . . I have something that belongs to TJ, and I don't know how to get it to him. Can you give me his new cell number?"

His hesitation is like a kick to the gut. I've slept wrapped around TJ's warm sexy body, his baby is growing inside me, and now I'm having to wheedle and cajole a way to reach him.

"How about I tell him you're trying to get in touch?"

"That would be great." Although he'll probably ignore the message, so I have to make Cy realize it's no joke. "Will you please tell him its important?"

"Do you want to ship it here?"

I lay a hand on my belly. "No, that won't work. But I'm not joking, it really is important. Also, is he . . . I mean, is TJ even in the country?"

After another awkward rebuff, I thank him and hang up. At least, Cy will tell TJ I'm trying to reach him. Hopefully, the man will be curious enough to respond.

$♥$♥$♥$

Two weeks later, another doctor visit goes well with Sherri at my side, and still no TJ on my radar. Tonight, I get a brilliant idea. At least, I think it's brilliant, but I can't be sure because I swear this pregnancy brain thing is real. I'm lucky I haven't been fired. I got lost at work the other day simply by getting off the elevator on the wrong floor.

Anyway, I won't be at Bonvier, Inc., much longer. I was fortunate they would even hire me when I was already pregnant. But Mrs. Moxley thought my long resumé of job hopping and wide experience was totally an asset. And she and the CEO are fully on board with me taking a long maternity leave, even though I haven't been there anything close to a year. Someone will fill in for me, and my job will be there when I'm ready to go back. I can possibly see a career stretching out ahead of me.

What was I thinking about? I laugh at myself, with my attention span of a gnat and energy of a sloth. Sherri cooked and I cleaned. What I mean by that is I put the plates and silverware in the dishwasher and left the pan in the sink before sinking into a chair to yawn my head off. While she's out with Dan, I'm ready to go to bed after a bowl of chocolate pudding with sliced bananas, my latest obsession.

What was it? Oh yes, my brilliant idea to reach TJ. The Parisi Hotel. In the foggiest fog of my baffled brain, I recently recalled TJ mentioning Marcus Parisi was in real estate and found him his island home. What if I contact him and . . . *Then what?* Not wanting to forget again, I put a note in my phone.

The following morning, from my desk at work, I look up Marcus Parisi to see if his company is the same as his name. *Bingo*. It's in North Carolina. I wait until my first break of the morning and call.

"Parisi, Inc.," says a cheerful voice.

"May I speak with Mr. Parisi?" I ask, then lower my voice in case anyone is listening. "I'm calling from Jordan Asher's office."

"Hold, please."

My heart is thumping, and I'm damp down my back under my stretchy, soft sweater dress, not a very nice feeling. Playing with the chunky necklace I'm wearing that's supposed to make the rest of me look slimmer, I wait. The next voice that comes on is *not* Marcus Parisi's.

"Hi, I'm Robin LaPointe, assistant to Mr. Parisi. Can I help?"

She sounds nice, so I'll give it a try. "I'm . . ." I clear my throat, "I'm Brooke, Mr. Asher's assistant. Jordan Asher. Do you recall the island he bought through your company?"

"Sure, on St. Regnal."

I want to high-five someone, but I'm alone. "Yes, St. Regnal. Exactly. Lovely place." Now, how do I get off the call without raising her suspicion? "Would you know if they're having some cell phone issues? I can't seem to reach my boss."

Rolling my eyes at the stupidity of that question, I'm already typing "St. Regnal" into the search engine.

"You want *me* to tell you if they're having a problem?" the assistant asks incredulously. "Like what? A tropical storm? It wouldn't affect your boss anyway. He's got a satellite phone."

"Of course. Sorry, I'm off my game today. All month, really." Then I wince at how stupid I sound. "Anyhoodles, thanks for . . . the reminder."

"Of course," Robin says, sounding a little less friendly. "Brooke, what did you say your last name was?"

"Whoops, gotta go. Another call is coming in. Thanks again." I hang up and start reading the Wiki site about TJ's island home.

A small tropical island, St. Regnal has a centuries-old town at one end with all the modern conveniences and even a four-star hotel. And the other half is privately owned by an anonymous buyer as of two years ago. Bingo! I did it. Maybe I could have been an investigative reporter after all.

Smiling, infinitely pleased with myself, I stomp my ankle-booted feet under my desk. With a gasp, I jump up and rush to the nearby ladies' room because the baby got excited when I did. His or her head is bouncing on my bladder. I barely make it, but that's OK. I have found him!

"How does that help you?" Sherri asks me when we're sitting down to pasta later. "You still don't have a number, certainly not someone's satellite number." She opens her laptop and types, then shakes her head. "I searched his name on St. Regnal. I get nothing."

"I know. I tried that already." I'm shoving fusilli in my mouth at a fast pace, trying not to feel defeated and desperately wanting a glass of wine, which I've forsworn ever since the day I peed on a stick. "I thought I'd made a breakthrough, but this baby is going to come before I can contact him, isn't it?"

Sherri reaches over and covers my hand with hers. "It," she repeats, softly. An old joke between us, and I laugh, but soon my laughter turns into sobs. And through my tears, I say, "I should fly to St. Regnal."

"No," Sherri says. "No flying until *after* the baby comes. What if TJ's not there, and you're on a tropical island without a good hospital?"

"Of course they have a hospital. Don't they?"

We look it up, and they have a small one that doesn't handle major surgery, so Sherri deems it unacceptable. She also threatens to call my parents if I try to book a ticket. "Besides, I can't get away, and you can't go alone," she says, always looking out for me. "In fact, *you* can't get away without losing your job. And, Brooke, you're going to need the money and the health insurance, right?"

"I wouldn't if I could find the damn billionaire father." My mind goes over the possibilities yet again. "I could mail a letter to him care of St. Regnal."

"You could," she agrees, but her expression looks as doubtful as I feel. "What about his parents? You could try them again."

I groan. It was a disaster. I actually found a number that worked and spoke to his mother in Virginia. But I couldn't get myself to tell her I was carrying her son's baby. I gave her my name, though. Then I heard his dad tell his mom to hang up. "It's another blasted reporter. Tell her to leave us alone," he said. She hung up on me.

Sherri sighs. "You're going to have to be an adult, stay put, enjoy the upcoming baby shower, and trust in the universe."

Argh! That makes me want to rip my hair out.

"Sometimes the universe, like babies, needs a little push," I say, but I know she's right. I've tried and I've tried. Maybe when our kid is graduating from high school, I'll find TJ so he can come to the ceremony.

26

Jordan

Enough fucking signs, enough shooting stars crossing the sky over St. Regnal, and definitely enough of my cousin's wife reading my horoscope. Also, I've had plenty of people telling me that Brooke is trying to contact me, including Cy, my parents, which really pissed me off, and strangely of all, Marcus Parisi. It finally sinks in. This won't be over until I face her and tell her to leave me the hell alone.

When the last of my guests leave St. Regnal, I'm on my jet for a half-day's flight to Boston's Logan Airport. After I deplane, the mutts continue on to Maine. The whole way, including the limo ride, I'm fighting the ridiculous excitement of seeing Brooke again after all these months. The last emotion I should be feeling is anything close to happiness.

I should still be angry after her recklessness sent reporters to my parents' house and mobs to the Thirsty Moose. Not to mention the drones that circled Rangeley, searching for a house that matched the photo. With the old-growth trees, the drones didn't stand a chance.

But I'm not angry so much as wildly disconcerted that I could have been entirely taken in by a pretty face, a shapely body, and a perfect pair of tits. *TJ, that better be the last time you let your cock lead you.*

When the driver pulls up to Brooke's building, I'm about to head inside to her second-floor front door when I see a couple out of the corner of my eye. They've just turned the corner onto the tree-lined street. I stare because there's something familiar about the woman.

As they get closer, I realize two things—one, the woman in the oversized flannel shirt is very pregnant, and two, she's Brooke. Like I'm playing a fast-paced video game, I take in the entire scene. She's holding onto a man's arm, he's looking down, talking to her. The autumn leaves are crunching underfoot, a squirrel darts in front of them, Brooke gasps, looks up, sees me.

Holy hell! I'm all over the place. Admiration at how perfect she looks. Angry that this stranger is now *her* guy, enjoying the warmest, most yielding, sexy woman I've ever touched. Filled with wonder that this same woman is now carrying his child. And it's all clouded over with a thick haze of sheer jealousy that has no outlet.

"TJ," she calls out.

I stand here like a dope. Too late for anything except to offer her congratulations. Part of me wants to walk deliberately to the limo and drive off right when she comes close. But it's not like me to be a sore loser. Maybe because I'm not used to losing—not the game, nor the girl.

"TJ," she says again, just ten feet away. "You're here."

"Obviously," I say, then swallow the bitter tone. "I heard you wanted to talk to me." Now I wish I'd called her instead of this full-of-myself gesture of coming to see her in person, thinking she'd be so dazzled by my appearance. "I wish you hadn't involved my parents in this."

"In *this*?" she asks, sounding confused. Then the guy releases her arm, and she glances up at him like she'd forgotten his existence. Good. "This is Dan."

I don't give a shit, but I nod, giving him the look that any guy gives another who has the woman he wants. Dan starts to offer his hand, which surprises me because I'd like to break every bone in it. Maybe he finally notices my mood since he stops short.

"I can't believe you're here," she says.

I swear her soft tone makes me want to draw her to me and hold her in my arms. Right in front of Danny-boy. Although with the girth of her stomach, we couldn't get very close.

Taking in her thick, shiny hair, longer than before swinging past her shoulders, and her gorgeous bright eyes, I tell her the truth, "You look great."

Before she can respond, Brooke gasps again and clutches her large stomach.

"*Oh*, God," she says, looking down, which is when Dan and I both see her pumpkin-colored leggings are wet. "My water broke," she announces. "Isn't that a weird phrase? Maybe it's *waters*, but it's really amniotic fluid."

By her babbling, I think she's in shock. I don't know if I should make her lie down or carry her inside, but I need to do something.

"Should I call Sherri?" Dan asks, drawing his phone from his pocket. "She's got the birth plan."

Why wouldn't this man know his own baby's birth plan? What a tool! Why is Brooke staring at me with those big brown eyes, sending me a message?

"I tried to find you to tell you," she says softly.

To tell me what?

And then the penny drops, as my mother says. I examine Brooke, who's standing with her legs slightly apart to brace herself, still looking unflinchingly back at me. While I'm working out what's going on, she nods.

"Sweet Jesus," I mutter. "You're having *my* baby."

All she says is, "I'd like to sit down."

Since Dan is no longer touching her, but now in an animated conversation, I assume with Sherri, I rush forward and finally take Brooke's arm. "Do you want to go inside?"

"It's too early," she says.

Is there a problem with labor starting at four o'clock in the afternoon? "What do you mean, sweetheart?"

"The baby shouldn't come yet." She stumbles over the words.

Trying to stay calm, I say, "I'm not sure how these things work exactly, but I don't think the baby really plans these things. Maybe it's not coming yet."

"It," she repeats and starts to giggle.

I feel badly using that word. "Do you know the sex?"

"No." Then she frowns. "But once the sac breaks, then the baby has to come out. I think within forty-eight hours." She looks up at me, and I see fear in her chocolate-brown eyes. "TJ, the baby's three weeks early."

I don't hesitate, I sweep her up into my arms because she's still a little thing, even with baby weight. "Open the car door," I say to Dan, who hurries over and yanks open the back passenger side. I lower Brooke onto the seat.

"What hospital?" I ask, waiting to tell the driver.

"*Um* . . . Sorry, I'm . . ."

"Mass General," Dan says behind me. I close the door and get in the other side, even as Brooke opens the window and speaks to him. "Tell Sherri I'll meet her there."

"OK," he says, touching her hand. "You hang in there, superstar."

I think about what I'd want if she were my partner, and what Brooke probably wants, which is Dan. "You can come with us if you want," I offer magnanimously.

"No," he says, shocking the hell out of me until his hand moves up to Brooke's shoulder. With an encouraging nod and what I take to be a tender glance, he adds, "Sherri told me to get the hospital bag with all your things. I'll meet you guys there."

OK, he's being responsible. That makes sense, except if I were him, I'd get in the goddamned car to be with my woman, no matter whose baby she was carrying.

We speed off toward Mass General. This is not how I imagined our first meeting. In the car, she is alternately calm and then panicky, holding my hand.

"I can't believe you came. How did you know? Everything's going to be fine, right?" she asks, but she doesn't want any answer other than reassurance, which I can only fake. Because what do I know!

"For sure, you'll be fine. The baby will be fine. I'll be fine," I end on a joke.

She nods, looking down at her wet lap. And then she starts to squeeze my hand.

"You're doing great," I say. "Are you in pain?"

Brooke doesn't answer. She's simply breathing loudly, looking down, eyes closed, other hand on her stomach. After a minute, she leans her head back and opens her eyes.

"That was my first contraction. I guess the baby *is* coming. It must have been the shock."

What shock? Then I realize what—or rather, *who*—shocked her. *Fuck!*

"Are we almost there?" I ask the driver.

"Yes, sir," he says, at the same moment as he pulls into the emergency drop-off. I'm out of the car and rounding it in two seconds. When I go to scoop her up, she bats my hands away. "Don't lift me. Just get me out of this low vehicle."

"Give me your hands. Swing your feet out," I order. She does both, and I pull her to standing.

"Good?" I ask.

"Yes," she says tightly. "I can walk. At least until the next contraction."

By the time it happens, we've gone through registration. I'm following the nurse who's pushing Brooke in a wheelchair when she says, "Here comes another one."

In the elevator, going to the labor unit, Brooke is silent, dealing with what's going on inside her like a champ.

I'm about to become a father. *Hot damn!*

$♥$♥$♥$

I guess I thought it would be quicker. As I said, I don't know anything about this. Since I'm adopted, as was my sister, I have heard exactly zero birth stories. I certainly never asked my aunts or cousins to give details of their labor.

It's been five hours. The multiple medical personnel who've checked Brooke out seem unconcerned about the length of time or the baby's early delivery.

"Heartbeat is good," the most recent doctor says before he goes away.

"Sometimes, these sweet little buns bake for different lengths of time," an older nurse says. "And you parents are usually off with the date, give or take a week. Baby might be not as early as you think."

When she leaves, Brooke says, "Who knows which condom was faulty."

Whenever Brooke muses on which time we had sex producing this baby, Sherri pretends not to hear, as she's doing now. Although she checks in with us and is supposed to be the one rubbing Brooke's back and getting her whatever she wants, I'm here. So, she stays a few minutes, then wanders out to give us privacy.

She and Dan arrived together with the all-important bag that had—I'm not kidding—a framed photo of Mr. Busby as Brooke's focal point to stare at during contractions. The photo is now set up in front of her. She's determined to go drug free, and somehow, looking at her black demon of a cat is supposed to help.

When Dan and Sherri came in the first time and then left after a few minutes, I finally asked Brooke, "You and Dan.

How's that going?" Because I've already decided I'm going to fight for her.

Her eyes are wide, then she puffs out her cheeks and blows the air out, resting between contractions. "He's great," she says. "Handsome, solid, dependable."

I hate him.

"But you've got it wrong. It's *Sherri* and Dan."

Suddenly, I love Dan. He was helping my woman along the street when he's merely her cousin's boyfriend.

"A great guy," I say, agreeing with her. "Handsome, solid, dependable, and *not* involved with you."

Brooke laughs, which is a preferable sound to her grunts of pain. "How is it that you're here now?"

I hesitate. The last thing I want to do at this moment is berate her for loose lips. "Let's focus on getting this baby born."

Raising an eyebrow, she says, "Maybe distracting myself is my way of getting this baby born while in pain."

"I see. Right. OK. I've been on an island—"

"St. Regnal," she says.

"Yes, and thanks for not selling anyone that nugget." I meant it with gratitude, but she is immediately defensive.

"I didn't sell anyone *anything* about you."

She says it so calmly, as if the trueness of her words is irrefutable. "Your name was listed in the last article," I remind her. "It spoke about us, remember? In Boston."

She rolls her eyes. "Did Cy tell you I wanted to speak to you?"

"Yes. He said you had something for me."

She points at her stomach.

"*Oh*," is my brilliant response.

"Cy knew immediately that I was telling the truth about not having anything to do with either story," she says.

This is news to me. "How?"

"Because there's really only one motive. In fact, you just mentioned it. Selling for money."

It's so egregious, it makes me sick to think about it. "And?"

"Why would I throw away a billion if we'd stayed together as a couple for a few thousand from Boston Media Group?"

I think about that, and the logic smacks me in the face, the way Brooke once did, except much harder. I knee-jerked to the wrong conclusion, thinking the worst of anyone trying to get a story and sell it, because of what happened with Livvy.

"Cy's smart," I admit. "He's especially *people* smart, which is why he's great behind the bar."

She smiles, but it instantly becomes a grimace as she's gripped by another contraction. By this time, I know to let her squeeze my hand if she needs to, or if she jerks a thumb behind her, I rub her back with a tennis ball, which was also in her bag. I've noticed she doesn't speak at all during the contractions. Brooke closes her eyes and shuts herself off while dealing with whatever's happening inside.

$♥$♥$♥$

It's four in the morning, and the nurse tells us it's time. "Baby's head is crowning," which doesn't mean he or she is wearing a bejeweled crown as I've learned. It means we're all about to meet one another.

Brooke is exhausted. I am, too, but I don't even let myself think such a selfish thought, not after what she's been through. Entirely naked, as she has been for the past hour, she's squatting on the bed, leaning over a hand rail that's attached to the frame. She's fierce each time she bears down when told to push, even though her eyes have sought mine once or twice, looking defeated. That's when I do what Sherri told me to do.

"You got this. Look how far you've come, like ten whole centimeters." *Wait for the laugh that does not come.* But she makes an appreciative *ha* sound. I'll take that as a win.

"You're almost done. Two more pushes, max." The doctor frowns at me. "Maybe three, but the hard part is all behind you. Just breathe and look at Mr. Busby."

She raises her eyes to the black fiend. "OK, Brooke," the doctor says, "your partner is right, after all. Maybe just one more push when I tell you. Ready?" Brooke nods.

"Now push," the doctor says. "Slow, steady, great."

Brookes' entire frame goes from taut and strong to marshmallow fluff, and she starts to release the bar. I ease her back onto the bed as our baby takes its first breath and then cries. Tears flood my eyes. I still can't believe I'm here. I didn't miss it, but part of me is ruminating on how I nearly wasn't even on the same continent as the woman I love while she had our baby.

Brooke's staring between her own legs while the medical team examines our . . .

"You have a healthy girl. None the worse for an early entrance." And suddenly, gloved hands are holding her in our direction. Brooke gets a hold of our naked daughter and pulls her against her chest.

"Wow!" she says, transfixed by the dark peach fuzz on our baby's head and her blue eyes.

"Wow," I agree. Leaning over, maybe with the worst timing in the world, I claim Brooke's mouth under mine for our first kiss. But I simply need to kiss her, to show her how much I love her, and to impart how ecstatic I am in this miraculous moment.

As our lips fuse, pure tenderness fills me and overflows. I hope she can feel it, too.

When I raise my head, she stares up at me before nodding and returning her attention back to the newest member of the human race. Baby Girl Asher.

27

Brooke

Well, that was an exhilarating and utterly exhausting forty-eight hours. Not to mention unexpected. I mean, I knew I had a baby inside me, but I thought she was staying put for a few more weeks.

Yet here she is. And TJ is here, too. Double prizes, double miracles.

I want to stop time right now while everything is perfect. Close the book, stop the tape, keep the status quo. But all too soon, we're being shoved out of the womb of the hospital, with its helpful staff and plenty of diapers and free advice. We're on our own. Just me, TJ, the limo driver, and those awaiting us at home. Sherri and Dan, who went on ahead with all my old stuff and my new stuff, such as baby's first footprints and yet *another* guide on breastfeeding. Everything except baby herself.

She's in my arms as I leave by wheelchair, climbing directly into the back seat of a limo *after* TJ affixes the baby car seat. Who cares that it took him nearly ten minutes of swearing to get the base properly tight and unmoving to his and the nurse's satisfaction?

"Your daddy has got this," I tell our baby and the waiting driver, and then, we're finally on our way.

I don't even blink an eye at the luxury of the latest limo, but that may be because I'm scared shitless at how they're letting me take this brand-new baby out into the world. They don't even know if I'm competent. She's anchored and strapped in between us, eyes closed, doing what she has been doing ever since she came out of me, sleeping. And neither one of us is talking.

I haven't forgotten that TJ kissed me. On my lips. Not the best possible moment, considering I was a sweaty, exhausted mess, but life-altering nonetheless. It meant, I think, that we're going to give this thing between us an actual try.

Glancing over at him, he sends me a genuine smile. I can see a little fatigue around his eyes, since he never left my side in the hospital, sleeping on a reclining chair in the room that left his feet hanging off. Now, on this short ride, I have no idea what he's thinking, but it has to be weird for him since he went from zero to baby five minutes after seeing me.

Our new little family of three is going home to Sherri's and my condo. My parents, who came by the hospital this morning to take photos, *oohh* and *ahh* over their first grandchild, and meet TJ, offered me their spare room. That would not go over well with Sherri. Plus, no offense to them, but the condo feels like home.

My room, which isn't nearly as big as the guest room at TJ's Maine house, is all the private territory I can claim. Mr. Busby, on the other hand, claims whatever and wherever the hell he wants, which is evident as soon as we walk in. As I open the door, before Sherri can get to me for a hug, he greets me with yowls and meows, annoyed at my absence.

The baby isn't in my arms because TJ is carrying her in the car seat, so Mr. Busby jumps from the floor, pushes off of my leg and comes flying up toward my chest. I catch him as I always do. That's how he claims me every time I come home.

"Show him our baby," I say to TJ.

"What? Really?" He looks doubtful.

"Just like you'd introduce a new pack member to your dogs," I remind him. "I'll hold him. It'll be fine."

Mr. Busby sniffs Baby all over her head, with TJ ready to whip the car seat out of reach if necessary. And then he's done, ready to spring out of my arms. "I think they'll be great friends," I say confidently, making Dan laugh.

"If not, that baby is outta here." And he jerks his thumb.

Sherri elbows him in the gut, but I thought it was kind of funny.

"Now what?" TJ asks.

"Good question," I say. "I guess she can stay in her seat as long as she's asleep, right?"

"Never wake a sleeping baby," Sherri chimes in with the old adage. "But when she's ready for bed, Dan put the crib together as promised."

"No!" I exclaim. "What a hero," I say to Sherri's excellent guy. I hope the two of them stick because he's the best boyfriend she's ever had.

"Freshly washed mattress pad and fitted sheet are on the mattress, bumper tied to the railing, all set," my cousin tells me.

"I have to go see." TJ is still holding the car seat. "Put her on the coffee table," I suggest.

He frowns. "Do you think that's safe? What if she rocks and falls off?"

Sherri laughs. "Then Brooke has given birth to Wonder Woman, and we'll be searching for her golden lasso." Finally, we go in for a big hug. "She's here!" we say together, before staring at Baby.

Then we head into my bedroom, which looks even smaller with my bed pushed against one wall and the crib to the right of the doorway.

"It's cozy and perfect," I say. "Thank you. Sorry about having to share coaching duty during delivery." Not that I'm sorry TJ came, but Sherri had put in a lot of hours.

"Not a problem," she says. We eye one another. "Is he back to stay?"

"Here?" I gesture around the room. "I don't think his stuff will fit." My little joke falls flat, but I don't know what's going to happen. Running my hand over the taut sheet, I feel my rounded belly with my other hand. Greatly diminished, but still a post-partum bulge. "It is really weird that she's not inside me any longer."

"Easier to buy her first pair of shoes this way," Sherri says, making me laugh. "She doesn't have to stick a foot out."

"Wasn't worried about that."

"You'll have your killer bod back in no time," she promises.

"Also, not a worry," I say. "As to your question, TJ and I haven't discussed the future. We've barely spoken about anything, although I think he believes me that I didn't sell him out."

"About time."

"Brooke," comes TJ's flustered voice. "She's awake!"

"I think I'm going to be hearing that a lot." We hurry out into the living room.

$♥$♥$♥$

It's like I'm back in college when, on rare occasions, my roommate and I both had guys spend the night. Sherri and Dan are sequestered in her room, and I can faintly hear her TV. Without discussing it, TJ came with me into my bedroom, and we closed the door on the world.

Obviously, sex is out. We're lying here, listening for the smallest peep from our daughter, while holding hands in the dark. I should instantly fall asleep, but I'm overly excited by all the newness around me. By a daughter in the crib and by this man in my bed.

"I'm glad to be back here with you," TJ says. "I missed the hell out of you."

"Me, too." Something's been bothering me, and I get it off my chest. "I'm sorry I called your parents. Your mother sounded freaked, and your dad got seriously annoyed. I was getting desperate to reach you."

"No, I'm sorry. I shouldn't have freaked. Obviously, I overreacted." I feel him shrug in the darkness. "I thought they'd followed orders and gotten an unlisted number."

"They probably did after a crazy woman called begging them for their son's contact info."

"Talking to Marcus's assistant was really clever," TJ says, making me smile.

"I didn't know it would lead to him calling you."

"When I heard I had an assistant named Brooke, it was the last straw. That and Cy telling me you had something important to give me. I couldn't ignore you any longer." He leans over and strokes my cheek, then with his fingers under my chin, he turns me to face him. "I can never apologize enough."

"Sure you can," I say cheerfully. "You can start by doing all the diapers for the remainder of our daughter's babyhood."

When he starts to laugh loudly, I clamp a hand over his mouth.

"Sorry," he mutters against my palm, and the tickling heat is an instant turn-on. If only there wasn't about six weeks of celibacy ahead of me. But I have stitches and other healing to do, so I remove my hand.

"What happens next?" I ask, because I need to know what his reappearance means.

"I don't know exactly. I wasn't expecting to become a father yesterday. I guess we should move in together and raise our daughter. We can start looking for a house, or ask Marcus Parisi to find us one. Do you want to stay in this area?"

I'm flabbergasted by how easy he makes it sound. "Why would *I* get to choose where we live?"

"I can work from anywhere. Do you intend to keep your job?"

My next question should be, *do I need to keep it?* But I merely say, "I like my job, but I'd rather be home with our baby." Is that clear enough? "My parents are here, and Sherri, of course. On the other hand, your parents are in Virginia, and I assume you have other family."

"We can have more than one house," he says matter-of-factly, like he's talking about another pair of pants or a spare sweater. "I want to keep my house in Maine, but Boston seems as good a city as any. I haven't seen much yet, but I had a great tour guide who I hope will show me more."

With that sweet comment, we roll onto our sides, facing one another.

"May I kiss you?"

"Yes, please."

TJ slides his free hand into my hair, cradling my head as he leans forward. When his lips touch mine, firm and warm, fitting my mouth perfectly, it's the single most intimate act of my entire life. I guess that's why fuck buddies don't necessarily kiss and why we waited.

His soul is expressed in this kiss. Dare I say, his heart is, too, as I learn the meaning of *tender*. I give everything I have and everything I am back to him. Tilting my head, I part my lips. At my invitation, the tip of his tongue licks along my upper lip, then glides inside. I swirl around it with my own, and he moans.

In the next instant, he's sucking my tongue, and I am desperately wishing intercourse was on the table. But as I stroke my fingers down the front of his chest, thinking of going all the way down to touch his arousal, he stops me with a hand over the top of mine.

Breaking our kiss, drawing back, he says, "I don't think that's a good idea. In fact, the nurse took me aside, you know which one I mean. She'll hunt me down if I so much as grind against you for the first month."

"I don't think that's what she said," I counter. "I think there are things we can do, or at least that *I* can do for you."

"You're a crazy lady," he says, but TJ's smiling in the dark. "I just wanted to kiss you. Nothing else. That was perfectly satisfying."

"Liar," I whisper and free my hand to squeeze his erection with my fingers.

He groans. "Stop it. I'm no saint, but *only* kissing is happening for a while."

"Fine." I pull back, but I admire the hell out of him. Relieved, too. Sore as I am and weary, it would've been hard to put my money where my mouth is. Or my mouth where my hand was.

"Have you picked out a name?" he asks.

"Sherri said it was bad luck, along with telling anyone I was pregnant before the second trimester. And buying any infant clothes before the baby's birth was a no-no, although the superstition doesn't apply to gifts. She also wouldn't let me eat anything ice cold."

"Not even ice?" he asks.

"No."

"Ice cream?" he persists, making me smile.

"I had to let it get melty."

He nods like it all makes sense. "That's a lot of potential bad luck. Glad you avoided it," he says. Then he clears his throat. "Brooke, do you want to bounce some names around now? I mean, can I help?"

I don't like this timid TJ, acting a bit as if he's walking on eggshells. "Of course you can. She's half yours. Besides it'll be a hell of a lot easier now that we know she's a girl."

"I guess so," he says, still sounding too serious. "Do you have any family names you want to honor?"

My hearts twinges for him, thinking of his adoptive parents losing their daughter. Right now, with new life sleeping a couple feet away, I can begin to imagine the devastation and the strength it must have taken for them to carry on rather than go insane with grief. That's why, although something too far out like Tiberia is not going to happen, I do have an idea.

"I like the sound of Olivia Asher," I say. "Both for the *olive branch of peace* idea and the echo of your sister's name." When he's silent, I add, "Unless her last name is going to be known as Danbury, but I think Olivia goes well with either."

"Thank you," he says quietly, then adds, "It's perfect. Also, when I filled out the paperwork while you were busy learning to burp her, I wrote her last name as Asher. It never occurred to me to do otherwise."

His presumption doesn't bother me. I'm thrilled he's giving her his name. He never even asked for a DNA test. "We still have nine days to complete that form with her first name."

"I think we got it in one day."

I nod, just as our daughter starts to fuss. "Well, Olivia, welcome to the family." I get out of bed. "Let's see what isn't perfect in your world."

As it turns out, we have a pretty easy night. TJ and I get a lot of sleep, as does Olivia. I also stick her on my breast every once in a while, even though not much is happening yet in that department. TJ was very interested in that procedure! I'm simply trying not to worry that she'll starve to death before my milk comes in.

Over coffee the next morning, TJ texts Marcus about finding us a house.

"You don't think that's premature?" I ask, even though I want to build a life with him. It's just we're doing things in such a weird order compared with how it went with Juan.

"Not too premature," he says. "After all, our baby is already here, and you don't have room to swing a cat in your bedroom." He looks at Mr. Busby on my lap. "No offense."

Sherri comes out of her room during my wavering and debating, which is mostly with myself, while TJ sits back and listens.

"Why don't you two take a walk?" she suggests.

"Olivia shouldn't go outside yet. I don't think."

"Olivia," Sherri repeats, then claps her hands together. "Nice! I'll watch her and you two can get some fresh fall air."

I start to protest. "Relax," my cousin insists. "She's the easiest she'll ever be. Not eating, not pooping. Let Aunt Sherri pretend for half an hour."

"Technically, you're second cousins, but OK." I let our pretend nanny shoo us out the door because hospital air and then condo air have left me depleted. Oddly, the first thing we discuss is how TJ is now on Team Dan.

"Seems like a nice guy, and he's obviously into Sherri."

"Agreed," I say, still feeling like I'm impersonating someone else by holding his hand as we walk along Bowker Street. Am I his girlfriend? His fiancée? Merely the mother of his child, and the woman who can't wait to have sex with him again?

"Almost as much as I'm into you," TJ adds, chasing away my doubts.

My heart flips. Now we're getting somewhere. Because it's weird sharing a child and talking about moving in with someone whom I've only just kissed for the first time. Not to mention how he thought I had betrayed him on an epic scale, up until a couple days ago.

"Maybe as much as I'm into you," I respond, and he squeezes my hand. I'm looking forward to getting to know him better once we're living in the same house. "So, what's the plan?"

A car screeches to a halt beside us. Without hesitation, TJ pushes me behind his body with a sweep of his arm.

"Jordan Asher?" asks a small man with a mustache and a baseball cap, even while he's already snapping photos with a big old-fashioned camera. He doesn't seem particularly threatening though, more distasteful than anything.

Is this guy what I represented by going up to Maine?

"Get out of our way," TJ says.

"Are you Brooke Danbury?"

I don't answer, but I peek around TJ in time to get my photo taken.

"Looks like you're going to have a baby," the reporter adds.

Now that pisses me off. I'm still round but nothing like a pregnant woman.

"Jordan, is it yours?" the guy persists when we both stay silent. "Are you going to deny your own baby?"

"I asked you to move out of our way." I can feel TJ's tension like a forcefield around him. And then, to my shock, he reaches under his leather jacket and withdraws a gun.

"Whoa!" The reporter says. He's so stunned, he doesn't even take a photo.

"I consider you to be aggressive," TJ tells him, "That's why I'm going to shoot you in the leg in self-defense, which this lady behind me will testify to."

The words are hardly out before the reporter is diving for his car, crouching low, and getting in. My mouth is still open when he peels away at breakneck speed.

"Are you all right?" TJ asks, slipping the gun back into the concealed holster.

I shake off my frozen stupor. "Where did that gun come from?"

He shrugs, which that tells me nothing. "Was it in bed with us last night?" I demand.

"Of course not," he scoffs.

"What about in the hospital?"

"Nope."

"What if Olivia gets her hands on it?"

"Are we discussing Wonder Woman again?" he asks. "Because if that baby who can't even open her eyes for more than thirty seconds manages to fire this handgun, then I'll let her protect us. Look, I'm not going to apologize for wanting to keep you safe."

I think about A-lister celebs and their bodyguards. It figures that TJ would want to do the guarding himself. After all, his games are all about hand-eye coordination. Sherri can catch a bar of soap as it falls or snatch a clementine out of thin air, even when I toss it to her left hand.

"I bet you're a crack shot," I muse.

He nods, looking grim. "Let's just say I could've predicted which of his leg bones I would shatter."

Yikes! Not for a minute did I ever consider that I would be affected by this world of paparazzi and those desperate to make money off a photo. I doubt that guy will ever return. Maybe it will blow over. After all, TJ is now old news.

"I don't understand why photos are such a big deal. They're pretty benign."

"Tell that to Princess Diana and my sister."

The implication is clear. "Did Livvy die because of a reporter?"

His mouth is a straight, tense line. He nods.

Shit! "You should have told me," I say softly. "I'm really sorry." Then, because we've reached the neighborhood park and because I'm sore and already tired, I sit on the same bench from months ago. But he doesn't join me. He's pacing back and forth in front of me, and I can tell his thoughts are going a mile a minute.

"Do you want to tell me what happened?"

When his expression becomes guarded, I add, "Since I'm now in the middle of this situation as mother of your child?"

His gray-green eyes lock on mine. TJ doesn't look like a happy man who just discovered he's in love with the woman who gave birth to his baby.

"I'd already been propelled into the stratosphere of famous people and was getting ready to move, since I no longer needed my Silicon Valley job. She came to visit me in San Jose after her birthday. I'd given her the Miata. Had it delivered to her door, and it had felt damn good to buy her whatever she wanted."

"You don't have to say more," I tell him.

"I need you to understand why I'm over-the-top furious when these scumbags think they can approach and take what they want. Livvy and I came out of a restaurant, and the paparazzi were there. Naturally, they thought she was my date. Suddenly, because of my money, despite being a geeky tech-guy, I was news and so was the woman I was with. At the time, naïve to how reporters work, I thought the best thing to do was separate and sent her back to my place in my car. It never occurred to me some assholes would follow my sister. I'd bought myself a convertible Audi. When they gave chase, she drove it too fast. Rounding a curve, she lost control and was ejected. She died on impact."

I cannot help gasping. I want to hug him, but he's still pacing. I know his pain is old and my comforting him now will do little. Maybe more for me than for him. Still, I'm wringing my hands when he finishes.

"I moved immediately. Went to her place in Houston, where she was practicing law, and drove her Miata across the country to Maine."

We remain silent for a few minutes. Then I get up, deciding walking side-by-side will help. TJ falls in beside me, remaining silent, obviously ruminating and lost in the past. I need to bring him back to me, so I try for normalcy.

"I'm willing to see what Mr. Parisi has to show us. It would be great to live within a half hour of my parents. I'm glad you got to meet them yesterday."

"They didn't hold it against me for knocking up their daughter," TJ says, but his stiffness belies any levity.

"I'm pretty sure they realize I could have done a lot worse." I wrap my hands around his muscular arm like a stage-four clinger and lean my head on his shoulder. Despite what just happened, including the reporter and TJ's gun, I'm looking forward to blending my life with his.

We take a few more steps, with TJ glancing over at each car that goes by. Finally, he asks, "How are your parents going to react when we aren't living together?"

Come again! I stop in my tracks again. "I thought we were going to look at a house for all three of us."

"I'm sorry, Brooke. After what just happened, I can't put you and Olivia in danger by living with you."

28

Jordan

I'm jerking Brooke around, not intentionally, but she isn't thinking straight. What if we'd had Olivia with us? What if I hadn't had a gun and that asshole refused to move?

In both scenarios, my mind goes to the worst that could happen, which is a blessing when designing multiplayer, choose-your-own-adventure games, but a nightmare when it's everyday life. Especially when nothing bad happened while my adrenaline is still spiked and ready to fight.

"Are you messing with my head because of that reporter?" she asks, her tone is one of confusion.

"I'm not trying to mess with any part of you. But it's clear that you'll need a house bigger than your room at Sherri's to raise our daughter." I run my hand through my hair, thinking aloud. "I guess I'll need a house, too, when I come to—"

"To what? To visit? Is that what you're planning, to be an absentee dad? How will that help?"

I pivot and start walking back toward her condo. I need to get away from Brooke and Olivia in order to keep them safe, and I want them to move as soon as possible because the press is onto this place. They need a house that already has an alarm system or that I can easily secure.

To that end, I text Marcus that it's become urgent, then I say to Brooke, "I hope Marcus will have something to show us by tomorrow."

"Forget it," she says. "If I'm raising Olivia by myself, I'm not doing it rattling around alone in a big house. I'll stay with Sherri."

"You don't have to work," I promise her. "And I'll hire you a nanny. Plus, we're going to install state-of-the art security and alarms."

She grabs my arm and stops me. "You want me to live in a prison that I don't leave even for work, with a stranger as our daughter's caregiver?"

It sounds ridiculous when she puts it like that.

"And what will you be doing?" she demands. "Will I be able to reach you, or will your number be unavailable to me again?"

"Of course you'll be able to reach me, every second of every day."

I know there's a lot more to unpack in what she said, but I just want to get Brooke indoors where it's safe.

"You know what, TJ," she says. "I'm starting to think that you're a commitment-phobe as much as anything else. I think the person you really want to protect is yourself." And she slams past me, heading for her brownstone with long, determined strides.

It's not true. At least, only peripherally. I would protect her and Olivia with my life. But if anything happened to either of them, just because we dared to be in public and in the path of some reckless paparazzi hunting for a photo, then it would destroy me. So, I guess protecting them is, in fact, protecting myself and my sanity, too.

Moreover, if Brooke can't see the danger that being attached to me causes, especially to our daughter, then that's on her. I'm going to proceed as if we're in agreement. New home, macked-out security, and what I haven't mentioned to her yet, a round-the-clock bodyguard. If Livvy had been protected, she'd be alive.

$♥$♥$♥$

My God, is this woman stubborn! I'm back at the Parisi Hotel, and Brooke just hung up on me for the third time. Sherri is the only one who may be able to get through to her. When we returned to the condo and explained what happened, Brooke's cousin was shocked.

"I think it was a good thing you weren't alone," she said to Brooke, "and especially not just you and the baby."

Brooke rolled her cocoa-brown eyes. "If I'd been alone, the reporter probably wouldn't have even known who I was or approached me," she fumed. "I certainly wouldn't have needed a gun."

"Bingo," I said softly. That's the instant she realized what I'd already figured out, that we can't be together for safety's sake. But she wasn't going to admit it.

"Don't look at me like that," she stormed at me. "There aren't reporters behind every bush."

"He took your photo, and he knew your name. You were seen with the world's 'most eligible bachelor billionaire.' Someone at the hospital is going to talk about you having a baby, and the records will show she's mine. And while that jerk today didn't know about Olivia, it's just a matter of time."

I picked up anything I'd left in the bedroom, kissed Olivia on her forehead, and left. Now, a day later, I have two houses to look at, but the infernal woman won't go see them. Absolutely refuses.

I dial Sherri's number. "Hi, it's TJ."

"I'm not supposed to be speaking to the enemy," she quips, making me sigh.

"You know I'm not the enemy."

"What can I do you for?"

"Get Brooke to agree to move into a house with security."

This time she sighs. "I honestly don't think that our condo is a problem, so you're on your own there."

"What happens when you move in with Dan? Will Brooke come too?"

A long pause, then, "I don't know if or when that will happen. But I guess we can cross that bridge when we come to it."

Don't either of these females have any imagination? Obviously not enough for self-preservation. "How will you feel if some psycho breaks in and kidnaps Brooke or Olivia?"

"What?" she exclaims. "When did this go from paparazzi to kidnappers?"

"It could happen. For years, no one knew where I was, but I've already had a couple fake extortion threats recently."

"Fake?"

"No one has my number, so they call the bar or my parents' house before my dad dropped their old number. The message was always simple: pay up or someone gets hurt. And the message had to be passed on to me by someone I care about."

"I'm so very sorry." Sherri sounds stunned and sad. Then she adds, "But you said they were fake."

Obviously, she can't see me shrug. "No one has been hurt. My parents have a security system and an unlisted number. The bar is no longer mine, and whenever someone calls asking for me, every employee laughs it off and says I'm long gone and hangs up before a threat can even be made.

"I can see why you're paranoid."

"I promise you I'm not paranoid. Merely cautious. But I can't stand by while Brooke refuses to use common sense. She lives in a place that has a wide-open door from the street and easy access to your second-floor condo with no other means of egress."

"We have a fire escape," Sherri says.

"I feel so much better knowing that Brooke can escape out a window with Olivia on her back as she climbs down a flight of rusty iron rungs."

"Point taken."

"Will you help me?"

"I'll try."

"I know you're at work, but I'd appreciate it if you could call her now. There are two properties for us to see."

Another huge sigh. "You're going to get me removed from the best-friend spot."

"Good thing you're family, then. She can't change that."

Miraculously, five minutes later, thanks to Sherri, Brooke calls. "You can pick us up, me and our baby. We'll be the ones wearing full-body armor and tinfoil hats."

"Don't joke," I say.

"If I don't, I'll be crying."

Fair enough. I pick her up fast in a rental BMW before she can change her mind, and we go to the first house where someone from Marcus's company will meet us. As we pull up to a hulking house with a secure concrete enclosure, Brooke says, "Nope. No way."

"We haven't even seen inside."

"It has a fu—" she cuts herself off and glances at Olivia. "An effing ten-foot wall in front of it. It's worse than I imagined. Next."

"Let's go inside and then you can say no." We do, with me carrying Olivia in her car seat. I admit the place is ugly, but it's built like a fort. We make it as far as the dark front hall, with the wall outside blocking most of the natural light from the first floor. Brooke does say no as soon as she sees the Realtor.

"Hi, I'm Craig."

"Thanks, Craig, but no thanks." Then she looks at me. "I'm getting out before lockdown happens. I'll wait for you in the car. I hope the guards release you for good behavior."

The Realtor's eyes are huge. "I hope the next house is a little more welcoming," I tell him, and the man nods.

Having hooked the car seat in again, I remind Brooke that this is because we're looking so close to the city. If we go out to the suburbs, then we'll find a little more space between a secure fence and the house. Also, more land overall.

"Whatever," she says, watching out the window like a sullen child.

Brooke has dark circles under her eyes, and I wonder if Olivia woke up a lot in the night. When I ask, she says, "I'm not going to give you a blow-by-blow every night for the rest of our lives. If you want to know how she's doing, then sleep next to her. You and your gun."

"You're being really difficult, and I only want to help."

"Help this," she says and flips me the bird.

"Really? Is that how you're going to behave?"

"What are you going to do about it? Paddle me?"

I get an immediate hard-on because our sex was the best I've ever had, and because I've been celibate for nine months. The look on my face must be of a sorry hound dog.

"Never again," she snaps, still talking to the view out her window. "Think. Of. That!" Finally, she turns to me. "How are you going to feel when I meet a great guy like Dan, dependable and available, and we shack up? How will you and your little gun fit in then?"

My little gun? "Brooke, I am not rejecting you."

She sticks her palm out in a classic nineties talk-to-the-hand gesture and glances away again. I grab hold of it. "Look at me."

Brooke sighs and turns to face me. I very much wish I could turn her over my lap and spank her. We'd both enjoy it. But she's still sore in her lower region. Instead, I try to keep a clear head.

"Can we take this one step at a time? I'm not going to form an attachment to anyone else, because there's no one I want more than you. Plus, I'd be bringing all the same problems with me."

She wrinkles her nose, considering my honesty, I guess. "There's no one I want more than you." Her voice is soft and thoughtful.

That's good to hear, and I'm processing it when she adds, "But, I'm not staying alone the rest of my life. You've basically said being together is impossible. I'm going to try my hardest to put up some defenses against lo . . . against *liking* you anymore than I already do. I also don't want to be nice right now, OK?"

Not OK, but she makes all valid points. Still, I don't release her hand. I set it on my leg and hold on while I drive us to the next house. The fence is practically invisible, with slender iron pickets and decorative spires on the posts. The gate opens for us. We pull onto a short semicircular drive, going all the way around the half-circle until we're facing the street again, leaving room for the Realtor.

The plot of land is not palatial by any means, but there is a small front lawn on either side of the driveway, and it's large by urban-living standards. Despite the Victorian-looking fence, the house appears modern although not sterile. I think it's inviting, minimal, clean. If Brooke likes something antiquated, however, then this won't suit her. I should know what she likes and am ashamed that I don't.

The Realtor's car pulls up behind ours, and Craig hops out. "A better first impression?" he asks.

"For me, it is."

Brooke is silent, eyes wide, taking it all in. I think that's a good sign.

"Obviously, this house is polar opposite," Craig says. "The other one had some good points, but it relied on old-fashioned security, like—"

"Ugly fortress walls," Brooke chimes in.

"Right. Despite the wrought-iron fence, this one is all futuristic. It's been totally redone as a smart house with integrated, invisible top-of-the-line surveillance equipment, biometric pads at all entry points, and AI-assisted lighting, and remote-controlled CCTV cameras with infrared sensors and thermal imaging. There are alarm sensors at all doors and windows, a biometric gun safe with rapid release, interior audio-enabled cameras, and a front gate with more cameras and digital keypad access."

"Why did the gate open for us?" I ask.

"I could see you from a block back and opened it."

"That's powerful," I say, impressed already.

"No offense while you two play James Bond," Brooke quips, sounding snarky, "but I want a house that feels like a home. May we see inside?"

Craig and I exchange a glance. I know he's thinking I have a bitchy wife or girlfriend. But he's not my problem. Satisfying Brooke is my only priority. As we walk through the foyer and into the living room, with me carrying the unwieldy car seat, she touches a wall, moves farther inside and looks at the view of the back garden. Next, she exclaims over the gourmet kitchen and gives me a quick glance when we discover a pool and hot tub. The pool starts indoors and then continues outside under an arch.

I can tell by Brooke's relaxed demeanor while we tour the generous-sized rooms that she likes it, or at least doesn't hate it. Craig knows when to stay silent and even leaves us alone. Marcus has a good salesman in this guy. It's me who asks her a little too eagerly, "What do you think?"

Brooke is studying the detailed blue-and-white tiling in the master bathroom. She turns abruptly and walks past me. But I hear her words over her shoulder, "This one is fine for me and Olivia."

Even though that's the situation I wanted her to accept, I feel a tightening in my chest, let down, shut out, wishing I had taken more time to figure this out before announcing how it had to be.

"We'll take it," I tell Craig. Multimillion-dollar house chosen. What's next on the agenda?

"My parents are arriving in two hours. Will you come with me to pick them up?" I ask Brooke. "They couldn't wait any longer to see their granddaughter."

Her expression momentarily softens, then she shakes her head.

"I look forward to meeting them, but I'm not going to the airport with you. That'll send them the wrong message about us. Plus, think of the danger to me and Olivia, riding in the same car. Bring them by the condo any time this afternoon."

When I drop them off, Brooke won't let me carry the car seat or walk them indoors. Stubborn lady. But I'll do anything to keep them safe, even lose the woman I love.

29

Brooke

Living in a mansion, in Brookline, only twenty minutes from Sherri and a half hour from my parents, I should be the happiest Cinderella in the world. Enjoying a modern-day fairy-tale, except *without* the prince. But hey, the rest of the story all checks out, since I now have a lifestyle any woman could only dream of.

And Mr. Busby loves racing around the big space like he's found his second kittenhood.

I didn't wait for my maternity leave to be over before making my decision. Taking Olivia with me to Bonvier, Inc., yesterday—in a limo—I introduced my sweet daughter to my kind boss and explained how my situation had changed.

"I won't be coming back."

Mrs. Moxley was so understanding, she made my eyes water. "I would do the same thing," she said. "In fact, I did. I interrupted my career to raise two boys, and now I'm working because I love it. Wouldn't have done it any other way."

Previously, we've talked a lot about business, this company, the world in general, but I decide to be nosy, having never asked her personal questions. In my defense, I had a human growing inside me the whole time I worked for her, and that tends to keep you in your own little world. "Is there a Mr. Moxley?"

Her smile tells me the answer. "Mr. Moxley—Peter—is living his best life, too. He's a painter. That's how we met, in art school. But I went into the business side while he was in fine art. By the time I get home, he's ready for my company. We cook together, go to plays, visit our boys and their families. We're having a great time."

"Sounds wonderful," I say. But I'm even more doubtful of my own happy ending unless I cut TJ out of my life. I don't want to be the single mother who watches my daughter gravitate toward her friends' homes for warmth and joyful noise. And later, her in-laws will think I'm strange, too. A love-and-sex-starved spinster who's taken care of by an absentee billionaire. I feel ready to cry.

"Brooke," Mrs. Moxley says, still rocking a sleeping Olivia gently in her arms, with all the experience of a three-time grandmother. "You look like you've seen a ghost."

"The ghost of my future," I mutter.

"Are we talking Charles Dickens?"

I shrug. "Olivia's father and I are not together."

She frowns. "That's a shame."

"But I love him." I state the truth because it feels so good to say it out loud.

"Then that's a tragedy. Is it irreconcilable?"

"He's a billionaire."

"How dreadful," she quips. Then Mrs. Moxley smiles. "I'm teasing. I know who the father is. Everyone knows, Brooke. You and Mr. Asher have made a gorgeous little girl."

Everyone knows. I've been coming to terms with that fact for two weeks, ever since a story came out that the bachelor gaming billionaire might not only be off the market but is a doting new father. There were photos of him carrying Olivia in her car seat as I moved out of Sherri's condo, although we never saw the photographer.

And the world didn't shatter during or after the two-day media circus. I remained holed up in my new house with our baby and my parents who stayed over, while TJ kept away. The public interest blew over. After all, someone having a baby isn't that noteworthy. No harm, no foul.

"I'll let you get back to work," I say. "How's your new assistant?"

"Much less pregnant than you were," she says and settles Olivia in her car seat. "You were very capable with every task I gave you, by the way, although I doubted I'd be keeping you after this little cherub arrived."

While she walks with me to the bank of elevators, she adds, "As long as neither you nor your billionaire has given your heart to someone else, I see no reason why you can't use your capable brain with its psychological training to figure out the emotional issues keeping you from being together."

She leans in to kiss my cheek. "I was going to say 'keep me posted,' but I suppose I'll hear about how it all turns out on the evening news."

On the way home, naturally, I become fired up. What the hell is wrong with me? I have the stick-to-itiveness to work my way through a bunch of *ugh* jobs. If I can drive up to Maine and, against all odds, find a grumpy billionaire recluse, then I can damn sure make TJ come to his senses.

As long as he hasn't given his heart to someone else, which I know he hasn't. The actual caveat is determining whether my billionaire has, in fact, given his heart to *me.* Quite plainly, does TJ love me enough that he can't live without me?

Only one way to find out.

$♥$♥$♥$

I'm jittery as Mr. Busby when he walks around the edge of the pool. One slip and he's a mad, wet cat. One slip, in my case, and I may push TJ away forever. This evening, he's standing in my living room, with the fire crackling behind him, and I wonder how to begin.

After watching him drive up on the motion-activated camera—no limo tonight—I opened the gate and disarmed the front door. Sometimes, the amazing security system feels like overkill, but when I'm alone at night, my mind is at ease. As usual, I made TJ remove his shoes at the entrance, and now his feet are sinking into the high-pile carpet, anchored by a cream-colored, overstuffed sofa and two fawn-colored chairs. I bucked the continuing trend of gray and white for a relaxed, warmer vibe.

"It always reminds me of Rangeley," he says.

I hope he means it makes him feel content and at home. He's here for dinner because I lied, plain and simple. After assuring him that Olivia was totally fine, I told him there was a serious problem that we could only discuss in person.

We go first into the nursery, where she sleeps during the day with the monitor trained on her sweet self. At night, she has another crib right beside my bed. Silently, we do that age-old parent thing: stare at our offspring with awe. Mr. Busby has a favorite spot in here on the cushioned recliner that also rocks and swivels. He and TJ lock gazes for a moment, appraising one another before we tiptoe out to the living room again.

"I'm sure she'll be awake soon," I say, "probably the minute I serve dinner."

Since my parents left, I mostly eat on the sofa, with the TV on for company and Mr. Busby nearby. Tonight, I laid the dining room table and hope it's not the only thing getting laid. Having cooked my version of a gourmet meal, lamb curry with carrots and potatoes, I aim to impress him. My first time cooking for TJ, frankly, I'm a little nervous.

"Smells great," he says.

"That's either our dinner or those outrageously expensive tall candles on the mantel."

This feels so strange, like a first date. It's been ages since we were in-person face-to-face alone. Whenever he's been over before, my parents or Sherri and Dan were here. And while we were still figuring out how this would work, he had an urgent call from an old boss in Silicon Valley. Some things have to be hands-on apparently, not just computers but people, and I intend tonight to be the night.

While he worked magic on some mainframe in San Jose, Olivia grew out of her newborn clothes, my stitches healed, and I decided to fight for my man. We video-chatted whenever the time difference allowed so he could see his daughter. During those brief interactions, I remained happy, relaxed, and independent. I didn't ask him details of his life, and I occasionally closed the chat before *he* was ready.

I may've played dirty by wearing a skimpy tank top and no bra a few times. After all, it was bedtime for me on the East Coast. As soon as his handsome face disappeared, I'd put on my snuggly flannel jammies. My nipples were always pearled because I was so damn cold.

Playing it cool seems to have done the trick. He flew back to the East Coast last night, a private, red-eye jet ride, and here he is, unable to keep his eyes off me.

"Red wine?" I offer, sashaying away from him toward the kitchen, knowing his eyes are on my ass.

"Whatever you're having," he says.

I turn. Yup, eyes on my caboose in black jeans, topped with a pumpkin-orange sweater.

"Apple cider because I'm nursing," I remind him.

He nods, his gaze fixing on my breasts. "I'll have the milk." His eyes widen, realizing what word just came out of his mouth. "I mean the cider, of course. No, make it red wine, after all. Thanks."

I have the wicked notion that he'd like to give my nipples a quick suck, but I'm saving every drop for Olivia.

"She's starting to look like you," he says once he's seated on the sofa.

Personally, I don't see it. If anything, she reminds me of TJ, but all I say is, "Perfect as usual."

"Still no nanny needed?"

"Nor wanted. Absolutely not, but the housekeeper you hired has been much appreciated." I nearly turned her away when TJ sent her to my door a day after I moved in. My mother practically shoved me aside to welcome Naomi.

"You'll thank me later," Mom said. She was right.

A place this big is a full-time job, which I can't do while doing anything else, particularly not while raising a baby. I mean, we could live with dust and dirty dishes. It wouldn't kill us. But two weeks ago, I was so depleted I could still barely get a shower into my routine. Vacuuming and laundry would have had to wait until she was in kindergarten.

Diaper, feed, clean, dress, watch in awe, feed, diaper, feed, do laundry, diaper—pretty much non-stop. I cherish the peaceful, relaxing time when I'm nursing Olivia. And I also enjoy the moment she lets out a big breath and falls asleep, but only if I've burped her first and put her down to sleep. If she falls asleep at my breast, we're sunk. Milk usually comes streaming out of her little bow-shaped lips, riding on an air bubble. And the waste of precious breast milk makes me insane.

Especially at four in the morning.

I unsettle TJ by sitting on the plush carpet in front of him, putting my cider on the low coffee table and leaning my elbow on it. Looking up at him, directly into those stony-green eyes, I can see he's already turned on. The fireplace, which I've become a master at lighting, is warm at my back. My heart is racing because I want this to work so bad, and I don't know what I'll do if I fail.

"You look as if you have something on your mind," he says.

I nod as he takes a sip of wine. "I miss that. You're lucky I keep a bottle around to torment myself."

"It's very, very good. I bet a small sip won't be a problem."

"You're probably right." Slowly, with a hand on each of his knees, I rise up between his legs. "Pour a little into my mouth," I ask.

He breaks out in a wicked grin, and I tilt my head back so he can give me a single sip.

"*Mm*. That is good." With a small moan, I dip my finger into his glass and paint the wine across my lower lip before trailing my finger down my neck and straight to my cleavage.

"You're being naughty," he says. "I'm starting to think I was set up by the most beautiful, sexy woman I know."

"Is it working?" I ask.

In answer, he sets his glass down and draws me closer. Covering my mouth with his, we kiss like we've been separated for a billion years. My pulse pounds, and everything I've been trying to put into cold storage flares to life. When he sucks on my lower lip, the sensation wings directly to my clit. A few gentle tugs with his teeth, and I'm drenched.

Releasing my mouth, he licks his way down the red-wine path I offered until he reaches the V neck of my sweater. Sliding his hands underneath, he palms my breasts, which are straining against the bra cups.

"You are more than a handful now." His touch is almost too gentle, like he's cautious. His next words confirm this notion. "I wish I could bend you over my lap and spank you for teasing me, but I don't want to cause you any pain down there."

The last thing I want is for him to be thinking about my labor right now or treat me like I'm made of glass. "You always took care of my needs," I say. "Let me do something for you."

Without waiting for his reply, I reach for the zipper of his jeans, but he captures my hand on his fly, letting me feel his hard arousal.

"Take your sweater off," he orders in the tone I love during sex. My lady parts flutter, and I start to obey, but first . . .

"Jordie, dim the lights to twenty percent."

TJ barks out a laugh. "You named the house AI after me."

I shrug, as the room becomes the perfect ambience and dimness for my body, which is not yet back to pre-pregnancy stage. It'll do, and I'm sure TJ won't find fault, but no need to shove my new bulges in his face, so to speak.

"I knew Jordie was a name I'd never say," I tell him truthfully and pull my sweater off over my head, shaking my hair back into place. Normally, I wear nursing bras with handy Velcro tabs so the cup opens easily without having to remove the bra. But tonight, I went all out with the old black lace, and my breasts are spilling over.

"Beautiful," he says, running his fingers over the upper swells, dipping into the cups to touch my hardening nipples.

"Bra off," he orders.

I unhook it with a sigh of relief, letting the girls bounce free. I nursed Olivia until about five minutes before TJ showed up, which is the only reason I'm not leaking all over the place from the bra's pressure.

"*Yowza!*" he says.

"Don't get too excited," I warn him. "They won't remain like this forever."

"Your breasts were fabulous before, and they're superb now." Leaning forward, he cups them, causing me to close my eyes with need. As his thumbs caress my nipples and I arch toward him, he adds, "They'll always be perfect, whatever size they are."

"Good answer," I say, and then I remember I'm supposed to be trying to drive him crazy so he cannot imagine another night or day without me.

Opening my eyes, I stare into his gray-green orbs, catching the reflection of the flickering candles behind me. Keeping eye contact, I pull his hands off my breasts and gently press my palms against his chest to suggest he get comfortable. Catching my intention, he hooks his arms along the back of the couch and lets me finally free his cock, which springs out, fully erect.

"Hey, old friend," I murmur.

TJ chuckles. "I'm so stiff it was starting to hurt."

"I can take care of that," I say. On my knees between his splayed thighs, I circle my fingers around the base, lean down, and take him into my mouth. Licking and sucking, while squeezing with one hand and massaging his taut balls with the other, I perform the blue ribbon of all blowjobs.

It's not easy. He's long and thick, as expected of a man his height. But I have all the time in the world—or until the dinner burns. When I glance upward, I see TJ's head is back, his eyes closed, and he's softly groaning. The sexy sound sets my body aflame, and I'm tingling head to toe, but mostly tits to clit, to be honest.

"I'm going to come soon," he announces in a gravelly voice. I know he's giving me the option to disengage and work him with my hand.

Instead, I smile against his shaft and start humming, adding a little vibration. He makes a gulping sound. When I look up again, his eyes are open and intense, watching me pleasure him.

I lift my head. "I want you to come in my mouth, but I want you to possess me first. Make me yours. Do you understand?"

He nods. I circle my lips around the head again and close my eyes as I feel him sink his hands into my hair and cradle my head.

"Mm-hm," I say encouragingly. I want this. I want TJ to be in control, with total freedom to thrust.

He knows it, too. With his hands inhibiting my ability to move, he takes over, gently at first, guiding me along his shaft then dragging me back, over and over. My tongue rasps across his warm skin, but there's little else for me to do except breathe through my nose and cover my teeth with my lips.

"God," he says, then groans again. Suddenly, he holds me still, and he's the one moving, thrusting fast and deep until I can feel his cock at the back of my throat. It's exciting, naughty, and makes me soak my panties. Spectacularly freeing—I give him mastery over how he takes his satisfaction from my mouth.

Another sexy, wild sound is torn from him as he sends his cum across my tongue and down my throat. I've never felt more powerful during sex, and I feel my own mini-climax shiver through me.

At the same time as he pulls out, the buzzer dings in the kitchen, and AI Jordie says, "Your kitchen timer is going off."

TJ and I look at each other. "A lot of things are going off at the same time," I joke as he does up his fly and I put my sweater on. Getting to my feet, he takes hold of my arm. "What about you?"

I don't tell him that I had a little orgasm. "Your pleasure is my pleasure," I remind him. "Besides, dinner is ready."

With that, I hear Olivia start to cry on the monitor. Jordie announces, "The baby is crying."

Of course she is.

30

Jordan

Eating with my girls is a trip. Olivia is having a snack, and it's such a sweet sight to see her breastfeeding. Brooke is probably over the novelty, however, cradling our daughter with one arm and eating with her free hand.

"Now I understand why everything is already in bite-sized pieces and all in one delicious dish. I'm really grateful you took the time to cook," I add. "I should have offered to bring food with me." I was just so damned excited to get from the plane to her door.

"I've figured out how to make most meals easy to eat with one hand." She tells me what her days are like, and I soak it all up.

"I have a little news from Rangeley," I tell her in return. I've been putting this off, because she might take it badly considering the consequences. "Turns out Tracy was the one who went to the media. Both times."

Brooke's mouth drops open, then snaps shut. Her expression is pure shock. "Why would she do that after working for you for three years?"

"With Sherri sending all those gamers there, and Cy making a big deal out of it, she realized the truth. When she got mad, she lashed out."

"Did Boston Media Group pay her well?"

"I'm sure they did since they sold the story and photos worldwide. But that's not why she gave them a story. Think about it. She went to *your* former employer."

Brooke frowns. "Sorry, I'm not following."

"She wanted me to think it was you, and I did. I went nuts, didn't I? And it's a miracle we're still speaking to one another."

"Tracy wanted to frame me in particular because . . . ?"

"Jealousy." I've learned how strong an emotion that is when I thought Brooke was carrying someone else's baby, even for a minute.

"I barely spoke with her," Brooke says, her tone brittle as she realizes all the damage Tracy did. "We agreed on your hotness level, and she was surprised you'd taken me skiing. But she said she wouldn't date her boss."

"Maybe that's what you heard, but it was more that she *couldn't* date her boss because I told her flat-out that was the rule the first time she expressed an interest. Combine that with finding out I'm a billionaire and she felt slighted, to put it mildly. More than that, she was mad at you for sweeping me off my feet. I'm the idiot who mentioned to her that we were together in Boston."

Brooke's mouth creates a silent *O*.

"Tracy had photos of me that I didn't even realize, and had followed me home once to take a picture of my house."

"A stalker," she says quietly.

I shrug. "A hopeful girlfriend before she knew I had money. And then a psycho bitch when she found out I did."

This brings a slightly bewildered expression to Brooke's face, followed by a shake of her head. "She got back at me *and* at you in one revenge cut."

"More delusional than that. She kept contacting me when I was on the island. Tracy hoped after I'd assigned the blame to you, I'd fall for her sympathetic support and see what and who I'd been missing for three years." I need to make it up to this amazing woman nursing my baby, but I'm not sure how.

She sips her cider, not seeming bothered by how egregiously I misjudged her. "How'd you find out?" she asks.

"From Cy. Tracy spilled her guts after a bender, and Cy fired her on the spot. But she's a local, so let the bad-mouthing of Jordan Asher begin."

Brooke winces. "You can't roll over for that. Besides, it might hurt Cy's business. I think you should let it be known Tracy was behind the entire world finding out where you live. No one wants a disloyal employee."

My turn to shake my head. "Very few people apart from you and me think she did anything wrong. Most people would do it in a heartbeat for the right price."

"But not me," Brooke says, giving me a dose of her chocolate-brown stare.

"I know. And I'll never make that mistake again. I'm ready to grovel at your feet and apologize every day for the rest of our lives."

My words elicit a slight smile from her. Then she frowns. "I have to say this really infuriates me. I want to drive up to Rangeley and tell Tracy what an utter asshat she is for making money off of you, and telling people about us."

"Listen to yourself," I say. "I knew all along you weren't the type to be a scummy reporter who would sell my privacy."

"Sure you did," Brooke says, with a roll of her eyes.

I clarify my statement. "I hoped that was the case. And I figured it out that first week. When you left, I was still convinced you were a decent human being."

"Until the first story came out," she says.

I nod. "It made me doubt that I could really believe anyone."

Strangely, she's the one reaching out her free hand to comfort me. I take hold of this slender woman's firm grip and never want to let go.

"After what happened to your sister," Brooke says, "I understand why you feel the way you do. But I think you can relax your protective instincts just a little. Let me take over some of the burden."

I'm beyond touched. "My copper-haired tiger!" I want to run my fingers through her silken hair, but the table is between us.

"More like a sluggish mama hippo than a tiger, but I could do some damage."

"I recall you have a quick, sharp slap."

She smiles. "Whoops! Did I apologize for that? Since it's a night for saying sorry."

"You did already," I tell her, because it doesn't matter in the face of what I've put her through.

Nodding, she rests Olivia on her shoulder on a bleached-white cloth and starts the burping process while herself yawning.

"Tired?" I ask. "Stupid question, I guess."

Brooke yawns again. "Even outside the womb, Olivia is flat-out exhausting."

"She's bigger," I say.

"Babies grow," Brooke says. "Blink and you'll miss it."

I've been missing too much and wondering if I've waited too long to figure out a way to have a relationship while not putting my girls in danger. Every time I tried to keep a conversation going with Brooke while face-timing from California, she had to end the call. I was starting to think she was done with me, and I wouldn't have blamed her.

But when she gave me that incredible BJ, I started the evening thinking either she's still into me or she wanted to give me the perfect demonstration of what I'll lose when she falls in love with some normal guy, like Dan. I spent the dinner in doubt because even before the timer went off and Olivia woke up, Brooke seemed to have no problem turning down my offer to reciprocate. It's a challenge I accept and intend to overcome before I leave.

So, why do I blurt out something lame? "I'm thinking about the fourth game," I tell her, just as Olivia releases an impressive belch.

Abruptly, Brooke gets up from the table. "I'm going to change her diaper and lay her down again. Say goodbye," she adds, barely pausing as she turns her back so I can see Olivia over her shoulder, her little eyes closed with contentment.

Next time I see my daughter, she might be an inch longer. It'll seem like she's ready to ask for the car keys. Getting up from the table, I grab all the dishes and go into the kitchen. When I've rinsed and stacked everything in the dishwasher—probably done wrong, but at least I did it— I'm looking forward to a few hours in Brooke's company in front of the fireplace. Then I remember the hot tub.

Wandering out onto the patio, I can't help looking up. The view is OK, but nowhere near the starry sky in Maine or on St. Regnal. Too much light pollution from Boston and the airport and neighboring suburbs.

I hear Brooke open the sliding French door behind me.

"Have you used it yet?" I ask, gesturing to the tub.

"My dad got it working, and he and my mom used it. But frankly, I'm usually ready to go to bed as soon as its dark. Sitting in a hot tub feels like another chore. Besides, I'd be so far from Olivia."

"Not that far," I counter. "Do you want to go in now? With me?"

"No, that's OK." She spins on her heel and goes indoors.

Denied again. I follow, and she goes all the way to the front door. "Brooke, is everything OK?"

"Sure. Yes, fine. It's been great to see you, but I hear my soft, flannel sheets calling my name."

Great to see me? "Really?"

"Yup. Soft as clouds, one hundred percent combed Egyptian cotton. I'll be out by the time you start your engine."

"You're throwing me out?"

Her laughter sounds genuine. "Your expression," she says. "The essence of being thwarted. Throwing you out sounds a bit dramatic. Don't tell me you're annoyed because sex isn't on the agenda?"

She makes me sound like the bitter, low-scoring gamer on a leaderboard. "No, it's not that. You seem different. Where's my try-anything-once girl who wouldn't have hesitated to let me get the jets going on the hot tub?"

She crosses her arms. "I'm a single mom now."

"I never think of you that way. We're in this together."

There's that laugh again, although less jolly. "When I have to get up two hours after I hit a deep REM, believe me, I know I'm a single mom."

"Let me stay tonight." *What the hell did I just say?* I wasn't planning on staying over and meeting paparazzi on my way out in the morning. My car is outside, announcing to the world that I'm here and that I care for this woman and our baby. They can be turned into weapons against me or taken from me in the blink of an eye. For all I know, I was followed from the airport.

"Not a good idea," she says, a classic knock-back that I wasn't expecting. In gaming, we call it a *gank*, and it makes me want to double down on my insistence that I stay, even though she's the one making sense.

"With all due respect, Brooke, I think I can stay if I want to. We haven't put anything in writing that says otherwise. I bought the house."

Her eyes are huge. "You bought the house for me and Olivia, and you made it clear you weren't going to live here."

"I'm just asking to spend the night. I spent six hours on a plane, and I don't want to drive back to The Parisi. Why should I?"

"For *all* our safety," she points out. "That's paramount."

It dawns on me belatedly that she's messing with me. "Jordie, make sure all the security systems are activated and all exterior doors and windows are locked."

"Done," the AI says.

"Kind of high-handed," Brooke says. "Anyway, do you want dessert? I have pumpkin cheesecake." She saunters away as if she hadn't claimed exhaustion a minute ago. I've just been played by an expert.

$♥$♥$♥$

Waking up later than usual, because I'm adjusting to the time zone change from the West Coast, it only takes a second to recall I'm in Brooke's bed. She's sound asleep beside me, and Olivia is snuffling around in her crib next to us.

The night, according to a sleepy Brooke at two a.m., was a typical one, with our daughter waking up every couple of hours. The pattern was the same each time, a quick feeding and then both my girls conked out.

The last thing Brooke said was, "Bottle-fed babies may sleep a little longer, up to an hour, but I'll be damned if I . . ." She was snoring softly before she even finished her sentence.

Now I know why she really didn't want sex after dessert last night, and why her eyes only lit up after she'd changed into pajamas. "Aren't these the best?" she asked, turning in front of me in a shapeless red-tartan shirt and boxy pants.

"The best," I agree. The last thing she wanted to hear was how turned on I was by her slender frame and large tits cloaked in flannel. But I was. Still, I couldn't help asking, "What happened to that cute tank top you were sleeping in a few days ago?"

She giggled and rolled over. "G'night, TJ." That was the first time she basically passed out on me, but it happened three more times.

Olivia snuffles a little more loudly, sounding like an animal. I dart out of bed in my briefs and scoop her up. I can't feed her, but maybe I can distract her so Brooke can have ten more minutes. Silently as possible, we leave the bedroom and go down the hall.

"Jordie," I whisper, "turn the heat up to seventy."

"Done."

The floor is cool underfoot, and I hope "done" means it warms up quickly. I'll set a regular schedule so Jordie heats up the place before Brooke and Olivia get out of bed. Luckily, there's a blanket on the back of the sofa. I remember resting my head on it when Brooke gave me the best blowjob of my life.

What was she trying to prove? I already know she's the one for me. Plus, I learned she's a great cook. Not that it really matters, because I can hire a private chef in a heartbeat, but it's nice to know more about her.

Sitting on the sofa, I lean Olivia against my bare chest and cover us both with the blanket. I run hot, so I know she'll be fine as long as she doesn't get too hungry. Not much I can do there. I wonder if Brooke will store breastmilk, like the lactation nurse talked about in the hospital. She said it would allow me to bond with our baby by being able to bottle feed her with the same "best stuff."

That was before I freaked out and pulled a gun on a reporter.

"What am I going to do, little one?" I ask softly. There's no place I'd rather be than right here, or wherever Brooke and Olivia are. But the what-ifs swirl through my imaginative brain, as easily as thinking up new situations for my next game.

My daughter's eyelashes are dark, fanning her pale cheeks. Her lips are slightly open, and she's making adorable whistling noises. She's like a meme of every perfect baby all mixed into one.

And I have her right over my heartbeat, another thing I remember from the hospital. Skin to skin, heart to heart, she seems to be sleeping soundly. I don't drift off, though, not wanting to waste a minute of daddy-daughter time.

How will I drive off later and leave my little nugget? I start to picture doing the opposite. Staying. Living with Brooke, sharing and blending and compromising. Raising Olivia like a family.

I'm still musing on this, thinking about bringing my dogs here and also about rude paparazzi getting zapped by an electric fence when I hear Brooke's footfalls behind me. She races into the living room, wild eyed.

"*Oh*, God," she says, looking at us.

"*Shh,*" I say, but it's too late. Olivia yawns, wriggles, and starts rubbing her nose back and forth on my chest. Her eyes are still closed, but she's determined. When she doesn't find what she's looking for, she starts to wail, and I learn that I'm terrified of a crying baby.

"Shoot, I'm sorry," Brooke says, plopping down beside me and undoing her pajama top. She's wearing a bra, which is a surprise, and she seems to be tearing the cup off before I realize it's Velcro. As efficient as a combo strike in a fighting game, she has Olivia peacefully sucking within seconds. It's a sound I've heard all night.

"She's good at that."

Brooke nods, looking unsettled.

"What's up?" I ask.

"As soon as she latches on, my mouth goes instantly dry. I'm so thirsty."

Jumping up, I say, "I'm on it. What do you want?"

"Plain water, please."

"Ice cubes?"

"Nope."

"Is it in the fridge?"

"Nope. Filtered water pitcher on the granite island."

"A squeeze of lemon."

"Nope. Please, TJ. *Plain* water. Now."

I was trying too hard. "Sorry." I rush over with a full glass, spilling some before handing it to her. Brooke drinks the entire glass.

"More?"

"No, thanks. Sorry I freaked out and woke her up. It's the first time in six weeks that I've awakened and seen an empty crib."

"Totally understandable. If you want to squeeze out some milk sometime—"

"Express my breastmilk," she corrects.

"Right, then I'd be happy to feed her, too."

She stares at me, looks down at Olivia, then back up at me. "It was nice having you in my bed last night."

No woman has ever said that to me when sex wasn't involved. Probably because I've never slept with anyone when we didn't have sex. I'm not so stupid as to say any of that, though. "Every two hours is rough on you."

She nods. "I'm a little tired now, but I'll be fine after coffee."

I spring back up. "Sorry, I'll get that started."

"Sit," she says. "Jordie, make coffee."

"Making coffee," the AI says.

"I filled the coffee pot before we went to bed. It's not high-caffeine because of Olivia, but the smell and taste fool me into feeling energized."

I sit again, feeling like I might be replaceable by a more-efficient version of myself. Certainly, Jordie knows more about Brooke than I do.

"Don't worry," she says, reading my mind. "Jordie can't do *everything* you can do."

"Funny woman," I quip. But I know for a fact male robots with sexual capabilities are already in the works. She's not being serious, though. Speaking of which, I finally remember something that was uppermost in my mind when I drove over last night. Upon seeing Brooke, it vanished from my brain, until now.

"You said there was a serious problem we had to discuss in person."

"I did, didn't I?" She takes her time, touching Olivia's head, yawning, stretching her one free arm. "A gardener. Sherri's Dan has offered, but I hate to take advantage of his good nature. I've got a few piles of leaves, and I'll need snow removal in a couple months."

I'm waiting for the serious problem, when she adds, "I don't want you to think I'm lazy. I'll be happy to rake and even shovel when Olivia's bigger, but I don't want her in a backpack at this age. What if I lean over and she falls out?"

"Into a pile of leaves or snow?"

"Right," she says. "I think the coffee's ready."

"Shall I ask Jordie how you take it?"

"Don't you remember?"

I smile because I do, from our mornings in Maine. Once we both have a cup, hers with a lid in case it spills onto Olivia, I address the *serious* issue that I realize was a ruse to get me here. "I'll hire a gardener."

"Thank you."

"Well, shit," I say. "That *was* difficult. Good thing we could tackle it together." Her cheeks grow pink, just enough to show her embarrassment at the worst lie ever. I'm almost insulted she couldn't think of something better.

Then I show Jordie up by frying bacon and eggs. "Shower time," Brooke announces. "I keep to a schedule. And this is the time when Olivia sleeps deeply for some reason. Her belly's full, she's had a little stimulation, and she has to sleep it off."

My mind races ahead. "We'll save time by showering together."

"That's ridiculous. It'll take longer, and one of us should watch her."

"How do you usually watch her when you shower?"

"I have a waterproof monitor in the shower."

"Another problem solved." I don't accept no. We put Olivia, freshly burped, down in her crib, and I grab Brooke's hand. The bathroom, I noted last night, has been feminized with good-smelling soap and shampoo, but I'm interested in only one thing.

"Strip," I tell her.

"Jordie," she begins, "turn on the heat lamps. Jordie, turn down the—"

I clamp a hand over her mouth. "Full light, lady. You're as gorgeous as the day I met you."

Her tongue tickles my palm, stiffening my cock.

"Sorry, I didn't get that," says the annoying AI.

"Jordie, shut up," I say. "You," I point to Brooke. "Are you going to make me tell you twice?" I can't help the grin that stretches my mouth. "Because there's no way you won't be spanked if you do."

She pauses, and I wonder if she's going to go for door number one, a shower together, or door number two, a spanking first. With a flip of her hair over her shoulder, she turns her back to me and unbuttons her pajama top.

In under a minute, we're in the spacious shower, each with our own large shower head, but we've met in the middle. Brooke locks her hands behind my neck, making her breasts rise up, and I claim her mouth like I've wanted to do all morning. It's a slow, sweet kiss. I hope she can feel my love for her. I know she feels my arousal when I drop my hands to her ass and tilt her against me.

"*Mm,*" she moans, and our tongues become quickly engaged as the steam rises around us.

"Kissing you is so good, I'm sorry we waited."

In response, she sucks my tongue.

"Are you . . . Can you?" I ask.

"Yes," she says.

Backing Brooke against the shower wall, I part her legs with my thigh, and instantly change my mind about thrusting inside her. Instead, I drop to my knees to worship her, the mother of my child, even more luscious and beautiful than the first time I saw her naked.

Opening her pussy lips, I hope I can give her as good as she gave me. With my first lick, she fists her fingers in my hair. With my second, she hooks her leg over my shoulder. And then her body undulates against my tongue. I grab her hips, anchor her, and grind my mouth against her clit.

"Yesss," she says again, like she's hissing. "Fingers," she urges, and I insert two inside her, stroking her G-spot while I suck her hard little nub.

"TJ," she whispers. "Fuck me."

"Come first," I demand, and use my teeth to gently nip at her clit before tugging it.

By the tensing of her fingers against my scalp, I know when she climaxes, a long shuddering orgasm against my mouth. I don't hurry to pull my fingers out of her until I know she's satisfied.

"I'm so ready for you," she says.

"We don't have to," I offer because I still don't want that nurse coming after me, beating me with a bedpan.

"I've been dreaming about your cock. Give it to me." She's still tugging my hair, but now she's doing it to make me stand. As soon as I do, she fits the head to her channel, wraps her arms around me, and urges me forward. "Please, TJ. It's been so long."

Surging into her, I hope Brooke knows what she's doing. Because I'll feel like a real jackass if this hurts or tears her or—

Suddenly, I pull out.

"TJ?" Her tone is desperate.

"Condom," I say, my voice sounding strangled. The first time in my adult life that I've forgotten.

She laughs, and I wonder if she's loopy from lack of sleep. "Brooke, this is serious."

"I'm protected," she says. "Birth control."

"Jordie, resume intercourse," I mutter and thrust inside her again.

31

Brooke

It's a clear, cold November day, and we've decided to take our daughter out. Together. We haven't said anything directly about TJ moving in. I don't want to bring it up and rock the currently even-keeled boat, but I believe he's thinking it wouldn't be such a bad idea.

Ever since I woke up and found Olivia in the care of another human being, her father, I've been receiving surprises—like the way he held her against his naked chest, the way he made my breakfast, and the way he managed to put her in a clean onesie. It only took him three tries.

"Let's go to the Fresh Pond Reservation. Hardly anyone will be there this time of year." I never feel much anxiety taking Olivia out, because my body has everything she needs right now. I toss a couple of diapers for her and a bottle of water for me in the ridiculously oversized bag that's decorated with lions, tigers, and elephants, courtesy of my mother. Later, I know I'll need to stuff it full with sippy cups, crackers, fruit, teethers, and a change of clothing, maybe for both of us.

"Shall I get a bellhop for Olivia's luggage?" TJ asks when he sees what I'm holding. Just for that, I slide the turquoise and purple bag onto his shoulder. Of course, somehow, he looks like the sexiest dad alive. *A DILF?*

When we pull out of the gate and onto the street, almost immediately, a car pulls away from the curb and follows us. Or at least, that's what TJ says.

"Reporter or paparazzi on our tail." He goes from jovial to tense in the span of a heartbeat.

I turn in my seat and take a look. It's a balding, middle-aged guy. Sure enough, he's snapping photos while driving. Seems dangerous for him. Suddenly, he's falling back, and I realize it's because we've sped up.

Facing forward again, I look at TJ's grim expression, reminding myself it's not his fault. He's been traumatized. He zips around a car, weaves in and out of traffic seamlessly. After all, he's an experienced gamer. But as we both know, accidents can happen.

"Just ignore him."

"He won't go away. He'll follow us to Fresh Pond, and we'll have to deal with him there."

"Then let's do that," I say. "But please slow down and stop looking in the rearview mirror. Or I'm going to rip it right off this expensive car."

He glances over at me, and I nod seriously, because I'll do it, too. "Do you remember Franco's line from *The Gumball Rally*?"

"Never seen it," he says, and I rest my hand on his thigh to let him know we're in this together.

"We'll have to watch it some time," I say. "There's a race car driver in it who says the first rule of Italian driving is 'what's behind me is not important,' and he throws away the rearview mirror."

TJ laughs. "That's ridiculous. I think you'll find they stole that from Enzo Ferrari. He said, 'What's behind you doesn't really matter.'"

"OK, same difference. Keep your eyes on the road and let's enjoy the day."

I have to hand it to TJ. He manages to drive normally for the remainder of the short trip and keep his attention focused forward.

When we get to Fresh Pond Reservation, it turns out I was *almost* right. It's not completely deserted, but there are only a few cars parked and no one in sight. The other visitors must be walking through the 166-acre park that encircles the reservoir. With this much open space, it's the perfect place for a paranoid billionaire and his family. Of course, the paparazzi boldly drives right in behind us.

"Stay here," TJ says.

I roll my eyes. It's not like this is a movie. I open my door and stand beside him.

"I literally just told you to stay in the car," he fumes.

"Spank me later," I tease. "But I'm not a 'stay here' kind of person, or I wouldn't have been knocked up by you in the first place."

"*Oh*, I will spank you."

"Promises, promises," I tease, but then the bald guy is snapping photos as if he's on safari and we're a pair of rare cheetahs. But he doesn't know he's the one who could be shot.

"Excuse me," I call out.

"Brooke. You can't speak to him. What are you doing?"

"Excuse me," I say again, ignoring TJ. "Can you stop doing that?"

"What?" asks Mr. *Razzi*, as I'm going to think of him, like a real human being who can be reasoned with. He does momentarily lower his camera.

"Can you let us have some private time? Or at least tell us how long you're going to be here."

"*Um*. Are you Brooke Danbury?"

"Yes."

"Why are you still talking to him?" TJ demands.

"What's your name?" I ask. "Seems only fair."

"You can't sue me. I'm staying far enough away."

"Not interested in suing," I say.

"I am," TJ mutters. "Get the hell away from us."

"Don't mind him. You make him cranky. How would you like to be our official photographer?" I ask, as inspiration seizes me.

The bald man cocks his head. "What do you mean?"

"Well, I can't guarantee exclusivity since others are bound to find us occasionally, but rather than chasing our car, which is dangerous for you and for us, if we're going to do anything interesting, then I'll let you know. You can have the best photo."

"What?" both men exclaim.

"Provided you then leave us alone *after* you get one or two. Like now. Say we stop looking surly and Mr. Asher puts his arm around me, then after you get this beautiful backdrop," I gesture behind us, "you drive away so we can live our lives."

Letting his camera dangle from its strap around his neck, Mr. Razzi reaches behind. Trigger-happy TJ apparently jumps to conclusions. He draws his gun so fast it's a blur in my peripheral vision as the photographer brings out his wallet. He puts up his hands as though he's being robbed and even holds his wallet out.

"Please lower your gun," I say. "Definitely *not* self-defense. And this man's going to think you made your money by robbing people."

TJ does as I ask, sliding the gun back in its hidden holster. I swear he spent too long in the Maine woods thinking everything—and everyone—was a threat, such as bears and wolves and reporters like me.

Mr. Razzi pulls a card from his wallet and holds it out gingerly. Stepping forward, closing the distance, I take it.

"How's your baby?" he asks.

My natural motherly instinct nearly makes me explode all over him with outrage and vitriol. Instead, I continue my negotiations. I notice he's wearing a wedding ring.

"Do you have kids?"

"Yep, and I'm trying to support them."

"By being a blood-sucking—" TJ begins.

I hold up my hand in his direction and address this photographer. "Then you understand that children are off-limits. Obviously, there can be *no* babies involved in your photos of us. Except for one shot," I add.

"Brooke!" TJ is getting louder.

I look at the business card. Frank Soltea. "You can take a single photo of our baby girl, and hopefully make your fortune, and then the paparazzi will be hounding *you*, not us."

Frank and I stare at one another, gaining a mutual understanding. Then he says, "The kid's photo's not worth that much anyway. It can get me banned from some tabloids. What people really want to see is whether you two are together. Is he," and he jerks a thumb at TJ, "a bachelor or off the market?"

"Enquiring minds want to know," I mutter and look at TJ.

His expression is utterly unamused. "Not having this conversation with him."

I don't want to let my feelings get in the way of our privacy, but they're a little hurt that he won't declare publicly that he's with me and not just the father of my baby. My eyes fill with tears, and I look away.

That's when I hear TJ tell the paparazzi, "Not that it's any of your fucking business or anyone's except Ms. Danbury's and mine, but we are together and I am 'off the market,' as you so crudely put it. Like I'm a piece of goddamned meat."

My eyes are wide and so is my smile.

The photographer isn't fazed by TJ's ranting. "A kiss would go a long way to satisfying people's curiosity."

I'm still staring at my guy. "What's it gonna be?" I ask him, walking back over to TJ. "A few photos for Mr. Soltea, or do we spend the rest of the day trying to keep a step ahead of him?"

The muscle in TJ's jaw is popping so hard, I worry he won't be able to eat tonight. And then, I see him make up his mind.

"One kiss," he says, as if it's punishment.

Gee, thanks! "Great," I say.

"And one photo of the baby in its car seat," Frank adds. "I'll take it through the car window."

"I thought you said it wasn't worth much," TJ protests.

The photographer shrugs. "The three of you tell the story," he says. "You want to give me her name?"

I glance at TJ. I honestly can't see any reason why not. It's not like her name is Elon Musk–level weird or anything. TJ nods.

"Olivia Asher," I say with pride.

Frank whips out a small pad from his pocket. This time, TJ doesn't flinch or play Dirty Harry. "Olivia," he says as he writes the single word. And that's it. I can't help smiling to myself that he needed to record this.

"Do I have your word that you won't hound us at every turn?" I ask him.

"Yes, ma'am. Now let's have that kiss."

It almost sounds like I'm supposed to kiss him. I feel weird closing the gap, grateful when TJ makes the move toward me.

"All right, but hurry up," he gripes. "We're not zoo animals."

How romantic! Suddenly, I feel extremely self-conscious . . . until TJ slides his arms around my waist and kisses me as though we've been doing it for a while. Relaxing, I slide my arms up and lace my fingers around his neck, leaning into him. Our mouths open and our tongues start dancing. In the next instant, he tilts his head and widens his stance, so I fit better between his legs and so his face is closer to mine.

When TJ nibbles on my lower lip, my ears start buzzing, and I breathe in the warm, familiar scent of him. When I tilt my head in the other direction, we're on stage two, deep and connected. His hands move into my hair, cradling my head, holding me still for his tongue to ravage my mouth. I can't help the moan that rumbles up through me, since I'm now reminded of last night.

A car engine starts, and we break apart. Mr. Soltea waves and disappears.

"Shit!" TJ says, but I start laughing.

"I don't even know if he took Olivia's photo," I say, feeling like the worst mom on earth while glancing through the back window to make sure she's still asleep. We would have heard her displeasure if she'd woken up.

"I forgot that maggot was even here," TJ says, opening the back door and unhooking the car seat as gently as possible.

"Shall I put her in the front pack?" I ask, having shown him how I can carry her close to my chest.

"Let's put her car seat in the wheelie thing," he says. "Don't want to wake her. Plus, she looks warm and snuggled."

With TJ pushing her carriage, we finally stroll onto the path. The chilly, blue-gray pond in front of us looks pristine, with sunlight making it sparkle like a gem. We pass a hawk perched on a maple that has already lost all its leaves, but there are plenty of chokeberry shrubs filled with brilliant red berries.

After we've walked for about twenty minutes, I stop and take out my phone.

"Don't pull your gun on me, Sheriff," I say. "Although if you have handcuffs to go with it, I'd be interested in those later."

TJ starts to laugh. I take a selfie of him and me, then we crouch down to include Olivia. Seems a good time to bring up the confession he just made. "So, you're off the market, and I'm the one who brought you home in my shopping cart."

"Ha!" he says, which tells me nothing.

I think I have to come out and say it. "I love you, Tiberius Jordan Asher."

He doesn't look surprised. "I know that," he says, which is probably the worst thing you can say to someone who has declared their adoration for you without knowing if it's reciprocated. I might shrivel up and die if he doesn't . . .

"I thought that was a given," he adds. Then he sees my expression. "*Oh*, shit! I mean for both of us. I figured you knew I loved you, and you felt compelled to tell me in case I didn't know."

Ohh-kayyyy. Good thing one of us has a psych degree. But I'm still silent, so he adds, "I love you, Brooke. I love you with all that I am, and I'm not talking about my bank account. Although, if you asked me to toss every fucking dollar into this reservoir, I would do it."

My heart has just expanded. I'm as warm and toasty as if I was sitting in front of his massive stone fireplace in Maine. "I love you, too," I say, cupping the side of his face.

"I know," he says. "You just said that."

Olivia starts to cry as I start to laugh. "Don't you want to hear me say it a couple billion times?"

"No," he says, and we start walking again back toward the car, which instantly stops her crying. "I already felt it in here." TJ thumps his chest.

I love that chest. I love this man. "I might like to hear it more than once," I tell him. "Maybe daily, if that's OK."

He leans over and kisses me swiftly. "That's fine. I can do daily."

"And we're going to live together. Right? The three of us? As Mr. Soltea said, 'the three of us tell the story. *Our* story.'"

He drapes his arm around me so we each have one hand pushing the carriage. "He's only one of many, you know. There'll be others, but I admire how you handled him."

"Everyone knows already," I tell him. Then I repeat it more slowly, thinking of Mrs. Moxley's words. "Everyone knows about us. And about our baby. So, living apart accomplishes nothing except to give the world the impression that you were done with me by the time Olivia came along. Kind of like my fav New England quarterback."

"Not following your logic," he says.

"Tom Brady's girlfriend, Bridget, was pregnant when he got together with Giselle. She had the baby under a lot of tabloid madness and then faded from the limelight as he moved on and got married."

"*This* isn't like that."

"I know. What's wrong with the world knowing that we love each other and have started a family?"

We stop in the middle of the path, and he kisses me once more. We stay fused at the mouths until Olivia starts fussing again, and I feel my milk let down. I know I have to get her into the warm car and nurse her. I break away first but am thrilled by TJ's next words.

"Absolutely nothing wrong with that," he says. "I'll tell the world I've fallen in love with Brooke Danbury."

32

Jordan

My palms are sweating. I can't recall the last time that happened. Wait, yes, I can. It was when I suddenly found myself in a labor room at Mass General.

I arrive home to the house I've only been living in for two days, with a bunch of flowers and a ring from the best jeweler in Boston. One of a kind yet traditional with, I hope, an acceptable amount of creative flair.

Taking the front step at a jog, I stop at the door, clear my throat, and breathe deeply for a second, trying to calm my heartrate.

"What are you doing?" asks Brooke's disembodied voice. "Are those flowers? Hurry up and come in!"

Hard to surprise the woman when she can spy on me from the moment I pull into the drive. I did manage to squirrel away a bottle of prosecco yesterday. The mini-fridge in the entertaining area was totally empty, and I'm not sure Brooke has even noticed that we have a bar in the living room. While I know she shouldn't drink much while breastfeeding, I think we should toast to us. *If* she says yes.

The door swings open before I can put my finger to the biometric pad.

"*Oof.*" She has barreled into me as I try to take a step inside. Wrapping my free arm around her, I pick her off her feet and back her into the warm entry hall while giving the door a kick closed.

"You are so strong," she gushes.

"You've totally crushed my roses," I say.

"Do you mean the flowers? Or is that a euphemism?" she asks, patting the front of my jeans.

Two seconds together and she's already giving me a boner. Releasing her, I hand over the two dozen long-stemmed red roses. Perhaps an old-fashioned symbol of my love, considering we jumped into sex, then had a child, and are now living together for the first time.

"Beautiful," she says, burying her face in the bouquet. "I'll find a vase. My mother gave me a heavy crystal one that she dragged all over the world when we used to move. She said, 'Take it. I don't ever want to have to pack it up again.'"

My heart is pounding, and I'm not really listening. I don't doubt that Brooke loves me, but marriage is a tricky concept. She's been engaged before and walked away from it. Maybe she prefers we remain as we are, either for now or forever. But to me, it's like adoption. I felt more truly my parents' son when they presented me with the paperwork. Making it official made it more real, and that's how I feel about getting married. Again, maybe a little old fashioned, especially for a guy who deals in otherworldly, space-age games.

After removing my shoes, I follow her into the kitchen, glancing at the monitor to see Olivia sleeping soundly in her crib. That means we have at least three minutes from the first snuffle to when she'll start crying.

Tossing my coat over a chair, I watch Brooke fill a large vase with water. I planned my meta strategy, my point-blank area of greatest effect as if this was a deathmatch, a free-for-all, a last-man-standing type encounter. I even rehearsed my words. But looking at her, loving this woman as I do, I can't recall anything clever or witty.

"Dining room," she begins, carrying the flowers with her. "No, the coffee table. Then I'll see and smell them more. I'll put a couple beside the bed tonight, too."

"I can always buy you more," I point out, not having guessed she would be so delighted. I file this knowledge away in a mental loop code, which I'll repeat for her as often as possible.

Brooke laughs. "I'll never say no to fresh flowers."

But will she say no to a wedding ring? Should I wait? Have great sex first, like last night and the night before that, and then spring it on her when she's in that relaxed post-orgasmic state? I pull her down onto the couch beside me while she admires the roses.

Then I drape my arm around her, and we lean against one another. Olivia snuffles in the background. Three-minute countdown begins.

"I'll get her," Brooke says.

"Let her wake up slowly. I want to talk to you." Time for the rush, sacrificing everything to overwhelm an opponent. Or, in this case, a lover.

Resting her left hand on my right thigh, she gives me a squeeze. "Everything all right?"

"Damn near perfect," I say. "So perfect, I don't want to mess it up or have anything change."

"*Oh*, boy," she says, then sighs. "Something always changes, TJ. The seasons, my favorite type of cake, Olivia's diaper probably in a couple minutes. What's up?"

"There's at least one thing that won't change," I say, taking her chin between my thumb and fingers and tilting her face to look toward me. "How much I love you."

"Wow," she says, blinking up into my eyes. "You just gave me an all-over body shiver."

"By telling you I love you?"

"Yup. Makes me all tingly. I mean, think about how far we've come from you hoping I'd freeze to death in a snowbank."

"I never hoped that, or I wouldn't have come to rescue you."

"With all the irritability of the grumpiest grump."

"I knew you'd be trouble, and you were. Big trouble."

She dissolves into laughter, and I can't help leaning down and kissing her. Olivia is murmuring, something she does softly when she still has her eyes closed. We still have a couple minutes. I nibble Brooke's lower lip and then rest my forehead against hers.

"You brought trouble *and* liberation. Who knows how long I would've stayed shut off, missing out on life?"

"Wasting yourself on meaningless sexual encounters every few months."

"Few months?" I tease.

She draws back so we can see each other's eyes. "Few *weeks?*" she asks, sounding serious.

My turn to laugh. "So meaningless, I can't even remember how often or with whom."

She pokes me in the ribs. "Good answer."

"Speaking of which, I'm hoping for a really good answer to my next question." I take a breath and give up on the flowery speech. I just need to put it out there.

"Ms. Danbury, will you marry me?"

Her gorgeous mouth opens, but no sound comes out.

"Come on," I say, feeling nervous again. "You can't be totally surprised."

"Of course I'm surprised. You just moved in a second ago."

"Sometimes things move quickly, like in a good multiplayer game."

"Multiplayer?"

"There are three of us on this team." Olivia chooses that moment to let out a baby roar of impatience. It's formidable. "See what I mean."

"Shoot," Brooke says, and wiggles her shoulders, looking down at her own chest.

"Milk delivery?" I ask, having discovered there's such a thing as a nursing pad to stop leakage. When I found a few of them in the bedroom, I thought they were either some kind of contraceptive or a small, soft wipe for cleaning Olivia's face, which is what Brooke found me doing with one.

Now Olivia is crying impatiently.

"Be right back."

I don't begrudge Olivia stealing Brooke away. If our baby needed me in the same fundamental way, I'd be honored. When she's gone, though, I bring out the ring box and set it down on the coffee table in front of me. I didn't get an answer. Seems like I missed the chance to seal the deal. I should've waited until I tied Brooke up later and refused to free her or let her climax until she agreed to marry me.

"*Oh*, my God! *Oh*, my God!" I hear over the monitor, making me jump. My first thought is a bad one, that something is wrong with Olivia. The screen is not in view, but I can clearly hear the speaker. Then Brooke adds, "Your daddy just asked me to marry him. Gracious, you have soaked this diaper, my girl."

The juxtaposition of our sublime future with our baby's here-and-now need makes me smile into the momentary silence while Brooke must be putting Olivia on the changing table. My heartrate returns to normal.

"What do you think?" Brooke asks our daughter. "Shall we make it official? Don't look at me like that with those big, knowing eyes. I mean, it's all fine and good for you, having two parents who are crazy about you, knowing that will continue for the rest of your long, happy life."

I hear kissing sounds and Olivia cooing, the only way I can describe what isn't yet a laugh but expresses her infantile joy.

"Your toes are scrumptious. Do you know that?" More kissing sounds, and I'm growing jealous. I want to kiss my daughter's toes, too, but maybe Brooke will disclose what's holding her back.

"Your daddy says he loves me, but—"

I hold my breath. Is she going to say, "But I don't love him back as much as I should?"

"But what's the prenup going to look like? The power is all on his side, along with the wealth, of course." Brooke pauses, then adds, "Baby girl, it's thrilling to think you won't ever have to worry about financial matters. No crappy jobs for you." Then she sighs, and I hurry down the hallway, not wanting to miss her next words.

"But what am *I* bringing to this union? Apart from how much I love you and your father. I'll tell you a secret, little one. I adore being your mom, and I'm having a blast cooking for your daddy, too. Maybe none of my jobs worked out because they weren't as fulfilling as being a wife and mother. I think I've finally found my passion." She pauses. "But what if I'm meant to be a psychologist at the University of . . . Utah?"

I've crept closer to hear that last line.

"Then Olivia and I will come with you."

Brooke whirls around, her cheeks red, holding Olivia to her chest like a shield.

"Eavesdropping," she denounces me.

"You were broadcasting into every room of the house that has a receiver." Her expression tells it all.

"I forgot," she says. "Used to being alone here, you know."

"I know. But you don't have to be alone again unless you want to. Even when Olivia reaches that age when she's embarrassed to be seen with us, you'll still have me. I'll follow you wherever you go, for as long as you'll let me. Utah has great skiing and hiking, not to mention bison."

"What about to the North Pole?" she teases.

"I'll build us a fire, sweetheart, and keep you warm."

"To Ben Nevis?"

I make a face. "There's no skiing on that mini-mountain, but I'll learn to eat haggis."

"To a volcanic island in the Aleutian Islands?"

"Best idea yet. You would look so sexy going topless and wearing a sarong skirt that just skims your ass."

"You can't say things like that while I'm holding our baby." But her eyes say she loves it. She loves me!

"I just did. Come on, Brooke. Don't let what-ifs about the future scare you out of marrying me. Don't be a dumb-ass like I was."

"Was?" she asks.

I laugh, and Olivia coos as if she has her mother's wit.

Then Brooke smiles. "OK."

"OK?"

"OK, I'll marry you. Right this moment, though, I have to nurse her before my boobs explode." Probably the least sexy thing I've ever heard about tits, and still I'm turned on. She squeezes by me. "Come on, Mr. *Linter*, show me the ring."

She likes teasing me with my made-up name every once in a while, especially during sex when I take out the paddle.

"First, a glass of water," I say, remembering the most important thing for Brooke as soon as our hungry baby latches on. "Coming up."

33

Five months later, Athens, Greece

Brooke

When we step onto Marcus Parisi's superyacht, I'm instantly glad that we have only a small sailboat, a dinky Sunfish, for goofing around in the shallows of our home on St. Regnal. Owning the island home, as well as our spacious house in Boston, and the winter lodge in Maine are time consuming enough. This looks like one massive headache.

Staff are moving smoothly through the crowd, smiling tolerantly while carrying trays of drinks and hors d'oeuvres. Guests are asking for everything from sun umbrellas, hats, and sunscreen—*be prepared for the Greek sun, people*—to watermelon daiquiris.

"I just heard a woman ask for a watermelon daiquiri," I whisper to TJ, like it was an everyday drink that should be on hand.

"Really? I think I'd rather have a piña colada," he quips, "and getting caught in the rain."

I snicker at the song lyrics, when Marcus, TJ's real estate friend, overhears and stops to talk to us, bringing his wife with him by the hand.

"Please don't tell me it's going to rain on all my clients and friends," he jokes, his topaz-colored eyes looking happy.

"The weather wouldn't dare be uncooperative," quips his wife, Lindsey, a smart, honey-blonde.

I've met them both a couple of times. They're relaxed, cool, non-stuffy billionaires. *Our* kind of billionaires.

"I think TJ's nose is burning," I say. "That's making him long for some cloudy weather."

Lindsey pulls a tube of sunscreen out of a loose pocket on her turquoise-blue sundress and hands it to TJ. "Having grown up on an island, I'm always prepared for sun emergencies."

"Adam, over here," Marcus invites a tall, dark-haired man to join our group. Then he looks at TJ and me. "Have you met Adam Bonvier, another client of mine? Also, a friend."

As my ears perk up at the last name, my eyes recognize him. "The man from the painting," I say, sounding like an idiot, but he smiles, knowing what I mean.

Turning to TJ, I explain, "I used to work for Mr. Bonvier's company, when you were AWOL," as I call the time between when we made Olivia and our reunion limo ride to the hospital.

They shake hands, and I am struck by the coincidences in our vast universe. Although, maybe the billionaire cosmos is just that much smaller, making it hardly surprising to have three of these powerful men on this one yacht, docked at the Athens Marina, alongside other superyachts.

"I think my husband makes friends of *all* his clients," Lindsey remarks, winking at Marcus. "Look how packed this ship is! Where's Clover?" she asks Adam.

"Already talking business with one of your clients. She sent me for a bottle of water or some fruit juice."

"I hear congrats are in order," Marcus says. "Perhaps you'll want a larger house in a few months?"

"Definitely not," Adam says. "Ten thousand square feet is plenty. Any bigger, and I would lose track of my gorgeous wife. The baby will have to suffer the cramped space."

"You two are practically neighbors," Marcus tells us. "The Bonviers are on Beacon Hill."

Adam, whose slate-gray gaze is nearly as mesmerizing as TJ's, looks us over. I guess we pass inspection when he says, "Then we'll have you to dinner soon. Do you play golf?"

TJ shakes his head. "Skiing, tennis, basketball."

Adam's polite smile breaks into a grin. "You're on. When you come to dinner, bring your court shoes. We'll go one on one. See you all later."

After he disappears into the crowd, I ask, "Does Mr. Bonvier have a basketball court *in* his house on Beacon Hill?"

Marcus nods. "Just the shooting area. Like a quarter court."

"Marcus can find anyone the perfect house," Lindsey says proudly. "Adam's wife, Clover, is a hot ticket. A go-getter. And their chef is amazing."

"You'll enjoy yourselves if you go to dinner," Marcus agrees. "We'll catch up with you later." They move along to welcome other guests to their gratitude party, which they host yearly for everyone who does business with them. We're staying in a villa outside of town, and Olivia is with our traveling companions, Sherri and Dan, for the evening.

TJ snags us a couple cocktails that look like sunset in a glass, and we head over to the railing.

"Like a billionaire's club around here," I say.

He laughs. "We probably all carry the same credit card."

Not that TJ would notice, but the three of them together were kind of amazing. Thinking of their combined wealth is one thing. But, damn, they're all so handsome *and* friendly.

Apparently, we'll be going to my ex-boss's house. And then we'll be expected to reciprocate, like we did with Marcus and Lindsey a couple months ago. They were really fun dinner guests.

But did Marcus mean something else when he said we'd *enjoy* ourselves? I have an unpleasant thought, probably irrational, but this ultra-rich world is still very new to me.

"What's that look for?" TJ asks me. "Like you've swallowed a bug."

I blurt out, "You don't think they're swingers, do you?" Not that Adam Bonvier and Marcus Parisi aren't perfectly drool-worthy men, but they're not *my* TJ. "I mean, you're not interested in that, right?" My voice ends on a high squeak.

TJ's expression is priceless, easily readable as he goes from aghast to amused. Finally, he starts laughing, disbursing any concern I was imagining.

"God, no," he says when he can speak again. "Just because we share an ability to make massive amounts of money, it doesn't mean we share anything else, except admiration. But if either one tried to make a move on you, I'd get out my gun again."

His rifle is in Maine, and he has stopped carrying the handgun after I explained that it seemed overkill at the supermarket. Besides, Mr. Soltea and his ilk have left us alone since our intimately small New Year's Eve wedding. No more bachelor billionaire stories to tease the ladies with. Basically, we're a boring couple, and I like it that way.

As for TJ, he's made peace with a few things, even donating his sister's Miata to charity.

"I'm glad you said that because I'm not into watching you with other women, either."

"Never going to happen," TJ promises. "Although . . . ," he trails off.

"What? Out with it." I'm back to imagining he wants more than merely me.

"I've been thinking of getting a large mirror for our bedroom. Would you be into watching *us*?"

The idea sends a shiver down my spine. *Watch myself with TJ?* I nod. "I'll try anything once."

"Damn," he says, leaning down to kiss me. "I want to eat you where I can look over and see the reflection of us, of your beautiful breasts, with me between your legs."

Just like that, I'm wet and ready. He takes my empty glass and sets it beside his on a nearby tray. "Let's go make use of a stateroom. Parisi must have about a billion on this boat."

"We can't!"

TJ grins. "Let's go."

I cannot believe we're doing this, but I want my husband so badly right now, I'd follow him anywhere. I'd strip naked on the bridge of this yacht if he told me to. And he long-ago discovered the trick to dealing with me is not to give me a choice.

With no idea how many guests are staying on board versus those, like us, who rented a place on shore, I do know everyone is currently on one of the open-air decks where all the partying is happening.

Forget what I said about being boring. Like the naughty lovers we are, we go into the first unlocked room we find. TJ starts laughing. It's a mini-gym, complete with weight benches *and* a wall of mirrors.

I stare at it. "Do you always get what you want?"

"Everything off," he says in the voice I never disobey, all traces of laughter gone. "Everything," he adds while locking the door.

Thankful there is a lock, I'm trembling while I undress. Not too much to take off—just my copper-colored silky sundress and underthings. Unhooking my bra, I toss it on top, then face him in my thong.

"You did not just disobey me, did you?"

I partly want to laugh because this man with the frightening tone is such a pussycat. But I keep a straight face and play along.

"I guess I need a spanking."

"Face down on the weight bench," he says. TJ grabs a towel from a stack of clean ones and lays it across the closest bench.

He's wearing a grey polo and navy-blue shorts with a canvas belt, which I watch him remove. I swallow. *Oh, shit.*

"Your hand is fine," I suggest.

"Not your choice, though, is it?"

Although it usually is, I don't argue. I'm literally throbbing between my legs. Hurrying to the bench, straddling it before lying flat on the towel, I drape my legs down either side.

"Nice view. You ready?"

"Yes," I whisper. Then he does absolutely nothing. It's one of my favorite parts, knowing he's watching me while I'm so turned on waiting for the first strike.

"Turn your head," he orders. "Take a look."

When I do, I moan from the view. *Do I really look that sexy?* He's standing behind me, belt in hand. I wiggle my ass a little, watching the horny girl in the mirror do the same while the reflected TJ tests the belt strap on his open palm. Then we lock gazes in the mirror, and he swishes it down onto my butt cheek.

"Wow," I say because it is actually a mind-fuck watching *and* experiencing it. After a few lashes that bring delicious heat roaring between my legs, making me squirm against the firm, padded bench, the "punishment" becomes sensory overload. Closing my eyes on the scene of TJ turning my ass cherry red while my clit pulses and swells, I'm already shuddering.

"I'm going to come," I confess, gripping the metal legs of the weight bench.

In seconds, he's on his knees, dragging my thong aside and setting his wicked mouth to my pussy, kissing me from behind like a tender lover. I convulse in wave-upon-wave of pleasure as his tongue performs its magical flicks.

When I finish riding this intense, unexpectedly fast orgasm, I take a few calming breaths and struggle to stand, belatedly hoping the guests didn't hear my loud moans. While I'm looking around for where we can have intercourse, TJ is already re-threading his belt.

"What about you?" I ask.

In answer, he retrieves my dress and drops it over my head before handing me my bra.

"That *was* totally for me, sweetheart. Don't you understand yet how this works?"

I smile at him. "Your pleasure is my pleasure, and vice versa."

"You got it." He looks around. "Bathroom through there if I know my yachts, which I don't to be honest."

"But you do know your gyms," I joke with my legs still trembling as I go toward the closed door to get dressed properly. "I'll meet you on deck."

$❤$❤$❤$

It's amazing how both our lives have changed in a relatively short time. On a daily basis, we're still getting to know one another, like favorite movies, music, and ice cream flavors. But in other ways, we know everything important about one another.

TJ knows three things for sure: that I don't care about his money, that I think the way his mind works is really cool, an especially beautiful process when he's creating a gaming world, and that Mr. Busby *rules* while his dogs *drool*. Regardless, I love having Duffy, Beau, and Grady with us again. Each one is fun on four legs. I can't wait for Olivia to be old enough to play with her fur family.

Colin and Emma stayed in Maine, maintaining the house for whenever we want to go up there, the three of us, plus the dogs and our cat. It's like going home each time, and then coming back to Boston is also like coming home. I am the luckiest woman alive because everywhere I go with TJ and Olivia is home.

And I am the private chef in our Boston house. Cooking and baking give me great satisfaction. After each long day, I realize all over again that wife and mother are what I was meant to do all along. At least, at this stage of my life. In the future, who knows? The possibilities are endless.

My husband asked me to help with his next game, Bright Destiny, creating the characters' personalities and motivation. Being a part of it at its conception is a blast.

And while I know TJ was severely traumatized by his sister's death, he's come a long way from the paranoid man I first met, hiding under his sexy cowboy hat. He's still happiest when it's only the three of us, but he has loosened his stranglehold on trying to control every situation that arises.

Except for in the bedroom, which he controls perfectly, with palm or paddle, silk ties, and passionate kisses.

I recently discovered that he wants more kids. A lot more. Not a billion, but a sizable brood. I'm OK with that. Become the mom to a pack of little Ashers? I'll try anything once.

The End

ABOUT THE AUTHOR

Jane McBay is the pen name of *USA Today* bestselling author of historical romance, Sydney Jane Baily. She wanted to write about strong, sexy men who know how to treat a woman BUT aren't wearing top hats and shiny Hessian boots.

Trading carriages for limos and horses for private jets, she's dreaming up mouthwatering billionaires with big . . . hearts. They're paired with clever, passionate females who have a hard time resisting these intriguing men. *So why bother?*

Give in, have fun, fall in love.♥ They do. And you will too! *NO* cliffhangers. *NO* frustration. *ALL THE FEELS*. You're welcome!

Contact her through her website, JaneMcBay.com.